VIA Folios 149

Italian Love Cake

ITALIAN LOVE CAKE

Gail Reitano

BORDIGHERA PRESS

Cover art by Jenny Kroik

Library of Congress Cataloging-in-Publication Data

Names: Reitano, Gail, author.
Title: Italian love cake / Gail Reitano.
Description: New York, NY : Bordighera Press, [2021] | Series: Via folios ; 149 | Summary: "In a rural New Jersey town, on the eve of WWII, young Marie Genovese looks out from her apartment window above the Five & Ten and wonders how she'll save the failing store she's inherited from her mother. Forced to bake for extra money, Marie dabbles in herbs, and hopes to change her fate. But when a herb-laced cake causes a wealthy local banker and Marie to fall in love, her troubles only compound-a family friend plots to take the store, her brother is involved in a fascist hate crime, and Marie becomes pregnant by her married lover. Enter the mysterious Aunt Ada from Italy, who brings a skill with herbs and knowledge of the family's Italian past. Soon Marie will face a choice: accept the protection of her wealthy lover, or defiantly break cultural norms by remaining independent. In a time similar to today, full of fear, economic uncertainty, and the controlling behavior of men, a powerful line of women, living and dead, helps Marie decide. ITALIAN LOVE CAKE is a story of a rare feminist awakening in 1939"-- Provided by publisher.
Identifiers: LCCN 2020050431 | ISBN 9781599541600 (trade paperback)
Subjects: LCSH: Women-owned business enterprises--Fiction. | Italian Americans--Fiction. | Baking--Fiction. | New Jersey--History--20th century--Fiction.
Classification: LCC PS3618.E57266 I83 2021 | DDC 813/.6--dc23
LC record available at https://lccn.loc.gov/2020050431

Printed in the United States.

Published by
BORDIGHERA PRESS
John D. Calandra Italian American Institute
25 W. 43rd Street, 17th Floor
New York, NY 10036

VIA Folios 149
ISBN 978-1-59954-160-0

TABLE OF CONTENTS

For

Nick & Ava

I thrived. I lived
not completely alone, alone
but not completely . . .

LOUISE GLÜCK
"Formaggio"

1938

Littlefield, New Jersey

CHAPTER ONE

One day I was the child of someone and the next day I was alone.

I was twenty-two when my mother died, the same age she was when our father must have been planning his escape. My mother, Carmela, had just given birth to Sammy, my youngest brother. Three years later our father, Giuseppe Genovese, walked out, leaving three of us under seven. He also left behind a struggling Five & Ten and a scandal that clung to our mother as shame and misfortune do to any woman, let alone one as young and attractive as Carmela.

Our father's whereabouts were a mystery. When my mother died, we had no idea whether he was still alive. My brothers and I never talked about him. Being men, I believed it harder for them to grow up without a father. For my part, I couldn't stop thinking how at the age I was now, Carmela Genovese had already been married, and left.

After Mom's funeral we'd gathered in the living room and no one talked. Friends brought casseroles and desserts, and Mr. Esposito, an old family friend, whom we called Mr. E., allowed my brothers to have too much wine and so they'd fallen asleep before the final guest left.

We lived in the apartment above the Five & Ten, and as I stood alone in the living room, I noticed how I'd failed to draw the curtains as I usually did in the evenings. I wondered if my neighbors across Littlefield's main street peered at me from behind panels of yellowed lace. Their windows were open to the stifling air, as were mine, allowing in a terrible humidity that stretched northwest to Philadelphia and southeast to Atlantic City. It was always that way in summer that humidity hung like a shroud over southern New Jersey. Littlefield sat in the middle of a flat plain of mostly farms, where in summer blueberries ripened on bushes, and in fall cranberries floated in bogs, all beneath a vast blanket of pine. The town spread out for miles, but we were at its center.

I smoothed my skirt and caught my reflection in the glass. If my neighbors happened to be looking, would they see a woman, or the girl I'd been mere days ago? My hair looked good, dipping to my shoulder in a gentle curl, and my dress hung in stylish folds, mainly because it was too big for me, one of Mom's. Her death had happened so fast following a diagnosis of cancer, and there were too few days when she had been well enough to talk. Every single day that I nursed her, I forgot to eat, and every night I cried myself to sleep. As I sat by the bed holding her hand, I worried constantly about my responsibilities. I became completely self-obsessed. Did she notice? From time to time she looked hard at me, as if trying to read my mind.

Her final words were:

> *Be strong.*
> *Don't let men push you around.*
> *Look after your brothers.*

The lights still blazed from the funeral party, but with the guests gone and my brothers asleep, a cold panic descended. I was thinking about what was ahead of me. I would somehow have to manage the store and my brothers, and I was terrified.

Normally, before going home, Mr. E. would have seen to it that the doors were locked behind him, but he wasn't himself, and into the confusion and grief a stranger had entered. I was in the kitchen doing the last of the dishes when I turned and saw a man I didn't recognize standing in the doorway. At first I thought he was a friend of my brothers, but he was older. He had kind eyes and seemed a little lost, and maybe for that reason I wasn't afraid. His face was smooth, as though he'd just shaved, and his clothes were clean and pressed. It looked as if he'd come to pay his respects, yet he was late by several hours. *Had he known our mother?*

I noticed his fingernails were dirty. He must be a farmer, I thought, the suit ill-fitting but well looked after. His hair was slicked down but you could tell the cut wasn't good. Right away I recognized him as someone the town would expect me to be dating. He was also an Italian, possibly even a good prospect. Farmers never wanted for food.

"Come this way," I said, leading him downstairs, intending to let him out.

But once we'd reached the downstairs hallway—in one direction was the door to the street, in the other the one leading to the Five & Ten—all I could think of was the overwhelming air of loss in the apartment and I didn't want to go back upstairs. Nor did I want to be alone.

He followed me into the store. I walked aimlessly down an aisle, as I often did at night. He came up behind me as I hesitated by the cash register, which I was glad I had remembered to lock. I felt his hand on my shoulder as gently he turned me around. He pressed against me and I felt the edge of the counter on my back. He kissed me long and hard. His breath was sweet, manly, and I failed to detect cigarettes or beer. His body felt hard against mine, and this went on for a minute, before he stepped back abruptly and made a gesture of helplessness, his arms open at his sides. He waited, hoping I'd say something, and that's when it occurred to me that he couldn't speak English. When I didn't say anything, he began, "I new to town. Just come." So he was an Italian, fresh from whatever port of entry and probably in the market for a wife.

He bowed slightly, which struck me as funny. Maybe he was embarrassed, ashamed for having kissed me. Whatever it was, a second later he turned and I watched him walk back in the direction of the hallway, to the little door that gave out onto the main street and listened until I heard it close.

I remained by the cash register, leaning on the counter, unable to move for many minutes. I looked around at the Five & Ten. In every item, in every display, was evidence of the love and care our mother had put into the store.

I headed back upstairs, feeling more tired than I ever had, and that's when I heard them. My brothers, Gino and Sammy, were in the hallway outside the kitchen. Maybe they thought I was in my room with the door closed, sleeping soundly, or maybe they weren't thinking at all. They couldn't have known that I was on the stairs, just on the other side of the wall.

I heard my brother Gino say, "We get Marie out of the way, and we're all set. We can save the damn store. We can do it. Salvie's onboard."

Salvie Esposito. Mr. E.

I listened hard, but heard no reply from my youngest brother, Sammy.

Gino spoke again, "We're the ones should be running things around here."

What exactly was he planning? Gino was tough, but he was also a coward. If he had dared to say this to my face, I would have hit him. As it was, I didn't want my brothers to know I'd overheard their scheme.

I looked at the dingy hallway, the familiar walls with their scarred paint. I took in the worn treads and the narrow stairway that led to the store. This was the center of our universe. All of this, what had been Mom's world for the last seventeen years, was now mine.

CHAPTER TWO

We were still in the Depression. I saw the same customers, women who'd been Mom's friends, and who remained loyal but had very little money to spend. Jobs were scarce, neighbors shared what they could and complained, sometimes they wept. A strange tension simmered beneath every conversation, every look, and at the moment when a woman reached into her wallet, you saw the threat of despair. People were talking about the Depression and whispering about the war in Europe, yet in Ferrara's Market there was optimism.

"Won't be long now," said Eddie Ferrara to the woman ahead of me in line at the check-out. "Just you wait. We'll see an upturn." If Eddie weren't so sweet, I would have contradicted him. I alone went to Ferrara's Market with the grim task of stretching what little was left in my wallet. It was doubtful Gino or Sammy even knew the cost of food. Thank God they rarely complained when night after night our meal consisted of beans and a little pasta. The cost of everything was rising, higher every time I picked up a sack of flour or sugar, and I needed these ingredients constantly now that I had started baking to earn some extra money. I walked the aisles, remembering which items Mom bought and which she considered too expensive, and I sailed straight past the imported olives.

Because the Five & Ten was barely surviving, I'd weakened and allowed Mr. E. to have goods that had nothing whatsoever to do with the store delivered to my loading bay. I was afraid to ask him what was in those sacks that tended to arrive at night, figuring the less I knew, the better. Weekly, in exchange, Mr. E. handed me an envelope of cash, which he liked to press into my palm with a meaningful look. Sometimes there was urgency, the pressure on my hand a little stronger. "For you, Mari." In his broken English he pronounced my name without the "e," accent on the first syllable.

But even with the extra money from Mr. E., I still couldn't afford the stock I needed. So I ordered the same old junk, my standard shipment from Corley, six notepads with the thinnest paper imaginable, four yo-yos—the children loved them—and women's socks with tiny rose appliqués that fell off after two washings, though the quality of the socks themselves was good. Also a few notions, and necessities such as sewing kits, scissors and baskets.

The other day, just as I was finishing up an order, in walked Mrs. Romasello. "Where are the boys?" she commanded.

"You can ask me," I said, stepping up to the counter, my tone strident.

I was still smarting from Gino's comment. *We're the ones should be running things around here.* Not that Mrs. Romasello wasn't capable of riling me under the best of circumstances. Didn't she realize it was I who stayed up late and combed the catalogues for just the right weight and price? Did she really think Gino, Sammy, or the resistant Kenny, who had worked for Mom and now worked for me, knew what a tea towel looked like? When she continued to stare, I went into the back room and stood in the doorway as Mom once had, her pretty legs strict parallel lines, as if their only function was to form a sturdy base from which to fire off orders. "Somebody go out and help Mrs. Romasello."

My brothers and Kenny were on the couch drinking sodas, and when they looked up it was as if I'd interrupted a meeting of the League of Nations. From the small radio barked the voice of that horrible priest, Father Coughlin. *Support Italy and you will feel stronger.* Ever since the Depression, there weren't just the inflated prices to contend with, but the angry voices of men. They shouted, and I saw more women with black eyes and bruises on their arms. Coughlin was a priest, but he sounded like a dictator. Maybe the two were now one and the same.

"Shut that thing off!" I said.

When Gino obeyed I was floored. But it was Sammy, so different from his lazy, resistant older brother, who got up immediately and went out to serve Mrs. Romasello.

My brothers and I had once lived happily together, but since Mom died the apartment felt small, full of their male odors and moods, and every conversation contained wildly childish outbursts or masculine bravado. To Gino I was a hindrance, the older sister to whom he looked for his basic needs, endless cooking and cleaning. For Sammy, who was younger than Gino by several years, I was less of an annoyance. He seemed appreciative of all I did, but he could be influenced by Gino. It was my greatest hope that Gino would fall in love with someone and move far away. To that end I decided to go to the movies on a Saturday night. If he was seeing someone, there was a good chance they would be there, and if I knew the girl, I could exercise my influence by making sure her family knew what a big prize my brother was. The other reason to go on a crowded Saturday was to see the picture, *You Can't Take It With You*, with Jean Arthur and Jimmy Stewart, a man and a woman from different social classes who fall in love.

I needed the distraction of the movies. I'd been once already this week, on Wednesday because it was "Dish Night," when to encourage attendance they gave out a free dinner plate. I was working toward a service for six.

As I looked around, I thought perhaps some of these people might become my baking customers. It was a different crowd on a Saturday night, full of people for whom an extra ten cents was no big deal. I couldn't believe there were still people around who had money. It wouldn't hurt for them to see me—this new Marie who could earn $2.00 for one and a half hours of work.

My cake baking was going well. Mrs. Ricci's daughter had called to say that her husband had managed to land a new job. At first I didn't understand what this had to do with me. "It was your cake, Marie. That's what did it." Then Mrs. Tilton stopped by, and I believed this was the first time she'd ever been inside the store. She not only praised the cake I'd made for her son's birthday, she bought a packet of cocktail napkins. "You know, Paul had a crush on a girl. Now they're going steady."

As people were taking their seats I hurried up to the balcony to see whether Gino was there. The balcony was where couples went to kiss. I'd been kissed in the store, but to be seen in public, even in the darkened balcony, was a freedom that was denied me as the owner of the Five & Ten. I couldn't afford a hint of gossip. I'd been lured by the idea of couples in love and showing their passion, but now I was left with the thought that with Mom's death I'd been robbed of my youth.

I took my seat downstairs just as the newsreel started. Hitler was marching along a small main street that resembled ours in Littlefield, except for the towering mountain behind. A large crowd cheered and gave that stiff-armed salute, even the children. The camera flashed on the face of an attractive young woman in the crowd. Her expression reminded me of the rapture of Saint Theresa, a look I recognized: eyes rolled back, a soft smile, lips parted.

Finally, the movie began, and I immediately identified with the love interest played by Jean Arthur. Her family, while comfortable and far from poor, was no match for Jimmy Stewart's family of bankers, and she worried endlessly over whether or not she would be accepted. However, the man remained determined to follow through on his love, and by the end his family adores her.

I walked home in the warm haze of a beautiful summer evening. I tiptoed up the stairs. It was late, but instead of going to my bedroom, I mounted the two worn linoleum steps to a tiny room off the kitchen that I called the ex-voto. The room was, in its entirety, an offering to my mother. Packed away and stored there were her clothes, keepsakes, and the small ceramic knick-knacks we'd grown up with. After she died I gave her cut crystal bowl a place of honor on the breakfront in the living room, but other things remained packed away, their contents a mystery to me. Sometimes when I visited the room I opened a box at random.

Mom, I'm here.

I always first announced myself. I took a seat on the floor and began sifting through blouses, scarves, and delicate underthings. Here and there a small circle of embroidery covered a hole. Among her many dresses and skirts, I searched for a piece that resembled the clothes I'd seen in the movie, something that wasn't too far gone for restoration. After examining several items I managed to find a skirt that bore not a single stain, rust mark or blemish. It was long, what they called a sailor skirt, with the hem edged in navy blue grosgrain ribbon. Carmela was likely in her early twenties when she had last worn it, the age I was now.

To the extent that ghosts are real, my mother was there in the room with me. I even felt a brush of wind as my eyes fell upon a postcard that had fallen from one of the boxes. It was written in Italian, so I could only read the signature. *Ada.*

Who was Ada?

I spent the next two nights altering first the waist—Mom had been a fuller-figured woman—then shortening the hem. On the second night I got up from the sewing machine and stretched. I tried the skirt on and realized I didn't have the right blouse; it needed something light and cottony to offset the heaviness of the sail cloth. Tomorrow I would leave my brothers to mind the store and dash over to Paola's Dress Shop. Of course, I wouldn't tell them where I was going. Gino in particular hated when I spent money.

As summer advanced, I felt each and every rise in temperature in my legs and in my stomach, and a slick of perspiration was visible on my bare arms. I replayed the kiss in the store. I could hardly concentrate for the feelings in my body that were stronger than anything I could remember and which added to my lethargy. My mood was tense and I was abrupt with the boys in the store.

On Saturday the picture was *Holiday* with Kate Hepburn and Cary Grant. Though I arrived early, the theater was already full. This time I made sure to keep my eyes closed through most of the newsreel and avoided the sight of tanks rolling into Germany. Unfortunately, I managed to catch the throngs of school girls in white blouses, backpacks thumping as they marched and waved. The support for Hitler was frightening. I looked around the theater, but couldn't read the expressions on the faces of people I'd known my whole life. Were they as shocked as I was? Or were they captivated? They seemed frozen.

I wore the sailor skirt and the perfect blouse, double breasted with elbow-length sleeves that puffed slightly at the shoulders. It was thrilling to note how my clothes weren't that much different from Hepburn's, her columnar skirts and tailored blouses. Nor was my figure, slim at the waist and only slightly fuller at the bust and hips. Of course my hair was like my mother's, full and dark and wavy. I was feeling glamorous and carefree, in heaven under the soft yellow lights, until I looked around and saw that practically everyone was in a pair. Married couples. A few younger ones, too, those who weren't in the balcony.

The movie's premise was ridiculous. Were we expected to believe Cary Grant's character was prepared to walk away from a successful banking career and a wealthy fiancée to satisfy his itch to travel? After the lights went up I saw faces drunk with contentment. Here we were, still in the Depression that felt like it might never end, yet we were meant to believe that in America anything was possible. My mother had believed this; I wasn't sure I did.

I saw him just as I rose to go. Walking up the aisle was the man who'd turned up in my kitchen the night of Mom's funeral. He wasn't wearing the suit, but a pair of worn work trousers and a short-sleeved shirt. His arms were muscular. He must be a laborer, I thought, or maybe he performed heavy work on a farm, which had been my first impression. His hair looked better in its unkempt state without being slicked down. He was tanned, or maybe he was naturally dark, which made him seem rough, tough looking. I slipped into the crowd leaving the theater. The man was behind me. I wondered whether he'd seen me.

The evening was beautiful and clear, and the crowd dispersed slowly as people milled around and talked, wanting to avoid for as long as possible their stifling interiors. I hesitated by the ticket kiosk and waited to see whether he would look in my direction. He had walked off to the side and was leaning against the glass display containing the posters advertising coming attractions. I was glad there was no one I recognized, because I didn't want anyone to see what I was about to do. I waved at him, and immediately he came over. He offered me a cigarette.

"I don't smoke," I said.

He smiled and lit his own. I waited to hear his voice again, while dreading those halting sentences should he try to explain where he'd come from, what he was doing, or about to do. I didn't care about any of it. I wanted nothing to do with Italy, that old place, nor to hear the optimism of the newcomer. We Genoveses had arrived not so long ago ourselves, and already there was much to protect, to prove. I didn't want to hear about his struggles. To Mom's advice on her deathbed, I had added my own:

> *Fight.*
> *Don't let them see you can't handle what is thrown at you.*
> *You are an American now. Keep pushing ahead.*
> *Look after your brothers, but only to a point...*

The man took a step closer. He turned his head to the side and exhaled a stream of smoke.

"I walk you," he said pointing toward the corner, and we set off.

I was careful not to look around in case I caught the eye of someone who knew me, but no one took any notice. Meanwhile I was reliving his kisses, his pressing into me, and simultaneously the feel of his penis, and the hard counter against my back.

I let us into the downstairs and walked ahead of him down the hall leading to the store. I couldn't take him upstairs because my brothers were there.

The street lamps spilled light across the counters, and there was the familiar smell of floor wax and the lavender water I sprayed, all of it comforting. Abruptly, the man whose name I didn't know wrapped his long arms around me. He kissed me with more passion than on that first night. And when he put his hands on my breasts and squeezed, not hard but insistent as his thumbs brushed across my nipples, the sensation erased all resistance. He took my hand and pulled me into the back room where we unpacked stock and the boys listened to the radio. We continued to kiss, and he moaned. I had never heard a man moan before. Soon we were making a kind of music, and we collapsed on the dingy sofa where the men ate their lunch. He slid his hands up inside my skirt, he kissed my knees. He was gentle, practiced, not that I would know, but it all felt so natural, and he seemed genuinely surprised which caused me to relax. When finally he entered me, though it hurt, it was a good pain, and I felt released from worry, from obligation, and the watchful eye of the town. It was a one-time thing, and I never saw him again.

CHAPTER THREE

My clothes from the night before were scattered across the chair in my room. Sunday was my day to straighten up and get ready for the week, but I was tired, and I'd missed Mass for only the second time in my life. The other time I was almost too young to remember; it was the day my father left. The essence of a trauma is carried on the wind, and on that day there was a vague sense of unease in the apartment. I remember that Mom couldn't get out of bed, a day like today, in summer—or maybe I was told that later, that my father left in summer.

I felt off-kilter from the moment I opened my eyes. Then two things happened right away. Someone was pounding on the downstairs door and yelling. I looked out the living room window to see who it was, and there was Kenny staring up at me, motioning to be let in. I pulled on my robe and went down.

"Corley says if he doesn't get a check, he's picking up his stock tomorrow."

We stood in the doorway in full view of the main street that was thankfully still asleep. I always worried about being seen talking to a man, even Kenny, who was happily married and everyone knew worked for me. I wondered what he saw when he looked at me. I was no longer a virgin. I felt mussed, refreshed, like how a bird must feel when it fluffs its feathers after a dip in a cool fountain.

"Corley called yesterday, but I couldn't find you," said Kenny, out of breath.

"He cannot pick up the stock," I said.

"That's what I told him."

"Tell him I'll have a check tomorrow."

He shrugged. "All that soda glass. It cost."

I thanked him and closed the door. I went to dress, and had just settled into a cup of coffee when the downstairs bell rang. It was Mr. E., as if he knew something had happened and wanted to investigate.

"Mari," he said. From behind his back he produced a large bouquet of gladioli, which I had already seen hiding there. He also brought a basket of zucchini, and in a separate bag a burst of fresh squash blossoms, which I would fry stuffed lightly with mozzarella and basil.

He presented his gifts with a whiff of seduction, the manly bringing of sustenance, the provisions one expects from a father.

I stepped aside, allowing him to enter first, honoring the seniority of the older man with the acknowledgement that he had the power to make things easier for me, that is, if I would let him, which I wouldn't. Not only was he fifty-five years old, but he carried with him an air of the past. He had helped my mother, now he was helping me, but that didn't entitle him to more.

"Where are they?" he asked, looking around for my brothers.

"Asleep," I said, going into the kitchen to put water on for a second pot of coffee. As I moved about the kitchen, my body pulsed. I felt changed having had sex.

There was a note of urgency in his voice and I wondered what business he had with my brothers. Mr. E. took them places, and it was good they had the older man to confide in. There were matters I couldn't be privy to. Boys needed that. But for some time now I'd sensed a tension between them and Mr. E. I wondered if he'd gotten them involved in some shady business. Twice now I'd caught Gino, Sammy and Kenny huddled around the small black Philco listening to Father Coughlin spew his poison. And only last week, when I asked Kenny why a shipment of new stock hadn't been unpacked, he said, "The shipment's from Feldman."

I didn't care who the shipment was from. "I need it out on the floor. Now!" I said, raising my voice. I had been waiting for these items, a good stock of kitchenware, including a nice shiny, cheap set of cutlery I was sure I could sell.

Abruptly, Gino switched off the radio. "You know, Marie, we should be buying *Christian*. Feldman isn't the only supplier."

I couldn't believe my ears. Feldman was the only one to ship even when I hadn't paid him. He had loved our mother. He would do anything to help us and the store.

"If it weren't for Feldman, the shelves would be empty," I practically screamed, before pointing at the radio. "You think those bad men help us? People already think Italians are thieves and liars. Now we're haters, too? You just repeat what you hear. You're a parrot!"

Mr. E. tapped the table. "You know, Mari," he said, bringing me back to the present, "this is a nice apartment."

"I'm happy here," I said, distracted.

"I love your boys."

It was as if they were my sons.

What would our lives have been like if Mr. E. had managed to convince Mom to marry him? I knew he'd angled for that. My brothers loved him. I also knew they talked about me. *Marie is fragile. Marie is unstable.* Which only reinforced what an old fashioned Italian man like Mr. E. believed about all women, that we would make any compromise so long as we were taken care of. It would suit the three of them to have me permanently wedded to the kitchen. Me cooking the produce Mr. E. brought, and my brothers happily, hungrily eating.

"Salvie, please don't encourage them to listen to that priest," I said. Whenever I used his first name he knew I was serious.

"He has some good things to say."

"I don't like all this talk about Jews and Christians. We all have it bad," I said, my voice rising.

I was thinking about Ruth and Gersh Oletsky, our Jewish friends and neighbors who owned the haberdashery two doors down. I recalled a conversation once between Mom and Mr. E. as they stood by the back door.

"I fought in the war, Carmela. Twenty years ago now. Then I come to New York, and I know what to do."

She had nodded as though she knew his history, like he was going over old news.

"Carmela, we support Italy."

"Fooey," she'd said.

"We won in 1918. After that we join the *Fasci di Combattimento* for ex-servicemen. We fight communism, and Mussolini help the little guy. We organize, and let him know how it goes."

"You let him know, Salvie?"

My mother cocked her hip to one side, a look of skepticism on her face. "I don't like it," she'd said, dropping her voice.

Was Mr. E. a fascist?

"Mussolini can count on us."

"He thinks too much of himself."

"Carmela," I would hear him say. "Carmela, do you hear me? Do you understand?" A question followed by silence. I could see them on the landing. I watched her shake her lovely head, then with her arms folded across her waist, her chin at an angle, "Of course, Salvie, of course." *What had been the question?*

"I don't have the money to pay Corley," I said, quickly. The weekly amount he pressed into my palm was no longer enough. God knew how I was going to afford to pre-order enough stock for back-to-school supplies, and if we didn't have strong sales then, we wouldn't make it through until Christmas. We'd always managed to lurch from holiday to holiday, until this year, eight years after the Crash, and we were still in a slump. I hated myself for it, but there it was. My need. Our need.

He placed a heavy hand on my clenched fist.

"You know, Mari. Things get better."

I relaxed my hand and slipped it out from underneath. "We've made it through before," I said, "but this is different."

On his face was a patient smile. "It's not so good for my business either."

"Olive oil always sells," I said. He had an importing business in New York to which he traveled back and forth. He always seemed to have extra money, and deals going on.

"You know, you're a good businesswoman, Mari. Better than your mother." He exhaled with exaggeration.

"No, Salvie. Not better…I'm…" The word I almost said was *young*, but stopped myself.

"We could team up, Mari. You and me. I take care of you. I give you all the money you need."

I kept my face neutral. I'd had too much coffee, and my stomach began to gripe.

He picked up his hat. "I pay Corley. No problem."

"I want you to promise me you won't get them involved in anything," I said, referring to my brothers. I followed him out of the kitchen, and just as we reached the top of the stairs, he turned to face me and took my hand. "I want children, Mari."

Surely he was kidding.

"You know there can't be anything between us," I said quickly.

He cast a look downwards and took in my figure like he inspected the quality of a tomato, a piece of produce. He looked directly into my eyes, "With you, Mari."

Mom had been nothing if not direct. If I'd inherited anything it was her forthrightness. Anyone looking at my life could see that honesty was my only luxury. Once I saw her slap him, though I might have imagined this. It wasn't like I didn't have rage. The difference was mine went to sleep, mollified by the appearance of a man bearing a gift. Each gift a future, a promise held out like I'd won a prize in a contest.

"Have Gino call when he wakes up," he said, his tone more abrupt. He proceeded down the stairs with a lively step. He was putting it on, showing me how young he still was, if one's fifties could be considered young.

"You know," he said, with the bright, public street behind him.

"What?" I wore my hands on my hips.

"We Italians have to stick together."

"Roosevelt doesn't want a war," I said.

"Believe me. It happen. Tell Gino to call." He put on his hat, then stepped out into the sun.

Back upstairs I went straight to Gino's room. "Gino, wake up, you lazy thing. Up! Mr. E. says to call him."

At that Gino threw his long, hairy legs over the side of the bed, where he remained rubbing his eyes. "When did he call?"

"He was here. He just left."

He became alert. "Why didn't you wake me?"

He shuffled past, and we were almost clear of one another when he leaned in and kissed my cheek before continuing to the bathroom.

CHAPTER FOUR

Another plodding week passed as I put the boys through their paces and tested the strength of my authority. I forced Kenny to stay late and rearrange stock in an effort to spark a few summer sales. It was our slowest time. But even with a lack of customers, there was always too much to do. I'd hoped this busyness might distract me from the hole in my life left by Mom's death; it didn't.

I'd managed all right those first few weeks, but now, suddenly, I seemed to have no energy. This situation was made worse by Mom's friends, Mimi Rizotte and Ruth Oletsky, who seemed to see me as my mother. All our conversations centered around money, the terrible economy, and the gossip they'd heard. They shared stories of other's misfortunes because they knew scandal couldn't touch them. They were married and settled, whereas I felt my every move scrutinized. *Why was Marie Genovese still single?*

Most days I sat alone in the store going over the books, choosing stock, managing as best I could, when I should have been out with girls who'd been my classmates, Angie and Tina, who had the lives I wanted. Angie had a car, wore beautiful clothes and flirted with men, and Tina, who had married young, could still be seen laughing with friends as they crowded into the Sweet Shoppe.

I had taken to napping in the afternoon. When the sun bore down in a hard stream through the store's windows, I went upstairs to my mother's bed, which now belonged to me, and lay staring at the ceiling. Too hot to sleep, I combed my list of worries: money, the store, being alone, having to manage the men. To that list, I added one more: the frightening prospect that I might be pregnant. My period was late by a week. Yet I had no desire to see the man again. I had felt nothing other than the urge to have a man, to feel him inside me, and now that I had, the next time would require a new ingredient, a feeling I knew existed, but had yet to experience. Love.

Unable to sleep, I got up and went to the ex-voto. There, placed high on a shelf, were Mom's cookbooks, six in all. I took one down, got comfortable on the floor, and had just opened it when I heard Gino's footsteps.

"What's wrong with Sammy?" he said, bursting in. "He won't unpack the paper supplies. I told him a hundred times."

It was so hot, everyone's mood was frayed, but Gino's large frame filled the doorway menacingly, which I knew to be an act. I was used to ignoring him, but today I couldn't cope.

"Take the rest of the day off. Both of you. And go somewhere else. I want to be alone. Get Kenny to man the store."

Gino stared in shock. "I'll tell him," he said, backing out.

"Do what you have to do, but go," I raised my voice in anger, and I saw his look of surprise. Yes, that's right, I wanted to say, I won't put up with your crap today.

As soon as he'd gone, I opened the first of my mother's handwritten cookbooks, this one covered with stylized images of bowls of fruit, what I recognized as wallpaper from the one and only remodel of our kitchen. Carmela had folded the cover according to how the Sacred Heart nuns had taught us, tight fitting, with a tricky last fold as constrained as religion itself.

I opened the book to the cake section. Mom used to say you couldn't underestimate the warming comfort of wheat, provided you used the whole grain, and preferably home ground. Mimi Rizotte could get her hands on a special type from a friend in the next town who dried the washed grains by tying them up in a towel. She then wrapped the towel around her head and left it in place until the grains were dry. Was the flour made from those pampered kernels that much better than the one I bought from Ferrara's? All I knew was that my brothers could be mollified by food, especially sweet things.

I gathered up the cookbooks and took them back to bed, and there I spent the rest of the afternoon studying the step-by-step instructions recorded in Carmela's large, round cursive that made her seem alive, young. I slipped in and out of daydreams as I recalled watching her bake. It was Mom who had taught me to love a house, its contents, its equipment and rituals.

I continued to lie there, the room becoming oppressively hot just as my eyes fell upon the recipe for Italian Love Cake. There were several small food stains on the page. I wondered, had Mom found this recipe in the *Ladies Home Journal*, or had it come from our family? Reading the list of ingredients, I didn't notice anything that could cause a cake to bring about a state of bliss. The base was a simple yellow batter, the ingredients the usual flour, sugar, and eggs. The ricotta, however, would make it costly.

I got up and went downstairs to get a Pyrex baking pan. I had only recently stocked the miracle soda-lime glass that would go into the oven without cracking. The store was quiet, and Kenny was in the back room with his feet up as he smoked a cigarette. Seeing me, he leapt to his feet. "Gino and Sammy were supposed to help me unpack those," he thrust his chin in the direction of a pile of boxes. Then slowly, without looking at me, he dragged himself over to the unopened stock. I spared him my look of disgust, and instead went out to George's cheese shop. There, with the last of the week's household money, I bought the ricotta.

I measured and mixed and sprinkled in the last of my anise. My friend Angie and I used to walk the Lake Park in summer, and on both sides of the path anise grew, turning the air fragrant with its licorice. Because Angie and I were young and liked to talk about the future, I would forever associate the smell of anise with hope. I decided to add a pinch of mint as well, described in one of Mom's books as helping with money and lust, which made me laugh. But then I became confused when the recipe called for the batter to go in first, then over that I was to pour the ricotta mixture. In Mom's hand were written the words, *the rich cheese sinks to the bottom and forms a fluffy cushion.* How in the world could the batter and cheese switch places in the oven?

I decided on a thick swath of vanilla pudding frosting into which I would sprinkle the rest of my field mint, a perfect counter for a cold stomach. I was thinking about Gino, how I doubted his digestion was good, or why else would he be so difficult?

Then I made two wishes. One, that the cake would turn out well, so I hadn't wasted my money. And two, that Gino might meet a nice girl and move to the moon. If I might be granted a third, I wanted to be released from this endless parade of days in which I cooked, cleaned, and worried.

During the long, one hour and twenty-minute cooking time, I opened the oven door twice, risking a loss of temperature that could easily ruin the cake while hoping to observe this magic, the switching of the layers. I became lost in a secret dream, of the cake firming, its layers shifting, as if all the clouds in the sky decided to float down and kiss the earth. So potently did the sweet fragrance combine with the strange transformation taking place in the oven, I was reminded of love. Not that I knew what it was, or what it was supposed to feel like. Those brief minutes on the sofa in the back room weren't love, that much I knew.

When the cake had cooled and I had finished the icing, I called down to the store. Kenny answered, and just as I suspected my brothers were there too. Always, when I was angriest, they stuck around, fearing what? That I would kick them out forever? Did I have that power? I told Kenny to grab my brothers and come up.

I cut them each a slice of cake and watched as they ate. They were smiling, in heaven over the deliciousness I'd put before them. It could have been the right time for a truce, except my mood alternated between expectation and defiance, and I was ready, if one of them made the smallest criticism, to murder all three.

CHAPTER FIVE

Gino and Sammy must have bragged about my cakes, because out of the blue I received my first important commission. Priscilla Ashworth called, or rather, her housekeeper. I tried to picture Mrs. Ashworth. Had I seen her in town? As the wife of the richest man in Littlefield, she was bound to be a snob, and she was married to a banker. People blamed bankers for the Depression. I imagined their house, which everyone knew was down a long lane that terminated at the lake, to be like a Hollywood set from the movies I loved, full of rooms with tall ceilings, and a sweeping staircase.

Until that point I had only tried three of Mom's recipes. The Boston Cream Pie had been a disaster, as had the cheesecake. I needed a couple more passes at both. The lemon chiffon for Mrs. Ricci's son-in-law had turned out a little dry, though he'd still landed a new job. But right away my Italian Love Cake had been a success.

"What kinda cakes do you bake?" I detected a slight irritation, as if the Ashworths' maid might have been a baker herself and was overlooked for this particular event.

"What is the occasion?" I asked, stalling for time as I searched for another name to describe the yellow cake with the glorious shifting layers.

She hesitated. "The Mister's birthday. Turning thirty-eight. He's not happy about it."

I was sure Priscilla Ashworth wouldn't approve of personal information going out, and wouldn't have liked the comment, *He's not happy about it.* Perhaps realizing this, the woman cleared her throat and asked more formally, "What kinda cakes do you have available?"

"I make a very fine vanilla cake with a light cheese icing. It's called…" My palms were sweating. I wanted this job, but I had no less ethnic-sounding name for Italian Love Cake.

"You didn't ask me how many," she said, interrupting the silence, but more gently now. I could tell she was in a hurry to get the order going, to get off the phone and report back to her boss that the cake was taken care of. "There'll be six, maybe seven. But I think six. If more, I'll call you," she said.

"When do you need..."

"Week from tomorrow." She gave me the date and took down my address. "Someone'll be by to pick it up at three."

We hung up before discussing a price, nor did I have to struggle to come up with another name.

I had all the ingredients laid out. But a cake for Mr. Ashworth, who on most days could be glimpsed pulling up to the curb in his long, black Packard, prompted a wish, one having to do with our position in Littlefield. Unspoken among Italians was the desire to impress the richest Anglo-Saxons. From the center of my living room I had an angled view of the bank, which reminded me of classical buildings in Italy. Its imposing columns and ornate molding seemed to say, *Money and prosperity can be yours, if only you work hard.* I worked hard. But still I had no money.

At first my brothers seemed flattered to be left in charge on our busiest day. But they soon became annoyed when they remembered that they liked to take off early on a Saturday to chase girls. I left them in the back room tying up their aprons, and promised to be back in the store by four, after the cake was picked up. Gino was none too pleased, but Sammy, who was always the first to support me in my plans, winked at me.

I prepared the topping and icing and put both in the icebox. With my body pleasantly restrained by the strings of my apron, which felt both professional and alluring, I didn't even mind when I went to get the butter in its special compartment only to discover that my brothers had used the last of it. This meant I had to make an inconvenient trip to the store and lay out still more money on an already expensive recipe. I grabbed my wallet, rushed to Ferrara's, and was back in less than twenty minutes.

For someone about to inject a stray ingredient, I felt as confident as a witch at her caldron. I willed the silky batter to accept—I had no more field mint—my sprinkle of anise, which I'd read could be used to encourage employment. Its other properties were the promotion of fertility and passion, which were good things, too, but what really appealed to me was the idea of further commissions. Then I thought, why stop there? I had a small jar of fennel, gathered from Mr. E.'s garden. Fennel's properties were as appealing as those of anise, its relative; both were calming as well as able to heat the blood. I pictured Mr. Ashworth getting in and out of his car, the only image I possessed, that of his elegantly suited body topped off by a proper hat. He moved with restraint, like an important man, and I wondered, did he ever have the urge to cut loose?

While the cake was baking I couldn't concentrate on anything, so I wandered around the apartment. Mom had done what was necessary to make the place a home. We were a legion of homemakers, and to her efforts I'd added my own touches, a small fabric orchid pinned to each lace curtain, where it was captured off to the side during the day. I always closed the curtains in the evening, all the women did. The shelves and a sparse collection of curios were freshly dusted. I made sure Mom's cut crystal chaffing dish was positioned dead center on the breakfront. Inside, all her best linens were still there, stored like holy vestments to be used once a man came into my life. Without having to open the drawer, I pictured them crisp from their last damp ironing.

I walked around drowning in the smells of Italian Love Cake, a fragrance so full of hope it made me want to dress up, to adorn myself the way Mom had done whenever appearances mattered. I'd always admired how she dressed in defiance of her manless situation; it wasn't in her nature to don the weeds of the widow. Rather, she celebrated what she had, her competence and skill, and a nice figure she liked to show off. So, regardless of the messy procedure to come—the application of the icing—I slipped into my new sundress, one I'd been saving. Yellow sunflowers burst on a caramel ground, with nicely fitting darts at the bodice and with wide straps for sleeves that set off my arms. I even slipped on my best sandals, and did something with my hair, piling it up as if to escape the heat.

The doorbell rang promptly at three, and instantly I was thrown into a panic. Not being a professional baker, I did not have any of those stiff cardboard rounds on which to place the cake. Nor did I have boxes. Why had I not thought to get one? Why didn't I stock them in the Five & Ten? Perhaps it was something I could look into, adding baking supplies. What was now an emergency situation meant I would have to use one of my own plates. Really, I only had Mom's crystal dish, and it disturbed me to let this out of the house where it might get chipped, or worse, never be returned at all. But it was either that or one of the Wednesday dishes. Not only did I not want to break my set, but a second, more uncomfortable thought was how plain it might seem. This cake was going to Mr. and Mrs. Ashworth, and with that frightening prospect the floodgates opened to a slew of insecurities. What if they didn't like the cake? What if they thought it too Italian and therefore inferior? I headed downstairs to answer the bell.

I opened the door expecting to see the maid I'd spoken to on the telephone, but standing there was Mr. Ashworth himself. He looked different up close, compared with the bird's-eye view from my window, where I sometimes caught a glimpse of him leaving the bank, his posture bent toward the mission of returning home, his features shaded by a Homburg. Up close, without the hat, he was handsome.

He greeted me with a polite smile that seemed pasted on, and a stiffness at odds with the warmth that briefly flared in his eyes. In the next second he seemed a little stunned, like he'd come face-to-face in close quarters with a powerful fan. Yet there was no judgment in his expression that could easily have communicated our difference in status: *I know you know who I am.*

Mr. Ashworth took a step forward, which meant I had to retreat up the narrow stairs. But his demeanor was such that whatever I said or did seemed a non-issue. He was here to pick up a cake, and whatever that took he was prepared to go along.

I was glad now that I had thought to change out of my flour speckled dungarees, but he appeared not to notice either me or the dress. Rather, he seemed a little distressed. Was it the heat? Or was it that life itself was a trial for this man? I didn't know him. It might have been the case that he was simply morose as a rule. God help anyone stuck with such a man, I thought.

"It's hot," I said inanely. We had reached the landing that offered the first glimpse of my rooms. A breeze, one of the first of the day, caused the lace sheers to balloon out attractively, before the dead heat resumed.

"May I please have a glass of water?" he asked.

"Of course," I said, happy to have an excuse to break the awkwardness.

We stood side by side for just a second taking in the image of the perfectly arranged living room. The dark sofa, a richly colored carpet that was the finest piece in the apartment, and two overstuffed velvet chairs on which I'd placed my two best linen squares, which had been my maternal grandmother's. I'd put them there to reduce the hot, scratchy feel of the velvet in the heat. The chairs were aging, regally, but still, and as I watched him inspect the room, I wondered what he saw.

I could study him now. He was a slight man, tall with a crop of sandy hair, which I had never seen because on the street he always wore a hat. The hair was vigorous, cut in a surprisingly boyish style that conjured images of a more playful Mr. Ashworth. He wasn't classically handsome, but there was something restless in those round blue eyes. He looked good in a suit, and I imagined his legs to be strong, even athletic, hidden beneath the generous cut of his trousers. He would eventually lose his hair, I could see that. But I considered men to be at the height of their physical beauty around the age Mr. Ashworth was now, in his late thirties according to an indiscreet slip by his housekeeper.

I handed him a glass of cold water and he drank deeply. Then he looked off toward the tall sash windows that overlooked the street and across the way toward his bank.

"Why don't you sit down," I said, "and I'll get the cake ready."

The cake had come out extraordinarily well, and it looked beautiful on Mom's cut crystal plate with the delicate gold edging. I wondered why I had not thought to use this plate before. What was I saving it for? And why did I consider it too good for my brothers and me but perfect for the Ashworths? Here I was sending it out with the possibility it wouldn't be returned.

My next worry was how to keep the cake cool. Almost as soon as I removed it from the icebox I worried the custard might begin to melt. I needed a box, and there was only one option, the beautifully preserved hatbox that had belonged to Mom. Along with the Turkish carpet and the gold-edged plate, it was a piece she'd treasured, something that would never, not for a long time, be thrown away. Her hatbox was the perfect size and round. The outside was a soft pink, not far off the color of cake boxes I'd seen. The inside was patterned with small yellow roses and once housed Mom's lace and seed-pearl-capped wedding veil. I hurried down the corridor to the bedroom, took it down from a top shelf and inspected it. I lifted the lid to smell and was pleasantly surprised to detect nothing other than the faintest hint of lavender.

Carefully, I lowered the cake into the box, fastened the lid and tested the strength of the satin cord handle.

Mr. Ashworth stood when I came into the room. "I don't recommend you carry this by the handle," I said, smiling as I handed him the box. His mood seemed more composed, as if the shaded apartment and water had calmed him. But there was an air of the end of a party, like when a child's balloon loses altitude and slowly settles to the floor. Just then I remembered it was his birthday.

"Happy birthday," I said, unable to manage the words Mr. Ashworth, which felt too formal.

He took the cake by the cord, then placed his hat back on, which freed his other hand to support the box as a cake should be carried. "Thank you, Marie," he said. At the sound of my name I felt my throat close. I was extremely thirsty and thought I might be getting a headache. "Are you sure you want me to take this box?" He lifted it slightly. "It's beautiful," he said, smiling.

"Oh no. Please take it. And don't forget to put the cake in the icebox as soon as you get home."

"Okay," he said, "thank you. Have you been paid?"

"No. I guess not. But there's time for that."

Did I think a banker didn't carry money? That a man as rich as Mr. Ashworth couldn't be expected to pay, to reach into an elegant pocket and withdraw a special wallet in which there would be an embarrassing number of large bills?

"What do we owe you?"

"I don't know," I said.

"Really? You don't know?" he laughed, an unexpected sound that obviously gave him pleasure, a laugh heard by family and friends at elegant gatherings where he was the center of attention. At once he seemed to become someone other than Mr. Ashworth in the chauffeur-driven Packard, and the air of defeat left him.

"What kind of cake is it?" he asked with some exuberance.

"It's called Italian Love Cake," I said, because the moment seemed to call for honesty.

He looked directly at me, "What's in this cake, Marie? Chocolate, vanilla, almonds?" His eyes were alive.

"Wait until you taste it," I said, as a flash of heat spread across my face.

How would Mom have described her cake?

"*Torta deliziosa*," I said, before doing the unthinkable. I raised the fingers of one hand to my lips as though I intended to send his cake off with a kiss, but then stopped myself as my fingers left my mouth.

His response was another hearty laugh. "Marie," he said, "what's in this *torta deliziosa*?"

There was no mistaking his teasing, the intention to prolong our silly conversation.

"Vanilla, ricotta, butter icing," I answered, my heart thumping.

"My God," he said, shaking his head. "Guess I'd better get it home and into the icebox."

I followed him until we were both at the bottom of the stairs, when, without turning, he said, "I'll have Ella call you and you can let her know what we owe."

Then he was gone. The cake was gone, on Mom's special plate, in her hatbox, on its way to the Ashworth mansion on the lake.

I sat where Mr. Ashworth had and gazed out through the sheers at the stone lintel of The Peoples Bank, obscured in places by clusters of leafed-out maples. I was there for quite a while, looking at the view and trying to imagine what Mr. Ashworth had seen when he stood in my living room. I was still sitting there when Gino and Sammy stormed in. "I thought you said you were coming down," snapped Gino, his large fists clenched. Sammy hung back with an amused smile.

"I forgot," I said, because truly I had.

"I have a date," said Gino, in a softer tone, and I sensed he knew something had happened for which I had no explanation. I saw him notice my dress, which had been hanging on the door to my bedroom in a kind of display after I'd altered the bust.

After they left, I remained in the living room staring out at the sky from Mom's chair. It was then I felt a heaviness in my stomach, the first twinge of what I knew was my period arriving.

CHAPTER SIX

The phone started ringing, and soon I had more orders than I knew what to do with. Several local women telephoned wanting to know whether my ingredients were fresh. These were the Italians—this wasn't something an Anglo-Saxon would ever ask, because really, how would she know? I didn't like myself for forming a low opinion of my best clients, especially as they were more appreciative and never balked at the price. If the icing was a little runny or if I'd added too much sugar, or not enough, they appeared not to notice. I observed their lower standards and felt superior. I even discriminated against them in subtle ways, like charging an extra quarter, or changing the pickup time to one that suited me better—call it the ghost of my feisty mother.

Finally, the Ashworths' maid telephoned to ask what they owed. Ella apologized and said the Ashworths had been out of town.

"How did they like it?" I asked.

"Good. I think."

Only good? Had there been no reaction? Well, it didn't surprise me, as they were probably too spoiled in their eating habits to make a fuss about something as trite as a birthday cake. Really, it was just there to hold birthday candles and be a pretext for singing.

"The cost is $2.25," I said, adding a little extra. Ella said the gardener would drive her into town later and she would pay me. And, she said, she had my plate. After lunch I went through my stock catalogues in search of cake baking supplies; I had already decided to order half a dozen boxes. Then an image popped into my head of Ella throwing Mom's hatbox onto the kitchen floor and stomping on it before tucking it into the trash.

Ella was a tall, thin woman with large, kind eyes and a short bob with a tightly turned under-curl at her rounded jaw. She was a Negro, and I recalled having seen her before in town.

"Here," she said, handing over the money and Mom's plate in perfect condition.

I thanked her, and was about to ask about the hatbox when Ella said, "Goodness!" her eyes drifted to the money now in my hand. It was thrilling that I'd managed to earn so much for a cake. Meanwhile,

I was studying her pert uniform and trying to imagine what it was like to have a steady job in a mansion working for rich people, and I, too, felt jealous. But the uniform with its starched collar made me wonder about the formality of life inside the mansion.

What I'd taken for rudeness when we'd first spoken on the telephone was really a painful shyness. Yet something in her eyes was wise, and if circumstances were different I might have tried to woo her inside for a cup of tea and some gossip. I actually thought about it, but abandoned the idea, because I wouldn't have been able to resist asking about Mr. Ashworth.

The next several days were filled with routine. We were closed on Sundays, and because Mondays were slow we did the stock taking. By Tuesday everyone's mood picked up, and with an uptick in business, the week began. The store got busier as the school year drew near, and it was good news when finally we struggled to keep the shelves stocked with pens, notebooks and spiral binders. Still, I typically ran out of money just as I needed to order more stock, so it was good I was taking in extra with my baking.

I was in the back sweeping up after a delivery when Gino came in. He was in love. I knew this by noticing how often these days he showered and shaved. He mentioned he was saving for a zoot suit, and I warned him not to waste his money. "You'll look like a criminal," I said. He exploded, accusing me of being staid and a prude.

"Someone's out front to see you," he said, raising an eyebrow. He plugged a thumb in the direction of the store and winked. I followed him out, noting the arrogant swagger he'd only recently developed.

Mr. Ashworth was leaning against the penny candy counter and staring at a display of hairnets. On the counter next to him was the hatbox. Gino made an irritating clicking sound with his tongue but then, thankfully, he moved off down one of the aisles where he was sure to be listening.

"Hello," I said, too brightly. The shop tended to be cold in the mornings, and I was glad I was wearing a sweater that fit me well. I didn't always wear nice clothes to work. Mr. Ashworth was hatless and his tie was loose and askew, as if the heat was already getting to him.

"I can vouch for the good quality of that Italian Love Cake," he said. The words struck me as bold. I noticed how nice his smile was. He seemed different, happier than he had on his birthday.

I thanked him, but then there didn't seem to be much more to say. A customer came and went. Gino appeared briefly behind the cash register, then disappeared again.

"Better be going," said Mr. Ashworth, looking around. Had he noticed the bare shelves? He, a banker, would see the state of my operation. Flustered, I wouldn't remember saying goodbye, nor whether I'd remembered to thank him, first for the return of the plate, and now the hatbox. Then he was gone.

How did I know that Mr. Ashworth didn't often smile? He had seemed taller in the store than he had in my apartment, or when, on occasion, I spotted him leaving the bank. Every day since we'd met, at five p.m. no matter how busy, I dropped whatever I was doing and rushed upstairs to the window. What was his body like hidden beneath the lightweight serge of his suit? His face was often shielded, but I could clearly see his neck, a smooth and graceful nakedness. I pictured him in meetings, talking on the telephone, or to his secretary. I had always found the bank's façade a pleasing view. But since that first encounter, each glimpse felt like an intimacy, an imposition on his privacy and an intrusion on mine in the cool darkness of my apartment.

CHAPTER SEVEN

At first I ignored the buzzer because I had too much to do. But when it sounded again more insistently, I went down hoping it wasn't the Jehovah's Witnesses who'd just moved into their new building on Chew Road.

"I think you have the wrong address," I said.

"No. You are Marie? Marie Genovese?"

She was an Italian from Italy. You could always tell. But it wasn't just the accent, they looked different. They had swarthier skin, fuller lips, and wore less make-up. I of course was an Italian, but I was fascinated by those considered to be *the real ones*.

She was attractive, in her mid to late 40s, with long hair that suited her, making her seem youthful, beautiful. Her skirt was of a fabric too heavy for the weather and cut in an unflattering way, shapeless and scratchy looking, which I assumed was what European clothes were like. I couldn't help but stare. The jewelry she wore was delicate, so unlike the cheap, chunky costume most women had, or the junk I sold in the store. A gold necklace was so thin you almost couldn't see it, and in the tiny cross glowed pale stones.

"Sono la sorella di tua madre."

I could almost understand her standard Italian, like the nuns had taught us, without a hint of southern dialect.

"Mi scusi?" My Italian was limited. We had been learning Italian until one day those beautiful little books with the cream-colored bindings suddenly disappeared. And when we asked Sister Bertino what had happened, she said we weren't to mention the books ever again. I later learned that Italians were coming under suspicion over our support for Mussolini. Some even considered us to be traitors in our own country.

"Tua madre, Carmela. Sono la sorella. Tua zia."

My mother's sister? My heart beat loudly in my chest. My hand went to my throat.

"What is your name?"

"Ada Parodi."

Mom had never mentioned she had a sister. I led her into the living room, and she took a seat in one of Carmela's overstuffed chairs. She had a confident smile, and when she crossed her legs, my composure was further shattered by a vision of Mom in her apron and long skirt.

Ada Parodi then launched into the story of how she'd come to America, from Savona in the region of Liguria, in northern Italy. Had both my parents come from the north of Italy? We had believed our mother to be from the south.

Reading my mind, Ada said, "Papa from Savona. Mama from Napoli."

So my maternal grandfather had been a northerner? I never considered that Italians moved around their own country the way Americans did within theirs. It was one thing for Italians here to have come from different parts of Italy, only to meet and marry here. But how did my grandparents manage that in Italy? How did my maternal grandmother from the south, and my grandfather from the north, meet? According to Ada, their father came from Savona, and on a trip south to Naples to visit a friend he'd met my grandmother. They married and settled in Arzano, a small town north of Naples, where the sisters, my mother and Ada were raised. Ada didn't know the exact neighborhood in Naples where her mother was from. They never went back there.

At some point Ada migrated north. Pride crept into her voice whenever she mentioned Liguria. She had switched suddenly to very poor English, so I didn't catch much apart from Savona, Liguria, and buses. She had been taking the buses, but where she came from they were different. They stopped anywhere, all you had to do was wave your hand.

Her voice was familiar, deep and full of vibration whenever emotion crept in. I asked how she had found me, and she mentioned the family she was staying with, the Mortellites.

"Here in town? I don't know them," I said, noticing the vibration in my own voice.

Her large eyes narrowed in disbelief, as if I were the unreliable one. Her eyes were hazel, the same color as mine, the same as Mom's.

"Are the Mortellites from Savona?" I asked.

She laughed, "Oh no, no no. Mortellite. Sono di Napoli."

I never knew which names were from the north, and which from the south. Most Italians in Littlefield came from the area around Naples. Of course, we Genoveses were from Genoa, and we had always been proud to claim the north, with its reputation for less poverty, more dignity.

"Mom never mentioned…"

Ada began wandering the living room. She was tall, taller than I. "You cook?" she asked, sniffing the air.

"I'm baking."

"I love kitchen," she said. "I know. È incredibile."

That was a word I understood. Yes, it was *incredible*. Abruptly, her facial expression changed and a smile overcame the serious face there a second ago. So far, she'd made no attempt to hug me or act in any familial way. "We not see us. For years," she said. "Parodis."

Did she mean she hadn't seen her sister, my mother? What a jolt it was to finally hear our mother's birth name spoken. Parodi. Carmela Parodi. Ada stood at Mom's breakfront and ran a hand across the smoothness.

"She never mentioned you," I said. Why not admit I was frightened? A stranger claiming to be my aunt turns up from Italy.

"Posso vedere la cucina?"

"Oh, yes, I'm sorry. I'll make coffee."

Looking around my tiny kitchen, I wondered if she thought it fancy compared to the poor south of Italy where my grandmother had been born. Or did she see what I saw; a small room perfectly adequate for the making of delicious food, even if the whole place was in desperate need of paint and better equipment.

"I teach," she said, looking around. I was about to ask what she taught when she said, "I teach you cook."

I recalled a day when Mom and I were in the kitchen. I was nine or ten at the time, and I listened as she chatted, until with sudden seriousness, she said, "You're lucky you don't have a sister. All you would do is fight."

At the time it was easy to dismiss our mother's distress. Weren't grownups always worried about something? But then Mom had turned to me and with quite a bit of emotion, said, "*I'm* the one who always baked. We *always* needed bread. *I* was the one to make sure it was on the table." She might as well have said, *I have a useless sister who I argued with all the time, and it never occurred to her to help the family.* Was that why Mom had failed to tell me about Ada?

Ada came to stand close to me at the stove. I had a tray of cookies baking, and a lentil soup was simmering. She hung her long, well-shaped nose over the steaming broth while making waving motions to scoop up the aroma.

"What is this?"

"Lentils, and tomato."

She took my arm and turned me around. "A love coming?"

Her eyes wandered the room before settling on the drawing of Ceres that hung above the sink. "In kitchen! Mama's!"

Had the drawing belonged to my grandmother? The picture was pleasingly worn, yellowed around the edges, with little bobbles where moisture from so much cooking had worked its way under the glass. Carmela once pointed at the drawing and said, *Ceres is proof that we come back.* My mother often said things that made no sense. She was of another generation, and though I didn't like myself for it, I rejected her superstitions. She had insisted on calling the goddess of agriculture, grain and fertility by her Roman name, Ceres, instead of Demeter, the Greek goddess we'd learned about in school. For her it was a point of pride that we used the Roman names and therefore claiming the gods and goddess for our own. Demeter was Ceres; Persephone was Proserpine.

I asked my teacher about Ceres because I was dying to show off that we had a picture of the goddess in our kitchen. She looked hard at me, weighing up whether or not to explain the myth; then she did. Proserpine had been abducted, brutally raped, and condemned to life in Hades. The loss of her daughter drove Ceres crazy, and that's when she cursed the earth and made it barren in the winter months. Only after she'd threatened to ruin the crops did her brother Jove, king of the Gods, agree to allow Proserpine to escape her captor husband in order to spend two-thirds of the year with her mother. And this became the season of growth, when wheat sprang up and the world greened and ripened. I liked that Ceres had used her power to strike a bargain.

"Let me?" Ada took Mom's cookbook and dragged a nail down the list of ingredients. "Sweets are better. The grain. Wheat from the ground. I like cake. You?"

"Yes," I said, thinking how with just a little flour Mom had been able to whip up the most delicious, pleasing sustenance: bread, pasta, cake.

But how strange Ada was. She spoke rapidly, her thoughts a torrent of unrelated subjects with connections she had no intention of revealing. At the same time she was nonchalant, like it was nothing to turn up on the doorstep of a niece she'd never met, enter her kitchen and start sniffing the air.

"Littlefield," she pronounced the name in two distinct words. "Water is good?"

Of course the water was good. In America every place had good water. Did she mean that Italy didn't? I had seen pictures of the Bay of Naples and the Gulf of Salerno. Friends of our mother's had visited these places that I'd come to know from postcards I found in the ex-voto. Water was everywhere. I'd heard Italians in town, most of whom had come from the dry, stony hills around Naples, say they'd come to the pine forests of New Jersey for the high water table. The could grow berries and other fruit here, and many had come to farm. Littlefield was also not very far from the sea, just twenty-five miles away to the southeast. But since I hardly ever left town, the Atlantic remained as mysterious as the vast Tyrrhenian.

"Divinazione dell'acqua!" Ada looked at me with an intense gaze. "I find water," she said.

Mr. E. had a friend who could cross a field holding only a forked stick, and if he felt a tremor, he knew water could be found directly below. Some people claimed to be able to read tea leaves and grains of corn. I had heard of Italians in town who used Tarot cards. I didn't necessarily believe any of it.

"Good for plants. They grow," she said.

The only farmers I knew well were the Rizottes, who owned the mushroom house; Mimi Rizotte and Mom had been good friends. As a shopkeeper in town, I felt apart from those who worked with soil and grew things. I thought of the man I'd had sex with on the couch in the stockroom the night of Mom's funeral, recalling the dirt under his fingernails. Not that I considered myself better. Not that I looked down on farmers. Only that the Five & Ten was across the street from a bank, a pharmacy, and a gas station. On our side of the street was the key cutter and two doors down was Oletskys' haberdashery. We all catered to needs beyond the basics of food.

Ada began inspecting things on the small side counter—my old mixer, Mom's mortar and pestle. "Plants," she said. "You learn."

"Do you mean herbs?"

She didn't answer. It struck me I knew next to nothing of my mother's life before she came here. Had she and Ada perhaps lived on a farm?

"Morta," she said suddenly, under her breath. Did she mean my mother? Of course Mom was morta. My stomach flipped over.

What a strange woman Ada was, not the least embarrassed to stand in my kitchen and make her appraisals, to stare nakedly at the circumstances of my life.

"I'm sorry, Ada, but I'm just so busy today."

"Everybody busy."

"It's the way it is here."

She gave a sly smile, and I was arrested by another glimpse of Carmela, of the teasing, playful side to my mother, employed to great effect in maintaining control over me and my brothers. Ada had a similar authority. It was overpowering.

"The store? Yours?" she asked quickly.

Surely she knew it was. I nodded. The sooner I served our coffee, the sooner I could get rid of her. "Yes, me and my brothers."

"Business good?"

"Sometimes," I said. It would be impossible to describe the rollercoaster of running a store in the Depression. I knew nothing of my aunt's circumstances, and a thought struck me. What if she believed the store might also belong to her? I felt myself withdraw, the familiar gripping in my stomach, in my heart. But as I brought our cups to the table I no longer wanted her to go. There was a companionable silence I likened to mornings spent with Mom in the hour before we went downstairs and our day began on the shop floor. Ada seemed, if not yet family, at least familiar. I even thought I noticed something of Sammy—a softness around the mouth, like a sensual, more relaxed version of me. Could it be I was more like my father, a Genovese rather than a Parodi?

Ada got up abruptly. "I come back," she said, and tilting her head, threw back her coffee in one gulp.

"Can I call you?" I asked.

"Oh, si."

In the living room I pointed across the street at the bus stop, but her eyes gravitated toward the tall granite bank building on the corner. She had been staring at it, and I almost said, yes, Littlefield has a bank. I told her the bus schedule, and she said, "Maybe I help you. I come back."

We exchanged numbers, and I promised to call. Then she looked at me as if a question had suddenly popped into her head, and she was debating whether or not to ask. I waited, but she didn't say more. I led the way downstairs, and on the threshold she grasped my hands in both of hers, "Don't worry," she said in a rush of emotion, "I see you soon."

I watched her cross the street to the bus stop noticing how she moved, how she tossed her hair and tilted her face to the sun. She bore an undeniable resemblance to Mom. But it wasn't until I was sitting in the chair she'd occupied that I remembered an Italian proverb told to me by Mr. E. At the time I didn't know what it meant. It was about having a *tail of straw*, which could mean you had a guilty conscience or a secret you didn't want others to know. I felt the weight of secrets. Mom had not told me everything. When was their last contact and how had Ada found out Mom had died? It was my tail of straw that prevented me from asking too many questions. I feared getting too close to the flame.

Every family had secrets. Ada's halting delivery was more than just a struggle with the language. She wasn't sure how much to say. Though how much did I really want to know, when becoming an American seemed to demand that we forget?

CHAPTER EIGHT

Oletskys' haberdashery carried everything from ladies' lingerie to men's neckties and hats. Their store was slightly larger than ours, with two full display windows on either side of a wide entrance. Mom had always envied them the extra space. We occasionally shared a supplier and shipping costs, and Ruth and Mom used to attend town meetings lest matters be decided by those who had never owned a store. That is, until Gersh started going instead, because everyone knew a man had a better chance of being heard.

Carmela often said that Ruth had saved her life after our father left. The Oletskys and the Genoveses needed each other, and it had always been that way. I continued to rely on them, especially Ruth; there wasn't anything I couldn't tell her, nothing I couldn't ask.

Ruth and I were sitting in my kitchen sipping tea and gazing out at the sky above the loading bay. It was on the tip of my tongue to tell her about the man who'd showed up late the night of the funeral, but with the arrival of my period some of the urgency had left me. I also wanted to tell her about Ada's visit, and was about to launch into it when I sensed she had something to say.

We were waiting for my cakes to finish baking—I had two to make, one for Mrs. Ricci and another for Mrs. Tilton, the librarian. I was whipping the icing and complaining about Gino, when Ruth interrupted me. "Marie, I have to tell you something." She sounded calm, but the look on her face frightened me. She went on, "I don't like to say anything, but Gersh stopped by your store last Sunday. He didn't think anybody would be downstairs, but the door was open. He needed help lifting boxes and wanted to see if the boys were around. And," she paused for emphasis, "he found Gino in the back room listening to *Golden Hour of the Little Flower.*"

"What's that?" I couldn't see the problem. It was such a sweet name. It sounded religious. "I don't let them listen to the radio during the week when they're supposed to be working…"

"Marie, that's Father Coughlin's program. He's poison," she said, her tone suddenly sharp. I hadn't recognized the name of the program, but of course I knew Coughlin. She went on. "He hates Roosevelt.

He started an organization called the Christian Front, and no Jews are allowed to join. Not that any of us would. He's even launched a campaign, *Buy Christian Only.* Imagine. He believes Jews are trying to impose slavery on the whole world. He thinks we created the Depression. Yeah, the Depression was our dream come true. Me and Gersh."

"That's ridiculous," I said. "Nobody believes that."

"Oh no?"

"I'll stop him. I'll talk to him. Did Gino help Gersh with the boxes?"

"No. He never asked him. Coughlin is a devil. Your boys shouldn't…"

"I said I'll talk to them."

I didn't mean to be short, but I was afraid to confront Gino. "I will," I said more softly. "I'll talk to him." With a smile I brought to the table a little plate of the trimmed edges from one of my cakes. I placed my hand on top of hers. "Please, don't worry."

"In Germany," she said with a defeated air, "They're putting us in ghettos."

"What ghettos?" I asked.

"Places where we can't go in or out."

I took her hand in both of mine. "Ruth, I'll talk to him. I will."

Ruth knew a lot. She was up on events in Europe, and she worried all the time about the Jews. Her voice broke as she described the fear and suffering. I thought about the Italians in Italy. I wondered what they knew, and whether or not they cared about events happening in other parts of Europe. Did they believe, as some in Littlefield did, that the world was better off ruled by dictators? I worried about there being so much support for Mussolini, but what could I do?

Socially, Gersh and Ruth kept to themselves, but they were active in town politics and took pride in the main street when not everyone did. I wanted to believe others reciprocated the Oletskys' kindnesses, but I doubted it. Mr. Gazzara was famous for leaving his garbage out until an animal distributed it all over the sidewalk. It was often Gersh who swept up the mess before opening hours, going well past the limits of his own store and onto the sidewalks of his neighbors. To show my gratitude, I brought them produce from Mr. E.'s gifts of food—bushels of zucchini, eggplant and sweet corn in summer, and jars of whatever I had canned in winter. I brought soup and stew. So long as I had the ingredients, it wasn't a hardship. I had to cook in large quantities anyway on account of my brothers.

Ruth stopped by often and complimented my displays. We joked that we catered to people who had more money than we did, careful to stipulate how grateful we were they existed. I admired the clothes she sold, few of which I could afford. I'd once bought gloves for Gino and Sammy, and Ruth made sure I knew they were of good quality. "I hardly ever stock these," she said, "too expensive." Then the funny click of her large teeth that glistened when she smiled. She always gave me a good discount.

Often, listening to Ruth, I felt the miracle of history. At least she knew her family's story. I had learned a small amount from Ada. It remained to be seen how much more she knew and whether or not she would tell me.

Ruth and Gersh first met in New York as teenagers and discovered that they'd both been born in a place called Woodbridge, not twenty miles from Littlefield. Their parents had come to southern New Jersey as part of an agricultural community owned by a wealthy Russian Jew who was recruiting families escaping the pogroms. Both their families had been seduced into joining a *back-to-the-land* movement that promised an agrarian heaven, but proved to be anything but. Like many immigrants they'd been lured by advertisements, like we Italians had been recruited to help build the railroads.

"What did we know of farming?" said Ruth. "I know. In the Old Testament we were farmers. But no more. It was filthy where Gersh's parents lived, and he was only ten years old when they shipped him off to live with cousins in New York. My parents stayed for many more years, and believe me I got to witness the filth. No plumbing. No doctors. My father complained he had no tools. Yet they expected us to use our own tools to clear the land, which was covered in trees. And the mosquitos were terrible. I hated it. Then, just as I turned fourteen, they sent me to live with relatives in New York. Two years later I met Gersh, and we couldn't believe we had the same story. After we were married we heard of a store going cheap in Littlefield and we scraped together every cent from every relative. And here we are."

Ruth had already heard the story of the poker game, how our father, Giuseppe Genovese, had managed to win the store. The story related a card game in a dimly lit room full of smoke, a scene from a Hollywood movie, which across many tellings became a kind of truth. In the center of the worn green felt under a bright light were all kinds of possessions, everything except cash which had run out minutes earlier. Into the pot someone tossed a sapphire tie tack, a watch, and a folded paper, an official looking document covered in small print, what turned out to be a deed. The deed was to a small, north-facing storefront on Bellevue Avenue directly across from The Peoples Bank. That was the paper that lay in the middle of the poker table when my father swept it clean. I don't think he cheated at cards. Then again, how would I know? I still have the tie tack.

One day we had nothing, and the next day we owned a Five & Ten. I was two years old, so I have no memory. What I can just remember is our father leaving us when I was seven. Mom took the three of us downstairs, and I remember Mr. E. took a step closer to her. I watched him stare at our beautiful mother. Unspoken was the shame of having one's father leave, which stifled all questions, about him and so many other things.

As I listened to Ruth's stories about Russia and the Ukraine, pogroms and famine, and how for the Jews left behind there was scapegoating and violence, I realized that I didn't have it so bad.

The next day I went to find Gino in the store, and I marched straight up to him.

"I want to talk to you," I said, leading the way to the back room where I wheeled on him. "I don't want you listening to that priest."

"What are you talking about?" he wore his big hands on his hips and leaned forward as though his back hurt him.

"Father Coughlin. I don't want to hear his voice in the store, and I don't want anybody knowing you listen to him."

"I don't listen to Coughlin."

"Don't lie to me. I heard you. And someone else heard."

"Who?"

"Never mind. I'll take the radio away if I have to."

Gino laughed, it was more of a snort. "Yeah, that would be real bad. And I couldn't get another one."

"Friends help each other. That's what friends do. And the Oletskys are our friends."

"What do you care anyway? Did you know they carry women's hairbands now? We sell those. They shouldn't be stepping on our toes."

"They also send us customers. That priest hates Jews. Do you understand? And who cares about headbands? We haven't sold one in a year."

My hands were shaking so badly I had to shove them down into the pockets of my apron. It was going to take more than a sprinkling of mint to soften him, and he wasn't alone in this new belligerence. Again the other day I'd had to ask Kenny why stock remained on the storeroom floor when the displays looked empty.

"I'll do it when I have time," he said in a rude tone.

"It's out of the kindness of my heart that I continue to pay you!" I called out after him, but he just kept walking, which caused Sammy to put his arm around my waist and whisper, "Marie, too harsh." He was right of course. I needed Kenny, and I needed Gino. And for now, at least, I had no choice but to put up with their crap.

CHAPTER NINE

I stood alone in line at the Rivoli on "Dish Night," one more plainly dressed woman waiting to receive her free plate. I'd gone the previous week as well, though I'd already seen the film, *Test Pilot*, a quiet "B" picture with Myrna Loy playing a Kansas farm girl. I planned to use my new plates on Thanksgiving and Christmas when we invited Kenny and his wife and Mr. Esposito. Thinking I might build my set more quickly, I asked my brothers to go to the movies on a Wednesday, but they flat out refused. "Are we so poor that we need free dishes?" they asked. "Yes," I told them.

Once the newsreel was over, I opened my eyes. Several rows down and to the left sat a smartly dressed woman in a dark blue blouse with a prim lace collar. What caught my attention were her gold earrings that flashed in the soft light. I had only seen Priscilla Ashworth once, but I knew who she was, everyone did, and seated next to her was Mr. Ashworth in a nondescript gray suit. I wouldn't have recognized him were it not for that shock of light brown hair and that smooth neck. Not a second passed that I wasn't aware of their presence, but as the lights went down, I kept my head locked forward.

After the movie was over, I worried Mr. Ashworth might notice me and be forced to make introductions, so I rummaged pointlessly in my handbag until most of the patrons had filed out. Quickly, so no one would notice, I slipped my free dish under my coat and stood to leave. But when finally I looked up, figuring most had already gone, our eyes met. His gaze was brief, but in that second it felt piercing, as if he'd happened upon a shocking incident and his brain was taking time to react, to decide what had to be done. He continued to walk behind his wife, who had gone ahead and seemed to be in a hurry. Others were walking slowly, discussing the picture, and there were quiet chuckles of delight. I realized how much I had wanted to see him, and for him to see me.

The next morning I was in an agitated mood. I paced, dusted, even damp mopped, though I'd done it recently. I rearranged stock. It helped our sales if I moved what little there was around in an effort to make the displays look new. I refolded tea towels and shifted a stand laden with sunglasses that Feldman had sold me to over by the housewares. If people had to hunt for what they needed, they would walk around for longer and were more likely to buy something. Woolworth's in Atlantic City was selling a line called Foster Grant, and now everyone was asking for sunglasses, which were a good way to refresh an old outfit when one couldn't afford new clothes. Feldman had given me a good price. But really I did all this because I was nervous Corley might turn up and repossess his stock. And by two o'clock, when this hadn't happened, I asked Kenny, who gave me a piercing look. "Esposito covered it," he said. Why did I come under scrutiny whenever Mr. E. gave us money? Kenny of all people benefited, because I couldn't pay him otherwise. Hearing the bill had been taken care of, I was relieved, but then a new anxiety, how this put me further into Salvie Esposito's debt.

I was in the kitchen starting dinner when Sammy came in. He leaned against the door jamb and stared at me as though I'd changed my hair color or come into the kitchen wearing an evening gown.

"What are you looking at?"

"Mr. E. wants to take us out for dinner."

"I don't feel like it."

"Come on, Marie. It'll be fun." Sammy never wanted to go out when it was just him and Gino.

"I have baking to do."

"Mr. E. will be disappointed," he said, leaving the room.

I hated to let Sammy down, but I had already decided. I was looking forward to a night alone. I would make myself a small plate with what was left in the icebox, some salami, and a salad with some delicious fresh tomatoes and a nice spoon of leftover ricotta from a cake order. The boys would be home late, so I would have the entire evening to myself, free to think about the married Mr. Ashworth, who if I happened to see again would be at a safe distance. He wouldn't have another excuse to drop in on me. He wouldn't need to pick up a nail file or a child's umbrella; he had servants for that. And there were no children, that much I knew. The day he'd returned the hatbox, two weeks ago now, it was only a gesture that confirmed his good breeding, the courtly manners that wouldn't allow for the box to be crushed or lost. But what of the electric meeting of our eyes at the movies? And how, ever since, I'd craved sweets, an urge that drove me not to the kitchen, but to my front windows in the hopes of catching a glimpse of him. What would it be like to stand close to that man with his beautiful suit, and to touch the crispness of that costly fabric? Would he smell like the bank, with its cool marble floors and air-conditioning?

Feeling restless, I went to the window and looked out. The bank's lintel was lit from below like a classical monument from the old world. Like photographs I'd seen of Italy's famous landmarks, statues of Marcus Aurelius or Bacchus towering over a fountain of cascading figures. Otherwise, the bank seemed cold.

I went to the kitchen and poured myself a glass of wine. Then I returned to the living room, where the curtains were open and I could be seen, but only by Mrs. Moriarity, who owned the apartment above the florist's across the street. Next door was the bank. Of course the one person I wouldn't have minded seeing me wasn't there, but down a long, winding lane, in a mansion on a lake.

I paced from the living room to the kitchen and back again. I went past the bedrooms down a short corridor and through a narrow door that led to a small balcony overlooking the store. I hadn't done this for years. There, a staircase we never used, led downstairs and into a corner of the stockroom. Most of the shops on the main street had this feature. There was also a tiny room that used to be an office, and which I hoped to use again someday, except Mr. E. had been up here recently and declared it unsafe, the floor rotten in places, the railings unstable. We talked about fixing it, but there were too many other needs. I went to sit with my legs dangling over the edge. From there I gazed down into the quiet store. Dust moats floated in the soft evening light, and the last of the day's heat rose and gathered around me. It was then that I felt my mother.

What are you going to do?

Mom and I had never really discussed anything personal. There was always too much to handle in the day to day. Nor did we talk about the future, mine or the store's. I had been too young to speak to her as I longed to speak to her now, woman to woman. I had many questions. What was love, and would I find it? And why did we always have to be so careful around men? I wished I had her to talk to. Was I about to blunder into a situation that could harm me? My emotions were like eggs in a damaged carton, broken, useless. True, I had Ruth, who was always practical, but I couldn't talk to her about my desire for a man. It defied description, this thudding heat between my legs. All I knew was I didn't want a marriage like Mom's friends had. Their grouchy husbands wore them out, diminished them, their beauty and spirits squashed beneath a string of demands. Mrs. Bertolli, Mrs. Romasello, Mrs. Cavuto, Mrs. Gazzara—what did those women do to deserve such husbands? Is that why Mrs. Cavuto was so short tempered? And Mrs. Romasello, as ignorant a busy body as there was, did she deserve Al Romasello, with his revolting cigars and mean tongue? I had trouble picturing these men as young, soft-spoken suitors, courting, bringing gifts. It was all the excuse I needed not to date, not to flirt. But my desire was less easy to push away. It wouldn't be tamed, not by hugging my pillow in the dark of my room, lying awake plagued by sounds, images, fragrances, and the chilled air of the bank, with its suggestion of aftershave, or was it the perfume of the tellers, or was it the smell of money, of prosperity?

My days were full of work. I went tirelessly from task to task, hardly pausing for breath. Then, without warning, my heart would constrict and my complexion would take on a bright sheen. I flew between fear and bravery. Order this, then figure out how to pay for it. Flirt with Mr. E. Secure a little more of a loan. *Were these loans?* Haggle with a supplier, while being glared at by Kenny, who treated me as though I was the cause of the Depression itself. My status as a single woman was an affront, a stain, a sin so grave it might bring us all down. Meanwhile, my brothers huddled together in the back room listening to that priest. Sammy cracked jokes, wanting to cheer me up, but my only real peace was with Mom in the ex-voto, where, in the dim light of the tiny room, I confessed my fears.

CHAPTER TEN

The two o'clock bus arrived from Philly. I looked at my watch. The bus was on time. I watched the passengers alight and noticed two groups of Philadelphians. There were the proper ladies down from Society Hill, who wore day dresses with little jackets and bright white shoes with perforated toes. Then there were the Italians, older women dressed in black too warm for the weather, their feet broad and knobby as Easter bread. They would have family in town, cousins, sons and daughters who'd moved to Littlefield knowing their female relatives would gladly make the tiring journey down to visit. They looked lost, unused to the quiet street, the slow procession of automobiles, such a contrast to the city. In their immigrant's garb they appeared wilted. Mom's friends were of a similar generation, Mrs. Rizotte and Mrs. Bellafiore, only they wore floral housedresses from the Sears catalogue; they rarely wore black.

Carmela used to stand where I stood now, watching the activity on the street below. Mom, did you ever think you could escape? Did you ever swoon in the heat as the curtains wrapped around your bare legs and clung, were you ever thinking about a man? Ever since he'd arrived to pick up his cake, in all the days since, I thought about him.

Among the crowd of passengers was a woman who was taller and younger than the rest. Her hair shone, and whereas the others were cast in shadow, she seemed to glow. Suddenly, she looked up and waved. My first instinct was to step back from the window at this invasion of my privacy. But it was too late, Ada had already seen me. I waved back, and performed a quick scan, wondering if anyone noticed me noticing her. What was I afraid of?

I watched her cross the street, her nice legs showcased by a skirt that was again too long and warm for the weather. Nevertheless, she had flair, and several people turned to look.

"'Ello," she said, walking directly toward me and up the narrow stairs. I followed her into the kitchen, where she pulled out a chair and sat.

"Warm," she said, fanning herself with a scrap of paper extracted from her purse. I put water on for coffee.

"What brings you to Littlefield?" I sounded formal, a little cool, and I wondered if Ada noticed. Of course I knew what had brought her; she'd been summoned by my need.

She leaned back and gathered her hair up in a ratty old snood, stretched and worn to accommodate copious tresses. She looked beautiful with her hair off her face. She looked beautiful with it flowing, and her resemblance to Mom made me catch my breath. What was the reason not to tell a child, a daughter, that she had an aunt? I blamed Italy. I was frustrated by this papering over, the hiding, the secrets, what seemed a national trait. At the same time, nothing escaped our sharp eyes.

We sipped our coffees, and just like the last time, the amount I wanted to say outweighed what I actually said. We talked about cake. Ada had brought me a rhizome of black hellebore, a poison.

"Be careful," she said.

"What can I use it for?"

Her eyes narrowed, her hand made a rapid flushing motion from head to foot, as if to dispel whatever needed to be swept from the human body, the mind, the soul. I was transfixed, also a little annoyed and surprised by her boldness, and the foreignness that at first I wanted to reject. Yet again, in her presence I felt refreshed, relieved of a burden. She stared at me with such a solemn expression, it was as if she expected a confidence. Maybe she was just tired, winded from the trip. She gave a long, low sigh.

"What is it, Ada?" I asked.

She waved me off. "Phew. I complain. Not good."

"No. Tell me."

"Men. *Pazzo. Pazzo.*"

Crazy. There were certain words known to all Italians, no matter how little they spoke the language. Ada's hand flew around her head. She rolled her eyes. So it wasn't me, but rather her own situation that had caused such a serious face.

I laughed. "What happened?"

I could see laughing wasn't the reaction she'd expected, but then she laughed too, only hers was cut short by a glare in which I sensed a dangerous mood.

"They no understand," she said with sudden vehemence.

I couldn't disagree. I, too, wanted to talk about a man, about *him*. His sudden presence in my life made the dullest routines harder to complete, but also sometimes a small task became engrossing, as though I was treading water in a warm lake. I'd been walking around holding my breath. Still, I hesitated to tell Ada the story of our chance meeting.

"Tell me," I said.

"The Mortellites! My God. They give me place to live. That's all." She leaned forward and with an abrupt tilt of her head gave a look of utter disbelief. "The brother-in-law. His wife, she die. Me? No. I no interested."

It was the first instance of our connection, which Ada, leaning back in her chair, seemed to savor. But then she sat bolt upright and squinted as though the sun had come blasting into my kitchen, though it hadn't. I had no idea who or what seemed to have temporarily blinded her, but I, too, felt a presence.

"You date?" she asked.

"No. I…"

Ada downed her coffee and stood. Wouldn't she wait for my answer?

"Don't go," I said, following her into the living room.

"Don't worry. I come back."

"When?"

"Soon."

"Are you okay at the Mortellites?"

She threw her head back and laughed. "Ha," she said. "You lay. You sleep. You eat. You go out. You need place to do. It's okay."

"Men can be trouble," I said.

She looked hard at me, as though she saw Mr. Ashworth walking around inside my head. She stood for a moment in the center of my living room before turning toward the windows, and staring out she looked from the bank to me and back again. I felt a brush of wind in the otherwise static air.

She straightened her skirt, pulled off the terrible snood and shoved it in her pocket. She looked better suddenly, softer with her hair down.

"Where are you going?" I asked.

Had she come all the way down from Philly, only to turn around and go right back?

She took a small mirror from her purse and reapplied her lipstick, a fiery red that she under-painted on full lips so that they appeared thinner, a straight, unamused line. I flashed on Mom, who had worn the same color, but had liked to paint her lips into a full, sensuous bow.

Ada turned to me wearing her street face. It was a mask. Who was this stranger?

CHAPTER ELEVEN

I was on my way to Ferrara's when I realized I'd forgotten my wallet. My bag felt heavy. It was time to empty it of the receipts and samples of merchandise that made their way into the large leather satchel. Thinking my wallet had to be somewhere near the bottom, I rummaged, and because I wasn't paying attention, we almost collided. We stood, practically chest to chest, before backing away embarrassed.

"I'm so glad to see you," he said. There was the boyish smile that just managed to lessen the more formal aspects of Mr. Ashworth in his three-piece suit.

"I'm glad, too," I said, not knowing what the words meant.

"Can I come up?" He was smiling.

It was suddenly as if he were a ventriloquist, and those passing on the street, though I wasn't aware of anyone, weren't meant to see Mr. Ashworth's lips moving; instead, it seemed the words came from another source, a dark, secret place close to the heart. I was aware of the need to be discreet but the boldness with which he asked to come up seemed designed to end whatever mystery there was between us. In that second, Mr. Ashworth seemed a much younger man.

"I have to go up anyway," I said, "because I forgot my wallet."

"Well, let me walk you," he said. The smile was unwavering now but his eyes had changed. They took on a strange seriousness, not hard, but opening to another possibility. As I turned to cross the street with Mr. Ashworth by my side, thank goodness there didn't seem to be many cars, nor did their drivers appear to notice anything out of the ordinary. Just a normal summer afternoon on the main street with the sun burning a little hotter and no hint of a reprieve from the scant breeze.

We mounted the stairs, and I was aware of leading Mr. Ashworth. I heard his steps behind me and felt the additional heat of a second body in close quarters. I was glad I'd remembered to spray the lavender water I made each year from the bouquets Mr. E. dropped off. And as luck would have it, I had just baked, so the door swung open to the scent of vanilla and butter.

"I have to do one thing," I said, turning to him.

He nodded. The corners of his mouth were curved in a faint smile, but his eyes were deadly serious.

I went into the kitchen and phoned down to the store. I told the boys the exterminator had come and they weren't to enter the apartment until I gave the all clear. "No problem," said Gino. "I'll tell Sam."

I hung up, my hand still on the receiver as I contemplated my lie and the tray of perfect cupcakes on the counter. I wasn't focused on anything in particular, but everything in the room became sharp as a paring knife. I didn't even care that I'd left him in the living room. Normally, I would feel a compulsion not to take too long, not to be rude, to not be that person who doesn't know how to extend hospitality to a guest. None of these thoughts occurred to me then.

I leaned heavily against the counter as the realization of what was to happen hit me. I had, after all, called down to the store.

"Marie?"

The sound of his voice startled me.

"Be right there," I called out.

The rollercoaster of our desire, simmering for days, was at last coming to its final dip and dive. Time slowed, or maybe I had been standing there for a while, because he was suddenly behind me, and I felt the warm pressure of his thighs against my buttocks, his arms around my waist. I turned toward him and there was no mistaking what we were about to do. The last word I would speak before we fell onto my bed was his first name, "Joseph."

It was painful, which surprised me because I had had that other experience. I could, if I wanted, count this as my first. And when finally we pulled away, our bodies detaching with reluctance, I could see he thought it was my first time.

"I didn't mean..." he said, trailing off.

"I did," I said. "I wanted it to happen."

He seemed surprised, but in the glow of our lovemaking that was like a confection of the sweetest, most chemically perfect recipe, I felt everything to be exactly right. Was this the change I had felt coming as I made his birthday cake? Could this man have been sent to me by my mother? The idea was crazy. If anything, he seemed more jolted than I.

"Marie," he said, gathering me in his arms.

"What is it?"

He shook his head. "I'm happy." Then, "I hope I didn't hurt you."

"No. A little. It's a good hurt."

This pleased him. There would be no need to confess the other lover. No embarrassment over the indiscretion of a *second* lover. But then the words were out before I could stop them, "You're not my first."

"Really?" If he was shocked, he gave no sign. Then time seemed to stop, until finally he spoke again, "I've been lonesome, Marie, for a long time."

"I've been lonely, too."

He sat up and twisted around to look at me. I wondered what the next moment would bring. It was as though we tiptoed across thinly frozen ice, the location of our destination mysterious, even perilous, but with the urgent need to cross whatever plain this was. For us to speak so honestly thrilled me. He lay back down, and together we stared at the ceiling. I was grateful suddenly for the attractive soffit paper with the cabbage roses, refreshed five years earlier by Mom, one of the last improvements she'd made to the apartment. The roses made me happy, reminding me of a debutante's bedroom, and I hoped he noticed how elegant the pattern was. But when I looked over I was surprised to see him wiping away tears. For the first time that afternoon I felt scared. Why was he crying? I didn't know what was in my own heart, but I felt similarly moved. "I'm so sorry," I said.

"You have nothing to be sorry for." He looked at me with tenderness. "I married well," he said, passing his palm down over his face. I noticed how strong looking his arm was, considering his job was lifting papers.

"God that came out wrong," he said, allowing his arm to drop heavily. "Marie." He smoothed my hair, drew me closer. We lay holding each other like children in a lifeboat. Would a sudden wave come along to capsize us?

Regardless, his confession seemed to seal our closeness. By marrying well, did he mean their money had come from Priscilla?

"Joseph," I said, stroking the hair of this stranger.

"Don't get me wrong. We loved each other. But that was ten years ago, when we first got married. And it was never right. Never."

He seemed angry suddenly, and I wasn't sure how to react. He didn't love his wife, yet they remained together? Was I the first, or had there been others?

Like most Italians, I hesitated to share my private thoughts. Instead it was the cool, Waspy banker who'd been the first to declare what our coming together had meant.

"It was arranged," he said.

He was trying to justify his marriage. Yet I didn't judge him. Looking at him, I saw a face I felt I'd known my entire life.

"How do you want it to be, Marie?" he asked, stroking my shoulder. He spoke casually, as if we discussed the weather. Was he referring to our next meeting, and the next? I experienced a thrill, as intense and pleasing as if he'd said he loved me. But what would happen when sanity returned and we realized what we'd done?

"Do you still love her?"

The room stilled. It was a warm day, and there was the sound of the fan going in the corner. He gathered me closer. He kissed me. "No," he said in a whisper.

I let him hold me tighter and for longer. I had no claim. In place of words I gave him a tender smile. We lay on Carmela's best sheets, the set with the small rose appliques stitched along the top hem. A delicate rosette, one I'd looked at a hundred times, rested in the space underneath Joseph Ashworth's chin.

"I think I have to get back down to the store," I said, worried the boys might come up.

"I should get back, too." Here he paused. "I don't know what to say, Marie. I have never…" He stopped. Suddenly we were exhausted, our confidences like little stones in our hearts. His restrained smile told me he was reverting back to the Mr. Ashworth people recognized, the banker who after discreetly closing my door would cross the street and enter his place of work, where his tellers would look up and fail to detect a change.

As I watched him go, I told myself to stop analyzing everything. Even if it was my habit, in this instance, thinking could wait.

It was a Thursday. That's how it began, and how it continued, at least for a while.

CHAPTER TWELVE

In order for Joseph and me to meet, I had to give my brothers a reason why they couldn't come upstairs in the middle of the day. I had at least one cake to bake each week, so I gave the excuse that I couldn't risk them opening and closing the icebox where I kept my delicate frostings and custards. To my surprise they accepted this. Of course, they liked the extra money my baking brought in, and they enjoyed having cake around.

Joseph and I timed his arrival for when the street was quiet, around two-thirty, after most clerks and shopkeepers had taken their lunch breaks and were back at their jobs. He would stay for an hour and a half, and by the time he left, the street was again busy. Still, I worried he would be noticed.

Ruth entered my kitchen one day and said, "My goodness. What's going on in here?"

Every surface was taken up with baking. I had reorganized the side counter where Mom's mixer now lived permanently, and stacked alongside it were my dry ingredients, cooling racks and icing spatulas. It was becoming impossible to make a cup of coffee or the smallest breakfast.

"My baking business. Can you believe it?"

"I don't know how you find the time. I'm exhausted after a day in the store," Ruth said. "All I feel like doing is putting my feet up and having a drink. Gersh would hate it if I was fussing in the kitchen at night. He likes to raid the icebox…when he thinks I don't see him."

"I try not to bake in the evenings," I said.

Often as not the boys went out, though not necessarily together. Gino was seeing a girl named Carla, who I'd yet to lay eyes on. But where was Sammy? He couldn't possibly have a girlfriend and me not know. Surely I would notice in that sweet face a glint fired by a woman's attention.

"Who are your clients?" asked Ruth.

"Mrs. Vitolo. She ordered one for her son. He's still sick, poor boy."

For Mrs. Vitolo's cake I'd planned something special and more daring. It would be the first time I experimented with the black hellebore Ada had brought. It was a purgative, and the doctor believed Jimmy Vitolo suffered from a kidney infection.

"Who else?" asked Ruth.

"Mrs. Fiedler. She likes cupcakes. I had never made them before… God, I can't think now," I said, hesitating to mention Priscilla Ashworth, so I made up a name.

"Who's that?" Ruth's eyes narrowed. "I never heard of them."

"They live in Franklin," I said.

Had she noticed my hesitation? She could smell fear; she was worse than Mom in that regard. How I hated to lie to Ruth. Would this be the way it was from now on, forced to hide my new self? Still, as I concocted my recipes, my heart raced with a new, exhilarating energy.

"Marie, are you listening?"

"Oh, Ruth. I'm worried about this cake. It's a new recipe, and if it doesn't come out, I don't have time to fix it."

"I'll get out of your way," she said.

"No. Stay for a while."

"You seem tired."

Not tired. Excited.

"You let your brothers take advantage." She gave me a frank stare. "Why don't you give the business over to the boys and let them pay you. Let them take care of you for a change."

Over my dead body.

"The store wouldn't be around for long!" I said.

She thought nothing of suggesting I forfeit the store. Everyone in town expected me to let my brothers take over. There were plenty of examples of women, who having run their father's businesses for years, gave up their rights once the old man died, and what property and money there was passed to the sons. The women continued to run things, because *Sis is good with numbers.* Though rarely was she compensated, apart from being permitted to continue to live in the family home, where likely as not she looked after aging relatives, cooked for brothers and any other males who happened to be around, uncles, friends, priests. Nor would she date, because she was always too tired. And after not so many years, she would be past it, a spinster, though still meticulous in her ledgers. Her final reward would be a lovely headstone in a medium price range, with the everlasting sentiment:

> *Here lies our beloved Sister.*
> *A good daughter to her father*
> *Devoted sister to her brothers*
> *Who always put others first…*
> *… and who, without fail, was considered last.*

"Tea later? When you're finished?" Ruth said, dragging me back. "What? Oh yes, sure. I'd love to."

After Ruth left, I sprinkled in some of the black hellebore from Ada's rhizome. It was an amount so miniscule—really I just waved my fingers over my mixing bowl—I doubted Jimmy Vitolo would be affected. I probably wasted my time; I only hoped I did no harm. I was thinking about Ada, and her offer to teach me about herbs, when my elbow caught the edge of Mom's cookbook and it slid to the floor. A card fluttered out, and I picked it up. The image was of San Lorenzo Cathedral in Turin. In a large, loopy hand was written:

> *The weather good. Sun out. I like here. No bandits. No malaria.*
> *Vedi?*
> *Cara, I learn. Soon, I speak!*
> *Love, Ada*

The date on the card was fifteen years ago. Had Ada been living in the north of Italy then? I tucked the card into the pocket of my apron, and opened my mother's book on rituals. I read about one that required a red ribbon, a horseshoe, and a coral necklace. I happened to have a coral necklace that had belonged to Mom. I was too young when I'd first tried it on, but now it suited me, glowing like a ring of fire and casting flattering light up into my face. The ritual was meant to bring luck, and though there was no mention of love, I took for granted that every spell pointed toward this secret wish.

I'd once walked into the kitchen and found Mom grinding substances in her mortar. *I'll show them! How dare he!* She'd repeated this several times, and I had the impression it was a situation she had dealt with before. I wondered, was her anger aimed at a man, or at the entire town?

I got started on Mrs. Fiedler's cupcakes, and as I stirred the batter I thought about the terrible things people were saying about Germans. Yet Mrs. Fiedler was a nice woman, and as American as any of us. So I sprinkled in some rue, for healing and protection. A spell could seek revenge; equally it could be employed for good.

CHAPTER THIRTEEN

I was grateful for whatever propelled my brothers out the door so I could contemplate my afternoon with Joseph. I had the boys drag a lunch table into the back room, which at first they didn't like because they were used to coming upstairs for lunch. Then I announced that from now on they wouldn't be coming up at all during the day, which might have made them suspicious were it not for my baking and the chaos it created in the kitchen.

Sneaking my lover in and out was always a risk. I imagined certain people in town, women mainly, waiting for any crumb of gossip. Though who would believe Joseph Ashworth would be calling on Marie Genovese? Unless, of course, he had a complaint about the front of the store, or was annoyed that we didn't often refresh our planters, which were his view from the bank.

My schedule became relentless. I went from the stock room to the floor, to the cash register, to my ledgers and order books, then straight into baking, and the next day I began the whole process again. With such a workload I should have felt tired, but as our affair deepened, my energy only increased. People commented that I seemed happier, that I laughed a lot, whereas laughing had once seemed frivolous, impossible. And my customers had new respect for this Marie who made cakes that were not only delicious, but which they believed, rightly or wrongly, helped them achieve their dreams.

Mrs. Vitolo called and wanted yet another, her third. "He's better, you know," she said. "It was the cake."

"Oh, Mrs. Vitolo, I'm so glad."

"I'll take the same again," she said.

I knew the Vitolos didn't have the money, so I dropped my price. Her son had recently had surgery. I aimed my intention and in addition to the tiniest pinch of hellebore, I added another of my secret spices, ginger, to help heal him. Really I needed galingal, which was what Mom's book stipulated, but it was hard to come by. I also believed it important to use what was at hand. And in truth, nothing was discarded—I sniffed at an egg and made a judgment, but mostly I approved it.

Then Mrs. Fiedler called. Could I use some sweet woodruff, she wanted to know. She said nothing about the cupcakes I'd made for her, which might have annoyed me had I not known her way of complimenting was to offer a gift in thanks. Sweet woodruff, according to Mom's book, was used to treat the kidney and liver, cramps and menopause, varicose veins and poor digestion. When I hesitated, Mrs. Fiedler said quickly that she often used it in ice cream and in sausages; it was also used to flavor the beer her husband made. I smiled into the telephone, "Why yes, Mrs. Fiedler, that would be lovely."

One afternoon, as Joseph and I lay in the filtered sunshine of my bedroom, he turned to me and said we should make another arrangement. The seriousness in his voice scared me, the words delivered so sternly.

"What do you mean?"

I didn't bother hiding the accusation in my voice. Was this the end? I cowered, pulled my robe across my body in shame and fear, and felt the familiar emotions of the orphan, a woman who'd lost her mother, and whose father had never been there to give her confidence around men. I held my breath.

"I only mean I will find us a place," he said, not noticing my panic. His upbringing and a rigid sense of honor meant he delivered any idea like a business proposition. I had worried for nothing. Okay, I thought, I will let you fix this for us, and I won't question.

"We should have a place to go. We can't keep sneaking around here. Your brothers or someone else could see me coming in and out."

That was true enough. I wanted to believe he didn't worry, just as I didn't allow myself those same thoughts. I changed the subject.

"What should I call you?" I asked, poking him in the ribs and enjoying the sound of his laugh. I didn't like calling him Joseph, which I imagined was what his wife called him. I had thought of *Giuseppe*, Italian for Joseph, but that had been my father's name!

"Joe, if you like," he said.

He seemed uncertain. I wondered if perhaps his first name embarrassed him, or maybe he would always be uncomfortable in a setting that didn't involve the bank, the Homburg and the chauffeur.

Not that he seemed to care for any of it. He was happiest once he'd
fallen into my arms and shed it all.

"Beppe," I said.

"Beppe? What is that, Marie?"

It was as if I would never get used to hearing my own name.

"Nickname for Joseph. Come here, Beppe." Then rather than wait
for him to come to me, I lunged across his chest, landing as gently
as I could on top of him. "Beppe. Beppe." I kissed him all over, and
soon we were laughing, until the fever took us again.

He told me about a house he owned, an old Victorian further up
Bellevue Avenue, where the road widened and the houses were larger
and set further back. Behind the house was a garage with a small
upstairs apartment outfitted with furniture and a small kitchen. He
had once used it for business associates traveling down from New York.
The apartment was close enough to walk to, less than five minutes
away for both of us.

Judging by the kitchen equipment, whoever had stocked the
place had never cooked. The pots were awful, well-used and needing
to be discarded. The dishes were garish and the glasses were cheap and
heavy, if impervious to chipping. I was further shocked to recognize an
item from my store—a large blue fruit bowl I had handpicked from
a craft catalogue. It amused me to see it here because I'd spent more
on that bowl than I had on any single item in the store. For months
it had occupied the centerpiece of a display I was particularly proud
of—the large glowing corner of my new housewares section. One day
the bowl was gone. And when I asked Kenny who had bought it, he
said he didn't recall, or maybe Sammy had been manning the register
that day, he couldn't remember.

Mom once complained that she sometimes got stuck with better
stock, the one or two pieces she had taken a risk on, then been forced to
watch them gather dust. When I asked her why she ordered expensive
things, she said, "What is life without beauty?"

The first time I met Beppe at the apartment, walking with my
head lowered, past the generous and deserted veranda of the large
house, I heard Mom say, *Isn't this an attractive setting?* We used to walk
together in the evenings, past the stores of our fellow shopkeepers
until we reached this quiet tree-lined stretch where the houses were

larger. She always commented on the trellis that separated this house and garage from its neighbors, covered in a sweet autumn clematis, the same one now shielding me from view. The season had begun to change and color was coming into the leaves.

Beppe and I were careful, but once, and I don't know how it happened, just as I was closing the door to my apartment and he was leaving the bank, we saw each other and there was a spontaneous outbreak of smiles. At that moment my friend Angie happened to be coming up the street. She headed straight for me and was about to say hello when she saw me smile in Mr. Ashworth's direction. I was sure she'd seen us because she looked away quickly.

A second later she was waving me down. "Hello, Marie. Hello."

I was aware of Beppe behind me as he walked away in the direction of our apartment. I could hardly follow him so I stopped to chat.

"How are you?" I asked brightly.

"I'm fine," she said, and we hugged.

Angie was pretty. More than that, she was beautiful, and I used to love going out with her. I treasured the memories of our first summer after high school, when the two of us walked to the Lake Park and took the path slowly. We talked about our lives, such as they were at seventeen, while the scent of anise mingled with the heavy musk of summer, and we imagined our futures stretching into infinity.

"Where are you going?" she asked.

"I have to go to Ferrara's."

"Shall I drive you?"

"Oh no. I like to walk," I said.

"But it's too cold to walk." Angie was forceful. She had been the ringleader in all our adventures.

"Oh, no, Angie. That's okay."

"I'll drive you. We haven't seen each other in *too* long."

Because her father owned the Ford dealership out on the Pike, Angie had a car, the only woman in our circle to own one. To continue to protest seemed awkward, so I climbed in and off we went. Ferrara's was up Third Street. I would buy something quickly, then rush back up Bellevue before Angie was finished shopping. But at Ferrara's she talked on and on and showed no signs of wanting to part.

"Angie, we should get together. I'm going to call you. But I'm in a hurry." I took her arm. She responded by squeezing mine, and I panicked suddenly, thinking she knew. I waited, expecting her to say something, but she only smiled. I left her in the pasta aisle, grabbed a small bottle of olive oil that I didn't need, paid for it and fled. I ran quickly along the quiet back streets until I reached the apartment. Beppe was waiting, and though he tried not to show it, I saw he was angry. We would have less than an hour.

"Where were you?"

"I'm sorry. I ran into my friend Angie and I couldn't get away."

"I thought you weren't coming," he said in a snappish tone.

Not coming? Didn't he know that I counted the minutes until our next meeting? Did he have any idea of the drudge that filled the hours between our sessions of love? His peevishness was all the more difficult to take given how easy I imagined his life to be. He had only to say what his plans were and no one dared question.

Suddenly the dowdy, cast-off furnishings were a reminder of the temporary nature of our affair, how this was far from a home, but a bedroom and two equally anonymous rooms, a place personal only to strangers. I should have known to expect it; a stab of melancholy that was the prelude to our easy coming together, unlike anything I had ever experienced. But if the power of our love shone a rosy light, it could also, with the slightest provocation, seem artificial. If there had been time, we would have argued; as it was, we accepted what minutes were left and without wasting a second more, we came together in a delirious storm.

CHAPTER FOURTEEN

In the renaming of Joseph, Giuseppe to Beppe, my lover became a more manageable male. Perhaps it was in reaction to my missing father, the desire to tame any man in my field of vision. I knew the reason that Italian mothers, sisters and daughters flattered their men by calling them names more suited to children, names that managed to stick throughout their lives. In town there was a Chiefy, a Shorty, a Tootie, and a Paulie. It made the men laugh. It softened them and, so declawed, they could be manipulated, loved. And so Mr. Joseph Ashworth became Beppe. For me, seeing his eyes soften again and again, accepting this compliment as if he had never been so closely considered, so adored by a woman, sealed our love. And God how we played. How was it possible that this man, so impeccably dressed and wearing his serious hat, the man who stepped from that large black car, was the same one who tumbled with such abandon in bed?

"I'm not sure I want to be named after Garibaldi," he said, laughing one afternoon as we lay in the glow of a pale winter sun.

I was just about to mention my favorite Giuseppe, Giuseppe Verdi, when he said, "Why can't I just be Giuseppe Ashworth?" We laughed for a full minute over that.

"What's wrong with Garibaldi?" I asked, after we'd calmed down.

"He was all right, I guess. Mussolini's a different story."

"Gino says we should get behind Mussolini. That he's doing good for Italy."

"Where does your brother get these ideas?"

"I found this newspaper in his room. It's called *Social Justice*."

"Show me a copy." He sat up and lit a cigarette.

"I can bring it next time. It's a Christian newspaper," I said, knowing full well what this would provoke.

"Marie, what they're preaching is hate. Hitler and Mussolini are in it together. Your brothers should stay away from their supporters."

"Supporters, here?"

"Yes. Here."

"But I'm afraid of these Communists," I said.

"They're not the problem. Hitler is using fear of them to spread Nazism."

I couldn't tell whether or not he was angry, but he shot me a look that made me hesitate to take it further.

For months, copies of *Social Justice* had been turning up in Gino's bedroom. I would find a stack, take one for myself, and carefully put back whatever debris had been piled on top. A week later the papers would be gone, replaced by a more recent issue. I found one with a hand note pinned to it, *Gino, you're a good paisan.*

"Beppe? Do you ever feel somebody might blame you?"

"For what?" He looked shocked.

"The Depression. All the suffering…here you are a banker…"

Coughlin was blaming bankers. He predicted there'd be blood running in the streets, and Christians would be slain by Communists. I knew it to be nonsense, but I wanted to give him a chance to refute the idea that those who controlled the money had, through their actions, caused the collapse we were living through.

"You mean causing the Depression?" He was suddenly mad. "That's nothing but a lie, Marie. Coughlin wants to stir up trouble wherever he can. Workers against bankers. Christians against Communists, which to him means Jews. He's a tool of Germany. And he's using Italians and anybody else he can to spread his propaganda."

"Mr. Esposito supported Mussolini when the Black Shirts were sent in to fight on the side of Franco." I wanted to hear what he had to say.

"Well, he's wrong. All of Europe is either against Franco or neutral. Mussolini's on the wrong side. As usual."

He ground out his cigarette, swung his legs out of bed and headed for the bathroom. I listened to the water running, and the banging of the medicine cabinet. Now that we had the apartment we could meet anytime; occasionally, we met in the morning, and he shaved.

"I think something bad is coming," I said when he came back into the bedroom. "Worse than we've had."

"Look Marie, the people causing the most trouble are either blaming the victims or pointing the finger at the only people who can help us out of this."

Was Beppe saying he was one of the ones who could help us?

He changed the subject by asking how the store was going, so I made up a story. It gave him pleasure to hear of the profits I was supposedly making. Except week to week we scraped by, and though I never said so out loud, I was afraid we might have to close the doors. Soon we wouldn't be able to afford the electricity, Kenny would refuse to wait for his paycheck, and Mr. E. would give his final ultimatum, that I *be* with him, or no more handouts.

As a woman I had much to prove. I wanted Beppe to respect my right to run a store, to be the one in charge, strong enough to weather the worse economic conditions. But if Gino was involved with the Italian Fasci, that reflected on me. And I hated that people saw Italians as the emissaries of that revolting loudmouth Mussolini.

I put my hand on his smooth, freshly shaven face.

"Marie, it isn't the fault of the financial system. That's still working, thank God. I'll admit, there were some rough spots…"

His words were meant to be calming, but I felt my anger rise.

"Rough spots? You call what happened rough spots?"

What about those who had nothing to eat, forced to line up to receive a tepid cup of soup, a slice of stale bread? Only once before had we disagreed, and that was about the apartment's furniture covered in a horrible dark brown stain. I'd mentioned how ugly I thought it was, and he'd blown up. "We're not buying new furniture." And for a minute it was as if we were married.

He pulled me further down underneath the covers. It was a bitter cold morning, and still early. "We have to fight this, Marie."

"Fight what?" I asked in a sleepy voice, wanting him to know that I wouldn't push him away.

"The insanity," he whispered. And those were our last words before thoughts evaporated.

CHAPTER FIFTEEN

This room, once my mother's, was pleasingly old fashioned, and I loved waking to the sight of the ceiling rosette that surrounded a milk glass globe that at night cast a warm glow on the mahogany furniture. In contrast to so much that was old and spoke of another time, my dreams had offered a glimpse of the future, maybe the result of what Sammy had told me about Mr. E.'s warehouse in New York. It had a conveyor belt. Or was it Mr. E. telling me about Henry Ford's assembly line? He had just bought himself a new Ford. "Mari, it used to take a day to make car, now they make one every hour. Machines. Thank God." Mr. E. said we were about to enter the future. What a funny idea, I thought. As if the lives we lived weren't our lives but a jumping off point to a better unknown.

In my dream was a main street like Littlefield's. There was a classical building in the middle of the block, a bank or the office of a new millionaire, and on the heavy lintel atop a row of columns was etched a name I couldn't read. On one side of the building was a shop with an awning, on the other was our Five & Ten. There we were in the full glare of the sun without a nice awning to keep the merchandise from fading. The street in front was wide, and the traffic was sparse. But unlike Littlefield's staid brickwork, in the dream each building was colorful, like in a children's picture book. Yet it was a familiar place, and being there made me happy, until looking up, I was startled to see a tall, needle-shaped building reaching way up into the sky. I had heard of skyscrapers, but had never actually seen one. It shimmered in the sunlight, and I was afraid it would threaten the quiet street, until I realized it was actually part of the town and I would soon come to love it as one loves the familiar. Others on the street hardly looked up as they went about their business, having already become used to it. Yet the idea persisted that as big and exciting and shiny as this was, those of us below would be left behind.

On the Sunday evening before Halloween I was in the back room unpacking candy for the next day's rush. I was listening to Orson Welles's *The Mercury Theatre on the Air*, when suddenly the music program was interrupted for an announcement. Explosions had been spotted on Mars, followed closely by the sighting of an alien spaceship landing in a field in Grovers Mill, not thirty miles away.

I almost fainted with shock. I was alone in the store so I telephoned Ruth, but neither she nor Gersh was at home. I thought about calling Mr. E., but the person I most wanted to speak to was Beppe. There was no way to reach him. I had no number, and it was evening. I walked around the store in a daze, until finally the announcer said it had all been a hoax. I wanted to personally murder Orson Welles.

A week later I was standing in front of my housewares section wondering why I hadn't thought to order more cooking equipment. Thanksgiving was only two weeks away, and already I was sold out of roasting pans. I stared at the empty display and felt like crying when in walked Mrs. Holloway. She needed three pans—she always bought from me this time of year. Unfortunately, she was after the one item I no longer had on the shelves, a cheap aluminum roasting pan.

"What's wrong, Marie?" she asked, and quickly I adjusted my face.

"I had a thought. You know these are much better," I said, and turning on my heels led her over to the new soda glass. Of course they cost twice what the cheap pans sold for, and they carried a higher mark-up, so I would have to make a good case. "These last forever, Mrs. Holloway. It would be an investment. And you can use them all year. I bake sheet cakes in them. They work great."

"I've heard about your sheet cakes, Marie," she said, picking up one of the square casseroles and turning it over. "I never thought of baking in this."

I waited patiently. I was learning the virtue of allowing a silence to grow, which often caused the other person to talk more, and sometimes they did exactly what you wanted.

"Okay, but I'll only get two. They're expensive, Marie," she said. *Two? My God!*

Later that day I even managed to sell a vase in the shape of a cornucopia adorned with wooden reeds. It was an item I'd been trying to unload all year because it was from the previous year's merchandise. Some items could withstand a gathering of dust, but others, like the cornucopia, resisted cleaning and had the unmistakable tinge of old stock.

In better years after Halloween, followed by Thanksgiving, we were able to coast until Christmas. This year Halloween had proved surprisingly brisk. The terrible War of the Worlds broadcast had had the effect of exciting people by scaring them, which oddly made the holiday more of an occasion and people spent more on decorations. Then, at Thanksgiving, we baked and stoked the home fires in gratitude for all that hadn't yet been taken from us. Even so, I wasn't able to put a single dollar aside for Christmas stock.

Feldman would continue to deliver, but the other suppliers to whom I already owed money began calling at odd hours, hoping to catch me by surprise. I was afraid to answer the telephone. I braced for a hard winter, and the way I got through the days was by reliving my hours with Beppe.

The heating in our tryst apartment was good, but it was still chilly, probably because the garage doors below didn't quite meet in the center, and freezing air blasted straight up the stairwell. When we had time, we huddled for longer under a pile of blankets.

Who didn't love winter and snow as a child? I had fond memories of snowsuits and matching mittens with strings attached, which Mom threaded through the inside of my coat so I wouldn't lose them, but I did anyway. Those years weren't so far past, and with the right trigger I could be that child again; a girl who loved snow and the woods, and tree-lined paths cushioned by rotting leaves. There was a time when I looked forward to all the seasons, spring's bursting new growth, even the boiling heat of summer, and in love with all the different clothes I got to wear.

But that walk to our apartment became interminable in the snow. At first it was just one more sensory experience on the way to the intensity of our sex, which I had become addicted to. Our lovemaking obsessed me, and I was anxious for that first glimpse of him as he took off, first his jacket, next his tie and then the careful enfolding of our arms before those first kisses. He was always tentative, which matched my mood perfectly, before seconds later we fell into a deliciously unconscious state, and we felt safe, nourished by the thought that we might never be released. Except we always were. Over and over again it ended, and we emerged, the same two people who arrived in a state of hope and anticipation, only to be returned to ourselves.

What a contrast to the summer, when our affair first began, when having enjoyed an afternoon with him I went home happy to spend the evening alone. Time could extend into infinity as I stared out my window into the failing light, while across the street the bank bathed in the yellow glow of the streetlamp, made me want him all over again. Only once had we been able to spend an entire night together, the time Priscilla had gone to visit her sister in Philadelphia.

"I'm free," he'd said, and there was no need to elaborate. And somehow I'd managed to send my brothers off to spend the night at Mr. E.'s with the excuse that I desperately needed a night alone.

I ironed my dress and got out the cookbooks. I rushed to Ferrara's for last-minute ingredients. I'm sure Eddie Ferrara noticed my breathlessness. In the hours before I was to see Beppe, I became extra sharp with the boys in the store, my mood unpredictable until evening rolled around and my kitchen became an efficient engine room. Finally, a breeze had arrived, accompanied by a gentle dip in the humidity, which seemed like gifts to us and us alone. I wore a shirtwaist dress, one I had been saving. It was made from the lightest olive-green silk, which set off the hazel of my eyes that I rimmed lightly in navy blue.

"Marie, you look great," he'd said, like he was the luckiest man in the world.

I'd worn my best perfume and a lacy apron that had belonged to Mom. Beppe's face was bright with pleasure as I dashed about the table laying plates and cutlery. I lit candles. We'd batted back sadness because it was playacting and we both knew it, and our evening's domesticity passed far too quickly. Sleeping had seemed a waste of time, though sleep we did between endless instances of making love, and we were tired in the morning and could easily have argued, but we batted that back, too.

I was convinced no one had noticed Joseph Ashworth coming and going from my apartment all summer. Before our arrangement changed, and we had the tryst apartment, I had felt protected, imaging the heat and the soft whirring of the fan able to mask the vibrations of our love. But once the weather turned cold, time contracted with such force it was as if the world came to an end every day around three-thirty, the hour I usually returned to my apartment after being with him. Evenings felt different, too. I loved my solitude, but the weather dampened my mood. I pictured him in that big house on the lake, sitting next to his wife. Did they listen to the radio? Did they walk the property? What did they talk about? These thoughts put me in a state as frozen as the ice-clad wires or the dingy piles of slush. And when a weak sun melted the snow, and my cheap boots did little to keep out the cold and wet, I grew resentful.

But someone had seen us. Unannounced, in the middle of the workweek, Ruth marched straight into my kitchen. At first I thought she was angry about the new goods I'd displayed in my window only yesterday, a stack of crisp-looking scarves. We were careful not to overlap in our offerings, but we'd agreed after Mom died that both our stores needed the business, and so we couldn't become too precious about a sale or two. Ruth's expression told me it wasn't that.

She leaned forward, hands on her sturdy hips. "So, when did it start?"

"Hello to you, too," I said, sinking heavily into a chair.

"Let's not beat around the bush, Marie. Let's just say I *know*," she paused for dramatic effect. I had been dreading this moment. I feared nothing so much as Ruth's censure.

"How?" I asked, weakly.

"I *saw*. And you better hope I'm the only one who did."

Saw? As in peering into my windows, or an open door? No, she must have seen him enter on the main street.

I found some wine and poured us each a small glass. "I've got to get back to work, Ruth," I said, taking a sip.

"I'm shocked by you, Marie. Your mother…" she began.

"Carmela knows," I said quickly. It just slipped out, the admission that I carried on communion with my dead mother. Did I really have to explain to Ruth, who'd known Mom so well, how strong her spirit was, how she spoke to me through her recipes and through her dresses and skirts, a great pile of them begging for youthful updating. Of course she knew about Beppe. And what was I supposed to do, lock myself away? Cook for my brothers until my hands were in shreds, age as I'd watched other girls in town do, unmarried, waiting to be

ITALIAN LOVE CAKE • 87

parceled off to the likes of the Cavutos, the Picciottis, the Scordos?

"I can't help it," I said.

What could I use if not my instincts, which told me I had every right to love him? I was young, not simply because of the number of years I had been on this earth, but due to the presence of my mother. I felt her, just as I felt ancestors I'd never known standing behind me, whispering to let me know my life was ahead of me, not behind. Their stories were lost, their lives gone, but mine had yet to be written.

A look of sympathy, or was it sadness, crossed her face. Ruth was from another generation, how could I expect her to understand? I had no wish to offend or shock her. I also knew, after her scold, she would settle down, and if needed she would help me.

With my secret out, I felt calm for the first time in months. Ruth and I sat in silence. The air had stilled, even the boys downstairs on the loading bay spoke in hushed tones. I wondered what they were up to.

"Ruth, I really have to get back downstairs."

"At least you admit it," she said, an expectant look on her face, a look Mom might have given me.

"Admit it to you? I tell you everything," I said, which wasn't quite true.

"Okay," Ruth said, "but be careful." Gently she patted my arm. She looked around the kitchen. "What are all these herbs?"

"I'm trying out some of Mom's recipes."

"I worry about you," she said.

I pushed my glass of wine away. "I shouldn't be drinking this." Ruth gave me a sly look, and I was quick to explain. "I'm busy stock taking."

"He's attractive," Ruth said, finally.

"Yes, he is," I said.

CHAPTER SIXTEEN

If Ruth noticed, who else knew about the affair? Instead of this news inhibiting me, I felt emboldened. I continued to dress up and wear plenty of bright red lipstick. I altered two more dresses belonging to Mom, and these I swapped out, alternating weeks so that I wouldn't seem to be wearing the same thing. I sported my legs, daring to hem my skirts slightly shorter than the fashion, and I indulged my love of shoes, adding ankle-strapped pumps to the neat wooden rack in my closet. Slowly, too, I changed how I related to Gino and Sammy, how I spoke to Kenny and my suppliers. I was more abrupt, and I didn't care what they thought.

My face glowed with the aura of physical pleasure that clung to me after an afternoon with him. Should I be spotted walking down Bellevue Avenue, away from the shops and toward the residential stretch where hardly anyone walked, people would consider it the eccentricity of an old maid. I continued to go alone to the movies on Wednesdays, dish night, and after the heavy curtain swished closed on the latest movie starring Bette Davis—a woman with appetites who was inevitably wronged—I walked home alone with the plain white plate tucked under my arm.

I was tidying up the office when Kenny walked in and gave me a broad smile. From a corner behind the desk he hoisted a bolt of fabric and thrust it into my arms. "For you," he said.

It was a nice mustard colored velvet I would have no trouble using, and I was immediately suspicious.

"Where did you get this?" I asked. Why was he giving me a present when he'd never given me anything before? It couldn't have been in thanks for reducing his hours before Christmas.

"Corley needs a check," he said.

"Tell him to wait." I was in no mood. I would pay when I could.

"Esposito said he can't help right now."

I put the bolt down and crossed my arms. I was meant to be grateful to him for the gift, but now I was angry he'd gone behind my back to ask Mr. E. for money.

"Tell Corley in a week," I said, in my most decisive tone.

Kenny let out a long, drawn out sigh to let me know what a trial it was for him to accept an order from a woman. He stood with his legs apart, and his hands on his hips like he owned Gimbel's. "There's a new supplier I think we should check out," he said.

"Oh?"

"The stuff is cheaper. Pretty." He waited for my reaction.

"And who is that?"

"My cousin. He has a wholesale business. Kitchenware and Christmas items."

So this was the reason for the present. He wanted me to order Christmas stock from his cousin.

"His stuff is cheaper," he said again.

It annoyed them that I sought out better quality. I could never make Kenny or Gino understand that the profit on one nice item far outweighed what we could earn from selling multiples, which were a thing of the past. Gone were the days when a nice tea towel generated word of mouth as it had in Mom's day. *Watch, Carmela would say, Now that Mimi has one, we'll soon see Rita and Genevieve. I give them two days.* Rather, it was the specialty items that got us through the leaner months, items that could take a larger mark-up, aiming at those who still had money to spend. Well-off women were seduced by crafts. I employed several local women to knit tea cozies and babies' booties, which sold well and fetched a good price, and I was able to pay the women a fair sum for their labors, which drove my brothers and Kenny crazy.

"Stock is my business," I said. "You worry about keeping the shelves full."

Kenny's face darkened. "You know, since money's tight, you could get credit from my cousin. I guess we could always try to get a loan, but they're not loaning to Italians."

"Who isn't?"

"The bank across the street. I know a bunch of guys who got turned down. The *Merigani* always get loans."

Kenny loved calling Americans the *Merigani*. It had begun as a mispronunciation, but soon became a useful slur.

"What are you talking about?"

"Bertolli tried. Tomasello. So did Macri. Nothin'. They said 'Come back.' What's that mean, come back? It means, you're a WOP. Don't bother."

"Kenny!"

"It's true. Ask any of them. They couldn't get a dime."

"I hate this talk."

"Suit yourself," he said, walking away with a stoop, like the conversation had made him feel old. How rude he was suddenly.

For the rest of the day he moved about clumsily, as though he'd been punched. I felt no such weakness. I was looking ahead to a time none of them could see, when a family could afford household comforts without having to go without food. I planned improvements. The Five & Ten would change, but it would still keep its warmth, the welcoming luster of old wood and floorboards, the cavernous feeling of an emporium.

But a week later, when the new stock arrived, instead of the goods I'd told Kenny to order, there at my feet was a pile of junk. The Christmas stockings and ornaments were of such poor quality I didn't even take them out of the box.

"Kenny, come in here," I yelled, but Gino rushed in instead.

"He's not here."

"Look at this." I held out ornaments in the shape of bells that dropped their glitter almost immediately. "This is junk, and I won't sell it! Where's Kenny?"

"How should I…"

"Find him!"

Fuming, I went to sit behind the register. Outside cars moved sluggishly in the frosty weather. I figured he'd gone to the bank to make our deposit. When finally he sauntered in with Gino, a smile on both their faces, I sprang from the stool. "What's this?" I held up a disintegrating Christmas ball. "You ordered the wrong things. I'm not paying. Tell your cousin to come and pick it all up. Now!"

"Marie…"

"Just do it."

I left the two of them standing there. How dare they ignore me. Of course it was now too late to get replacements, sales would be worse than expected, and we would end up owing everyone. Recently, it had come to my attention that Kenny put off certain customers. When Mrs. Rizotte came in for a strainer, he said he couldn't find them. Next he told her we didn't stock strainers, which wasn't true. Mimi was one of my best customers and a friend. I drew Kenny aside and told him that from now on his activities would be confined to the loading bay. He was to handle deliveries only. "Marie, I can do as much as you want around here. Ring up sales. Whatever you need." It was as if he hadn't heard a word I'd said.

Right after our run-in over the cheap Christmas ornaments, he began staying late. First he went around making sure everything was locked up, which had always been his job. Then one night, long after we'd closed, cigarette smoke wafted into my kitchen window from the loading bay below. When I looked out, there was Kenny sitting on the edge of the dock flicking his ashes, which he knew I hated. For the next several nights I heard him let himself into the rear office door using his key, and soon after that a truck would arrive. In the cold I could see clouds of breath as Kenny and another man smoked and talked. I couldn't make out what they said, but they began unloading large sacks from out of a truck, and after that first truck left, another arrived to pick it all up. Was this more of Mr. E.'s business? Whatever it was there were large quantities, and sometimes trucks arrived twice a night. Meanwhile, I had never seen Gino so busy. I was pleased to see him working, but his cooperation was offset by behavior I found appalling. Recently, right in front of me, he'd torn open an expensive gift box of macaroons and began shoving them into his mouth like he was starving.

"Gino!"

"Don't flip your wig, Marie. And don't worry, I'll be out of your hair soon." With that he stormed out, taking the macaroons with him.

What did he mean, out of my hair?

CHAPTER SEVENTEEN

Beppe called, and he sounded so happy I almost succumbed to the offer I knew he'd make.

"I could meet for an hour. Right now." I pictured him at his desk where he often worked late.

"I can't," I said.

I would have loved nothing better than to sneak off, but in the run up to Christmas there was too much to do.

"I'll miss you," he said. "I have to be away for a couple of days. I'm back on Thursday. I'll call you then."

I almost relented, but I'd already poured myself a glass of wine, ready to settle in for the evening. Maybe it was the strained relations between Gino, Kenny and me, but something told me to stick close to home. We exchanged goodnights. I said I would miss him, too. I wasn't off the telephone five minutes when Mr. E. called. A movie called "Forward America" was being shown at the Sons of Italy Hall. It was about the government's anti-chain store legislation.

"Marie, we go together," he said.

Since I'd already said no to Beppe, I had no intention of saying yes to Salvie Esposito. Besides, I planned to alter a dress. I suggested he go and then tell me about it later, but when he agreed so readily I was suspicious.

I took up my sewing and soon forgot everything, including the busy next day when we would redo the shelves to get ready for Christmas. I would mark down items that hadn't sold, and would try to salvage as many ornaments as I could from the mess Kenny had ordered. I planned to go to bed early. The hours passed, and I had just packed away my sewing and was rinsing my glass in the sink when I heard the commotion. From down in the street someone was yelling, "Take your hands off me!" I rushed to the window in time to see Mr. E. and two policemen attempting to restrain Gino. Sammy was hollering at his brother to calm down, and people had stopped to watch. Across the street a group of men, some I recognized as belonging to the Sons, looked almost bored, as though whatever was going on they'd been watching for a while.

A minute later it was Mr. E.'s voice on the stairwell, "You stupid son of a bitch!" Then the sound of a scuffle, and as I reached the stairs Mr. E. was attempting to corral Gino. My strong brother grabbed the older man by the collar and continued shoving him back down the stairs, until they were once again out on the street. I ran downstairs just as Sammy was attempting to pull Gino off of Mr. E., who was setting up to punch Gino.

"Back off, you coward," shouted Sammy at his older brother.

"My God, what's going on?" I said, finding my voice.

"Go inside, Mari," said Mr. E.

"I will not!"

Finally, a policeman stepped in, and glaring at Gino said, "We're taking you to jail."

Mr. E. turned to me, "I go with him."

After that things quieted down, but a clutch of men remained on the street talking. I wanted to ask them what had happened, but went instead to my bedroom and sat staring at the soft looking roses of the wallpaper. The pattern was calming and made me think of Mom. What was I going to do with my crazy brother?

Minutes later I heard Sammy's footsteps on the stairs, but I couldn't move.

I had terrible trouble sleeping that night and woke in a bad mood. Sammy was still in bed at eight o'clock, and while I waited for him to get up, I straightened the kitchen.

"Tell me," I said, when he finally came in.

"Gino passed around a hat. Said he was collecting for the New York *Fascio*. They say they're fighting communism. They're pro-Italy. They want to make sure America sides with Mussolini and doesn't enter the war."

"I thought you were watching a movie."

"Gino had a book. A black leather book, and he wanted all the men to sign it. Pledge their loyalty, show they were prepared to fight. To go out in the streets and beat up anyone who said anything against Italy or Germany. Some stayed behind to sign."

"Your brother is a fascist? Who else was there?"

"Gersh. And Marty Jacobs. They didn't sign of course. Then Mr. Jacobs called Gino a traitor, and Gino punched him."

"You're kidding."

Marty Jacobs owned a furniture store in the next town. He was a friend of Ruth and Gersh's and he often came to meetings in Littlefield to keep abreast of business here.

"Where's this book?"

"I don't know. Gino put it away."

"Who signed it?"

"I don't know. I'd left by then. The fight started inside the hall, but then moved outside. Gino tried to run away, but I caught up with him, and we started fighting. He couldn't manage to hit me. He tried, but I didn't let him."

Someone was ringing the doorbell, really laying on it. "I'll go," I said.

I opened the door and Gersh burst inside. "Marie, your brother! That movie was just an excuse."

"Come up. There's hot coffee," I said, leading him into the living room before going back into the kitchen to get us both a cup. Sammy had slipped back into his room.

Gersh sat forward in his chair, he shook his head, and with a dramatic flourish pulled from his coat pocket a paper. "Your brother got us there so he could pass out these." He thrust the paper into my hands. It was more of that Coughlin filth, a reprint of an article from *Social Justice*, the newspaper I'd found in Gino's room, called "Protocols of the Elders of Zion." It listed the horrors Jews supposedly were planning to unleash on poor, unsuspecting Christians, referred to as *goyim*. "The tyranny, oppression and needless poverty in the world are not of God's devising but are the results of planning by men who hate and detest the Christian principles of brotherhood." Coughlin went on to lambast Roosevelt and the New Deal. The word communism was mentioned a dozen times. Coughlin blamed the Jews for the coming war.

"What about the movie? What was it about?" I asked.

Gersh batted away my question like it was a pesky fly. "It's an old film. About legislation to stop the big chains from buying up little guys like us. It's an old idea. Been around for ten years or more. It was just an excuse to get us there. Then your brother passed around a hat for donations to help the fascists discriminate against us. And that book! If anyone finds that book, he'll get his ass kicked from one side of town to the other."

"What book?" I decided to let Gersh tell me.

"Your brother wants the signatures of a hundred men. Italians. Italy is on the wrong side, I'm telling you. Their love affair with Germany won't work out. The Sons pretend they do good, but they're full of hate and prejudice, just like the whole world."

"Not Sammy," I said quickly, "He's not a part of any of this. Gersh, I'm so sorry. I don't know what to say."

"Marty was there. The two of us, the only Jews. We were lured there!" He glared at me. "My parents left the Ukraine in 1885. Right after the tsar was assassinated, and the next tsar made it okay to go around beating up Jews. They blamed us. At first the number was small. Soon we not only got beaten up, but our property was stolen and the authorities did nothing. My father escaped the worst of the pogroms. Lucky he got out too, because the rest of the family was killed in the civil war thirty years later. Ukrainian troops turned on us. Everybody turned on us. When Gino punched Marty last night, I thought, my God, it's happening again. We came here for a new life. And we've been here longer than some of you. We were farming before the Italians even got here. Now everyone wants us dead!"

"That's not true, Gersh, my God."

"You don't know what's going on, Marie. And you better tell your brother to look out."

"I can't tell him anything."

"I still have family in the Ukraine. A famine, five years ago, and five million died. Stalin is stirring up tensions between Ukrainians and Jews. He accuses us of being communists. He's putting us in ghettos. And it's going to get worse."

"I'll get us more coffee, something to eat."

"No, thank you. I have to get home to Ruth. She's very upset. God help us," he said, starting to walk out. He turned. "What if people boycott us? In the run up to Christmas?"

I hadn't thought about that. The Five & Ten was just as vulnerable to the whims and prejudices of the town.

As soon as Gersh left, I grabbed my purse and rushed over to see Ruth, who was in the rear of the store folding handkerchiefs.

"Ruth, Gino's a complete ass. He fell under the spell of bad influences. I swear. He's an idiot."

Gino wasn't just an idiot, he was dangerous. But I wasn't ready to admit it. Ruth kept her head down and continued to fold. The store looked so beautiful. Pine boughs had been fastened between towers of merchandise, and colored lights sent warm patterns dancing across the polished mahogany counter. The Oletskys may have been Jewish, but they always decorated at Christmas time. It occurred to me that their customers, most of whom were Christians, might not notice the effort, and if they did, some would consider it a sales ploy. I knew differently. Ruth and Gersh were part of the fabric of the community, and as much as any of us they loved the ritual of the decorations.

I fidgeted with the strap of my handbag and allowed my eyes to rest on the busts of mannequins holding elegant velvet hats with feathers. Beneath those, the latest bras were displayed. It was a matter of economics—there were only so many mannequins and a large variety of goods to display. But there was also a deliberate eccentricity, a humor and a spirit in defiance of the straight-laced, fearful times.

"You know I love you, don't you?" I reached across the counter to take her hand.

I feared nothing so much as Ruth's anger. Like Mom, she could be stern, unforgiving.

"I'm so sorry, Ruth. I could kill him. I will kill him!"

She surprised me by smiling. "There's a limit to what you can do. They are boys. So unmanageable," she said, with a shrug.

"You wouldn't believe how they treat me, Ruth. Kenny has completely changed. Mr. E. is paying him more money, and he's supposed to do more, but he does less. I hate them all, but I need them. I'm trapped, Ruth. Trapped! I want Gino to go. I want him gone for good."

"You're lucky they stick around. At their age they could have left already to go start their lives."

"Not Sammy," I said, calming down. "He's different. Definitely not Sammy. It's that rotten Gino. It's Gino start to finish."

Ruth placed her hand on my arm. Her grasp was firm. I recalled her telling me that Italy had been mistreating its Jews, even before the Kristallnacht attacks in Germany last November. I had been embarrassed to admit I didn't know what Kristallnacht was. A word that sounded so pretty, but referred to the streets covered in shattered glass from synagogues, homes, and stores owned by Jews. Ruth had had to explain how countless numbers had been murdered in Germany during that rampage by the paramilitary. Now here was that same hate and prejudice right on our doorstep.

"Ruth…"

I had been staring at my feet.

"Let's not talk about it anymore," she said. I looked up and she was crying. I gathered her in my arms, and I smelled the remnants of cooking, which reminded me of Mom.

"Let's not," I said.

She walked me to the door, and just before I stepped out of the store, she grabbed my hand and squeezed it.

CHAPTER EIGHTEEN

The next day I walked slowly over to Ferrara's. I was embarrassed to be seen out on the street, thinking now that I would forever be associated with my brother's terrible behavior, but no one looked at me. Ferrara's windows happened to face the Sons of Italy hall. I always shopped the bins at the front of the store where they put the sale items, tins of olive oil and pastas that were out of date. Today, confronted with the ugly cement façade of the Sons with its freshly painted door, I was reminded of the hateful business that had taken place there two nights ago. Many in town, men whom Carmela had respected, and who respected us, were members. I was sure now that Mr. E. had instigated Gino's actions.

Just as I was thinking this, two cars with New York license plates pulled up to the curb. A half dozen men got out and hurried inside the Sons. Judging by their darkly handsome features and their long black coats, they were Italians. How I hated those coats which made them look like undertakers. But I was alone in noticing. The slicing of cold cuts never ceased, nor the bustle behind the tall meat counter, with the Ferrara men continuing to serve customers.

Later in the day, Mrs. Fiorello called. I braced myself, ready for her to mention the fight, and I was surprised when she didn't. She was calling because she needed a dozen cupcakes for her grandson's birthday. I tried to convince her to allow me to make *pizzelle* instead, since it was Christmas. I already had an order for Feldman, and it would be so much easier if I could just double the recipe.

"Young people love *pizzelle*, Mrs. Fiorello," I said, imagining the light, crunchy waffles with their tiny flecks of aniseed.

"No. I want cupcakes," she said.

I wanted to do something special to get her grandson started on his path to manhood. I would sprinkle in some anise, what with its expectorant quality and a reputation for easing tensions, it could address some of the challenges of being a young boy. And its licorice flavor would be delicately masked by a nice, rich chocolate.

I knew Mrs. Fiorello couldn't afford to pay me, so I suggested a trade. She had a beautiful bolt of silk charmeuse left over from her daughter-in-law's custom-made wedding gown. Her youngest son was marrying well, an Anglo-Saxon from the main line. While dropping off a large order of sugared almonds she planned to wrap in little mesh bags and give as wedding favors, she had invited me in to show off the gown's extravagant fabric. We were standing in her tiny sitting room with little natural light, yet the pale, ivory silk shone like the moon on water. It would be difficult to sew on, but it was of such obvious quality I agreed right away to take it in exchange for baking. I also gave her a big discount on the almonds.

Now I had two orders. Cupcakes for Mrs. Fiorello and a pound cake for the priests, ordered by Mrs. Delfina. I disliked baking for those lazy men and wished I hadn't said yes. But I was a little afraid of Mrs. Delfina, who whenever she came into the store managed to drag one of my customers off to the side. In Italian she would whisper, *comeetra, comeetra*, though it was more of a hiss. *What was this word, comeetra?* They knew I didn't speak Italian. They sent sharp looks in my direction, then took themselves off down an aisle where I couldn't see them. But I could still hear their rapid speech, their laughing and sniggering. Only later did I realize that *comeetra* wasn't an Italian word, but the sound of their furtive whispers: *come in here, come in here.* This was Mrs. Delfina's urgent plea to whomever she happened to find in the store—to come and listen to the poison she spewed about me. People thought her devout and kind because she worked for the priests, but she was neither of those things. I suspected that her words, far from harmless, caused me to lose customers. What if I sprinkled some poison and killed her and the priests all in one stroke?

It was early evening by the time I got home from Mrs. Fiorello's, and already it was dark. Kenny had closed and locked up. Instead of going straight upstairs, I went into the quiet store.

Mom, I'm here.

I always felt her at night, when the Five & Ten became a living, breathing animal, full of the wants of my customers, their hopes and dreams. A car's headlights swept across the window and in a flicker I saw the store as it would one day be, with gleaming new shelves, cases full to bursting with merchandise, and on everything a fresh lick of paint. We would not be in this Depression forever. And after the war, if

America entered the war, it would be as Beppe said, a boom. Not that I wished for war. I hated the idea of men fighting and dying. It was too devastating. But I could feel the war coming. Roosevelt had been preparing us with every fireside chat, even if many still didn't believe it.

I leaned the silk charmeuse up against a counter and pulled down the plastic that covered the bolt. So this was what well-to-do girls wore to their weddings. The silk came alive under the light of the streetlamp, but as magnificent as it was, it gave me less pleasure than the glow on my merchandise, the twinkle on a piece of foil, the reflection on glass. I finally let in a thought that had been bothering me since I'd heard it. Angie was engaged. I looked at the silk and tried to imagine what it would feel like to wear a gown made of such fabric.

CHAPTER NINETEEN

Mr. E. turned up and casually asked me if I had any cake to serve him. I motioned for him to take a seat in the living room.

"You eat my cake. You drink my coffee. Then you get my brothers into trouble."

"Mari…"

"How could you? The Oletskys are our friends."

He was nervous, but would I get an apology? He made himself comfortable on the sofa and I took the seat across from him. He was facing the window, and in the glare caused by a fresh blanket of snow, he looked old.

"The movie is important…"

"Don't give me that. It's old news. You did it deliberately. And what about that book pledging allegiance to Mussolini? Why do you do this?"

"That book nothing to do with me."

"So you know about it."

"Gino take it out."

"Why all this hate? Tell me!"

"I need favor, Mari. I'm stuck, or you know I not ask."

A favor? Now?

"Something come up, Mari…" Again, that aggravating shrug.

"Get to the point."

"I had a couple guys quit. And the holidays. I got a big shipment coming in. If you could spare them. For a month. In New York."

The boys? For a month? I laughed, thinking it was a joke.

He hung his head, the self-defeated manner of the conservative Italian man, a hint of the old country creeping in, each sentence a declaration of undeniable fact. No matter what I said, if he wanted to take my brothers he would take them. Though the immediate benefit I could see would be a month without Gino. I pictured a quiet, peaceful apartment. Except deliveries needed to be overseen, stock unpacked, shelves filled. If I had trouble leaving the store now to go and meet Beppe, what would it be like without my brothers? And we were heading into our busiest time of the year.

"Not before Christmas, Mari," he said, reading my mind. "I would never do that."

I badly needed a coffee, and rose to get us two cups. But just as I left the room, I caught his expression. Was it fear? As with all men, even the prospect of hearing a woman's *no* had the power to set the world careening off its axis.

"What about my money?" I asked, coming back into the room. If the mysterious evening runs on the loading bay continued, I should to be paid. But even as I asked, I dreaded what further demands he might make. With my brothers gone the extra money would become even more necessary. Mr. E. had gone from helping Mom to helping us and I never questioned his involvement. Was it purely generosity on his part? Sometimes I thought he was still doing it for her. Then again, maybe it wasn't a big deal for him since he was so well off.

"I already think of everything, Mari. And don't worry. I keep giving cash. You be okay. Or I wouldn't take them."

"You can have Gino, but not Sammy."

"Don't worry so much, Mari, the money will continue. And I don't take them until January."

"Not Sammy," I said again.

"I need both."

My brothers would go, and they would go for as long as he needed them. Having laid the first brick, he worked quickly to shore up his wall. "Kenny do the extra work. I pay him more. Of course."

He smiled, and a burst of warmth flooded his eyes. What a phony he was. He leaned toward me and in a lowered voice said, "We talk about store, Mari. I'm happy to help. But we talk. I make things easier for you."

There it was.

CHAPTER TWENTY

With Christmas rapidly approaching, I was busy, and one day in the late afternoon I received two telephone calls. The first was Ada. I was happy to hear her voice, but she got right to the point like this wasn't a social call.

"Hellebore," she drew out the syllables, ending with a lovely rolled *r* and a cheery *ay*. "Did you use?"

"Very small," I said quickly. The day after I'd delivered her cake, Mrs. Vitolo had telephoned to say her son was greatly improved. I had hardly used any of the herb, just a light passing of hands over the batter.

"Good," said Ada, without a hint of relief, but with pride, having steered me correctly. I was about to ask when she would come for a visit, when the telephone went dead. I stared at it in disbelief.

The next call was from Ella, the Ashworths' maid. She needed a large quantity of soup for a Christmas party.

"Mrs. A. thinks something warm," she said.

Mrs. A.

I detected a tone of judgment, as though she wanted to share an aside, as she had that other time, the comment about Mr. Ashworth not being happy turning thirty-eight.

"I can make soup," I said. The one I had in mind, a blending of clear broth, meat and greens was loved by the boys, for whom I'd made it over and over.

"Mrs. A. wants something light," said Ella.

"It's light, but hearty," I said quickly. "And warm. Perfect for winter. And it looks festive." I was nervous. In person Ella's careful hairdo, her warm eyes and perfect housedress softened an abrupt manner. I didn't like her nearly as much on the telephone.

"The base can be chicken broth, or I can use beef if you prefer. It's good either way. We can decide. It has tiny meatballs, and escarole, and plenty of fresh parmesan cheese grated on top..."

"Hmmm," she said. "I'll have to check. I'll call you right back."

What a year, I thought, beginning in June with that first call from the Ashworths. And now, with Christmas on top of us, there was to be a big party at his house, which Beppe had failed to mention. I had hoped his life was mildly disrupted by our affair, but with Ella's call I realized not much was changed for him. Would the soup be fancy enough? And what would I call it? Certainly not by its real name, *Italian Wedding Soup*.

Beppe was the only one who'd known the name of his birthday cake. Italian Love Cake. Now I would be making Italian Wedding Soup, a name that referred not to the legal joining of lovers, but to the wedding of flavors.

Ella called back. They needed enough for thirty. I tried to imagine a house that could fit so many people. I pictured Christmas lights wrapped around towering trees, garlands of mistletoe, and all kinds of outdoor adornments in a frozen lushness. No doubt a perfect amount of snow would arrive just as the guests stepped delicately from their cars and into the warm interior of the Ashworth mansion. I could see it all, every detail.

Christmas in my apartment consisted of Mom's sideboard with the pitiful tabletop tree. Each year I strung the tree's thin branches with ancient multi-colored lights that had faded over the years but had an adorable frill-like detail, as if each wore a skirt. I had loved these, right up until now. I could, I suppose, take a new box of lights from my holiday display. Why not? Who would keep me from robbing my own stock?

Though the Ashworths had no children, I pictured a train set, a grand one with winding, hilly topography, tunnels, and signal lights. A month ago, as Beppe and I lay in the pale sun of another winter afternoon, I almost asked him why they'd never had children. What made me think of it was my period was late. In the beginning Beppe and I had taken chances, but we had been much more careful lately. He could afford rubbers and so we'd used those, except for once or twice.

Italian Wedding Soup was the simplest of Mom's recipes, but it called for plenty of parsley, which, because it was winter I would have to buy, that and the escarole and the meat, all of it at Ferrara's.

I took down my mortar and pestle and ground some dried fennel seeds. Fennel's promise was protection, its power hinted at victory, success, even possession. Its flavor was close to that of anise, and since both would be masked by the cheese and the aromatic oregano, I added some anise, too. Its powers were broad, and there was much I wished for. I hoped the soup would neutralize gossip about me and Mr. Ashworth. I was sure people were talking; it was crazy to believe our affair could remain secret for long. Another wish. I wanted to believe, as Mom had, that a miracle could happen. That we might be lifted, carried as if mounting a chariot, swept off to a different life. Had the Parodis, my mother's family, been prone to a kind of wishful thinking? Or was it that gambling streak of my father's?

As the time approached for the delivery of the soup, my wish became more modest. I simply wanted the Ashworths to find it delicious, hearty. Really I had a single hope; that by tasting my Wedding Soup, Beppe would understand I wasn't a woman to be trifled with. And as he stood in his beautiful living room with the rumored cathedral ceiling, surrounded by the beauty of his life and the sounds of his friends and his family enjoying themselves, as the sparkling lights cast a glow on his world, I would invade him and take up residence. In that precious second, he would be thinking only of me.

CHAPTER TWENTY-ONE

Ella called again to ask whether I could also prepare some raw vegetables and a dipping sauce. Yes, I said, somewhat reluctantly, thinking about the brisk demand for desserts in the run-up to Christmas and how much time the soup was going to take.

I had already decided to limit my dessert offerings to a choice of two. A special dense fruitcake packed full of glazed fruit, a favorite among my Anglo-Saxon customers, and a steamed persimmon pudding. Both could be made in advance. The fruitcake I wrapped tightly and put in the downstairs cold storage. The persimmon pudding froze exceedingly well, so I put them in Mimi's deep freeze, in the extra space she'd let me borrow. I planned to stop taking dessert orders a week before the Ashworths' party.

Ella wanted to know whether I would be able to deliver the food myself. Now I hesitated.

"Is that a problem?" she asked.

"No. Oh, no. I can get my brothers to help. There's absolutely no problem."

They could even deliver without me, I thought. I could show them how everything should be laid out, kept warmed, and hope they would be polite and efficient for such an important client. Except I knew I would deliver the soup myself. Nothing could have kept me away.

I spent the afternoon at the kitchen table making a list of ingredients and quantities. Ella had said they would be happy to advance me the money to purchase ingredients. I'd said no far too quickly. What stupid pride was this? The size of the order would take a chunk out of my cash flow at a time when I could hardly afford it.

I cleaned the house in preparation for a marathon of cooking. Gino's room was a mess, and there were piles of laundry. Not that any of this affected my process in the kitchen, but any and all disarray destroyed my ability to think. It was a Genovese trait to consider absolute order the prelude to any serious undertaking, a need that superseded reason or a simple solution like closing a door.

So I cleaned. After that I walked to Ferrara's. Eddie helped me pick out what I needed, then disappeared into the back to cut me a large piece of cheese and to check whether they had enough ground beef. I needed four or five pounds, but they only had two ready to go. I took what he had and Eddie said he would come by later with the rest. He followed me out of the store, as if to walk me to a car, which of course I didn't have.

"How many people you cooking for, Marie?"

"Too many," I joked, tossing my hair and enjoying the captivated look on his face. It was as if I suddenly remembered I was young.

Ella called back to say the Ashworths preferred beef broth, so when Eddie delivered the order I told him I needed beef bones for stock. Later that day he dropped off a hefty bag.

I planned to begin making the stock that afternoon. That and the huge quantity of meatballs, about one hundred and fifty, would take me all day. They were small, not even an inch across, so it was a lot of patting into shape and rolling between flat palms to get the nice roundness. I set to work chopping onion, celery and carrot and threw it all in with the bones to begin the long boiling process. I was right in the middle of getting three large pasta pots filled and ready when the phone rang.

It was Beppe. We'd last met several days ago, and I'd expected a call. I tried to draw the scene. Was he telephoning from the mansion, from an upstairs room where he wouldn't be disturbed, or from a study off limits to his wife? We were hardly past the pleasantries when he said, "I'm sorry, Marie, but I'll be busy all this week."

"Busy?"

I stared at a pile of raw bones ready to be boiled down into a broth to be consumed by the Ashworths and their friends.

He spoke quickly, "Priscilla's sister is coming down from Philadelphia."

It should have occurred to me that the holidays would be different.

"I have a lot of cooking to do," I said quickly, "A big order. A party."

Would he mention he knew I'd been hired to cook for him? Did he even know?

"I'm making soup for thirty people," I said.

Seconds passed in which neither of us spoke.

"Did you hear me? I'm cooking the food for *your* party."

"Marie, I have to go. Can I call you tonight?"

Tonight? He never called in the evening.

"You can call at eight," I said, angrily, and hung up.

I felt sad, but I didn't stop working. Soon I had all the pots going, and once they'd begun to boil, I lowered the heat and went to take a bath.

The bathroom filled with steam, and when I lifted my foot from the water I could hardly see my toes. It felt dramatic to cry fiercely in the gloom that so perfectly matched my mood. The water relaxed me, and I soaked for a long time. It occurred to me to add some wine to the bath water and some salt—I had brought these in with me just in case—but for this particular ritual that I'd read about in one of Mom's books, I would need to pretend to be kneeling outside under the moon while holding a sprig of rue, which I now mimed dipping into the bath before anointing my naked body in the shape of a pentacle. Forehead, right nipple, left shoulder, right shoulder, left nipple, forehead. I was sure Mom had never used this book. She would laugh, calling it nonsense from the old country. What was a witch anyway but a woman who wanted to control her own life? Rather than spells, we used food. We brought bread to the table, ladled soup, served cake, and whenever I did these things I felt my mother's invisible hand.

How could these old beliefs be effective against the forces of our circumstances, mine and Beppe's? He was unhappy in his marriage, and I—and this was the hardest to admit—was at an age when I had very little control over myself. Was this constant sexual urge even normal? We were consumed with lust neither of us could resist. For me, an outlet, really the only *solution* if I weren't with Beppe, would be to accept a marriage arranged by Mrs. Macri, Mrs. Romasello, or Mrs. Mazza. Following Mom's death, all three had circled with offers of their male relatives and they'd seemed desperate to attach me to one of them.

All rituals were stabs in the dark. It was pure illusion to believe I had control over the store, my brothers, or the gossiping town. But I was determined to go my own way, to resist what was expected, to fight, even if it felt sometimes as if two enormous men had hold of my arms, two more my feet and they were pulling.

I was wrapped in a towel with my chenille robe thrown on top, when I opened the bathroom door and was hit by the meaty fragrance of the stock. For a second I thought of calling Ella to say I couldn't do what I'd been hired to do.

Beppe telephoned promptly at eight, but it wasn't a good call. When I asked him why we couldn't meet for a whole week, he said, "Please Marie. You need to settle down."

Was there an herb, a blending of wheat and chickpeas perhaps, cooked over a wood-fire, a concoction I might make for him to soften the humor?

"Why didn't you mention the party?" I asked.

"Marie, I don't know what to say."

In bed we were compatriots, keepers of each other's minds and souls. On the telephone, the distance grew. When exactly had I become a woman who waits, an appointment to be shuffled, cancelled at a moment's notice? I gripped the telephone and recalled the pentacle. Everyplace I had touched with the imaginary sprig of rue now began to tingle, my nipples, forehead, and shoulders. I dragged the telephone's cord out as far as it would go, and looked down at the loading bay, which was quiet. The moon was up. I felt calm.

"Marie, tell me what you want. Did you hear me?"

"Yes, I heard."

"Well?"

"I want you to take care of me."

I could have been more specific, and said what I'd rehearsed many times. *Beppe, leave her and be with me.* I waited for his reaction.

I heard him sigh, then he said it, "Marie, I love you."

CHAPTER TWENTY-TWO

The soup took more doing than I thought, and the apartment drowned in the smell of boiling bones, like I was living inside Ferrara's Market.

"Jesus, Marie, what are you doing?"

Gino and I had barely spoken since the terrible night at the Sons. He seemed to know if he wasn't careful he would lose a roof and a hot meal.

"Earning money so you two lazy good for nothings can live here and eat me out of house and home." He threw off that handsome smile that could almost seem charming.

"Listen, Gino," I said, over my shoulder, "I need your help to deliver this order on Friday. Soup for thirty people. I can't do it alone." I would rather have used Sammy for this particular errand, but he was getting over a bad cold.

"Sure. Where?"

"The Ashworths down on the lake."

Gino came around to face me, his hands on his hips, and I had to endure a slow whistle aimed at the air above my head.

"Can you help me or not?"

"Friday night?"

"Late afternoon. Around four."

"Sure. But Sammy has to stay in the store. We'll be busy."

"Will you see if he can?" I kept my head low to the act of rolling the meatballs.

I had revised my estimate and figured I'd better make two hundred. People loved them, and they were hard to stop eating, each one a tiny explosion of flavor and a buttery texture with a hint of cheese and the tiny flecks of parsley. The addition of an egg gave them a loose, airy quality that trapped the beautiful stock inside. If it had been any other client I would have skimped, but for the Ashworths, *for him*, nothing was spared.

I was fast, but it was painstaking work, and my right wrist began to bother me. My hands became incredibly soft with the constant application of fat from the meat. I loved the look of the rows forming, as I placed the tiny balls on trays lined with waxed paper, then the wonderful moment when I'd filled a tray and was forced to go on to the next, like finally pasting in the last S & H green stamp into my collector's book. Each time Mr. E. put gasoline in his Ford he was given a fistful of stamps, which he tended to pass on to me. Only two more books and I could claim a Sunbeam toaster.

Full trays were now scattered all over the kitchen, balanced on cookbooks and appliances, and because I couldn't fit them all into the icebox, I opened the kitchen window and worked in a heavy sweater until my hands became so cold I was forced to take a break.

The living room was toasty, so I sat there with my warm cup of tea while trying not to glance across at the bank. Since Beppe and I wouldn't be seeing each other, my relationship to the street had changed. I avoided walking into my own living room.

"Sammy," I yelled.

"I'm right here," he said, coming into the room.

"Can you please bring up the large pasta pot from the store?"

I would have to cook the soup in batches and I only had three large pots. Now my store display would be missing its centerpiece, the shiny pot with its sturdy lid. Like the blue bowl, it had been expensive.

"Sure, Marie."

"And try to order another blue bowl. And another pasta pot. A big one."

"With what budget?"

"Feldman will give us credit. Tell him we're expecting a busy week. He might have something in stock." I gave a stern look. I wanted to impress on him that Feldman was a true friend.

"You said we were done ordering for Christmas. We won't get it in time."

"Just do it, okay?" I stood close to him. I placed my hand on his cheek. "My baby. Just do it, please?"

Later that afternoon Ella called. "Do you have a large serving bowl for the soup? Mrs. A. wants guests to ladle their own. We have two large chaffing dishes but they won't be enough."

Even if by now Ella and I were accomplices, comfortable with our plain exchanges, I became short tempered. The only bowl big enough was the cut glass punch bowl that lived on the breakfront. Now, at

Christmas, it held large pine cones spray-painted gold. Next to it was the sad little tree with the faded lights.

"I'll look around," I said, "and call you back."

Ella gave me their home telephone number, which I had never had. Beppe's number.

Would I really send off another family treasure to possibly be ruined, as I'd sent off the plate, and the hat box that once held Carmela's wedding veil? Even so, while on the telephone with Ella, I began removing the cones from the dish.

Gino borrowed Mr. E.'s car. I'd never even considered how we'd get the soup there, and here was Gino behind the wheel of Mr. E.'s little black Ford. I was shocked that my normally thoughtless brother had arranged this without my having to ask.

I took an hour deciding what to wear. I had to be comfortable, which meant flat shoes, and since I'd be helping Gino carry the heavy pots, I would wear slacks, a thought that excited me. Mom had owned a pair of very fashionable slacks at a time when only wealthy women in the movies dared wear them. Hers happened to fit me. The style dictated that they be loose—the looser fitting, the more fashionable. I wore my nicest sweater, and on top Mom's camel hair coat, which I risked ruining with one slosh of soup. It was wide-sleeved and glamorous. I almost took it off again, opting for my plain dark cloth coat, but no, I thought, *It's Christmas, Marie. Live a little.*

Gino and I loaded the soup into the car and I wedged old towels around the pots so they wouldn't teeter. On the way there I kept warning him to be careful, telling him to slow down on the icy roads, though we crawled along at an extremely slow speed. Central Avenue was the most beautiful street in Littlefield, with houses much grander even than those on Bellevue. They were set far back, and there were no sidewalks, only broad fringes of landscaping that provided fleeting glimpses of the spacious homes behind, each surrounded by tall, mature trees. Except for the Ashworth property, which wasn't visible at all.

The Harbour was reached by taking the last right turn, at the end of Central, where I imagined the lake must widen. People in town whispered maliciously about the British spelling of harbour, with a "u," but it made me think of Manderley, the fictional mansion in

Rebecca, a novel I loved.

The tall gates were open. I wondered if they were ever closed, and if so under what circumstances. I pulled up my wool socks in an effort to stay warm, and looked over at Gino, who wore only a long-sleeved shirt and a thin cardigan. He had to be freezing, though he didn't seem to be. He was taking it all in just as I was. His neck in profile was square, trunk-like, but his nose was finely chiseled, handsome, almost delicate. How Italian he looked. Did I look Italian? I was reminded suddenly of my ethnicity. Whereas around Beppe I never thought about it. Maybe that first time when he'd come to pick up his cake, but never since. Now, entering the Ashworth property, I was hardly more than a servant.

We drove along an icy lane, icicles hanging from carriage lamps already glowing, though there was still light in the sky. Gino pulled the car up on a crescent-shaped drive. He'd hardly stopped when we were waved on by someone in a maid's uniform who stood at the front door. We followed her motions to the back of the house, where I allowed myself the first full look at the elegant Tudor. The rear driveway was larger than the front, a huge circle in which many cars that I assumed belonged to service staff were parked. Attached to the end of the sprawling house was a garage that looked as though it would hold at least three cars. The kitchen door was obvious. A bright yellow light shone from out of its clear pane and people were moving around inside. Someone had told them we were here, because as soon as we stopped the car, the door swung open. I saw Ella first and behind her an elderly couple; all three were dressed in black and wearing white aprons.

"In here," she called, beckoning with an impatient arm.

I leaned into the back seat and pulled the towels from around the five large pots. There had hardly been any spillage, but now we had to get them inside without incident.

Beyond the field of snow that stretched from the house to the lake was a square dock. My attention was abruptly pulled toward the lake, which I had seen many times, but only from the Lake Park with its worn paths and noisy crowds. Angie and I used to walk there in summer.

This lake was tranquil, the water frozen so smoothly it resembled a pane of glass. Everywhere I looked, shrubs were meticulously sculpted beneath their caps of snow, every inch carefully pruned and tended. I had never felt such envy as I stole a final glance, noticing how beyond the lake there was a view of still more trees, no other houses, just an uninterrupted vision of beauty. I was reminded of the feel of Beppe's fingers on my skin, an equivalent luxury. Now I wanted both—to have him, but also to be here.

I was aware of Gino standing behind me as I bent into the car to retrieve the first pot.

"I can't lift it," I said, stepping back.

He had been standing there silently, but now he laughed, "I was waiting for you to figure that out," he said, gently.

"Be careful," I chided, as he lifted the pot, though he seemed to be taking extra care.

A woman in a maid's uniform held the door open for us, and together, one on each side, we carried in the first heavy pot.

"I'll get the others," he said.

I hadn't been aware of the cold until my limbs began to thaw in the warm kitchen, and the sudden flush of heat made it difficult for me to keep my emotions in check. Finding myself inside his house, I felt numb. In addition, the maid who had opened the door for us stared for a second longer than felt comfortable. It had to be the slacks, and Mom's coat. She looked away just as Gino brought in the last pot.

It was then I remembered I'd forgotten to make the raw vegetables and dipping sauce. Thankfully, I'd remembered the bread. My error and the feeling of being too warmly dressed in Mom's coat, caused a hot flush to shoot up my neck and into my face.

Gino hoisted two of the pots onto the stove, the first to be warmed before being transferred to the chaffing dishes. The Ashworths' kitchen wasn't much larger than mine and certainly not attractive; actually, it was ugly and not nearly as efficient. The stove was in an alcove, making it awkward to move the heavy pots on and off. That made me wonder what the Ashworths ate and whether much cooking went on here at all.

With the soup delivered, all I wanted to do was to leave. I was suddenly afraid of seeing Priscilla Ashworth, or worse, having to see her alongside Beppe. Just then a young maid, who introduced herself as Helen, asked whether I would look at the buffet table and give my opinion about whether or not the set-up was right for serving the soup.

I followed Helen into the dining room where I had to fight with myself not to get lost in a detailed inspection, for there was much to look at. We'd entered directly from the kitchen through a door that swung both ways, which I guessed made the delivery of food and the clearing easier. The dining table was large enough to seat at least twelve people, and the dining room opened rather grandly onto a vast living room. This was the room with the famed cathedral ceiling, and I tried not to stare. It, too, was extremely ugly and not at all what I expected. I'd pictured pastel colors and silken festoons, luscious like a Mae West movie set, but the room itself, despite several pairs of French doors and large windows positioned high up, almost at the ceiling, was dark. The wainscoting was painted a deep brown, and mashed against it was dark brown furniture, the biggest pieces I had ever seen. On the walls were various tapestries and Oriental carpets. But what caught my eye and wouldn't let go was a very tall Christmas tree placed in front of a set of French doors, so tall it almost obscured the highest windows. Though it wasn't yet lighted, tinsel and ornaments glowed in what little light filtered in.

I was dragged back from my inspection when Helen pointed at the table, "We're thinking of putting one chaffing dish here and another there. I'll be ladling the soup. We'll refill after the first group is served. Can't tell if we need another bowl. Did you bring the bowl?" she asked, looking worried.

The bowl was still in the car. "I did. But it can't be heated," I said inanely, as if they might be dumb enough to set it atop one of the chaffing burners.

"Of course not," said Helen, shaking her head. "But we can heat the soup in the kitchen, and maybe I can serve out of yours first, while the others are in the chaffing dishes. What do you think?"

"I think the two chaffing dishes are enough," I said. "I don't think you need the bowl."

I decided on the spot that I didn't want them using it. I didn't want to give them a single extra accommodation.

"Or maybe we can use it to put the Christmas cookies in," said Helen. "Or the punch. Can I see it?"

I followed her back to the kitchen, where I found Gino leaning on the counter flirting with another young woman in a maid's uniform.

"Gino, where's the bowl?" I asked, feeling annoyed.

He looked up and grimaced. "In the car. I'll get it." He was irritated to be pulled away from his clutch with the maid.

Helen inspected Mom's bowl with its delicate gold edging. I was further annoyed to notice how right it looked in the Ashworths' house.

"I want to use this," she said, motioning to the young woman who'd been talking to Gino, "Please put this on the buffet table."

The woman went off with the bowl. *So many hands*, I thought. Why did I bring something so special to a household that wanted for nothing? I was busy hating myself when in walked Priscilla Ashworth.

"You must be Marie Genovese," she said, walking toward me with outstretched arms. She took one of my hands in hers, as though I was a long-lost niece, or a child. My heart was in my throat. The woman I'd seen with Beppe at the movies had seemed a little cold, whereas Priscilla was warm, confident, and there was no doubt who was in control. In the glare of the kitchen lights I could have been a harsh critic of her clothes, a dowdy blouse in a lilac color better suited to someone older and a plain gray skirt that was a little too long, and the black t-strap pumps that seemed too ordinary for an evening party at home.

"Come with me," she said leading me back through the swinging door into the dining room, which gave me the chance to study what I'd missed the first time. Arranged in front of two sets of French doors in the huge living room were many velvet armchairs and a grand piano. Opposite the piano was the tallest free-standing breakfront I'd ever seen, crammed floor to ceiling with china and glassware. Though there was plenty of room for all of it, the effect was that of a dark jumble, made worse by the busy patterns of the rugs that stretched from the dining room clear through to a smaller sitting room far beyond where we stood. That room was partially cut off by tall, dark, wooden panels, and above those, yet more carpets hung from a balcony lined with bookcases and brimming with books that looked as if they were frequently taken down and wedged back in.

In between saying how lovely I found the china and agreeing that the dishes were well placed for serving, I stole glances, but Priscilla Ashworth was watching me. What was all this insecurity about how to set a table? And why was I asked to advise how these wealthy people should be serving their guests?

Most surprisingly, in a corner of the dining room, near where people would be eating, was a fancy bird cage. Inside, a pair of squawking parakeets shed feathers and sent seeds flying in what looked like a fight. Apart from the lively activity of the birds, the place was as still as a mausoleum, and it made me sad.

I appraised the furnishings and answered Priscilla Ashworth's questions, but with every second that went by I worried Beppe would walk in. Then, just as I was thinking this, Priscilla Ashworth said, "I don't know where my husband is. I told him you were here. I said I wanted him to come down and look at the table. And meet you," she added.

I made an effort to smile. She looked as though she expected me to say something.

"I guess men aren't really interested," I said, at which she turned to me, and with some enthusiasm said, "They aren't, are they?" She laughed. It was a low, throaty sound that made her seem a more interesting woman than the one I'd met in the kitchen. I could see that Priscilla Ashworth had been a homely girl, a good sport. The kind of woman people like, men especially, because they're not threatening. Yet she had a spirit, what Carmela would have described as being "game."

God knew how long I would have to stand in my lover's dining room and pretend to be nothing more than a hired cook. Finally, she led me back in the direction of the kitchen and I followed.

Gino and I didn't talk much on the way home.

"Some place," he said, and the whistle again.

"Gino, I hate when you make that sound."

"What sound?"

"That annoying whistle. Stop it."

"What's gotten into you?"

"Nothing. I'm tired. If you'd been making soup for four days."

"How much they paying you?"

"I don't know yet," I said, looking out the window.

"You didn't give them a price?"

"No."

"Great business, Marie."

Instead of listening, I was in the forest across the lake looking back at the mansion with the lights blazing.

"Salvie says when a shipment of olive oil comes in he doesn't take a single order until he figures out a price."

I made a note of Gino's use of Mr. E.'s first name.

"That's different," I said, hoping to leave it there.

"Why? I see you forgot the vegetables they ordered," he was laughing.

"They didn't care."

"Priscilla Ashworth is a looker."

"Do you think so?" I asked, turning to him.

"She's all right," he said, seeming to lose interest.

"I think she's plain."

"I don't know. I think she has a pretty face."

I had no idea how much my brothers knew or how much they guessed. I'm sure they noticed that I went out at odd times during the day. Between meeting my lover and all the baking, several afternoons a week I was no longer in the store.

It was two miles back into town, but the trip was slow as the temperature dropped and the roads became icier. I slipped further inside myself with the revelation of the house. If one ignored the pile of messy half-read newspapers resting on several end tables, and the stacks of books wobbling in towers on the balcony floor—I assumed those would be cleaned up before the guests arrived—his house would have been too intimidating. As it was, the mess, what I considered unforgiveable clutter, made me feel a little better. It was shocking, given how people liked to say Italians were dirty, when in fact my house was tidier and certainly cleaner. How did people come to such conclusions?

At the same time, I was disappointed Beppe had failed to live up to my fantasy of a rich, elegant banker from a Hollywood movie. Still haunting me was the idea that I was no match and no equal, that somewhere in the scheme of life's hierarchies I'd landed on an entirely different scale, and that rather than share what I felt we shared, we stood stranded on opposite shores, an abyss between us.

By the time Gino and I reached the apartment I had put away the image of Priscilla Ashworth in her grandmotherly attire and erased the sparkle in her eye as she'd asked me whether the bowls were placed correctly on the buffet table. Had it been a test? Was she making fun?

Then, as evening came on, those images invaded once more, and I wondered at the cars driving up, and what the women wore. Particularly I tried to imagine what Beppe would look like on such a night. Surely by now I had seen all of his clothes, but tonight would be special.

CHAPTER TWENTY-THREE

Christmas came and went without a word from Beppe. It had been a week since the party, and if I counted the week before, when he'd been unable to meet, it was a long time. I knew he was with family, but I had expected at least a call. When Ella telephoned to find out what the Ashworths owed for the soup, I asked how they'd liked it. There was a long pause, and I held my breath. My wedding soup was delicious, there wasn't a person alive who didn't love it.

"They got loud," she said.

"Loud?"

"You know. Making noise. And dancing," she gave a snort, what sounded like disapproval.

"Well I hope they liked it."

"Oh, they liked it," she said.

She wasn't effusive. I wouldn't get another word out of her. Yet I continued to hope for an indiscreet slip. Might she mention how Mr. Ashworth had been full of praise for the woman who'd cooked them such a delicious soup? But no, Ella was her typical, restrained self. We arranged a time for her to drop off the money and hung up.

Next Ada telephoned, and it wasn't until I heard her voice, soothing and melodious with a peppering of Italian phrases, that I nearly broke down.

"Oh Ada," I cried. "I'm so glad you called."

I had the urge to tell her everything. That his life was as placid as mine was turbulent, that I had seen his house and it had unsettled me.

"I come?"

"Yes. How about tomorrow?"

"I come next week," she said. "Good?"

"Yes, I...." I tried to keep feebleness from creeping into my voice. I had been prowling the apartment with restless energy. I was miserable, a child in need of comfort. Hearing Ada, it was as if I spoke to Mom. I wanted to be held, like the time I had a crush on a boy. I was nine years old at the time, and I wanted to kill myself at the thought that he would never love me back. Mom fought a smile until I cried out, *Help me*, and her face crumpled. There was sympathy in that motherly look, but also amusement. The problem wasn't serious.

How would Ada react if I confessed to seeing a married man? Would she drop everything and come? Would she judge me?

"Good?" she asked again.

"Yes, good," I said, disappointed that I would have to wait.

She hung up, and I stared at the telephone. Why didn't I press her for an exact time? I wouldn't allow the boys to schedule so much as a delivery without first clearing it with me. I held them to strict times and arrangements. But with Ada it was different. She came to me, turning up unannounced according to some hidden clock. Stranger still was the feeling that I was the one being summoned. I had to sit down. I was too weak to stand.

Two days after Ella called, I still hadn't heard from him and I began to panic. While I waited I distracted myself by reorganizing the kitchen, turning it back into a room where regular meals could again be served. I was right in the middle of this when Beppe finally telephoned.

"I miss you," he said. "Can you?"

I could always detect lust in his voice after a period away, but this urgency was new; he sounded feverish.

"Of course," I said, patting the frequently washed counter with the palm of my hand.

"I miss you, Marie."

I knew he wouldn't mention the party, but I wondered if he knew I'd met his wife.

"I miss you, too," I said.

To hesitate would have been to introduce some unpleasantness, so I kept my tone light. Yet having met Priscilla, I could no longer pretend she didn't exist.

"I have to get out of the office. How about one-thirty?" he asked.

"You're in the bank today?"

He laughed. "I work every day."

I turned my head to lean back through the kitchen door in order to glimpse the bank's lintel, the sight of which made my lover's presence real.

"One-thirty is fine," I said, sounding calm, though I, too, was crazy with desire. I finished straightening the kitchen, then went to take a bath.

As usual, I arrived at the apartment first and was surprised to find it warm, recently dusted and there were fresh flowers in a tall vase on the worn pedestal table in the hallway. I had always hated that table. Now it brought to mind the ugly furniture in the mansion and my disappointment at seeing his life. I was certain now that these pieces were castoffs from the mansion—the blackened brass lamp with a frayed silk shade, two creaky cane chairs, a rickety side table.

Was it Beppe who had prepared our nest today? And who had arranged for the heat and the flowers? And with snow on the ground, where had the yellow irises come from, summer flowers, and what had they cost? On the same table as the flowers was a small box wrapped not in Christmas paper, but in soft white tissue with a large pale blue bow, fluffy and soft as a negligee. I opened the card: To Marie, Happy Christmas, Joseph Ashworth. I glanced at my watch. He was late by twenty minutes, which was unusual, particularly given his urgent call.

I sat down with the present in my lap and looked around as if someone might be watching. A thick covering of snow muffled the outdoor sounds, but even so the apartment was unnaturally quiet. Though the room was warm, I experienced a sudden chill, at the same time as I had the urge to flee. Maybe there'd been an emergency at the bank, or perhaps his watch had stopped.

I didn't know how long I sat there staring at the beautiful floral arrangement with the gift in my lap, which I couldn't bring myself to open after the hard slap of the signature: the stiffly formal *Joseph Ashworth*. Not Beppe, but Joseph, a name I no longer called him.

What if he wasn't coming, and the present was his way of saying goodbye? This thought caused me to jump up and rush to the small bedroom. The present slid from my lap and hit the floor, but I left it there. In the bedroom I looked frantically for a clue. But everything seemed in order, except for what was missing; not a hint of how much we'd given to each other within these walls. It was, in the bare winter light, just a room. I had to lean against the door jamb or risk fainting. The bedroom was cold, and just as I turned to go back into the living room, I heard the key in the lock.

Beppe entered and I froze. We looked at one another, before our eyes drifted to the gift lying on the floor.

"What happened?" he asked as if stumbling upon a crime scene.

"Nothing." I shook my head, wondering why I felt so guilty. I realized then that I had not bought him anything. What was even more shocking was that I hadn't even thought to buy him a present. Instead, I'd gone about my week making soup, being the hired cook, and when he'd called to say he wasn't able to see me for a week, I didn't exactly forget that it was Christmas, but nor did I make an effort. Now, here it was, intimacy without hope of commitment, that and the sordid business of a key to a tryst.

He cast off his hat and bent to pick up the fallen present, which gave me a chance to see his hair, the thick sandy top of his head, and in that instant there was no more judgment. Here he was, a little late, but again at the appointment of our love, and I wanted him.

I took off my coat and threw it over a chair. He took off his, and we were shedding garments as fast as we could. It had never before happened like this, and a far cry from the veiled suggestion in *It Happened One Night*, which I'd gone to see right after Mom died. In the picture a bed sheet becomes a chaste curtain, but the audience knew what was coming next. Of course the love scene happened off screen, whereas it was really happening now with Beppe. We stumbled awkwardly into the bedroom, which no longer felt as cold, and we were falling, our lives tumbling together. No matter what the card read, no matter how he'd arranged for flowers, planted the gift and then arrived late, no matter that I'd been inside his house and met his wife, everything fell away as we wove in and out of each other's arms.

I wanted to say it, *I love you*, and it almost sprang unchecked from my lips. Instead, I held him, my fingers cupping the side of his face as if to shield him from the light of day. "I'm sorry," he said, "I'm so sorry. I had so many meetings this morning, and I tried to cancel them, but I couldn't." Then he was laughing, full of a joy that was rare for him, as though what he'd said sparked enormous relief. He wanted me to know the effort he'd made.

"You have time, don't you?" he said. "You aren't in a hurry to get back?" The words rushed out, and for a second it was as if we'd swapped temperaments, he the more emotional Marie, I the more measured one.

"No, it's fine. I have time," I said, though I didn't.

"Good. Oh good," said with a mischievous glint.

After we'd made love we lay staring at the plain ceiling. I noticed water stains in the corners, a strip of peeling wallpaper. Though I'd seen them before, this evidence of neglect seemed full of portent and compromise.

"Shall I open it?" I asked, picking up the long thin box. Slowly, we'd started dressing, both of us now needing to get back.

"Yes, open it," he said, smiling as he did up his tie. I unpicked the tape, unfolded the wrapping. Nestled in the velvet box was the most exquisite bracelet, delicate gold with a dainty clasp of diamonds. He knelt on one knee in front of me and drew me toward him. "I will never hurt you," he said.

"I won't hurt you either, Beppe."

"I want to take care of you, Marie," he said, echoing my words from weeks earlier. I threw my arms around him. My heart flooded. A second later we pulled apart so he could do up his jacket buttons and I could pull on my coat. We had to rush now.

"I need a loan," I said quickly. The words were out before I could stop them.

He sat down heavily on a small Queen Anne chair next to the window. I couldn't recall either of us ever sitting in that chair. Sometimes it held clothes.

"I know you need it, Marie," he said, picking his words carefully. He had to have known. He'd been in the store to see the thinly stocked shelves. He had to have noticed the peeling paint on the wall behind the cash register. I sat on the bed in front of him but he wasn't looking at me. He got up and smoothed his suit. Would he let the subject drop? The fears of an hour before took shape, the warm apartment, his lateness, the flowers, the formal note.

"I have to look at the collateral, Marie."

"Collateral?"

"The value of the store."

"Oh."

"Let's sit down together and go over your books."

I nodded, but I was thinking, *This is me, Marie, the woman you say you love. The store isn't separate from me.* But any loan would be better than the drip feed of Mr. E.'s checks and his envelopes of cash, which put me in the way of physical obligation.

I almost asked Beppe whether there was any truth to what Kenny had said, that the bank hesitated to loan to Italians. The only discrimination I was aware of was against farmers, Italian or otherwise, who had a hard time borrowing money for the next year's crop, to buy the seeds of their future. They dressed in their best suits, ill-fitting and badly cut, and sat across the desk from men like my lover. I decided not to mention what Kenny had said. Why acknowledge a prejudice I could do nothing about?

1939

CHAPTER TWENTY-FOUR

I turned on the heater. I also made a fire in the living room and was comforted by the sight of the small flame, of the promise of warmth even before the logs fully caught fire. Then I cut myself a slice of leftover meatloaf and covered it with gravy made from a Steero cube. I'd once taken pride in eating well even when alone. But since the boys had left for New York, almost a month ago now, I had all but stopped cooking.

As usual, after Christmas, business dropped off with frightening speed. Yet there was still so much to do, and I was tired all the time. The stockroom needed to be cleaned and merchandise that hadn't sold packed up. But to Kenny's complaints that he needed more help, I shrugged. What could I do? There was no money for extra staff. Mr. E. was at least putting more in my envelope each week in exchange for taking my brothers with him to New York. The late night runs on my loading bay increased, and trucks were arriving twice a night. Even so, we were strapped.

You didn't often hear it mentioned, but we were all alarmed by Roosevelt's recent State of the Union Address: "A war which threatened to envelop the world in flames has been averted; but it has become increasingly clear that world peace is not assured."

It was all over the newsreels how Chamberlain had been cheered by Italian crowds on a recent trip in which he'd met with Mussolini. We were meant to feel optimistic that he'd gone to convince Mussolini to persuade Hitler not to make warlike moves, but I had a sick feeling in my gut. And did I imagine it, or were my customers more shaken than they let on? I could only base this on our terrible Valentine's Day sales, where the only special merchandise we'd managed to move was the usual small bags of conversation hearts and the paper cards children liked to give to their classmates. As the day came to an end, I knew I would be stuck with the more expensive items—the larger foil-covered chocolate hearts and heart-shaped ceramic bowls for holding jewelry. As usual we'd sold out of all the red items in the penny candy bins.

What had started as a celebration of martyrs in Roman times, our Valentine's Day became a celebration of martyrs as Kenny and I dragged ourselves through the dreary process of marking down items in the hopes of making a few more sales, anything to save us from another winter slump.

A week later when Beppe called to say that Priscilla was leaving the next day to visit her sister, right away I volunteered to make us dinner. It was so rare that we got to enjoy the comfort of my apartment, and with my brothers gone, I had this new taste of freedom, of being able to do whatever I liked any time of day.

Beppe wanted to go over my books and talk about a loan, which I was sure he would agree to. I wouldn't mention how, in advance of this money, I'd gone ahead and ordered a new icebox. The money was meant to be used for stock, but with my expanding baking business a decent icebox was a necessity. The newer model was bigger and wouldn't ice up, and would give me more room for batters and icings.

It was February 22nd, George Washington's birthday, so I decided on a strictly American meal, Colonial Mushroom Soup, Minuteman Broccoli Bake, and Please Be Mine cheese balls, all from the St. Joseph's Holiday Cook Book. I was hoping Beppe would notice that I not only knew what Americans liked to eat, I could prepare this food, *his* food, as well as I could ravioli or spaghetti. I had most of the ingredients I needed, except for the mushrooms which I would get from Mimi, whose husband owned the mushroom house. The young buttons would be fresher and more tender than anything I could buy in the store.

"No problem," said Mimi. "Lou has to go into town. I can drop them off."

While I waited for her to arrive, I prepared the Please Be Mines with a dough laced with paprika. I took the remainder of my fennel, ground it to a fine powder and sprinkled in some for *protection*. I wrapped each large green olive stuffed with pimento with dough and set them in the icebox to chill. What would Carmela think of my preparations? I felt my mother everywhere on this night. It wasn't simply the cooking, but my determination to get financing for the store.

Before Beppe had set up our apartment and we were still meeting at my place, we'd become practiced in the ritual of his arrival. I would wait behind my downstairs door until I heard a light rapping of a knuckle, then I would douse the lights before I opened the door and he slipped inside. I replayed this ritual over and over again in my head. Tonight it would be the same as in those early days.

I had been cooking all afternoon, and when finally I heard him, I experienced a familiar anticipation, the urgency of wanting to make love. Seconds later we were standing next to each other in the dark. He couldn't see my face, nor I his. He took me in his arms and the newspaper he carried fell to the floor, and we were Marie and Beppe from last summer. Mere months ago, our love had been more polite, our opinions kept to ourselves; lately we were bolder, we pressed points, we argued. Still, what hadn't changed was the feel of our arms around each other, and as we kissed, from the other side of the door came the clomping of a horse's hooves, and the sound of a car's engine like a loud clock ticking. The door felt thin, leaving us exposed to the world, and it was thrilling how no one could see us, though we could hear them, conversations carried on the wind before evaporating in the cold. People were going home. Briefly I wondered if he'd managed to reach my door without being seen. But I didn't care. He kissed me again, both of us spurred on by the danger of our secret.

As we sat down to our meal, I explained that the occasion of our first president's birthday had inspired me to make a theme of the food. At first he looked suspiciously at what he was eating. "Don't worry. It's just mushroom soup," I said.

Mimi's mushrooms were fresh and fragrant, and the cream couldn't dominate as it sometimes did. The Please Be Mine cheese balls, which was our appetizer, were extra crispy, with a slight tang from the pimento hidden in the olives. I served a special Chianti—the only Italian touch—a gift from Mr. E. who'd left it in the store with a note: *To Mari, thank you for the loan of your nice boys. I feel privileged to know you and yours, Salvie.*

Beppe leaned back and patted his stomach. "If they'd eaten like this before Concord, the British might have won!"

"There's no war tonight, mister," I said, imitating Carole Lombard in *Made for Each Other*. It felt good to joke. I was feeling drunk; nothing could bother me.

Beppe stared straight ahead for what felt like a long time, before placing his hands on the table as though he intended to get up. "Shall we take a look at those books now?"

I went to get the ledger. "I'm thinking of putting in a soda fountain, a milk bar. And I want to add housewares, more than I carry now."

He didn't react. "What are your salary expenses?"

I hesitated. He didn't know about the money Mr. E. gave me.

"What do you pay Gino and Sammy?"

"Room and board."

"Your brothers work for free?" he asked, his head bent to the ledger pages.

I couldn't answer. For at least a year now, their money had come from Mr. E.

Beppe looked at me over a pair of spectacles he'd only recently begun to wear, which made me think of the difference in our ages.

"My brothers take what I give them."

I squeezed the bracelet he'd given me until it left a mark. I gazed at the twinkling candles in their porcelain holders while I half listened to my tabletop radio tuned low to Danceland.

"I want to show you something, Marie." He stood up and went to get his newspaper. I had never actually looked at *The New York Times*. Mr. E. sometimes brought *Il Progresso*, but it was in Italian, so I couldn't read it. At least for now we'd abandoned the ledgers and I was relieved. I cleared the table so he could spread out the paper, but what he wanted to show me was right on the front page. "Read this." He tapped the headline, the first story on the front page:

"22,000 Nazis Rally Unmolested Here; Police Check Foes"

"This happened in New York yesterday," he said.

"What does that mean *unmolested here?*"

"The Nazis were pretty much left alone. But there were 100,000 protesting the rally."

He began to read: *Protected by more than 1,700 policemen, who made of Madison Square Garden an almost impregnable fortress to anti-Nazis, the German-American Bund last night staged its much-advertised "Americanism" rally and celebration of George Washington's birthday.*

"What is the German-American Bund?" I asked. He ignored my question and kept reading.

"Inside the Garden, all was peace, if not quiet, as various speakers praised the first President of the United States, Father Charles E. Coughlin and all friends of Nazi Germany. The 22,000 persons present cheered loudly. Outside a crowd was gathered estimated by the police at 100,000 persons, some of them vocally anti-Nazi..."

Abruptly, he stopped reading and looked up. "Your brothers are in New York, aren't they?"

"Yes. So?"

"They're there with Esposito?"

"Yes."

I was stuck on the phrase, *Father Charles E. Coughlin and all friends of Nazi Germany.*

He pushed his chair back and removed his glasses. "When are they coming back?"

"I have no idea."

Did he think there was a connection between this awful rally and my brothers and Mr. E.?

"How did Christmas sales go?"

"Beppe, I hate when you quiz me. It's like you don't trust me." I was becoming aggravated. The flirtatiousness of a minute ago was gone.

He retrieved the ledger, "Show me the salaries for your part-time worker."

"Here," I said, pointing.

"Show me the sales."

"Here," I said.

He looked for a second, "I don't believe these numbers. Tell me the truth."

"What truth? You act as if I'm lying. You think it's all so easy."

"I didn't say that..."

"But you think it is. Do you know what would happen if I accounted for every single transaction? If I paid taxes on every cent I earned? You don't know what it's like to have to feed two giant boys..."

"Men," he said, interrupting me. "They're grown men."

"They're my younger brothers."

"Why do you treat them like your sons? Isn't it time they pulled their weight? Stood on their own feet, and you stopped making excuses?"

It was true, I wasn't responsible for my brothers. That is, until someone thought I should treat them better, give them the store, or they got into trouble. Then they became my responsibility.

"What excuses?" I couldn't remember the last time I'd raised my voice to such a pitch. It was as if a tight hat had come off. "What do you want me to do?"

"Marie, you have to tighten your belt."

The words fell so easily from his lips. I couldn't believe what I was hearing. My entire life, every waking minute was spent trying to spend less, eat less.

"How do you tighten an already tight belt? Huh, Beppe? How do you do that?"

"We all live with too much," he said.

"You mean you do. I've seen your house. But not me. I don't live with too much. I alter Mom's old clothes. I collect free dishes on Dish Night. I see matinees so I can save ten cents!" With a stern look and a lowered voice, I leaned forward and said, "You don't understand anything."

I got up so abruptly the ledger fell to the floor with a crash. I kicked it and it slid underneath the table. I left him, fled to my bedroom and slammed the door. I sat there and waited.

"Marie. Please open the door."

Silence. One minute, two. Then I opened it. And of all things, we were laughing. What spell was this? He took a step toward me, and I forgot the ledger with its lies. I slid my hand down the front of his shirt to his belt buckle. There would be no more talk. But as we fell onto the bed, I couldn't stop thinking about an image from the newspaper. The anti-Nazi protestors at the rally, a woman and a group of angry looking men held signs mounted on rolled-up newspapers. Their mouths were open and they were yelling. In the foreground a photographer had just let off a flare to light his shot. In an adjoining photo, a mounted police officer tried to hold back the crowd. It was the horse's face I couldn't get out of my head, its expression, not so different from that of the protestors, head twisted up, teeth bared, a fearful eye rolled back.

CHAPTER TWENTY-FIVE

People had started mentioning the war. You heard the word in stores and on the street. Beppe wanted to make sure I understood that Hitler was bad and that Mussolini was his dupe. My political education might have been slow, but I understood more than he thought. Just because the Italians in town carried on as if everything was normal, that didn't mean we weren't ashamed and fearful. If and when America entered the war, and there was no reason to believe we wouldn't, Italian men would be called up along with everybody else. Still, I felt accused when Beppe explained how, since World War I, Italy and Germany had been courting one another. Then the Spanish Civil War gave them the opportunity to fight on the same side as they helped Franco hold on to power. In World War I Italy had been on the victorious side with the allies, now we were on the wrong side, the evil side. I listened patiently to what Beppe had to say. I knew he was right, but I didn't want to think about it.

I had to walk over to Mrs. Bellafiore's to deliver a cake. Luckily, the weather was cold, because I worried about the icing. Mrs. Bellafiore's cousin, an older man, was having difficulty getting his wife pregnant. The cake was for his birthday. I needed a pinch of periwinkle, which could regulate a woman's cycle—I assumed the cousin's wife would be having at least a slice—but I couldn't get my hands on any, so I substituted vervain. Since it was a lemon cake no one would be the wiser. As insurance against failure I sprinkled in most of my remaining anise to help calm the stomach of the older man, to improve the flow of urine and energize the prostate. And I'd reserved a sprinkling to dust across the dish of lovely rounded river stones Sammy had given me—an offering to express my gratitude, because my period had arrived.

Just as I was about to leave, Mrs. Vitolo telephoned to say her son was improving. The doctors hadn't been optimistic, but now they were. I had only used ginger, and thought, imagine if I had been able to get my hands on galingal!

I placed Mrs. Bellafiore's cake into one of my new boxes. They were a soft shade of blue, but they were flimsy, so I'd had to add an extra piece of cardboard, which I cut from an old packing box, and

onto this imperfect circle I placed the cake. Then I cast my intention—
that Mrs. Bellafiore's cousin would have a good birthday, and soon,
perhaps, father a child.

The Bellafiore's house was seven blocks away through a network of
short streets that I didn't often walk. I had never been inside the small
bungalow, with its screened-in porch like so many along Peach street.

"Oh, Marie. Come in. Come in."

The house was dreary, full of overstuffed furniture, on top of which
were tossed and tucked lengths of mismatched fabric intending to hide
the exploding cushions. The house smelled of garlic and oil, and in the
kitchen a stewing broth sent up jets of steam. It was the fragrance of
home, reminding me of Mom's kitchen, but also of Ruth's. Even if her
Jewish food was different, there was a common ingredient, cabbage.

I set the cake down on the kitchen table. "This should go into
the icebox, Mrs. Bellafiore."

"Oh, yes," she said hurrying over.

"When is the party?" I asked.

"Oh, tomorrow. Just small. My cousin and his wife. She's young,"
she said.

How young, I wanted to ask. Louie Bellafiore was old, too old to
be trying to become a father, and suddenly I doubted the effectiveness
of herbs in a cake.

I explained I had to get back to the store, but Mrs. Bellafiore
pointed to a chair. The Bellafiores were as poor as everyone else, but
there was a pride in the careful setting out of her chipped tea pot on
a lovely hand-crocheted doily. Her tea towels were also handmade,
fashioned from old tablecloths and aprons.

"I could sell these," I said, lifting one.

"Those old things?" she laughed, a pleasant, joyous little bell of
a sound. "You are popular now," she said, her wrinkled face folding
up into a smile. "You have a secret," she said in a conspiratorial tone.

Was she referring to the herbs? I hoped so. Or could it be Ada?
Was my aunt spotted coming or going from my apartment? How else
could she have known that Mom's sister had found her way to town?
Or, did she mean Beppe? There were too many secrets. Except Mrs.
Bellafiore was not at all snide, unlike so many in Littlefield who felt

the need to add a little extra, a probing question, a dangerous rumor.

"I hear your brothers are in New York," she said.

I held a smile in place. "It isn't easy in the store without them."

"It might be easier in some ways," she said, turning back to the stove to stir her pot. "That Gino is bad," she said, coming straight to the point. Since the fight at the Sons, I had been surprised not to hear more gossip.

"He is a handful," I said.

"Yes, a handful," she said, still with her back to me, "but he's no child anymore." This scold from the older woman hit me as hard as Mom's would have. She turned around to look at me. "You should be careful, Marie. People have had enough of him. The politics. Not everyone mind you. The men at the Sons think he's the bee's knees." She shrugged, softening her tone, "I don't blame you. Most people know you can't handle him."

I left after a few pleasantries that I wouldn't remember. We hugged goodbye and I fled the old house. But what I would go over and over again was the moment we stood at the door and she pressed the dollar into my palm, how her hand lingered over the bill. I realized then that she couldn't afford the cake, and that it wasn't just concern over her cousin's ability to father children, but a belief in my powers that had driven her to an extravagant purchase, a hope so strong it overcame her disapproval.

CHAPTER TWENTY-SIX

When Sammy telephoned, I was so happy to hear from him I burst into tears.

"How are you? When are you coming home? Mr. E. said a month. It's been almost six weeks."

"Gino won't leave."

"Well, you should come home. Without him. What are you two doing most of the time?"

"Nothing. Working. We go to meetings and we listen to the radio."

"What meetings?"

Silence on the other end.

"Why call if you have nothing to say? Can I speak to Gino?" I was sharp.

"He's out with Mr. E. We went to a rally."

"What rally?"

"I don't know what it was called. There were Nazis. I swear, Marie. Real Nazis. You wouldn't believe it."

Beppe had had a suspicion.

"Why did you go to such a place?"

"I didn't have a choice."

"You do have a choice, Sammy. Is Mr. E. there?"

"I told you. He went out."

"Is something wrong?"

"I'm all right," he said, with slight hesitation. "I hurt my arm is all."

"How?"

"I'm all right. We were helping Mr. E. load a truck. Mostly we lift crates of oil when the shipments come in. He needed us to get some guys away from his warehouse."

"Is that how you hurt your arm?"

"I'm not a baby, Marie."

"Where was this rally?"

"Madison Square Garden. I can't believe it happened here. In this country. You wouldn't believe.... But don't mention I told you."

"Are you kidding?"

"Listen, Marie. I love you. Don't worry."

"I do worry. I want you to come home. Do you hear me?"

That night I had a nightmare that woke me. Men wearing soldiers' uniforms were breaking down the door of my store. Once inside, they pulled down displays and smashed everything. I woke up shaking with fright. But it wasn't all the dream—actual noises were coming from the loading bay.

I pulled on my robe and crept downstairs. In the small hallway leading to the office I pressed my ear against the door and listened. There were three men, and one of them was Kenny. I peered into the back and saw them loading sacks onto a truck. Kenny was looking on, his body tense as he motioned for them to hurry. After the sacks were loaded, Kenny helped them pile what looked like crates of sweet potatoes up against the load until it was completely covered. Then the two men jumped in and the truck pulled out.

The next day Mrs. Fiorello came in and said she'd seen Mr. E. in town. I thought, how can that be? He often traveled back and forth, but all I could think of was that he'd left my brothers in New York. She was looking not at me, but around the store, and I realized her only mission had been to deliver this news and gauge my reaction.

"Thank you," I said, steering her out.

"Call me if you need me, Marie," she said.

I put Kenny in charge of the store and went upstairs to telephone Mr. E.

"Salvie, what are you doing in town? And where are my brothers?"

"My God, Mari. I'm embarrassed. Madonna mia."

"Where are they?"

"In New York. I just here for an hour or two."

"Do you have time for coffee?"

"What do I bring?"

"Nothing," I said and hung up.

I happened to have a couple of slices of love cake in the icebox. It always tasted better the next day, when the icing had fully married the cake beneath and the cheese beneath that. The subtle colors had richened, the thick ricotta was more yellow, the cake more golden, and the icing glowed like a snowpack in bright sun. I made a strong pot of coffee and sat down to wait.

Mr. E. arrived with a bouquet of roses.

"Thank you," I said taking the flowers. Then I indicated with a swift motion of my arm that he was to go ahead of me up the stairs. Today he wouldn't have the pleasure of inspecting my bottom.

After we'd settled in the kitchen I said, "I want to know everything, and no use telling me a story."

"You worry too much, Mari. Things are good. I have this for you."

He handed me the envelope, and it seemed a little fatter. I had always looked the other way in exchange for his help, and the arrangement worked so long as I made this compromise, never to ask, never to complain. I let him flirt and served him cake.

"The German Bund. What is it?"

"Where did you hear that?"

"I read it in a newspaper."

"What newspaper? What could you read..."

"In *The New York Times*," I said.

I flashed on the men getting out of their cars in front of the Sons of Italy.

Mr. E.'s head was lowered to his cake. "No use lying," I said, "Sammy told me everything."

"Everything what?"

"About his arm. How he got hurt." I didn't believe for a minute that Sammy had hurt his arm unloading a truck. Mr. E. avoided my eyes.

"Gino had a ticket. Sammy and me, we stayed outside. It was a night, Mari, I tell you. It was history!"

"What kind of history?"

"You would have been proud of Sammy. He tried to stop Bund guys from going inside, right in the middle of everybody. They shouting. Waving signs, 'Bund, go home. Back to Germany!'" His eyes grew big like he was right back there with the threat, the excitement. "Sammy saw the swastikas and went crazy."

Swastikas! In Beppe's newspaper, swastikas were plain as day on the Bund supporters; there was even a giant one right inside Madison Square Garden. And either side of a huge picture of our first president were the flags of the German American Bund, in the center a swastika.

Mr. E. continued, his eyes flashing, "I didn't think he had the nerve, the guts. He was swinging at the Bund guys as they went in."

"Who are these Bund guys?"

"Friends of Germany."

"Germans?"

"No! Merigani, Mari. The speaker was from Germany. He loves America."

"Where was Gino?"

"I told you. I only had one ticket. Gino went in."

"Where did you get the ticket?"

"Mari…"

"You lied to me."

"No."

"I'm not stupid."

"Italians were outnumbered, Mari! All Merigani. Plenty of them. More than us. And they support Mussolini, and Germany." He was careful not to mention Hitler.

"You took them to that terrible rally. Are you a Nazi?"

"No! But Mussolini, he say some good things."

He moved his cup forward, my signal to give him a refill. I took his cup and put it in the sink.

"When are they coming home? What else aren't you telling me?"

"Nothing. I don't hide secrets."

With a sudden movement, he grabbed my hand and applied so much pressure I thought it would leave a mark. "Take your hands off me," I said, pulling away just as the pressure ceased. "What is it you're running through my loading bay?" I had never asked him before. "Kenny was downstairs with some men and they covered whatever it was with sweet potatoes."

"It not a bad thing, Mari. And I pay you. Believe me, nothing bad going on."

I was thinking about the new icebox and how I would pay for it. I hadn't heard anything from Beppe about the loan.

Mr. E. got up and I didn't see it coming. He pulled me hard by the arm to get me to stand, then wrapped his arms around me and pressed his lips on mine. I tried to shove him away, but he was stronger than he looked.

"I missed you, Mari." We stumbled across the room until he had me pinned against the wall, and he pressed into me until I could feel him through my dress and apron. He put his hands on my breasts and squeezed. "Stop!" I yelled. There was a sickly smile on his face, as though he was both ashamed and excited. But he had no intention of stopping. What if he forced me? I managed to break free, and just before I tripped and fell I saw the picture of Ceres over the sink. I struggled to my feet, only this time I grabbed a plate from the drain board and threw it at his head. He ducked and it smashed against the wall, but that was enough to break the spell of whatever craziness had seized him. I was shaking so badly I could hardly get my balance. I couldn't find my voice to tell him to leave, but he was already pulling on his coat, taking his time. He looked around the room like he was seeing my kitchen for the first time. That's right, I thought, memorize it good, because you might never see it again.

CHAPTER TWENTY-SEVEN

I poured a mound of flour directly onto the counter and with a swift motion of my hand created a well in the center. Into this small volcano I cracked four eggs and beat them right where they were. Mom had never used a bowl. One of her books explained how this method favored the setting of an intention. I would add my usual garlic, oregano and thyme, a pinch of anise and parsley. Regrettably, I had no time to rub parsley into my forehead like I'd seen her do. Soon I was kneading, and I ended up with three perfect mounds of dough that I put aside to rest for an hour. Next I started on the sauce, which took longer, and I began to hum, feeling happy about the coming meal, if not the evening itself. My brothers were coming home. The food at least would be perfect.

After hours of work, first the dough and the sauce, then the rolling out and the cutting of the rounds to be filled with cheese, my mood was lifted by the sight of the sweet, freshly made ravioli and the anticipation of the piping hot ricotta within and its squirt of sweet liquid. What man, with the prospect of such a meal, would dare cross me? I vowed not to bring up the subject of the rally.

Standing before me were two grown men. My brothers were now stronger, more defined, and Gino was enormous. His shoulders seemed to have doubled in size. There wasn't an ounce of fat on him, and when he hugged me the hardness of his chest was like the marble of a statue. Sammy hung back, which wasn't unusual, but his expression was sour, like he was not at all pleased to be home. This hurt me, because Sammy was the one I most wanted to see.

"The place looks just the same," Gino said, hurling himself into an arm chair.

"Sammy, look at you. How grown you are!" I stepped forward and hugged my youngest brother, but his face shut down as though someone had issued a warning.

"Where's Mr. E.?"

"He had to get home. Said to say hello to you," said Gino.

Thank God, I thought. Then, coward!

"I have a present for you," said Gino.

"Will you call Carla?" I asked.

"Carla is history."

"How about you?" I turned to Sammy, "Any girls in the picture?"

"I've been dating someone."

"And?" I tried to sound playful.

He gave a furtive smile. "Nothing to report."

Gino went over to his brother and slapped him hard on the back. "Go on. Tell her, Sam."

"Tell me what?"

"Get lost, Gino," Sammy said, thumping his brother on the arm.

"I'll tell her," said Gino, stepping forward full of ceremony as though he was about to make a toast. "Sammy here is engaged."

"Engaged? Wait," I said, "let me put a pot of coffee on. Sit down both of you and we'll talk. I want to hear all about it." I ran from the room because I needed a second to get over the shock. As I readied the pot, I fought to compose myself. When I came back into the room they'd snapped open their huge suitcases and were pulling out presents among mounds of crumpled, dirty laundry.

"So, who is this girl?" I asked.

"She's a woman," said Sammy, locating a plump package wrapped in a delicate blue paper, the likes of which I had never seen, not in all the supply catalogues I'd looked through. With a smile he handed it to me.

"I'll say," said Gino, "She's twenty-seven."

"Shut up," Sammy said, pressing his dirty clothes back inside and closing his suitcase.

I refused to show surprise. "Does she live in New York?"

"Yes."

Gino wasted little time. "He's going to move there."

"Will you shut your fat face?" said Sammy.

"That's enough," I said, and hearing the coffee pot spluttering in the next room, I set Sammy's present down and went to deal with it.

"What's her name?" I asked, returning.

"Here, open this first."

Gino thrust a nicely wrapped box into my hands. Sammy had left the room with his suitcase. "She's Mr. E.'s niece," Gino said. "Name is Gloria."

Mr. E.'s niece? A year ago this would have seemed like good news, the knitting together of our two families. Now I recognized Salvie's scheming, another bid to take over my life, our lives. I unwrapped Gino's gift.

"How do you like it?"

Gino had given me what could only be described as an ugly scarf. The colors were garish, purples, reds and greens in a busy pattern that wasn't at all my style.

"Thank you, Gino." I got up and put my arms around him. I fought tears.

"You should see the stores they have in New York," he said.

"I'll bet."

"They're on every block. I couldn't decide. Do you like it?"

"I love it."

"Try it on."

He took it and draped it about my shoulders.

"Look in the mirror," he said, and taking hold of me, steered me toward the mantel piece. There we were in the mirror, brother and sister. Seeing us framed together this way I had a flash of our growing up, all our fighting and disagreements. But I was thinking about Sammy getting married. Would it really happen? It was too quick, and he didn't seem at all excited, in fact he seemed depressed. That's when it struck me that this was the end of what felt like a very long first chapter of my life. My youth would go quickly now, and with the departure of my brothers, once and for all I would be alone.

"Where are *you* planning to go?" I asked Gino, as I turned from the mirror. I tried to make it sound like teasing.

"Why? Trying to get rid of me? I'll stay here for a while if that's okay."

He seemed gentle, sitting with his arms between his knees, his hands clasped, relaxed in the family living room.

A second later Sammy came back with a cup of coffee and sank into the sofa.

"You look nice," he said pointing to the scarf. "I liked the other one better, but this one looks good, too. Here, open my gift." He handed me his present.

I never remembered them buying me anything. Christmas and birthdays usually involved a kiss on the cheek. Once, they'd pooled their money to buy me tickets to the pictures. When they were younger, several years running, they'd wrapped up small, inexpensive toys I recognized from our kiddie bins in the store. They would present me with these cheap items and laugh uproariously like it was the funniest joke.

I opened Sammy's present. Nestled in a small square box was a book. The cover was softly padded in a fine leather the color of spring foliage, and in embossed letters was the word *Recipes*. Inside, the lined pages were divided into sections. At the top were the shorter lines for the ingredients, and below those, running the full width of the page, were lines for the written steps. Mom had never owned such a beautiful book, and I could hardly breathe for the sadness I felt.

"I love it," I said. "I love both my presents," I added quickly, so Gino wouldn't feel slighted. Then I hugged Sammy, and whispered in his ear, "I love my present," and I felt his man's body. It hit me that soon he would be gone, and I didn't know how I would bear it.

"Are you hungry?" I asked, stepping back from our embrace.

"Starving," Sammy said, in a visibly better mood.

"Me, too," Gino said, "I'll wash up."

"Dinner will be ready in twenty minutes," I said.

The big pot of water was almost boiling as I lifted my delicate ravioli from a tray on top of the icebox. I began heating up the marinara sauce that had taken me the better part of the afternoon. I checked on the tray of baked eggplant in the oven.

I decided to use my new plates; I almost had service for five. I set the small dining table in the living room and lit candles. I even had a nice bottle of Chianti from Ferrara's that I'd spent far too much on.

"It's ready," I called. Sammy came in and helped me bring the steaming food to the table, and I poured the Chianti into Mom's cut crystal goblets. Sammy was the first to sit down, but Gino seemed to hang back, as if at any minute he might excuse himself.

"Sit down," I said. "Aren't you hungry?"

He sat.

"A toast," said Sammy, raising his glass, "To Marie. Our pain in the ass older sister who we love more than anything." He was laughing. He looked so grown up, more handsome than I remembered.

"How come you took off the scarf?" asked Gino.

"I didn't want to spoil it while I was cooking."

"You could put in on now."

"I could," I said, getting up.

"This is delicious," said Sammy. "I haven't had ravioli this good since the last time you made them."

I returned to the table wearing the ugly scarf, but Gino's expression wasn't mollified. He stared at the food.

"Aren't you hungry?"

"I don't eat pasta."

"Since when?" I was on the verge of laughing.

"It makes me lazy. Mr. E. says it's not good."

I was shocked. "Sammy, you too?"

"No. I eat everything. More for me," he said, elbowing Gino, who sent a quick fist flying toward Sammy's middle section. But at the last second Sammy crumpled and avoided the blow.

"Stop it," I ordered.

Gino said, "Italians eat too much pasta. In the future we're not going to eat it. We'll eat American food and get strong."

Where had he picked up such an idea, so foreign and ridiculous? It must have struck Sammy as absurd, too, because he seemed amused but was careful not to let Gino see. I braced myself for their bickering. I felt the freedom of the previous weeks evaporate.

"I don't know what else I can feed you," I said. "You can have the eggplant."

The one without the spell, I thought. In the dough was a special concoction of spices into which I'd impressed a wish—that Gino would go away, fall off a cliff, disappear.

"It's not your job to feed me," he said, helping himself to the eggplant.

I don't need you, says the child; what every child will eventually tell its parent. Well good, I thought. Why then had I felt so tied to him, to them both? Burdened by their hunger, their laundry, their need to kick me when it suited. Color rose from my neck up into my face. The scarf was too hot, and with a sweeping gesture I removed it.

"I believe in *Americanism* now," said Gino. It was a sharp declaration, as though he delighted in some new authority. I recalled the word *Americanism* from the article about the rally in Beppe's *New York Times*.

Sammy put his fork down, lifted his wine glass and paused; he seemed to be waiting for what his brother would say next.

"I eat polenta," declared Gino.

"Polenta. Where do you eat that?"

"In New York."

Polenta? I couldn't imagine. Neapolitans hated it. The Genoveses were from the north, but Mom had always cooked southern food.

"It's *northern* food," declared Gino. "Our father's."

Our father. The missing male and still the patriarch. I almost said, *A missing father is nothing but air. There are too many of them. He is an idea, an empty space, as useless as a spell without an intention, molecules without a spirit.*

"It's what I eat now," said Gino. "*We* are from the north."

"Does this have something to do with those lies in *Social Justice*?"

Gino sent up a loud guttural sound I never remembered hearing before. "The people have to be led. We have to make the others understand. We're strong…"

"Oh, shut up," I said.

Then, he did what he so often did, jumped up, and his chair almost toppled over before he caught it.

"Sit down. Who are these *others*?" I matched his look of defiance.

Sammy took a sip of wine without taking his eyes off his brother.

"Jews. Mainly," Gino said, still standing.

"Where are you getting this, this poison? Who is teaching you? I won't have this talk in my house. And you won't be going anywhere with Mr. E. anymore."

Gino surprised me by sitting down, but in that second he changed. His breathing became loud and steady, a deep animal breath. He poured another glass of wine and leaned back in his chair. "Salvie says I have to stay in training. Stay strong. So I can fight if I have to."

"You mean like the fight at Madison Square Garden?" I asked, relishing the shock it produced. "Is that what you mean?"

"My arm's good," Sammy said suddenly. "Healed up nice." He shot a look at Gino.

"You didn't answer me," I said.

"Yeah," said Gino. "We pummeled each other," he laughed. "How did you find out?"

The brothers exchanged a look.

"Mr. E.," I said, looking directly at Sammy.

"If you already knew, then why ask?" said Gino. "You should have seen it. Everybody was holding up signs. *Stop Jewish Domination. Jews Against Christians have to be stopped.* People were going nuts. Mounted police everywhere, the whole deal. The communists were out in force, but they were outnumbered. Then some asshole on a bullhorn was yelling out an apartment window. *Be American. Stay at home.* He yelled it over and over. How 'bout it Sammy?"

Sammy didn't answer. It was then I saw the gap between them, which had grown to be a mile wide.

"And listen to this. When the police went up to the apartment to check on that asshole, there was only a recording on a timer. That's it. No one there. It was nuts. And we were chanting back, *"Wake Up America! Smash Jewish communism!"*

"How could you!"

"Hey, we're back, and everybody's fine. Right, Sammy?" He jabbed his brother in the ribs, but this time Sammy batted his arm away with force, and Gino's big shoulder twisted back. It looked as though he might take another swing, but Sammy was prepared to stand his ground.

"I want you to go and apologize to Ruth and Gersh," I said to Gino.

"You're dreaming."

"I'm serious, Gino. You had no right to pass out that filth at the Sons of Italy. They're our neighbors. Our friends."

"So they own a store, big deal. Doesn't mean we're friends."

"Ruth saved my life. After Mom died..." I couldn't continue. I felt like crying, but I wouldn't give him the satisfaction.

"*Americanism.* That's what I believe in now."

"All these –isms. Everybody's got an –ism." It was the only thing I could think to say, a quote from Jean Arthur's father in *You Can't Take It With You.* Sammy laughed. I laughed too. The two of us together again, ganging up on Gino.

Gino got up and scraped his chair along the floor before heaving it against the table. He took a last look at each of us before stomping out.

Sammy and I sat in frightened silence until we heard the downstairs door close. I refilled our glasses. We finished our meal.

"Tell me about Gloria."

"I'm too tired," he said. "I'll tell you tomorrow, if that's okay."

"It's fine. I love my book."

He seemed happy.

Sammy had seconds of my ravioli and wiped his plate clean with a piece of bread. Then we went our separate ways.

CHAPTER TWENTY-EIGHT

Sammy had become more quiet. At first he seemed hesitant to talk about Gloria. I had to ask him several questions before he volunteered anything.

"She's sensible. You'll like her."

"When am I going to meet her?"

"Soon."

Gloria had moved from New York to Camden to live with her aunt, and Sammy had been traveling up to Camden on the weekends. He'd been home for almost three weeks and yet he hadn't brought her down to meet me. I pictured a plain girl with sparkling eyes and a direct manner. She'd brought out a different side to him, like he was thinking about things more deeply. Maybe what passed for shyness all these years was really a hidden maturity.

Aside from his frequent disappearances, it was terrible having Gino back. Without warning a fight would erupt on the loading bay, and if I happened to be in the store, hearing the commotion, I'd rush into the office. If I was upstairs, I'd hurry to the kitchen window and peer down. I didn't get involved, unless it was Gino and Kenny ganging up on Sammy, which happened more and more. To add to that tension, trucks were arriving at least twice a week and always at night. I would wake, smell cigarette smoke, and then hear the soft opening and closing of doors in the apartment as my brothers went to help. Recently, I overheard men in Ferrara's talking about illegal stills up the line in Toms River. Sugar was being run from right here in town. I listened to this gossip in plain sight of those telling it, so I could only assume they didn't yet suspect the source was the Five & Ten. Nor did I completely believe it myself until Kenny walked in just as I was opening a sack that had been left behind in the office.

"What are you doing?" he asked.

"I know about Salvie's business."

"Yeah, he's got the olive oil in New York."

"No. Business *here*. I know you're running sugar up to Toms River." I pointed to the sack.

Kenny plugged his thumbs into his belt stays and stood with his legs wide apart. "There's nothing going on here, Marie."

Back talk made me furious. Why did men push so hard even when they knew they were wrong? He needed this job to keep his wife happy and in line. Like so many men in town, Kenny had married a woman just like his mother, and the pretty, young Loretta would eventually become just as grouchy and avaricious as old lady Monastra.

"I'll talk to the others. This is going to stop," I said.

"What's the problem?" said Gino, appearing behind me suddenly. He sat down on a broken swivel chair that cast his huge body to the left, and it would have been funny, except we stared like boxers from our opposite corners.

"You think you're running things, Marie. But you're not. Salvie, Kenny and me are the ones." He'd left out Sammy. "The only money coming in the door, we're bringing. Without us, there is no store."

"I'm doing just fine without you."

"Yeah, with the money Salvie brings."

"Mom left me in charge…"

"Yeah, I know, you're in charge. And Ma said you have to take care of us," he said in a sing-song voice as though he was repeating a phrase he'd heard throughout childhood. "Now it's the other way around. We take care of you, if you're nice. You walk around like you own the place. Don't worry. If we find a buyer, we'll split it three ways. We won't cut you out. Or maybe we will." He laughed.

"The store isn't for sale. We all have to agree. All of us, and we're not selling." I put my hand on the file cabinet to steady myself.

"Without us there is no store," he said again.

"You? You're too busy chasing girls. And where were you before Salvie's deals? You weren't interested then."

"Yeah? We ain't making it on lipsticks here."

"I work myself to death. I make sure it looks good. Who besides me comes up with ideas to improve what we…"

"And what about Mr. Across the Street?"

"What are you talking about?"

"You're never here. You think everybody doesn't know?" he got up, pointed a finger in my face. "People know. Sammy, Salvie, Kenny, everybody. We have eyes." He swung his arm out to indicate the front of the store, the street beyond, and the bank. Kenny looked on, his eyes wide.

"Get out," I yelled. "The two of you. Get out!"

"Christ." Gino threw his arms up in disgust.

After they'd gone I looked around at the dingy office. It was like the light during an eclipse. First the sky turns a sickly green, then there's a glistening around the edges, as all around you everyday objects come into sudden, high relief.

CHAPTER TWENTY-NINE

Gino began leaving early in the morning at least an hour before I got up, which suited me. But it was harder to avoid one another in the store. He was angry most of the time, and I was out of patience. He complained about the stock I ordered, and criticized the placement of displays. I didn't hide my disgust at his opinions, but nor did I talk back. He could frighten me with a look. Soon, we were in a kind of stand-off, agreeing silently that if I didn't bother him, he wouldn't bother me. It wasn't exactly a truce, but the realization that we were too different, that our interests would never line up. He would sell the store in a minute, and I would never sell. We knew where we stood.

Beppe and I were meeting at least twice a week in the early afternoon. And in the time it took me to bathe, iron my dress and fix my hair, I became calmer. I looked in the mirror, passed my hands across my belly and along my hips. I stared at my reflection and my image appeared to float, to gather itself like a spirit leaving one home in search of another.

It was early June, and the air was full of that first hint of summer humidity. I was getting ready to meet Beppe. I closed my eyes and whispered, *Leave her and marry me.* It was the first time I'd admitted to myself what I dared not think might be possible; that my proper banker might actually change his life for me. And just as I thought this, the phone rang. It was Ada.

We hadn't spoken for weeks. She was laughing, as though there was someone in the room with her who shouldn't have been there, and they delighted in a private conversation. I had never heard her laugh before, a light peal of joy. Was the person in the room with her a man?

"Will you go?" she asked, in the same light tone.

Go where? Was she talking to me, or to the man? I didn't know how to answer.

She said, "Marie, you take trip?"

"Me? No. I have to work. The store. When are you coming?" I asked.

"I sorry. A thing happen. But I come soon. I call you, yes?"

"I thought you were coming to visit."

"I know. Sorry. I am."

She hung up. I was stunned, but I had no time to be annoyed, to question or puzzle over her words. I didn't want to be late for my meeting with Beppe.

I relished the feel of my long hair on the pillow. I watched him get out of bed, captivated by his naked body. He moved confidently, without a shred of modesty. I got up and made tea just as I would if he were my husband.

Once we'd settled back with our cups, he surprised me. "I could live differently," he said, looking around the simple bedroom of our tryst apartment. *Mr. Ashworth living with Marie Genovese?* The thought of it made my heart pound.

"I could, too."

"My sweet Marie," he said, gathering me in.

"We could make a plan," I said, in the same vague tone.

On his face was a smile, but there was a change in his eyes. "You know we can't. At least not yet."

"So we're playing house?" I asked playfully, even if behind my casual tone was resentment at him for introducing the subject then putting on hold any further discussion.

"God, no."

"What did you mean by living differently?" I tried to control the emotion in my voice, but I was losing patience with his casualness. He couldn't just throw out a statement like that, then refuse to discuss it.

He drew me closer. "Marie, we can't talk about this now."

"But you brought it up."

Everything came down to what he could and couldn't do. He dictated when we met and he felt free to cancel any appointment with the excuse of a sudden business trip. Were those trips real? It took every ounce of strength not to pull away. A young, single woman falls for a married man, then expects that man to act on his love. My situation was common. But when had I crossed the line into expectation? If I persisted, we would fight, and our arguments left me drained. I rested my head on his shoulder so he couldn't see my face. He began making love to me again, and though I wanted him physically, hatred welled in my heart. I didn't want to feel dislike for this man, but I struggled against the urge to scream, to heave him off me, hurl insults. And what of the conversation of a minute ago? Why dangle the possibility of our being together? It would have been easy to wound him. Instead, to his tenderness I became more aggressive and more demanding of my own pleasure, which seemed to please him. It pleased me even more.

We dressed in silence. It would be several more days before we saw each other again. Then, just as we were leaving, he said, "Can you take off on Friday and come back on Monday?"

I shrugged. I wasn't in the mood for games.

"I want to take you to the New York World's Fair. Marie, you have to be more excited than this. I've made all the arrangements."

I recalled Ada's words. *Marie, you take trip?*

"Can you? Can you go away with me?" He held my gaze. *We're okay, aren't we?*

What a luxury, I thought, not to worry how people see you. Mr. Ashworth came and went as he pleased. How dare I hold on to a sour mood.

"Yes. I think so."

"You *think*? That's all?"

He kissed me, straightened his tie, and winked. He was trying to play up the comedy of the situation. Might he trip or attempt a backward summersault like Buster Keaton?

"Until New York," he said.

I couldn't be mad. I was actually starting to get excited. I watched him leave. I always stayed for a few minutes to freshen the water in the flowers and do things around the kitchen. I liked to touch our three small bowls, the under plates, the flatware. I made sure the cups hanging on their little hooks all faced the same way.

CHAPTER THIRTY

It was the first anniversary of Mom's death.

"These are for you," I said handing Kenny a plate of my vanilla chiffon cupcakes. I wondered if Kenny remembered. But that wasn't the reason for the cupcakes. I wanted to soften him up before I broke the news that I'd be away for the weekend. I started to explain about the sick cousin I was going to visit, the daughter of a man we called Uncle Gerard, who wasn't really a relative, but who'd been a friend of our father's. I was in the middle of describing his daughter's pneumonia, when Gino walked in.

"How sick?" he asked, winking at Kenny.

Ignoring Gino, Kenny turned to me, "How long you gone for, Marie?"

"I'll be back on Monday."

"Don't worry about us. We'll man the store," he said, throwing a look at Gino, who made a loud sniffing noise before leaving the room.

I was hoping Sammy would stay in town to help look after the store. He'd been spending more and more time with Gloria in Camden, so I offered them the apartment. This was a scandal since they weren't married and Sammy acted shocked, but he accepted right away.

"Don't worry," he said, "We'll hold down the fort."

I could have told him the truth, but instead I repeated the lie about Gerard's daughter having pneumonia. We were sitting in the kitchen sipping our coffee, talking about who would do what in the store, when he said, "Hey, sis. No big deal."

Sammy said he would deliver the cake orders that were due on the morning I was to leave. He would also sweep the front sidewalk, and he volunteered to run errands. I had two cakes. One was for Mrs. Fiedler, whose brother was coming home from the hospital. The other was for Angie's birthday, and I planned something special for that.

With Sammy watching, I couldn't speak to the herbs as I usually did before adding them, though I did have my eyes closed, visualizing a full moon, mentally drawing it down until it hovered just above my head. I soaked the herbs in a little warm water and set them to mellow in a cup on top of the icebox, which I didn't think he noticed.

In five minutes they would be sufficiently diluted to mask the flavor of rue, the "herb of grace." Catholic priests used springs of rue to scatter drops of holy water onto the faithful. I preferred to harness its power by summoning Fauna, goddess of the forest. Why I believed Angie needed protection, and grace, had to do with Bobby Cavuto, her soon-to-be husband.

Was Mom in the room? Or was it a shape-shifting Fata, a fairy that had come to help not just me, but Mrs. Fiedler, Angie, or perhaps Kenny, who struggled with life as much as the rest of us. Or Sammy, who, despite being in love, seemed confused and lost when it came to the future. We'd fallen silent. Normally we would be carrying on about store matters. I wondered, did he feel Mom in the room? I wanted to mention that this was the anniversary of her death, but I was afraid to introduce a sad subject. Except, in his face I saw it. He knew. He had remembered.

It was a Thursday and the store was busy. In the late afternoon I was waiting on a woman who I thought was my last customer, when in walked Mrs. Cavuto, who demanded I find her a packet of paper doilies. Mrs. Cavuto taught summer school and she used them to decorate her classroom. I said I'd check in the back.

"They used to be out on the counter," she snapped. My mind was so full of the trip, it was easy to ignore her rudeness, and I was relieved when Sammy came from the back room and offered to help.

I caught my breath and took a last look around. How pretty the store looked with the afternoon sun on my displays. The stock was sparse, but I'd put love into the arranging. A collection of cloth flowers, some made into corsages, were on a large, mirrored tray, where their reflections made them appear more attractive. Next to them were boxes of good-quality model cars and a generous stack of oilcloth placemats. I'd had Kenny reorganize the peg board holding the notions, and just this week added packs of nails and screws brought to me by Mr. E., who was on a campaign to patch things up between us.

I performed a last inventory before going upstairs, my thoughts now taken up with outfits and shoes. Beppe had said we would do a lot of walking. We would also be riding the trains. We would stop for lunch on the way up and arrive at our hotel around four p.m., in time for afternoon tea. Would I need a change of clothes, or could I remain in my traveling suit? So many decisions. Sammy interrupted my daydreams.

"Can I take you somewhere? I mean, carry your bag?"

"That's sweet of you, but I'm just going across the street to the bus." Another lie. What I had to do was make it up Bellevue Avenue without running into anyone I knew, then slip unnoticed down the apartment driveway and into Beppe's car. I'd checked the bus schedule, so I could refer to a departure time. "You'll be busy in the store at ten," I said, "I'll just go across to the stop."

He followed me into the bedroom. "Look, I can carry your bag wherever you want. Is that all you're taking?"

I'd spent hours whittling my outfits down to an efficient bundle, yet I still didn't feel I had quite the right things. He stood in the doorway while I packed, his long arm propped against the jamb.

"That's it," I said, looking one last time at my selections. Everything was folded carefully into my old suitcase with the worn corners and faded stripes. The case was beat-up looking, but it was all I had.

"Do you want to borrow a bag?" he asked.

"Oh. Do you have one?"

"Mr. E. bought me one in New York."

I followed him into his room and watched as he reached up to the top shelf and took down a small overnight case. "I was going to give it to Gloria for a present, but here," he said.

"Are you sure? You can still give it to her. I'll take good care of it."

"No, you have it."

So, Mr. E. bought the boys presents. I wondered what he'd given Gino.

Excitedly, I transferred my clothes to the new bag, which was small and perfect to hold all I needed for the weekend. "Are you sure?" I asked, though my things were already inside, smoothed and ready.

"I'm sure," he said, smiling.

The next morning, the last thing I had to do was write a check to Feldman. I left Sammy downstairs in the hallway and rushed into the office. Normally, Kenny paid our bills, but I'd neglected to put Feldman's invoice into the stack with the others, because I wanted to do it personally. I often wrote him a note of thanks. I was constantly in danger of losing my suppliers due to late payments, but Feldman would always wait. I knew I had the money to cover it, because I'd deposited it myself. Using my key, I took the checkbook from the top drawer and opened to a fresh check. I had just noted the balance the day before, but now I saw the last check had been written out to cash in the amount of one hundred dollars. The amount itself was shocking—practically the sum I owed Feldman for all the Christmas stock. And why was it written to cash? There was no explanation. The window washer charged ten dollars, but Mr. E. paid him directly. I couldn't for the life of me figure out what else could have cost so much. On Tuesday I could go into the bank and ask to see the cancelled check. But I was leaving. I had no choice but to forget about it.

Sammy took my case and went ahead of me.

"What is it, Marie?"

"Oh, nothing," I said, as I locked the door behind us. I considered telling him, but the damage was done.

We paused on the sun-drenched sidewalk. "Which way, Marie?"

"Down Bellevue toward the Pike," I said, with an anxious thrill at revealing my true destination. But the look on Sammy's face told me he'd already guessed.

"Have as much fun as you can," he said. What an odd way to put it, I thought.

With the sun blasting so fiercely I ran down my list of outfits, and was glad I'd packed my lightest things. As we walked, I planned where I would ask Sammy to leave me in order to go the rest of the way on my own. I was worried Beppe would see me with my brother and realize he was in on our secret. We were three houses short of the large white house with the veranda, when I stopped. "Sammy, thank you," I said and put my hand on his arm.

"Marie, what's the matter?" He stared so hard I felt the tears coming. I wanted to give myself up to the trip, to the three whole glorious days ahead. "Tell me," he said.

"I think someone is stealing. Maybe Kenny. Or Gino."

I told him about the check. It frustrated me that I couldn't deal with the matter right away. I was also trying to hide on the main street, in full view of passing cars, with my lover about to arrive. It was infuriating that so much of my life had to be lived in secret. Sammy held on to my arm, but before either of us could speak, we heard the sound of a large motor as Beppe's Packard came into view. Sammy leaned down to kiss me. "You have fun, Marie. And don't worry about anything." He laughed, and it was rare for me to hear his young man's laugh, naughty, knowing.

Beppe had recognized Sammy, but all he said was, "So, he knows. I don't like it, but I figure you know what you're doing."

"Sammy can be trusted."

"Let's hope so."

I felt a tinge of annoyance. I understood the need to be careful, but his tone was irritating.

Beppe looked over at my clothes. I wore a plain black skirt and gored matching jacket that fit me well. Rather than an altered garment, the suit had been purchased new for the occasion of Mom's funeral, when I'd been a little thinner. My figure had since filled out, and with my woman's body, it fit me better than ever.

"Marie, you look great," he said.

"Thank you. So do you." And he did. He wore a suit I had never seen before. It was blue, not a dark navy, but a blue with more life in it, and I wondered if perhaps he had an entirely different wardrobe for trips to the city. I wondered so many things about this man sitting next to me.

CHAPTER THIRTY-ONE

As we drove north on Route 206, the relentless routine of the store fell away with the scenery speeding past and the feel of the smooth macadam beneath the floating suspension of Beppe's car. I straightened the lapels of my suit and settled back against the soft leather. It would be a while before we needed a snack, but I felt for the small package in my purse. With leftover batter I'd made two small cupcakes.

We stopped for lunch at a diner. It was thrilling not to recognize anyone, nor to have anyone recognize me, or *us*. The drive was long, but we alternated talking and listening to the radio. I was relaxing, and so was he. But at the Midtown Hudson Tunnel I became frightened. I had heard of it, a brand new tunnel hidden beneath the mud of the Hudson River, one and a half miles long and lined with gleaming white tile. Mr. E. had relatives who'd worked on it. So far only the center tube was open, but there would be three in all, and it would take years to finish.

"Wait until you see, Marie." Beppe seemed even more excited than I, and not at all scared, because he'd driven it twice before.

"It's not a very nice name, but the men who are building it are called *sandhogs*," he said and laughed. "You can only imagine the work. They have to set up air locks because of the pressure on their ears."

Mr. E.'s relatives must be sandhogs, I thought.

I had been scared as we entered the tunnel, but I got used to the darkness. I wondered how far underneath the mud we were. But the whole thing was over in less than a minute, and as we broke out into the brilliant sunshine I chalked up my fear to the naiveté of a country girl. It was the first exciting experience of the trip, and I couldn't stop smiling.

"Guess where we're staying?" he said.

I imagined a hotel room like the ones in the movies, with nice curtains and comfortable chairs. There would be two beds with satiny looking covers and fluffy pillows, and a nice view from the window. I turned to look at him in profile, aware that I was sitting in the spot where his wife sat, aware that we were traveling as a couple.

"Where?"

"The Waldorf-Astoria. I never stayed there and I want to."

I was glad he hadn't, because now we could experience it together. As we sped along busy Manhattan streets, I tried not to stare at the tallest buildings, because only people unused to cities did that. I took to the crowds and noise. The city felt young and right away Beppe seemed different. He stopped the car in front of the hotel and moved very quickly across to the awning where he spoke to a man dressed in a special uniform. The man called for someone to take our bags. Beppe was a step or two ahead of me as we entered the lobby, but he kept looking back with a satisfied grin. This was a different man from the one I watched leave his car in front of The Peoples Bank. That man seemed much older, each step measured, and I thought to myself New York must be the kind of place where a person could become the more idealized version of himself, even pretending to be someone different.

Before we checked in, he said he wanted to show me something, and I followed him into The Sert Room, a huge hall filled with tables and soft-looking velvet chairs. Beppe pointed out the murals painted by a man named José María Sert.

"This is where we'll have dinner tonight."

"What do they mean?" I asked, pointing at the huge panels. I experienced not a drop of fear as I admitted I didn't know the painter nor the meaning of the dramatic images.

"They're scenes from the novel *Don Quixote*," he said. He turned to me, took my chin into his fingers, "I didn't read it. I started it, but I didn't get very far." Then he laughed; we both did.

The Waldorf was such a grand place that even Beppe seemed impressed. The lobby hummed with activity, but sounds were dampened by a thick carpet, a quiet accentuated by the warm lighting. Several couples and small groups milled around.

The women wore clothes that stunned me, and right away I felt out of place. I didn't own a summer suit, which was what they mostly wore. My clothes were fashionable, I knew that, and I actually did see a couple of women staring. Still, my confidence wavered. What did they see? A girl dressed in what she *thought* New Yorkers wore, or a country bumpkin in her Sunday best? If this was the case, Beppe didn't seem to notice, and when he took my arm and we walked up to the check-in desk, he wore a proud expression as smoothly he said, "Mr. and Mrs. Wolcott."

I caught my breath and waited.

"Yes, sir, Mr. Wolcott."

A reservation was ready for us. I held Beppe's arm so tightly I thought he might notice and gently wrestle it away, but he wasn't as tense as I was. He was happy. I took my first full breath of the day.

Our room was a double, with a bath and a separate make-up and dressing area they called a boudoir. In the bedroom itself there was an ornate mirror over a fireplace and two slightly worn but comfortable-looking easy chairs. I pictured us in those chairs, Beppe reading the newspaper and me gazing out at the beautiful buildings. I was surprised at how easy it was to feel like a couple.

Not knowing what to do next, I stepped out of my shoes and went to stand by the window. A splash of afternoon sun had turned everything a bright gold. Beppe removed his shoes and stretched out full length on the bed. He looked over and patted the soft-looking coverlet.

"Marie."

I went to lie next to him and thought, what if my clothes become wrinkled, but my next thought was how we must look in such a room. We were like actors in an advertisement for the hotel rather than its guests. We looked good together, good enough to appear in a photograph.

He turned to me. "What should we do tomorrow?" But before I could answer, he said, "We should go to the fair."

"How will we get there?"

"I'm going to drive us."

I nodded happily. We would have days. We wouldn't have to go back to our separate houses for three whole nights. "Maybe we can have some clams?" I asked.

"Sure, we'll do that. You have a clamming rake in the store. Where did you get that?"

It was true. The boys had hung the rake on the rear wall over the doorway to the storeroom. "It was my father's."

He nodded solemnly, and I was thinking, here we were in New

York, where I suddenly felt free enough to talk about a part of my past. Often, a romantic scene in a movie would feature a beautiful woman wearing a dress that cost more than the Five & Ten earned in a year. Then time would abruptly shift, showing the heroine's humble beginnings, her insecurities, her fears. I figured it might be the right time to give Beppe my gift. I got up and went to retrieve my purse on the desk. I reached in and brought out a small vial, a tincture I'd prepared. "I made this for you."

"What is it?" he asked, amused.

"It gives you more energy. But it also helps you to sleep. I take it all the time."

"Really? What is it made from?"

"Rue. And anise."

"I like aniseed," he said, taking the bottle from me.

"Now don't forget to take it. I mean, don't throw it away."

He laughed, which told me I'd successfully read his mind. "I promise."

"I have something else." I took out the cupcakes.

"They've been in your purse this whole time? You were holding out on me!" He unpeeled the wrapper and took a bite. "Oh, this is good. This is very good."

We ate and laughed some more.

That night, after an incredibly delicious but simple dinner in The Sert room, we made love and went straight to sleep.

The next morning we decided to take the subway to the fair. "I want to show it to you," he said. "It will be faster, and we can people watch. I know how you love that."

I didn't care how we got there. I was just happy to have him make the decisions. New York offered so many spectacles, people in a hurry, some dawdling, reading newspapers, and their clothes made me to want to guess what each person did for a living. The women wore so many different hair styles and facial expressions. Everything about them seemed thoroughly modern.

I wore my outfit, the one I'd planned, the sailor skirt and the expensive blouse onto which I'd pinned a corsage of silk flowers, and a small straw hat with a veil. I felt fashionable, that is, until we walked outside. I noticed several well-to-do women who were far less dressed up than I, though their more casual daywear also seemed to be made of costly fabric, what Mom would have called *understated*. My hand flew to my collar, where I'd pinned the corsage, momentarily shielding it from view. The gesture must have alerted Beppe, because he took my hand, the one hugging my throat, and placing it warmly between his hands looked plainly into my eyes, "Marie, you've never looked more lovely."

I fought tears of happiness and embarrassment. So many desires were stirred by the sight of these people in this big city that when Beppe kissed me, a chaste kiss in a public place, it burned with special intent.

"We'll get on at 59th Street," he said. "We'll take the subway to Penn Station." A second later we were holding hands and rushing down the street. I had never been on a subway. But as we reached the entrance, we found it locked behind an iron gate. Beppe looked around, confused, before his arm flew up, and an instant later he had hailed us a taxi.

"We're going to the fair," he said, "Can you take the Triborough Bridge?"

"That's the way," said the driver.

We leaned back, and for a while we didn't feel the need to talk.

"You wouldn't believe what I read in *The New Yorker*," he said, breaking the silence. "You'll like this story. There's this hardware store here in town somewhere and a Japanese man walked in. He said he was from the local consulate. Then he started looking at a pair of calipers and he asked how many they had in stock. The owner said he had around a dozen. The Japanese man asked him if he could get more, a lot more, in fact he needed a steady supply. He put $1,000 in cash down on the counter. 'This is for the calipers that I want sent to Honolulu,' he said, and he gave the man the address. The owner went in back and looked up the address and saw it was near the Pearl Harbor Navy Base."

"Does this have something to do with the war?" I asked.

"Calipers are for measuring. So I guess the store owner might have been thinking the Japanese were using them to measure the instruments we have at the Navy base. In other words, spying. That's what I think, too."

"My goodness," I said, not wanting to believe that we were getting any closer to war. "Let's not talk about it."

"What would you like to talk about instead, my sweet Marie?"

He put his lips on my neck, and I pushed him away because our driver was watching. Also, I didn't like his tone. I felt dumb for not knowing that the Japanese might be spying on us. A second later though, we were laughing, then cuddling, and as obnoxious as we could be while the driver looked on.

Constitution Mall was breezy and my hat almost flew off. Flags were everywhere up and down the long smooth avenue and they fluttered like giant handkerchiefs in the wind. We strolled, passing huge statues of sleek figures that Beppe explained were in the Art Deco style. He said their fluid lines described the future, a time of movement and change. From his jacket pocket he took out a paper listing "Attractions of Note," and we stood close together as we read what was on offer. He wanted to see the General Motors Futurama exhibit about what our highways would eventually look like. He also liked the idea of the Railroads Exhibition, with Kurt Weill music and plenty of girls and Indians. I had a much longer list starting with DuPont; I was curious about how they were turning wood into fabric for clothes. I also wanted to see the Gardens on Parade with a showing of orchids and begonias. He wanted to see Foreign Buildings, whereas I wanted to see the United States Federal and State Buildings, which I was pleased to notice had been rated higher in interest value.

"We won't have time for all of it," he said.

"Let's just walk then."

We took our time wandering up the Mall and ended up in line to see the Futurama movie. I didn't care whether it was good or not because I was with him. Before the lights went down I could study the women in their small pancake-shaped hats that didn't ruin the view, whereas my own hat was larger and, I worried, less modern.

The film had a tediously serious narrator, whose male voice made every word seem like an inevitable truth: *Opportunity for employment of men, new highways of social and commercial development through the imagination and vision of men. Men of science broadening our mental activities. Men exploring and pioneering into new fields. Men endlessly...*

I wondered, did the future belong only to men?

We stepped out into sunlight and reached for our sunglasses. With so much talk of the future, I got to thinking about ours and what would happen after these three days and nights were over. I felt a gulf open up between us, like one of those gorges in the film waiting for its connecting bridge, or next desolate stretch of road.

"Shall we grab something to eat?" he asked.

"Yes, let's."

"Say, after lunch I think we should go see *The Hot Mikado*." According to Beppe's paper, Bill "Bojangles" Robinson was "packing them in" at the Hall of Music and this immediately grabbed my interest.

When we passed a postcard kiosk I said I wanted to write a card to Angie, and selected one in lovely pastels featuring the Trylon and Perisphere. Beppe explained how the huge, glowing white structures were meant to be symbols of hope. Though up close their surfaces were lumpy and when I mentioned this, he told me that originally they'd wanted to make them out of concrete, but because of the cost they were forced to use stucco over gypsum board.

I pictured Angie's surprise when she received my card and saw where I was. She would ask a thousand questions, but I would stick to my story about visiting my sick cousin, before explaining that I'd decided at the last minute to sneak off for a day to see the Fair.

Beppe was apprehensive. "Who are you sending that card to?"

"My friend Angie. Don't worry," I said, "she doesn't know anything about my life." I was aware of sounding offhand, but I hated to be questioned.

"Good," he said.

I wrote out Angie's address on the card, and at the last minute something witty came to me.

Dear Angie, May your life be as bright as Edison's electric light!
Love, Marie.

I thought about the cake I'd made for her birthday. It was true, I wished her life to be as bright as it could be and full of joy. For once, I wasn't jealous.

Beppe suggested we go directly to the restaurant, and by the way he walked with purpose I could tell this had been arranged. Le Restaurant Francais in the French Pavilion was one of the best at the fair. It looked out on the manmade Lagoon of Nations that was full of afternoon sunshine and sparkling water, and quite a few people were milling around the plaza. It had become quite warm, but inside the restaurant it was very cool, almost too cool. We were shown to our table high up on the third tier, and there were two more tiers above us, all with breathtaking views.

I excused myself and went to the ladies' room to wash my hands. I was staring at my reflection, admiring how good my hair looked under my best hat, when I caught the woman next to me staring. She wore a crisp-looking suit in a soft green color, like fresh lichen. Not only did she not return my smile, but looked me up and down as if I were covered in mud flung from a speeding taxi. Her look was so critical, my first thought was she must know Beppe and had seen us come in together. I returned to the table just as our appetizer of foie gras appeared, followed by a cold meat dish. Seeing Beppe so happy, I decided not to mention the woman in the bathroom, who I now realized had been looking at my clothes, my hair, my hat. I was dressed like someone from the country. I forced a smile and took my seat.

"Forgive me, Marie, these came highly recommended, so I ordered them. That's a saddle of lamb. Is that all right?"

"Yes, Beppe. It's more than all right."

"We have a bottle of wine coming."

"I don't think I can drink that much."

"Then drink as much as you want."

Decorating the platter were little savory extravagances elaborately crafted like the geegaws I sold in the store, only made purely of food. Jellied consommé had been molded into shapes like the detail around a Venetian mirror and "iced" with little curlicues made of apple marmalade. I had never seen such food. Before today, I hadn't known this kind of food existed. Especially now, with so many starving—ten years into the Depression and people were still lining up for cups of soup and thin slices of bread—it was numbing.

Afterwards, we walked and digested our meal and we spoke of nothing in particular.

"Do you want to come back tomorrow?" he asked. "Or should we stay here tonight? The lights at night are meant to be something. You know they project them onto the Trylon and Perisphere? We could grab a room nearby."

"What about our other room?"

"I guess it would be a waste of money," he said, but the way he stopped and looked directly at me, I could tell he wanted me to say whether I considered the idea crazy.

"If you want to stay," I said quickly.

"No. Let's get back. We're comfortable there, and tomorrow I can show you some of New York. But first let's take in *The Hot Mikado*." He used the very words I had been thinking, *We're comfortable...*

We loved the takeoff on the Gilbert and Sullivan musical. The costumes were extravagant and the headdresses spectacularly jeweled. I would have to see the movie, *The Mikado*, which had just come out, starring Kenny Baker as Nanki-Poo. I loved listening to Baker on The Jack Benny Program.

The dancing was sexy and most of the cast were Negroes, good looking and with more energy than seemed possible. The swing dancers wore short yellow pleated skirts that belled out as they twirled to blaring horns and trumpets; others wore close-fitting lamé pants that I thought I might try to sew for myself, if I was able to get the fabric. Such brilliant theatrics reminded me of the vastness of the world. Not in a lifetime could a person experience all the variety that was in New York. No wonder Gino and Sammy had been curious to the point of danger by attending that terrible rally. I didn't excuse their behavior, but now I understood that there were simply too many spectacles, too many new ideas to ignore.

Beppe and I were different suddenly, our bodies full of the swing and the jazz of the brass band. And as we left the theatre, the swelling sound still thumped in my head.

"Those dancers sure had energy," he said. "Bo Jangles is a thrilling performer. Those Shirley Temple movies don't do him justice."

"You don't think so?"

"No. I don't like how they use him."

"How do you mean?"

"The kindly colored man. It demeans him. I had no idea he was so talented. Say, Marie, should we try and dance like that?" he asked playfully.

"We could," I said, giving him a sly smile.

He took my hand, and we picked up the pace of our walking.

I thought about Ella, the Ashworths' maid, and what she would have thought of the dancers. The women in their short, short skirts and sometimes they landed with their legs around the men, who then tossed them over their heads before dragging them smoothly between their legs. Beppe interrupted my train of thought. Did I want to go back to the hotel, or on to another adventure?

"Another adventure," I said.

It was proving impossible to get a taxi at the entrance to the fair. A line of people waited, and we had no choice but to get in behind them. Then the wind came up, the sky clouded over, and Beppe became agitated. I was thinking perhaps it was because he didn't have the same influence here as he did in Littlefield. In New York he wasn't Mr. Ashworth with his chauffeur, but just another person wanting a car, and I felt disappointed for him that he couldn't produce this miracle.

How funny he looked, spoiled and grumpy as he gazed at the sky. I was worried it would start to rain and we would argue. I was also feeling tired, like the energy of *The Hot Mikado* had taken too much out of me, out of us, and now we needed to rest. But we were so far from our hotel. Beppe waved his arm in an attempt to attract a taxi. I didn't really believe he would cut in front of the others waiting, but for a second it seemed he would. I searched for conversation to distract him.

"Did I tell you? We might have found a second-hand soda fountain?"

I felt suddenly like a businesswoman. Could that be why the woman in the powder room had stared? Did she perhaps see a working woman with plans to expand her store? I tried to recall a movie that captured the right image. Maybe Rosalind Russell in *Fast and Loose*, but abruptly I was brought back to the present by Beppe's comment. "That's silly, Marie. You will never do it in this economy. And you have competition."

"Who?" I demanded, as a sharp gust lifted my skirt. Simultaneously, I reached up to hold down my hat. "Who is my competition?"

"The Sweet Shoppe. You'll never make a dent. And where were you thinking of putting the counter?"

"Where the register is now. Along that wall." It was the spot where I'd come upon him returning Mom's hatbox.

"It's too dark there. Why would someone sit at that counter when they could sit in a big window at The Sweet Shoppe?"

The words were harsh, and his tone shocked me.

"I'll put in a mirror. That's what people do. And I'll serve better ice cream. And sell baked goods." The idea had just popped into my head. I could think on my feet when I had to.

"Let's take the subway," he said, glancing at the hopeless line of people. At that he grabbed my hand and practically dragged me off.

"I'm going to need a loan," I said, adjusting to our rapid pace. It had seemed the logical moment to risk mentioning what we'd never fully discussed following the inspection of my ledgers. The loan I still hoped he'd offer.

"I don't think I can approve that, Marie," he said, looking everywhere except at me, as he tried to figure out our next move. When he stopped to ask someone where the subway was, I worked my hand free.

Approve? Perhaps I shouldn't have referred to it as a loan. I was ready to suggest he leave me and go on ahead.

"This is silly, Marie. Let's not argue."

I couldn't get over how easily he dismissed my plans.

"I'm sorry. Forgive me." He stopped walking and gently took hold of my arms. "I'm an idiot. We can talk about this whenever you want. But let's get to where we're going. I'm taking you to dinner at a very special place."

Dinner? We had not that long ago eaten a rich, French meal.

"Don't worry," he said. "You'll be hungry by the time we get there.

Besides, it's heading back to our hotel, in a roundabout way. It will be wonderful, you'll see."

We took the Long Island Railroad and had to change trains twice to get to East Harlem. East Harlem. It was rumored to be so poor. I looked over at my lover and tried to figure out whether this might be a joke. Despite having to change trains, we arrived while it was still light, and I was relieved the rain seemed to have missed us. It was a little cooler suddenly, which was nice.

Because it was a Saturday evening, the stores were still open and I wanted to go inside one or two, not because I hadn't been in many stores in my life, but because on almost every one was an Italian last name, just like in Littlefield.

"What is this place?"

"Marie, it's Little Italy!" said Beppe, laughing before taking me by the shoulders to quicken our pace. "What would you like to see?"

"We could go into some stores. That one," I said, pointing across the street at what looked like a variety store but that also sold hardware, items I had been thinking of stocking. Shovels, rakes and small tools were parked outside or in bins on the sidewalk. On familiar ground suddenly, I led the way. I hadn't known about this Little Italy, but I knew a good store when I saw one.

The interior was familiar, with its worn wooden floors and the pungent smell of wax and polish. Merchandise bins fairly shone with cleanliness and care, and behind the counter were the owners, husband and wife. I had only to glance at them to know this was a family-owned business, as no doubt most were around here. Even this far from home I felt a connection to them, though with Beppe watching I hesitated to show them the warmth I knew they'd respond to. For once I didn't care if he read on my face, plain as day, how much I loved the life of the store. Right then I knew I would never get rid of the Five & Ten, nor would I give it to Gino. I wouldn't begrudge my brothers money from it, but I would never close its doors.

A drama was going on inside the store. The woman, who I was sure was the wife, slammed an armload of plaid work shirts onto the counter, where they made a muted thud before toppling over onto the floor.

"Look what you do," screamed the husband, before looking up

and seeing us. Quickly I disappeared down one of the aisles, but Beppe paused to watch, letting them see what I knew they'd interpret as a rude curiosity. No doubt Beppe was thinking a man should not speak to his wife like that. Oh no? I thought.

In this Mom and Pop, I imagined a future for the Five & Ten. *Mom? Are you seeing this?* It was as though the doors of my mind were suddenly flung open, and in that moment the future was as clear and smooth as a new stretch of road.

"Let me buy you something," said Beppe, rounding a corner and out of sight. A minute later he reappeared with an ice cream scoop, one of those nice heavy steel ones made all in one piece. A reference to the fountain. And though I certainly didn't need his approval or his permission, here it was.

"Should I stock them?" I asked.

He laughed. "I couldn't say, Marie. But let's get two. For the fountain."

At the back of the store, floor to ceiling, were built-in bins. Each one was labeled with a small piece of cardboard in its own holder. There were nails, screws, hinges, and up high, out of reach of any normal-sized person, were less-called-for items such as door locks, keyhole plates and stamped brass pulls. There was a wooden footstool to help customers reach the upper bins. Not all these items would sell well, but they would all be in demand once we got out from under the Depression. Of course this store serviced so many more people. We were in a city, after all, not in a small town, but I had stopped thinking in a practical way. Nor would I get tangled up in any more debates with Beppe. He would always see things differently as they related to the economy, the desires of my customers, the running of a store. There was much he didn't understand.

"Are you hungry?" he asked.

I would have been content to stand right where I was for many more minutes.

"I'm starting to be."

"Good. Because I have a special place in mind."

"Is it far from here?" I asked, hoping we wouldn't have to get back onto the train.

"No. We can walk. It's close by."

Here we were in an Italian neighborhood. I couldn't imagine what kind of food he was prepared to eat, but it would not be what he was used to. It certainly wouldn't resemble the fare we'd had last night in The Sert Room, or the extravagant French lunch.

People were gathered on every corner, and when we walked toward a group of young women around my age, they turned to stare. I noticed they were dressed in dark suits with white blouses, almost identical to Mom's funeral suit, which thankfully I wasn't wearing. I was afraid Beppe might notice and think, this is what poor girls wear, the same look available cheaply and everywhere. I thought again about the woman in the ladies room at the French restaurant, and those I'd seen in and around the Waldorf, who wore color, seersucker. But a glance in his direction told me Beppe hadn't noticed. He was checking a paper he'd taken from his jacket pocket.

"Two more blocks," he declared with satisfaction.

A minute later we were standing outside a little corner place called Rao's. Beppe gave them his name and we were shown to our table, which was near the kitchen. "I don't like this table," he said to me. "I made this reservation weeks ago."

My heart nearly broke with joy at his consideration and all the planning. He wanted everything to be perfect, and it was. The aroma of food coming from the kitchen and the elegantly dressed waiters, and the customers who seemed at home, as if they ate here every night.

"They're known for their meatballs. That's what I'm having, but I think we should get an order of veal with lemon to share. What do you say?"

"I say yes. To all of it."

The meatballs were light and fluffy, which made me vow to use more egg and cheese and to aerate mine more. The veal was tender and pale in a light lemon sauce. I was proud to notice how this Italian food surpassed even the fussy French meal, though I was shocked to note that the prices weren't that much different. I had heard there were Italians who lived in the far north of the city, but I had no idea of the richness of life here. It was nearly overwhelming, the amount I didn't know.

For dessert Beppe ordered tiramisu and I an Italian cream cake. "There's no Italian Love Cake," he said, taking my hand. "That's an omission."

We had finished our bottle of wine, and with our desserts we sipped espressos. I had never eaten so much all in one day.

"It won't always be like this," he said, and I held my breath waiting for what he would say. "All this food. It's a big luxury. Even if we don't have a war. Even if…" here he stopped and looked away. There wasn't far to look because the kitchen wall was right there. He cleared his throat. The air was sweltering with heat from the kitchen.

"I love you, Marie," he said.

The suddenness of the words left me speechless. I wanted to say *I do too, Beppe*, but my thoughts were rushing ahead to the end of the trip, our car pulling into town, and a hasty goodbye followed by a chaste or passionate kiss. Which would it be? What could possibly follow this glorious weekend, even as we said how much we loved one another?

I looked across the table at him, and dry-eyed, clear-eyed, said, "I love you, too, Beppe. I always will."

CHAPTER THIRTY-TWO

As the landscape became once again familiar, we were dragged back. How strange to still feel like our New York selves, only now among the trees and rural pikes, the county-maintained roads that all looked the same, long, boring stretches lined with garages, farm stands and the occasional convenience store. My body still vibrated from so much lovemaking, but my heart was heavy.

He pulled into the driveway of our tryst apartment and spun the car around so that my door, the passenger side, faced the apartment rather than the street. He got out, came around, and we didn't look at one another. The air was so still and humid I felt faint, and the sudden quiet of the town threatened to undo the joy of the previous days. I preceded him into the tiny downstairs hallway. He carried my suitcase. I thought perhaps we might go upstairs and talk, but he said, "Marie, I'll leave you here."

We kissed. I watched him go. I wondered how I would get my suitcase home. It was heavier with all the new things Beppe had bought me—a small beaded purse and a black dinner jacket by an Italian designer I had never heard of called Elsa Schiaparelli, both from Saks Fifth Avenue. And a brass dish for holding jewelry edged in milky-blue marbles, with "1939 New York World's Fair" stamped in the base. I hadn't bought Gino anything, but I'd gotten Sammy and Kenny each a pen knife decorated in gold with images of the Trylon and Perisphere. I'd also bought several postcards I planned to use as bookmarks in Mom's cookbooks. All of those I'd insisted on paying for myself.

It took me several minutes to gather my wits. I wanted to leave enough time for him to get to his office, or home, wherever he would go first. I didn't want to see in which direction he went.

I checked my face in my compact. My eyes had a lovely clear quality that a small amount of tears can produce. Then I fled the apartment, leaving my suitcase behind in the hallway. Anyone spotting me would only see Marie who owned the Five & Ten, young Marie who sometimes surprised everyone by dressing up for nothing, walking with determination up Bellevue Avenue.

The biggest surprise, as I headed for the store, was the memory of optimism. How the ideas I'd seen, as Beppe and I walked together in an unfamiliar city, now gathered themselves into a bundle of hope. My energy, flagging since we'd crossed over into the countryside, returned in the form of an invigorating list of plans and improvements. Why had I thought it necessary to try to protect everyone? It wasn't possible. I provided Kenny with a job, but that didn't mean I had to put up with his nonsense. Beppe was right, what did I really owe any of them? Just because I was Gino's older sister didn't mean I was responsible for his behavior. I realized too that even if I were to meet Gloria and think her all wrong for Sammy, why should I care, it was their lives, not mine. I'd found new courage, and for the first time in my life, I felt free of it all.

There were plans to consider. There was the new stock I would order after seeing the hardware store in Little Italy. The incredible food we'd eaten had given me ideas for new cakes and pastries I could sell. These thoughts made me quicken my step as I headed for the store, ready again to put my arms around my life. I would face the problem of the missing money—I could hardly afford to let that go—but I finally understood what people meant when they said they felt refreshed after a vacation.

I arrived at the Five & Ten, and with the sun shining, I was transported back to the store in Little Italy that had given my plans such a boost. With enough capital I could transform the Five & Ten, and I wouldn't be limited by the usual dime store categories, the cheap toys and gadgets. I liked the idea of selling work clothes, but that would put me in competition with Ruth and Gersh, something I would never do. I would expand into hardware. Imagining a new look, I stopped outside to gaze at my display windows and was so mesmerized that at first I failed to notice the CLOSED sign hanging on the door.

Why was the store closed on a Monday?

I cursed whoever had made this decision. I would not give Kenny his gift. Did they think that because I was coming back today I wouldn't care? I didn't have the key to the store, so I let myself into the downstairs hallway and wasn't halfway up the stairs when I was greeted by a woman I didn't know.

"Marie, I'm Gloria." Having never met her, I wasn't prepared for the intimacy of grief. Her eyes were red and she was crying, which could only mean that something had happened to Sammy.

"What is it?"

In a split second, a spirit-like wind washed over me like someone stepped on my grave.

"Sammy's in the hospital," she said.

"Is he all right?" I ran up the stairs into the living room.

"I think so." She looked at me for a second, then collapsed down onto the sofa, her tears continuing. "There was a fight. It was terrible! Oh, God," she said, her head in her hands.

I sat next to her. "What happened? Tell me."

"Gino beat him up. He came upstairs, and he jumped on him. I never saw him like that. He was wild."

"Where's Gino?"

"He ran away. No one knows."

I looked around. It was then I noticed the empty space where Mom's cut crystal bowl had been. I scanned the room and saw the large tear in the curtain, and a hole in the oriental rug that I'd been carefully darning was now torn past hope of repair.

"They fought in here? I have to see Sammy. Where is he?"

"Our Lady of Lourdes in Camden. Uncle Salvie says he'll come over and drive you up. I've been there all day. I just got back so you wouldn't come home to an empty apartment."

As she spoke, I studied my brother's girlfriend. She was pleasantly plump, with a forthright expression, and right away I liked her. What a shame this had to be our first meeting.

"What else. Tell me all of it."

"The Oletskys. Their store was damaged." She looked terrified.

"Out with it!" I said, becoming impatient.

"I think it started there. I was here, making dinner, and I heard yelling outside. And breaking glass. Sammy came upstairs out of breath. He said we should leave. A second later Gino came in and that's when it started. I didn't know what to do, they were tumbling all over the place, so I went into Sammy's room and locked the door. I knew I should call the police, but I was afraid to come out, and I was afraid Gino wouldn't let me get to the telephone. Then I heard Gino running down the stairs with Sammy chasing after him and yelling. I ran down, too, but by then Gino was gone. Sammy was on the ground bleeding from the head. Somebody must have heard the noise and called an ambulance. I rode with Sammy to the hospital. He was unconscious the whole way. It was terrible. They wouldn't let me see him. Then Uncle Salvie arrived and we waited for at least an hour, but they still wouldn't let us into Sammy's room. Uncle Salvie told me not to worry, that he would take care of everything. He told me to come back here and wait for you."

"Is Sammy all right? Are you sure?" I was out of my mind with worry.

"He has a concussion. The doctor says he'll be okay."

"What about the Oletskys? What did Gino do?"

"He threw a barrel through their front window. A nail barrel, I guess. Mr. Oletsky was in there, but he only got a few cuts on his head."

I'd been so obsessed with the changes I wanted to make to the store, I'd failed to see the Oletskys' broken window.

"My God. I've got to go and see Ruth."

"No, Marie. Don't do that."

"Why not?"

"She won't see you."

"I could give a damn."

"Don't go. We have to wait for Uncle Salvie."

"I'm not waiting," I said, but when I stood up I felt faint and had to sit back down. A second later I was up and calling the hospital. Before getting the bus I first needed to find out about Sammy's condition. I spoke to a nurse who said he was all right. "His uncle just left."

Uncle? Salvie?

If he was on his way, I figured I should wait, otherwise I would end up stuck in Camden or forced to take the bus back home. I was too restless to stay in the apartment, so I left Gloria there and went to sit behind the cash register downstairs. I opened the cash drawer, an automatic gesture. There was money inside. I was thinking about Kenny. How in the confusion he'd probably left the store unattended. The money could have been taken, but there it was, still in the drawer.

I thought briefly of Gino. What was happening?

Gloria called down to say she was going to take a nap, and I left the hallway door open so I would hear the telephone if it rang. I stared at my cluttered display windows and the film I'd installed to keep the sun from fading the already worn-looking stock. It turned the street a sepia color, like an old movie. How I longed to replace it with an awning. The Little Italy stores had all had awnings, some with lovely stripes. I'd once loved the look of my store, but now, after seeing those others, it looked shabby. I promised myself that if Sammy was okay, I would go ahead with the improvements. If it turned out he was more seriously injured, I would go ahead anyway.

I heard the telephone and rushed upstairs. It was Mr. E. calling to say he'd pick me and Gloria up in an hour. He didn't mind driving back up to Camden. He was being very solicitous. Gloria and I got ready and were standing outside when Mr. E. pulled up. Though I didn't want to, Gloria insisted and so I sat in the front seat next to him. He gripped the steering wheel and I could tell by the look on his face that he was angry. Whenever a man didn't want to say the truth, there was that look. *How should I handle her? Give her the usual balm of comfort? Does she blame me?*

"You got him listening to that priest," I said, aware that Gloria, whom I had just met, was witnessing the history between me and her uncle. "And those newspapers." My voice rose in the confined space of the car. "Why?"

"Gino, he's…what's the word…influence…he fall under. It's my fault, Mari. But it's…just…politics. All the men talk. We kick around…"

"Talk leads to action!"

"He's a hothead."

"Look what happened. His brother's in the hospital. And what about the Oletskys?"

"Sammy is fine, Mari. And the store. Everything will be okay."

"I found some money missing."

"What is this talk?" he said.

I refused to say another word. I looked out the window and prayed we'd be there soon.

*

Sammy did seem fine, but his voice was weak. They had him sleeping sitting up in case of bleeding on the brain. Hearing this, I nearly lost my mind, but the doctor said it was a usual precaution.

As soon as Mr. E. left the room to get us some coffee, Sammy said, "Where's Gino? I want to see Gino." It took all my strength not to speak too loudly or show too much emotion. What shocked me was his tone, not angry or urgent, but full of sadness as if he, and not Gino, were responsible. He seemed to be in mourning, and I lamented the misplaced loyalty he had for his older brother, the kind of respect and forgiveness children dutifully show a father, even a bad father.

I took his hand, "Never mind about Gino. You think about getting better."

"Are the Oletskys all right?"

"I haven't seen them yet."

I felt guilty. If I hadn't been in New York, the fight might never have happened. Apart from my embarrassment and shame, my heart ached for how Ruth must be feeling. She would probably expect, given that Sammy was in the hospital, that I would be busy for a couple of days. But I couldn't delay making contact for too long. That is, if she would see me.

"Are you sure you're all right?" I took his hand.

He nodded, looking handsomer still, even though he was in pain. In addition to the head wound he had a dislocated shoulder. The doctors wanted him to spend one more night in the hospital.

I went out into the corridor to think, unsure of how long I should stay in Camden. I was like a *Linchetto*, a sprite who'd crawled out of her wine vat in order to play a trick on someone. And if I were a Linchetto, the person I would most want to play a trick on would be Gino. I wished him ill. I couldn't relax. I was too full of resentment at how rapidly the good effects of my trip with Beppe had evaporated.

"I think you should stay away from Sammy for a while," I said to Mr. E. right in front of Gloria. It was harsh, but I wanted to punish him.

"Mari...please."

I ignored him. We left the hospital and dropped Gloria at her parents' house, which was not far from the hospital, after which Mr.

E. and I drove the rest of the way in silence.

Back in the apartment, I went in search of Mom's coral necklace and hung it around my neck. I had read in one of her books that red coral was powerful, and I whispered my wishes in order. First, that Sammy recover quickly; next, that Mr. E. be subdued, manipulated into providing only help; third, that Beppe would rescue me from all of it.

CHAPTER THIRTY-THREE

The rot in Europe had finally reached us. Italy's *squadristi*, Mussolini's Italian Black Shirt Legion and Bundists were living right here among us. Mimi and I had seen it in the newsreels, Mussolini declaring, "The great, the beautiful, the inexorable violence." Now our own boys were rampaging and vandalizing, and stupid men signed a black book in allegiance. Were they fools enough to believe they might destroy the men who really ran this town, men like my lover? Because it wasn't the Italians who had the power, though I supposed this was the whole point, that they lacked power, confidence, self-respect and so gravitated towards the strongman. God help men's frustrations, I thought. There was no end to the damage they could do.

We hadn't run up a single sale since the Oletskys had had their store window smashed in by my brother. Usually by mid-week business picked up, but today, a Wednesday, only two people had come in. First Mrs. Delfina, whose only purpose was to stare. With her was a woman I recognized as a wealthy parishioner from Father Barnes's congregation. "I'm afraid this might poison me," said Mrs. Delfina, inspecting the glaze of an earthenware bowl before setting it back down with a loud crash. Luckily it didn't break. I looked up from my seat behind the cash register and got ready to say something, but just then the woman leaned toward Mrs. Delfina and in a loud whisper declared, "Imagine serving meatballs in a mansion!" Was this a reference to my Wedding Soup? Had she been at the Ashworths' Christmas party? Or might this be a reference to an Italian woman cooking anything for the likes of the Ashworths? Whatever she meant, she intended for me to hear it.

"A disgrace," said Mrs. Delfina, who made a clucking noise.

I fled to the back room, where I ordered Kenny into the store in case they needed help. Then I went upstairs and began cleaning, first the sills, then the baseboards, all of which I had done only recently. And when the buzzer sounded I almost didn't answer, but then looking down from my front window onto the street I saw it was Mrs. Fiorello, whom I was always happy to see. I brought her upstairs and offered her a chair in the living room, whereby she reached into a heavy-looking satchel and took out a freshly baked casserole.

"You're so kind, Mrs. Fiorello."

"How's Sammy?"

"He'll recover. It wasn't that bad."

"Oh, thank God."

I burst into tears. She came to sit next to me and put her arms around me.

"Don't you worry, Marie. Everyone knows the pressure you're under. Everything is okay."

I could have stayed forever, crying on her shoulder, but there was no putting it off. As soon as she left, I telephoned Ruth. Normally, I would have grabbed my purse and hurried next door, but their store was still closed for repairs. That morning I'd happened to look out just as a large van pulled up, and mounted on the back was a new sheet of glass, a replacement for the damaged front window. I flashed on a horrible image—Ruth's description of Kristallnacht—and a wave of shame overtook me.

Ruth answered right away.

"Ruth," was all I could say.

"I was wondering when you'd call." The same old Ruth, ruefully cynical at my discomfort. We were sad and diminished but perhaps our friendship was intact.

"I wanted to sooner. Sammy comes home today. I was waiting. I mean, he wasn't that hurt. Ruth, I'm so sorry. I know you'll never forgive me. I don't blame you. But I can't lose your friendship. I can't. How is Gersh?"

"He's okay," she said, "Just scratches."

That was Ruth. It was almost funny, the way she had of minimizing things, or maybe in the scale of what could have happened—measured against the hatred and terror Jews lived with on a daily basis in Europe, the terrible reports from home—scratches were really just scratches.

"Ruth, please. I hate him. I hate my brother. And I'm afraid of him. But he's gone. He took off right after."

"I heard he's living in town. With Esposito."

"No. Where did you hear that?"

Gino, at Mr. E.'s?

"We should sit down and talk." She sounded so calm.

"Yes. Whenever you want. Should I come over now?"

A long silence. "No. Not now." Then, "I don't blame you, Marie. We'll talk, okay? But not today."

I went straight downstairs and grabbed Kenny by the arm. He looked from his arm to my face. "Is Gino at Salvie's? And don't lie to me."

"No. Are you crazy?"

"Don't take that tone with me, Kenny."

"No one knows where he is."

"No one?"

Kenny was quite capable of lying to me, but his frightened expression let me know that in this instance he was telling the truth. I also knew my brother Gino. For all his loudmouthed bravado he would understand just how grave an act it was to harm the Oletskys.

I left Kenny in the store. Despite the heat I went to stand outside, ready to be my most charming should someone walk by. People would eventually forget, but it was going to take time. I swept the sidewalk until sweat broke through my dress. I gazed up at my display windows, at the dreary woman's torso, her face in a carnival mask, her neck adorned with costume jewelry. Who could ever admire such a display? And the row of used cowboy boots next to a kitchen stepstool over which I'd draped my best apron, and underneath, a ragtag collection of pots and pans.

As I stood in the sweltering heat feeling sorry for myself, I tried to imagine my new Five & Ten. Drawers and shelves full to bursting with building supplies. There would be multiples of everything, and choice, different levels of quality and price. I held fast to that picture. It had the power to save my life.

CHAPTER THIRTY-FOUR

I arrived at our tryst apartment to find Beppe at the round table engrossed in his newspaper. He looked up and slowly got to his feet. We embraced. We kissed, our passion ready to spring to life. But when we disengaged, I was about to speak when he sat down and continued to read. He raised the paper so I could no longer see his face. I knew him capable of hiding his emotions, but how could he be so rude, and on our first meeting following that heavenly trip?

Infuriated, I sat down and read the headlines on the front page of Beppe's *New York Times*: Rome Sees Danger on the Border of Libya. Britain Spending More on Warships. Nothing about the stories I heard circulating, about soup kitchens, workers' strikes, stores going out of business, children without shoes. I guessed you'd have to go well inside the paper to find those. People were hard up. In Littlefield, a man stood out in front of the gas station selling apples.

"What is it?" I asked.

He finished the article he'd been reading. Without answering me he turned to the back pages, to the tiny print of the stock market that was like an ancient language spoken by only a few.

"You are rude," I said, starting to pace, while trying not to see the dark varnish on furniture that reminded me of those horrible church confessionals with their musty smell, the noise of the old wooden screen sliding across like a death rattle as the fuzzy outline of the priest came into view. The priest, a threatening stranger, one able to forgive but only if the subject humbled herself, showed contrition.

"Talk to me," I said. "And stop reading that damn paper!"

He folded it, put it down on the table.

"Sit down, Marie."

There was surprising coldness in his voice. What had happened to *I can't wait, Marie. I've missed you, Marie.* He got up and started to pace. "Why didn't you tell me yourself? I had to hear it from my tellers. Everyone is talking."

So it was Gino, and what had happened at the Oletskys' store.

"You have no idea..." I said, bursting into tears.

"You let this happen," he said.

"Me? How could I stop it? I was away with you, remember?"

"I warned you about your brother."

"What could I do? I'm afraid of him. I've always been afraid of him."

"All that Coughlin nonsense. I kept telling you it's dangerous. They're serious, Marie. My reputation…"

His reputation?

"What about mine? Is it worse to have people know I'm the sister of a fascist? Or for them to know you're sleeping with me while living with your wife?"

"That's not what I mean."

"What do you mean?"

"I don't want this to end, Marie. But we have to be careful. Both of us."

"Don't you dare lecture me."

He sat down, shifted position, drummed his fingers on the table.

Every relationship I had was bound up in need. That terrible word. What did he know of having to make sacrifices, to cook beans meal after meal, to stretch a piece of salt pork until we wanted to cry *uncle*. At the same time, I did feel responsible. It was completely irrational for him to expect me to tame an animal like Gino, but there it was. My negligence. Like all women, I'd been raised to believe we were responsible for the bad behavior of men, especially the ones we raised, fed, made homes for. I went over and sat by the window so I wouldn't have to look at him. I stared down at the empty driveway and the house, this place that belonged to my lover, one of his many assets.

"Beppe, I need money. Right now. For improvements."

"How do you propose to pay it back?"

He didn't miss a beat, on level ground suddenly when the subject was money. Maybe we were alike, I thought, practical and clear headed when we discussed business.

He was looking away from me, toward the kitchen. "Look at me, Beppe. I need to do something quick. To make them forget. To erase what happened."

"People don't forget so easily, Marie. Besides, it isn't a good time to invest in more stock. Or make improvements. You should wait until business picks up."

"I can't wait. How will business pick up if the store doesn't look good? The fountain is exactly what will make people forget."

I studied his suit, the generous cut, no skimping on fabric there.

"What do you think I could get for the store?" I felt calm. Marie, the businesswoman. Not that I'd ever sell, but I wanted to judge his interest.

"It might be worth something," he said, "But it's a bad time to sell anything."

"If there's a war…I mean after. Business will be good. That's what you said."

"But you don't want to sell, I thought."

"I mean if I *have* to."

The fine-looking shoulders and neck made me want him, but I would do without him today.

"There are some good contracts going out," he said. I saw the wheels turning, his thoughts settling on opportunities.

"Contracts for what?"

"Things needed for the war. Mattresses for Navy ships. That's one I heard about the other day."

"What else?"

"Too many to tell."

"Name one or two."

"Boots. Soldiers need footwear. Government contracts are giving a good return."

"Can I get one?"

He laughed. "Not really."

"Why?"

"You'd have to manufacture something, and you need capital, and a premises."

"I have a premises."

"I can't give you money, Marie. You know that."

"Why?"

"Because of your brother."

I had expected him to say because people would wonder what was going on between us. Or because I was a woman, or an Italian, or because business was bad and it would be an unwise investment.

He looked at me with sudden kindness. "Come here, Marie." He motioned for me to sit on his lap.

"No."

He got up and walked over to where I was sitting, and gently, using two fingers, lifted my chin. He stared into my eyes. Even as I imagined the sun falling warmly across the floor and dancing on the bed covers, I remained frozen.

"I have to go," I said, gathering my purse.

"No. Look. I have some time. I don't have to be back right away."

"I do," I said.

CHAPTER THIRTY-FIVE

Sometimes when Beppe and I argued, I pictured the mansion, the calm water of the lake and the rhododendrons in a breeze. In my daydreams I sometimes stood on that dock and looked out, while trying to imagine what his life was like. What was my place in that life?

The first thing I did when I got back to the store was telephone Mr. E.'s friend to say I would buy the second-hand soda fountain. Right away I could tell he didn't want to do business with a woman, that is until I told him Mr. E. had asked me to call. How easy it was to get a man to agree once another man said it was okay. I had no idea how I would pay for it.

Just as I hung up there came those three distinctive knocks; Ruth never used the bell. So she was finally ready to see me. I was terrified as I opened the door and she stormed inside. We didn't hug as we usually did, but once we were seated upstairs in the living room, she leaned toward me and took both my hands in hers. "I don't want to fight with you, Marie."

I threw my arms around her. "I'm so sorry, Ruth."

We were both sobbing, and when we pulled away, she said, "I hope we can forget. I think we can."

"We can. It's all my fault. Please forgive me. Forgive *us...*"

"My God," she said, shaking her head. "What is happening?" I was stunned by the hopelessness in her voice. She looked around the room, "Where's the bowl?"

The cut crystal bowl, which had survived a trip to the Ashworths', had been smashed to bits by Gino.

"They fought in here," I said. Ruth tilted her head and I heard her thinking, *When will you admit your brother is a bigger problem than you think?*

"Will you and Gersh come to a picnic tomorrow night on the loading bay?"

"Dinner, outside? In this heat?"

"Will you come? You and Gersh?"

"I don't know. Maybe."

"Gino won't be here. I'm never going to speak to him again, Ruth."

"We'll see," she said.

"He's not living at Salvie Esposito's," I said quickly, hoping to dispel that rumor. "Please try to come. I need your opinion about something."

Not that I would be competing with them, but I figured now was the right time to tell her about the counter before she heard it from someone else.

"I'm putting in a soda fountain," I said.

First she looked at me like I was crazy. Then she smiled. "I was wondering when you would figure out you needed something."

"It's a big expense, but I have to attract more customers."

"How are you going to pay for it?"

Ruth was direct. She was waiting for me to say it was Beppe, but the truth was I didn't know where the money would come from.

"I'll get a loan," I said.

"Let me guess."

I smiled. "I can't say yet. You'll be the first to know."

"I could warn you, but I won't."

"Thank you."

After Ruth left, I went to look for recipes in Mom's book, the one with the pictures of the rivers and streams of Italy. Plates of tortellini and mortadella sausages were balanced on a stone turret and behind them the Due Torri towers in Bologna. In another picture, somewhere in Rome, a tray of grilled veal chops sat on their broiling grate, deliciously charred. I couldn't afford sausages or chops, but I would do the best I could with substitutions. I wanted our meal to be wonderful.

I would make my announcement after dinner, and I couldn't wait to see the look on Mr. E.'s face.

I planned a *struffoli alla napoletana*, small balls of pastry covered in honey and sprinkled generously with "jimmies," little vermicelli-like strands of sugar in many colors. This had been a favorite dessert when we were children. In the picture, a glowing pyramid of struffoli was photographed against the carved wooden door of La Chocolateria Gay Odin, the oldest chocolate and ice cream shop in Naples.

I left the storage room clutching Mom's book, thinking how tomorrow our loading bay would be transformed, its peeling cement and old pallets becoming our stone turret, our ancient ruin. Next I called Ada and invited her, and she accepted right away. "I bring wine," she said.

In the end the party included Sammy and Gloria, Kenny and his wife, Loretta, Mr. E., and Ada. Mr. E. said he would be late, Ruth had called to say she had a headache, but she thought Gersh might stop by later, which I doubted. I told no one ahead of time that Ada would be coming.

She, too, was late. By the time she arrived, Kenny, Loretta, Sammy and Gloria were already sitting around the table eating my antipasti, olives stuffed with a pork and chicken mixture I liked to use in braciola. I couldn't afford steak or veal, but my lighter version was just as lovely. I'd rolled the stuffed olives in bread crumbs, then deep-fried them. Everyone was eating and talking as I edged Ada forward.

Her hair was windblown, her blouse and skirt crumpled, and I felt guilty inviting her on a Friday night because the bus would have been even more hot and crowded than usual. She seemed less confident, and she held tightly to my arm.

"Meet our Aunt Ada," I said to the group. "Mom's sister."

Sammy gave a sad, sorry look as though I'd divorced him from the family. What unconscious state had I been in not to tell him about her? The affair with Beppe had clouded my judgment. In my defense, though, Ada's existence had never seemed quite real. I supposed that could be my excuse.

"Ada, this is my brother Sammy. A surprise, yes?"

I watched him watch her. He was already on his feet and extending his hand, all the warmth he could manage beaming toward her.

"'Ello, Sammy," said Ada, before she pulled him in for a hug.

I introduced her to everyone, one by one, before announcing that I had to check on the food. I'd made a pole bean salad, *Insalata di Fagiolini*, and meatballs with artichokes, *Polpette con Carciofi*. I had even splurged on mozzarella and prosciutto to lay across the meatballs. And I had avoided pasta, certainly not because of what Gino had said, but because it was too hot outside.

With Kenny's help, I'd transformed the bay into an Italian garden. In a tall vase were gladioli from Mimi's garden and we'd strung lights between the pillars. Ada had taken a seat next to Sammy, and the two talked intently. When finally, Mr. E. arrived he was looking tired, but at the sight of Ada he perked up.

I introduced them. "Ada is Mom's sister," I said.

"Madonna mia!" He threw his hands up and drew her toward him. I couldn't tell whether Mr. E. wouldn't let go or Ada was equal in this embrace, but like lightning their greeting left an afterimage, a bright electric glow. Kenny asked Sammy to help him with something in the store and the two left.

Ada used her foreignness to distance herself, pretending not to understand the simplest question when it suited her. People had started getting up and changing places. Loretta was now talking to Gloria, and for the next hour Ada and Mr. E. spoke nonstop, their conversation almost entirely in a southern Italian dialect. From time to time Ada threw back her head and laughed, and Mr. E. danced in his chair.

"Attention," I said, when Kenny and Sammy had returned and we were finally settled with our cake and coffee. At the last minute I'd decided the struffoli was too much work, so I'd iced a nice sheet cake instead. The time had arrived for my announcement, and I was just about to start when Mr. E. interrupted. He thought the bay was too hot and that we should all go upstairs.

"It's no cooler up there," I said in a snappish tone that I instantly regretted.

The sky had clouded over. It felt like a storm might be coming. I could tell Loretta wanted to leave, but I wouldn't allow anyone to go until I'd told them about the counter. Suddenly, the men were talking loudly about the war and Roosevelt. I interrupted them by clapping my hands. "I have an announcement."

I could have easily started with bad news. How there was nothing left in our bank account for upkeep, let alone for stock, and that the Five & Ten had hardly made a sale since the incident at the Oletskys', and that I held Gino personally responsible. But I said instead, "Salvie has a friend with a business. What did you tell me they sell, Salvie? Kitchen equipment?"

"Mari, I tell you. Restaurants. Commercial. For business."

He was distracted, wanting to get back to his conversation with Ada.

"Yes, that's right. Well, I got in touch with Salvie's friend, and I ordered a soda fountain." Here, I paused.

Mr. E. shot a look at Kenny, then at Sammy, before staring at me with an expression I couldn't read.

I continued, "I'm putting in a milk bar. It has a dark marble top and a stainless console. In the corner where the cash register is. And a mirror over the bar so the store is reflected. It will make it look bigger."

Mr. E.'s mouth opened and closed but nothing came out.

"I'm taking out a loan," I said, telling my lie. "The store will be my..." I searched for the word. "Collateral."

I had hoped to find at least one champion, but no one said anything, not even Sammy, who sat holding hands with Gloria. I recalled our mother's words, *I'm leaving the store to you, Marie, but take care of your brothers.* Sammy left all the decisions up to me; whatever I considered best for the Five & Ten was usually all right with him. Again, I had been thoughtless, this time by failing to discuss the counter with him.

I hardly looked at Ada, but when I did her expression was neutral, as though she hadn't heard, or if she did, it meant nothing.

The men weren't in agreement, that much was clear. Mr. E. was so tightlipped I could tell he was furious. Kenny looked completely shocked, but like Sammy, he was probably just annoyed he hadn't been consulted. I believe Sammy would have backed me, but he was angry that I hadn't told him about Ada.

Really, it was that they couldn't see the benefit of putting in a counter. People were so poor. One saw the same cars, the same suits and shoes. But I remained convinced that once the Five & Ten offered a glimpse of social life, and people walked by and saw the gleaming chrome and a row of shiny red stools, they would come in and spend money on a small luxury, a milk drink with a flavoring or chocolate topping. Their moods would be lifted, buttressed by something sweet. I also planned to keep my prices low, at least at first.

I was glad no one questioned where the money was coming from, since I didn't yet know. But I could tell they thought I gambled. Nor did they ask how I dared to make improvements while we were still in a Depression. The men were no longer paying attention, but finishing off my bottle of Four Roses and talking about baseball. They seemed more anxious to discuss how Joe DiMaggio and Bucky Williams had both been named most valuable player.

Suddenly Ada stood up and clapped her hands. *"Cantiamo una canzone!"*

Sing a song? We had no instruments, and what song would all of us know? The only one I could think of was "Santa Lucia" that was played every 16th of July for the feast of Our Lady of Mount Carmel. Mom had had the beautiful Caruso recording, but the version that stuck in my head was full of a cacophony of sour-sounding horns played by old men from the Sons, who each year followed the Virgin Mary down our main street on her rickety stand. No, I didn't want to sing. I wanted to talk about the counter. How could I be alone in my excitement?

Ada rapped on the table with her long fingers and everyone fell silent. The men looked up expectantly. "Okay. Okay. I do now," she said. She had already worked her magic on them and they became suddenly alert. Now they would sing, or do whatever else she suggested.

"What we sing, Ada?" Mr. E.'s voice had changed from his usual gruff tone to a soft expression.

"Vivere!" she declared.

"Ah," said Mr. E., *"To Live!"*

He raised his chin like Mussolini himself in a gesture of salute, and Ada beamed.

"Okay. Okay. I do now." She seemed nervous, but that was gone instantly once she began the song in Italian, her voice deep and rich. She was hardly through the first couple of lines when she turned to Mr. E. "You say in English," she said, commanding him to translate.

Ada was standing, whereas the rest of us were seated, watching her. I was captivated. I didn't notice at first the look of pain on Mr. E.'s face as he translated in a whisper:

My girl has left me
I'm free at last.

Kenny, unable to hear, said, "What? Louder!"

Ada continued singing in her mellifluous Italian, and I could see the young Catholic girl she had been, full of innocence as she sang on holy days. That joy from her youth had moved easily into adult songs of love and relationships. For the first time she seemed sexual. It was shocking, exhilarating, and immediately I thought of Mom. There was much I would never know, things a daughter is always slow to learn about her own mother. We had needed more years together, time we would never have.

Ada stared into the eyes of the men as she sang. Loretta was the only one who appeared bored, but it was Mr. E. who seemed stricken. It couldn't still be the counter, I thought. He'd gone from a carefree mood, with obvious joy at the food, and Ada, to this gloom.

After the first verse, there was a brief pause, full of tension, before we practically screamed in unison the refrain—

> *Vivere,*
> *finché c'è gioventù*
> *perché la vita è bella*
> *la voglio vivere sempre più.*

Ada sat down as the song continued. Her elbows swayed and she pounded the table in rhythm to the music. "Ancora!" she cried, and without further prompting, we went again into the refrain. I wondered whether we could be heard for miles, as far away as the farms, down lonely, winding roads through the endless pines. We were crying into the dark, but there was a bright, streaming light in our hearts.

After *Vivere*, everyone wanted another song, except Mr. E., who got up and with both hands on his back, groaned like he would need to be carried to his bed across town.

Ada obliged us, this time with a lighter tune called *Tulipan*. Though why we were singing about tulips "under a May sky like a Dutch cheese" was a mystery. Kenny explained that the song had been a number one hit for the Trio Lescano, Italy's version of The Andrew Sisters. But it needed a big band, or an orchestra, and there was only Ada pounding on the table and the rest of us struggling to keep up. Mr. E. sat back down and stared grumpily into the distance. And without offering any to the rest of us, he emptied the remainder of the Four Roses into his glass.

Tulipan was a crowd pleaser, but silly, I thought. Yet Ada received extravagant praise, which she responded to with a flamboyant toss of her hair, like a visiting star who'd decided to grace us with a rare appearance. When suddenly she announced she was leaving, Mr. E. made a fuss. "Don't go. Stay. I drive you. Later."

"No, no," she said over her shoulder as she headed to the office to retrieve her purse, and I followed. She turned to me in the doorway, and with all eyes on her, on us, she announced, "I come back. Don't worry."

Then she was gone. Kenny and Loretta got up to leave, but then Kenny took me aside and said, "Marie, about the counter." He wanted to give me suggestions about its placement and the rearrangement of the stock. That's when I knew he was on board.

Sammy hung back, and when he was sure no one could hear, he leaned close to my ear. "When did you meet her? How long have you known?" He was insistent, and as I feared, he was hurt I hadn't told him about his aunt.

"A couple of months ago. Isn't it incredible?"

"She's like Mom." There were tears in his eyes.

"At first I didn't believe her," I said, though of course there was no doubt. Physically, she was too much like our mother. Sammy made a move to go. I took his arm, afraid now to be left alone with Mr. E., who had gone around the corner to smoke. "Can you wait a minute?" I asked.

Mr. E. had been pleasant enough while speaking to Ada, but he was mad at me for ordering the counter, and there was the dark cloud of the song. Never far from either of our minds was the attack in my kitchen.

I asked Sammy and Gloria to help me clear the table and bring the dishes upstairs so I wouldn't be left alone with him. A few minutes later I thought I heard him leave. Unable to delay them further, I said goodnight to Sammy and Gloria. I was in the kitchen putting the last of the dirty dishes into the sink when he walked in. "Mari, the counter. Madonna Mia."

I kept my back to him.

"Did you know Carmie have sister?" he asked.

"Mom mentioned her once or twice," I said quickly. I didn't want to admit I hadn't known about Ada. Too much of our past was gone.

I also wanted to deny him the privilege of claiming to know more about our family than I did.

"Wonderful," he said.

"But you knew," I said, turning to face him.

"No. No."

"It seems like you knew her."

He looked off into the distance, trying to work out what to say.

"Mari, you could tell about counter. No need sneaking."

"I'm not sneaking. I'm doing what's right for the store." I bent to retrieve a fresh tea towel from the drawer.

"But, the way you say. In front of everybody."

I began rinsing the dishes. "Your friend will make a sale. And he will give you a little something."

"What, Mari?"

"I'm sure you'll get a kickback."

"Kickback. Off my own money?"

"I'm not asking you to pay."

He made a groaning noise that was meant to shame me. He sniffed. "What loan could you get?"

"I don't want anything from you. You're lucky I'm still speaking to you."

He took a step closer. "Listen."

"Don't you dare. Don't you ever get near me again. I'll call the police."

He held up his hand in surrender. "I sorry."

I was on my guard.

"I have a problem, Mari." He was quiet suddenly, calm as anything. "No one to drive the sugar this week. I get somebody, but tomorrow I need."

Me? Drive the big truck with the slipping clutch? He stood with his hands in his pockets, waiting for my answer.

"Kenny can do it," I said.

He grabbed my hand, and I recoiled from the feel of his warm, calloused palm. I felt like a Mafia wife. You like your cash, here's how it is going to be. Gone was the calm of a minute before. He cupped my hand in both of his and squeezed tightly.

"Having to ask, Mari," he shrugged like it made him weary, the greatest pain he could have experienced. He knew there was no way I could survive without my cut of the sugar runs.

"Would you have asked Mom to drive?"

He flinched at the mention of Carmela.

"I loved your mother," said in a whisper, without a trace of the faker he could be, full of drama, lies, pretending. What he said affected me, but I remained in control. "If you want me to drive, you have to pay for the counter."

"I thought you got a loan." He stepped back and smiled, pleased he'd been able to pry the truth from me.

"That's the deal," I said.

"Geesh," he thrust a gnarled hand into the air as if to scatter birds. "Yes, yes. I leave you now, Mari."

I gripped the kitchen table and waited until I heard the downstairs door close.

CHAPTER THIRTY-SIX

Driving at night in the plain white truck, with the moon casting leafy patterns across the macadam, I felt like I was in a scene from a movie. I wore Mom's trench coat and her felt fedora. Immediately, I developed an ache in my shoulders from handling the large, heavy wheel and having to wrestle to change gears. Into the cab wafted the earthy smell of sweet potatoes that were packed against the sugar. The sour, dusty smell tore at my throat. If I was stopped by the authorities, I was to say I was driving my father's crop of sweet potatoes up the line to the Reading Terminal in Philly. On the way I practiced my lines until the lie became the story.

In the middle of the night, Miss?

I work in a factory during the day, sir.

I pulled into the parking lot, and several men came out to meet me, their careworn faces resigned and practical. They were prepared to do whatever was necessary to feed their families, nor did they seem surprised that a woman drove the truck. So many things once considered out of the ordinary, even frowned upon, were now the price to be paid for maintaining life as we knew it.

The next day Mr. E. called to say he was sorry, but he would need me again the following Thursday. What happened to, *Just this once, Mari. I promise.*

Not only did I drive that Thursday, but again the following Tuesday, and the Thursday after that, as the number of runs increased. What with my full hours in the store, and my baking, there was no let up. Beppe and I hadn't spoken in a week, not since our argument. When he finally called, there was the usual lust in his voice. I wanted to see him, too, but I was wary.

I arrived first, and from the window of our tryst apartment I saw him coming up the driveway on foot, followed by a small truck. Two men jumped out and manhandled a large square box. I heard the key in the downstairs lock and Beppe's voice on the stairwell.

"Easy now. A little to the left."

I gathered my purse and hat, went into the bedroom and closed the door.

"It's a beauty," I heard Beppe say.

"It sure is," said one of the men.

I couldn't imagine. The apartment had not changed, nothing added or subtracted. I sat down on the bed, leaned back against the headboard and listened to a lot of shifting and scraping, as Beppe instructed them where to put whatever the item was. While I waited for the men to leave I stretched out fully. I was tired from last night's run up to Toms River, and I must have drifted off. I woke to the sound of the downstairs door closing, followed by the thrum of a truck's motor. A minute later I was jolted by the familiar organ music and the baritone announcer: *The National Broadcasting Company now brings you Young Widder Brown. The story of attractive Ellen Brown with two fatherless children to support. The story of the age-old conflict between a mother's duty and a woman's heart.*

The mournful organ swelled as my favorite program began, and I rushed into the living room to find Beppe kneeling in front of a large mahogany radio console.

"I didn't want to wake you," he looked up and smiled.

Young Widder Brown brought to you today by the makers of Errol Wax.

In Michael Forsythe's hotel room, Ellen Brown has spoken words which Michael had hoped she would speak. Ever since he fell in love with her months ago, after Dr. Anthony Loring believed a lie about her and discarded her, and was tricked into marriage by his wife Millicent...

I threw my arms around him and we kissed.

"You thought I didn't know you were in there?" He was laughing, but I was crying. He thought they were tears of joy, my pleasure at seeing the radio. If only that were the reason. I didn't know what I felt, except I wasn't myself. I no longer knew my own mind. Did I love this man or hate him? He wouldn't understand; I hardly did myself.

The radio we had in the store was a small desktop model with terrible sound. What had the console cost, and could I have paid for part of the counter with that money? Beppe pulled up a chair. He held my hand and together we listened to Young Widder's soon-to-be troubles with Dr. Loring. Did he notice how we were like a soap opera? A familiar story. A cliché?

Halfway through the broadcast, I reached for the knob and switched it off. There was the muted afternoon sound of birds and a strange ticking noise far off, as though the town was keeping the time of our love. Everything was too full and tender. Here we were hidden where no one expected us to be. It was as if we floated in space. No thought could be held for too long in the rush to fuse our bodies and the secret longings of our hearts. We made love that afternoon like it was the first time. Beppe thought it was the radio, that I was excited and wanted to show my appreciation. I could now come into the apartment whenever I wanted and listen to *Young Widder* or *The Lone Ranger* or *Stella Dallas*, while pretending to be Marie without responsibilities. Ever since our trip to New York I had more nervous energy, and I was managing on only five hours of sleep, a pace I couldn't continue.

"You're different," he said.

"I guess. Cup of tea?"

"Yes, but don't go yet."

After we'd made love a second time, I got up and put on the robe I kept in the otherwise empty closet. I was anxious to escape into the kitchen to think. For days now I'd been worrying over the fact that *my friend* hadn't arrived. I suffered burning in my stomach and waves of nausea. I was no longer in any doubt that I was pregnant.

Beppe called out, "We can't stay long. I have to get back."

"And I have a shipment coming in," I answered, as I warmed the pot and started making the tea. I was rushing, that had to be the reason, because just as I turned to get the cups down, my arm swept carelessly across the shelf that held my prized blue bowl. I watched in horror as it hurtled to the floor, and that was all it took. I burst into angry tears. Beppe rushed in to find me kneeling on the floor, holding the two largest pieces of the shattered bowl.

"Leave it, Marie. You'll get cut. Here, I'll help you," he said, offering his hand.

A sadness that had been gathering for longer than I could remember broke loose. I was shaking and I couldn't stop crying. Beppe's face was destroyed. I imagined him looking at the smashed bowl and thinking women were mysterious, our emotions confused, that and our habit of moving too fast in the kitchen.

CHAPTER THIRTY-SEVEN

It was as though the world had tilted and I was just hanging on. It was so oppressively hot and overcast, with air so thick I could hardly breathe. I had once loved late summer, but in my present mood and the heaviness in my body, I wondered how I would survive.

It was at the end of a long day, in which we had seen not a single customer, when Angie surprised me by coming into the store. I felt guilty for neglecting our friendship. Was she here for something specific, kitchen towels, loose powder, a honey caddy? But the way she sidled up to a bin so distractedly let me know she wasn't here to shop.

"Business good?" she asked.

"It's all right."

"I see you're getting in some new things."

"They're selling better quality at Miller's, so I thought, why not here?"

With a little cash set aside from all the driving, I'd purchased a nest of colorful bowls and a half-dozen stemmed glasses. I still owed my suppliers, but at least we wouldn't seem to be going out of business.

"Dad's dealership should have that kind of cash flow," she said with too much exuberance.

It was pure flattery, putting me in the same category with her rich father. She was here for information, so I met it head on. "I got a loan," I said.

"Oh? From The Peoples Bank?"

There it was.

"No. A family friend," I said, preparing to weave a story.

"Who?"

"You don't know him." I was most like my mother when I frustrated their curiosity. "Let me show you the new stock."

Beppe hadn't approved a loan, but he brought me gifts. A carton of men's work shirts and snap caps, which I convinced myself wouldn't be competing with the Oletskys—though in the end I decided not to put them out. But I gave a prominent position to a display of small hand tools, which sparked memories of New York. I had Kenny take down the old peg boards that were worn and peeling, and replace them with the tall, fresh-looking unit. Then, so as not to make the rest of the store look bad, we worked on the surrounding shelves, waxing them to bring up the shine.

Angie stood patiently as I took down items for her inspection. She wasn't getting what she'd come for, a hint about my relationship.

"Wait," I said, "You must see the new egg beaters."

They were stacked in a gleaming tower, and next to them, a pile of crisp table linens, small squares and rounds with cheery patterns. These were a gift from Kenny, from a supplier friend of his, who could get his hands on good domestics at a fair price. Kenny was still making reparations for the cheap Christmas stock, so I'd promised to order more from his friend.

Angie's eyes fell upon the replacement blue bowl. "I like this," she said. "How much?" The Pullias were one of only a few families with spare cash. I could have named any price.

"I'm sorry Angie. It's already sold."

"Sold? To who?" she asked, looking indignant.

"A lady who lives down on the lake. I never give out the names of my customers. Let's just say they can afford it."

I was determined to bring the bowl back to Beppe's and my apartment, to replace the one I'd broken. Life was good, and bad, and women had their arms around all of it. We dealt as best we could with enormous piles of troubles. If we could make ourselves happy by giving in to the occasional luxury, why not? I wanted to believe my fate, one handed down through an unbroken chain of women, a life full of chipped crockery, frugality, and drudgery, might be cheated by the vision of that bowl. Meanwhile, Angie seemed lost, as though the bowl had acted on her as well, causing the most fantastic dreams. Maybe she could escape the horror of the mating ritual. In her case, a trip to the altar with Bobby Cavuto, with his big ears and bad temper. Angie, I thought, why don't you fight me for it? Buy the damn thing, take it home and let it sing to you. Then one day, when something goes wrong, and you're high with emotion and running to keep pace, you'll move your arm too fast—likely as not, you'll be in the kitchen—and down it will come, smashed to bits. And you'll think, not only have I wasted my money, but maybe my whole life.

Because it's years into the future, and the whole time you've been putting up with Bobby Cavuto.

"I've got to go, Marie," she said, jarring me from my daydream. She touched my arm. "It's nice to see you. I was thinking we should get together."

"I'd like that."

"Are you all right, Marie? You look a little pale. You should go sit down."

"I was up late," I said, smiling.

As soon as she left, I asked Kenny to look after the store and I went upstairs, but I couldn't relax for long. The second icebox in the storeroom was completely full with my baking supplies. In the heat I couldn't afford to leave anything out. And with sacks of flour everywhere around my kitchen, I wondered where I would put it all.

I was thinking about Angie's comment about my cash flow. I had to admit it wasn't as bad as all that. It was a small miracle I had so many cakes to bake. My most pressing problem was how I would I get it all done.

CHAPTER THIRTY-EIGHT

We were having an Indian Summer, which normally I enjoyed. But every morning I woke feeling nauseous and though I tried not to, I ended up losing my breakfast.

Sammy telephoned to say he would be driving down from Camden on Saturday. After the fight with his brother that put him in the hospital, two months ago now, he'd been spending more and more time with Gloria in Camden. He still worked in the store on weekdays, but I rarely saw him on weekends, and I sensed he wanted to talk.

I had a nice lunch prepared. I poured us each a glass of wine, and we sat in the kitchen like the old days. The apartment had been so quiet without either of my brothers, now Sammy filled the room with his manly shoulders.

"Have you heard from Ada?" he asked.

"No."

His eyes were full of emotion, so boy like, I thought, cool and sad at the same time.

"I liked her," he said. "Maybe we should invite her up to Camden for dinner. It would be closer for her, coming from Philly. Can you believe Mr. E. was once engaged to Mom?"

"What?"

"You didn't know? It was back in Campania."

That's when Sammy told me the story. Mom had thought Salvie was too old for her. He would have been around thirty then, and she was seventeen. So this was before she'd met our father and they'd come to America. I recalled the lines of the song Ada had asked him to translate: *My girl has left me. I'm free at last.* And his expression, crestfallen, but also angry.

Sammy leaned across the table and lay his forearm on top of mine. "It's okay, Sis. I thought you knew. At the party Ada told me she'd visited and told you about Mom, so I thought..."

I recalled the moment when Ada was leaving the party, how she'd leaned in close, and I'd thought she'd said, *Be careful with Esposito.* But her breath was rich with red wine, her accent thicker than usual, and I couldn't be sure of her words.

"Marie?" Sammy was shaking my arm.

"I can't believe it."

"I know," he said laughing. "We're all related."

"No. Mr. E. isn't related to us."

Gloria was Mr. E.'s niece, and of course Sammy wanted us all to get along. I liked Gloria, but that didn't change my mind about Mr. E., the vulgar way he treated me and the violence he encouraged in Gino. Sammy didn't know about Mr. E.'s *passes*, a gentle word to describe what were really attacks. I thought of telling Sammy and only hesitated because of Gloria. I wondered, had Ada known Mr. E. was in Littlefield?

I said, "I can't understand why Ada didn't tell me she knew him from before."

But Sammy seemed to have lost interest, and I felt old, from the generation still obsessed with what had gone on back in the old country, too preoccupied with the past.

"Have you heard from your brother?" I asked.

I'd spent not a second thinking about Gino, but I wanted reassurance that he wasn't coming back.

"I doubt he'll show his face. I went over to see Ruth and Gersh. I apologized. I feel responsible."

"You? How did you have anything to do with it?"

"I should've stopped him."

"You couldn't. No one could."

"Marie, I came for the rest of my things."

Though I had known this day was coming, the words landed on me like a hammer.

"You'll have your life back," he said quickly.

What life?

"We're only in Camden. You can come up. I want you to see our apartment. And when we come here, you can make us dinner." He laughed, knowing how I hated to be asked to cook.

"If you ask nicely," I said, teasing him. I tried not to appear sad.

"I already talked to Kenny about taking over some of my responsibilities. He said it's no problem. He can handle it."

Sammy had always been my ally in any dispute. If a supplier was difficult or if Kenny refused to do what I'd asked, Sammy often stepped in. Without him here, would Kenny again try to trick me into buying inferior merchandise from one of his relatives? Who would stand up for me? A long silence followed in which neither of us spoke.

"You're not going to work here at all anymore?"

"I can do a couple of days a week, for now. I'm trying to get a job at Campbell Soup in Camden. He took a sip of wine. "Listen, Marie. There are a lot of single guys around. And you're great looking."

"Get to the point."

"You should be dating someone you can be with."

Someone to be with. What if I told my sweet brother I was sure I was pregnant?

Sammy went to pack. I cleared the table and tried to keep busy so as not to hear the empty hangers clanging, the opening and closing of the closet door. I pushed open the window so I could be distracted by the sound of Kenny whistling on the loading bay. When finally Sammy's cases stood in the hallway, I had to lean against the wall.

"Marie, I gotta go. Walk me down?"

"Sure. Oh sure."

There was a noise in the distance like someone drove a tractor down the main street. Sammy and I stood for a minute in the downstairs doorway, "I bet it's DeLucca's truck," he said. "The clutch is shot." He was so serious. I studied the strong neck twisting in the direction of the vehicle that had made the noise. He still had one foot in the town.

"Guess I'd better go."

We hugged, and the smell of his neck was as precious to me as that of a child's, making me want to hold on tighter.

"Let me know how you're getting on," I said. "And don't forget to send my love to Gloria."

I turned quickly and hurried up the stairs so as not to see him go.

CHAPTER THIRTY-NINE

I was jarred by the sound of the downstairs buzzer and ran quickly into the living room to peer down. I was afraid it was Ruth, and there'd been another incident. But then I made out the shape of a woman's straw hat and the suggestion of a skirt, which told me it wasn't Ruth, who would have been bare-headed and wearing her apron.

Ada stood on my doorstep. She was dressed too warmly, but she didn't appear to be bothered by the heat. In contrast to the night she'd come to dinner, she was serene, self-possessed, and carried what looked like a doctor's case with a brass latch that could be locked. Stepping toward me, she held me at arm's length and looked me up and down.

"Ada, we have to talk," I said.

I had been rehearsing what I would say. I was furious she hadn't told me that Mr. E. had been engaged to our mother, and that Ada had known him from before. But I couldn't stay mad, because Ada's hair under the straw hat was captured in a snood at the nape of her neck, the same way Mom had once worn hers. She took me in her arms and we hugged. A second later she was charging past me up the stairs. I followed her into the kitchen, but I'd lost the urgency to confront her, and instead watched her pause to stare at the spot where I'd set out my tools: sifter, spoons, spatula.

She snapped open her bag and I got a glimpse of what looked like an apothecary, with rows of dark vials full of leafy shapes and matted mossy substances. Each bore a white label with the vial's contents written in Italian, followed by the English. Her fingernail lingered on the vial marked, *digitale/foxglove*. Then she handed me a red rose, which I hadn't noticed before, and without explanation took down Mom's mortar and pestle. She extracted a small bottle of chlorophyll from her bag, went to my kitchen window and looking down at the loading bay, said, "Downstairs. We go."

"What do you need?" I asked. She didn't answer, but stared frankly in a manner that didn't allow for questions.

"Dirt," she said, holding out her cupped hand.

My big pot of basil was in need of refreshing, so I led her onto the sunny main street and, checking to make sure no one watched, steered her toward Ruth's planter. Without hesitation Ada plunged her hands into a burst of red geraniums and came away with two generous scoops of soil.

Back in the kitchen she filled a cup with water then led me into the living room. Her eyes drifted to the bottle of corked wine I kept on the sideboard, evidence of my nightly sip. I expected a scold, but she only uncorked the bottle and poured a tiny amount into a small glass bowl.

"Sit, Marie."

Ada knelt on the floor in front of me. On a piece of paper she drew:

"What is it?"

"Digitale." She got up, disappeared briefly into the kitchen, and came back with the rose. One by one she tore off the petals and lay them in the shape of a triangle around the drawing, while directing me to look down at what she was doing. When all the rose petals were laid, she began speaking in Italian:

Presentarmi a questo spirito. The rest was rattled off with such speed I had no hope of understanding. She put the mortar and pestle down on the floor, while continuing to tap the pestle rhythmically against the mortar as she recited this list:

> *Seme / seed*
> *Germoglio /sprout*
> *Radice / root*
> *Foglia / leaf*
> *Bocciolo / bud*
> *Fiore / flower*
> *Frutta / fruit*

I recognized only certain words, *fiore, frutta, seme*. And at this demonstration of Ada's old world superstitions, I pictured Mom saying, *Da da da fortuna! Get away from me. You are bad luck.*

She raised the mortar and passed it over the paper with the drawing. To the cup of water she added three drops of wine using a dropper she'd pulled from her bag. Next she dipped the pestle into the water and applied it to the rim of the mortar as she said in English: "Spirit of digitale, please join. I release seal. Now!"

"Marie!"

I was jarred awake by her urgent whisper, "You want what?"

Her handsome face was inches from mine. She reminded me of La Befana, the witch on a broomstick, as she held up a long index finger, "You want? Not too many words!"

Forced to think quickly, I said, "I want…" She nodded, encouraging me, and the wish flew from my lips. "I want my daughter to inherit the store."

She picked up the paper and placed it into the mortar, then rested the pestle on top. The weight of the pestle pressed on the paper and created what looked like a piece of frilly dough awaiting its sweet filling. Her eyes were closed. *How had I not noticed the similarity in their hands?*

"You leave this," she said, pointing to the set-up on the floor. "Twenty-four hours. Then pour water. Paper must soak. Put in a ball like this. Squeeze. Make round shape. Then bury with dirt. Clean this," she said pointing at the mortar and pestle. "I leave now."

I opened my mouth to speak, but she held up a hand, "It is done," she said, packing up her things.

Heavy-lidded and drowsy, I led her downstairs. Then it happened the minute the door closed behind her. I forgot everything. I returned to the living room and noticed the altar. It was then I received what the religious text of St. Teresa of Avila called the gift of tears. My understanding, from what we'd been taught in Catholic school, was when God gave us tears, he gave us the gift of tears, and we were never to apologize for crying. Not that I started crying right then, but that I felt enormous relief. It was the most shimmering bliss, then it was gone.

My strength returned, I went to the kitchen to begin a batch of cupcakes, and the whisk was never so efficient, the ingredients never so smoothly blended. My old oven even managed to hold its temperature, and condensation failed to form on my kitchen window. I had welcomed a stranger, one I still did not know, but who knew me.

CHAPTER FORTY

I was sluggish, lacking in energy, and my breasts felt as though they were about to burst through my dress. But as bad as I felt, I dragged myself to Ferrara's because I needed flour, and there I caught sight of Mrs. Romasello. She had never been a friend of Mom's. Carmela had thought her an ignorant, merciless gossip. She glanced in my direction, then turned abruptly and disappeared. I thought, *Viola knows.* She thinks I've gained weight and can't wait to tell her friends. I could have fled the store or caught up with her and forced her to say hello to me. Instead, I finished my shopping and left carrying my heavy bag, careful not to look right or left in case there was someone else wanting to stare. It was then I noticed the black cloud forming. How I loved a good electrical storm, and I wished for lightning, huge claps of thunder, and the pleasure of that release.

I was almost at my door when I saw the Ashworths' sedan pull up outside of Dan's Stationery. A second later Priscilla Ashworth was swinging her legs out of the car. She paused and gave a brief, distracted smile in my direction. I was sure she hadn't recognized me, but I felt a sudden connection, two women sharing a man. Later that afternoon I lay doubled over in my bedroom, having thrown up everything in my stomach. Lightheaded and dizzy, I telephoned Ruth.

"Can you come right over?" I wanted her to hold me as Mom would have, as Mom had done whenever my imagination exploded and I invented a worry. This time the fear was real. I had crossed a boundary.

"I'll be right there," she said.

We sat at my kitchen table, and my nerves burst. "I feel so sick, Ruth. For a few weeks now. I have no energy. And I'm throwing up—not just in the mornings, only it's worse then."

"Do you think you could be?"

"Maybe."

She stared at me with such intensity, I started crying.

"What have you been using?"

"Using? He has…"

Ruth waited.

"Rubbers."

"I see."

"But we don't always. You know, I count the days. And once or twice—and I hate doing it—I washed inside with Lysol. Just a mild solution."

"Okay now, you listen to me." She covered my hands with hers. "Everything is all right. Take your time and tell me."

It made me extremely agitated to say out loud what I'd visualized too many times—a scandal the whole town would soon find out about. I was sure customers were coming in just to ogle and they rarely bought anything. Perhaps more telling were the faces I no longer saw. Mom's friends and their daughters who'd once come in to pick up a lipstick or a fan, to buy school supplies or tea towels, no longer did. Was it the Depression, Gino's behavior, or was it finally my transgression? It was a miracle the phone continued to ring with cake orders, but for how long?

"Does he know?"

"Not yet."

"And you went to New York," she said.

"How did you know that?"

"Sammy told me."

"When?"

"That night..." She paused and stared at the floor. She meant of course the night Gino threw the nail barrel through their window. I almost apologized again, except I knew Ruth didn't want it mentioned.

"Sammy told you I was with Beppe?"

"Beppe?"

"Joseph Ashworth. I call him Beppe."

"Oh." Ruth smiled. "Where did you go in New York...with Beppe?"

"The World's Fair. It was so wonderful, Ruth."

She didn't say anything for a full minute. "So what now?"

"I don't know!" I cried out, just as a gust of wind rattled the kitchen window. It was a *folletto*, a knot of wind, which everyone knew was a spirit, one who turned up in the middle of a *situation*, particularly one having to do with sex.

"You should see a doctor," she said. "Have you done that?"

"No."

"I can take you. She got up and started to fix us some tea. "There's one I know of. In Roseview."

"I think Angie's mother knows who he is."

"Now that's interesting," said Ruth with a sharp laugh.

"He's one of *those* doctors?"

"Unless it's too far along, but it doesn't seem so. He'll say whether you are. You don't want to go to Agnoli here in town."

"God, no!"

She looked directly at me. "I had one once," she said. "It was the wrong time. The wrong man."

Who was this man, and why couldn't she have a baby with him? Was that before Gersh I wondered? I had so many questions.

"You didn't want children?"

"I wanted them. But with Gersh. Not with that other man. Then it didn't happen, with Gersh."

"Did you regret, you know, the other one?"

"No. Never." I could see she didn't want to say any more about it. "I'll find out about the doctor. I can take you. You have friends in town, Marie."

"So do you," I said.

We held hands. I thought about mentioning Ada, but I was too emotional. Ruth smoothed my hair like I was her child. As soon as she left, I went to the ex-voto and took down Mom's *Materia Medica*. Rather than one of those doctors, how much better it would be to calmly sip tea in my own house. I pictured the herbs arranging themselves under my fingertips. The tea would be bitter, but I could bear it.

CHAPTER FORTY-ONE

Please help me, Mom.

As I whispered these words, I felt the warmth of her arms around me as I sat in the little room where I kept her things. The ex-voto's sole window was high up, and with a storm coming the room no longer felt part of this world. From my seat on the floor I watched the tops of trees on Orchard Street bend and sway. Normally, I opened the *Materia Medica* and flipped to a page at random, but today after several tries, having been offered cures for heartburn, aching joints, and warts, I went deliberately to the index and looked up abortifacients.

I read about each herb. Pennyroyal, blue cohosh, cotton root bark, angelica, mugwort, and even parsley was reported to work. I didn't yet have a plan, nor did I know what I wanted. I closed the book, placed the spine between my legs, and allowed it to fall open to a page where a very thin blue ribbon had been tucked into the binding. I had never noticed it before, but I recognized it as a stay—those small straps added to the inside of a gown's bodice to keep it from slipping from its hanger. *Mom, which of your dresses had this come from? And did you have a pregnancy we never knew about?* The page described artemisia, or mugwort, the "mother herb."

In the chalky light, with the ribbon in my hand, I conjured my mother. Just as Bernadette must have squinted to see the sudden image of the Holy Mother, a flash of blue and silver dissolving at its shimmering edges, my eyes misted over as I willed her to intervene. I curled up next to the book and fell asleep.

So much sleeping. It took me with gentle force. I became tired several times during the day, but at night I got a second wind. The Five & Ten was a lovely place after everyone had gone home, full of age and care and history. I dreamed my mother leaned on the penny candy counter, a smile trained on the children whose eyes became saucers at the sight of those clear jars full of sweetness and color. And in that moment, I heard her say, *Here, take another.*

CHAPTER FORTY-TWO

My kitchen was an oven. Not only was I working harder, I barely had time to fix my hair, or to loosen the waists of my work dresses. I was tired all the time, yet on my cheeks was a rosy glow, as though I'd had too much wine. Looking at me, no one would have guessed at the turmoil inside.

It was the warmest September in memory. Usually my cake business went dead just as the children were going back to school, but this year the phone didn't stop ringing, and already this week I had two orders. I sat in the store and watched the lazy ceiling fan make its slow turn, then the small screech as it tilted before righting itself on an endless rotation that marked the minutes when business was slow. I went into the back room to clean up a mess left by Kenny. He always managed to leave a little cardboard, some excelsior or string on the floor of the stockroom, which I would stuff into an empty cardboard box with the message, *I cleaned up your mess. Now you can do the rest.*

As I was walking back into the store, I saw a woman standing outside. At first I thought she was window shopping. She gazed at my displays, leaned in closely and cupped a gloved hand to the glass. Who wore gloves in this weather? Nor was it possible to see inside past the yellow film I'd installed to help cut the glare. Then I recognized her. Could she see me as clearly as I could see her? Why not come inside, I thought, and we can talk. But Priscilla Ashworth only stood there for several more seconds before turning abruptly and walking away.

Mrs. Bellafiore, who I was always glad to see, came in and lay her large satchel on the counter, a soft smile on her wrinkled face. I loved Mrs. Bellafiore, and no less since the day she'd given me a stern warning about Gino. The words had felt harsh at the time, but just days later Gino launched his awful attack on the Oletskys.

"I thought I'd bring these," she said. From out of her bag she took a stack of crocheted doilies in bright fruit-like colors, lemon, peach, orange, blueberry. "You said you could sell these. I thought we should try." She had the same direct manner as Mom.

"They're beautiful, Mrs. Bellafiore. How much do you want for them?" I hoped she understood I couldn't pay her anything up front.

"Oh, I don't want anything," she said, and clutching my hand with sudden pressure, delivered her news. "Louie's wife is expecting."

So these were in payment. My God, I thought, old Louie Bellafiore had managed it, and all it took was one of my cakes. I stepped out from behind the counter and hugged her. "That's good news," I said. "But I can't accept these. I would love them in the store. I want them, but when they sell, you will be paid."

"I won't accept it," she said, tears appearing.

"Please don't cry," I said. Just then I was gripped by a wave of nausea, which Mrs. Bellafiore noticed.

She put a hand out to steady me. "Don't worry, Marie. And let me know," she said, pointing at the doilies.

I displayed them next to my stack of table linens. It was good to have a bright shot of color. It was also good to have something to do, which made me forget, if only for a few minutes, the sight of Priscilla Ashworth.

When Kenny returned from lunch I rushed upstairs to rest, but immediately the phone rang. Without so much as a hello, Mrs. Vitolo launched straight into what was on her mind. "Marie, do you think you have special powers? Like you can make something happen if you want to?"

I heard the skepticism in her voice. She, like so many Italians in town could play the *scold*. Whatever magic I possessed, she doubted my right to have it. Yet she wanted to believe. It was as if I were Bernadette in the garden with the nerve to have seen the Virgin.

"No, Mrs. Vitolo, I don't think I have special powers." If I had the power to make anything I wanted happen, by now I would have a gleaming new store with lines of customers stretching around the block, my lover would leave his wife, Sammy and Gloria would come to live with me and work in the store, and I would fire Kenny.

"He's recovered, you know."

Gone was the skepticism of a minute ago. Jimmy's doctor was no longer of the opinion that he had a heart condition. Rather he believed Jimmy suffered from nothing more than a growth spurt. It had been a year since Mrs. Vitolo had ordered that first cake, now her son was better.

"I'm so happy," I said.

"You did it, Marie."

"It's just good luck, Mrs. Vitolo," I said.

We hung up, and I had just sat down when the telephone rang again. It was Beppe wanting to meet.

"Marie, we have to talk…" There was a smile in his voice. He was trying to sound light. But I could tell there was something on his mind.

"I can't," I said.

Could it be the loan? We hadn't spoken about it since the argument when he'd given Gino as the reason why he wouldn't consider it. If it weren't for the sugar runs and the money Mr. E. gave me for allowing him to use the loading bay, the store would no longer be open. Thankfully, my baking business was thriving. Beppe had to have known I still needed the money. *You'd better be careful. I'm in no mood.*

"I'm alone in the store," I said.

"Where's Kenny?"

"He's not here. And I'm expecting a delivery."

Loretta had cut herself while chopping vegetables. She was fine, but feeling faint and Kenny had gone home. A further annoyance was not knowing the exact time of the shipment. But Beppe insisted, and so I did something I had never done, I put a sign on the door saying I'd be back in an hour.

On the way up Bellevue Avenue, I was calmed by the gentle whoosh of oak leaves in a warm breeze. Yet in their color was a hint of Fall and my mood wasn't the best. I wondered if I might tell Beppe about Ada. I would thank him for the items he'd bought me for the store, and the new cake mixer. What I wouldn't mention was his wife peering in the window; nor would I tell him about the pregnancy, at least not yet.

He was already there when I arrived. He stood abruptly, on his face a look that told me something had happened between our phone call and now. It was exactly like the last time, after Gino's fight at the Oletskys'. This lover, this proper man who valued politeness and propriety above all else, managed to hide his feelings until the moment he had me in front of him.

"Why, Marie? I don't understand. Why does anyone need to manufacture illegal liquor anymore. Since it's *legal.*" He flung his arms out wide. His voice rose like a professor grilling a dimwitted class. "It's not worth the risk."

"For money?" I asked.

"It's illegal, Marie,"

"I never know what's in those trucks," I said quickly, which wasn't exactly true. "I was only driving what Mr. E...."

"You drove the sugar up yourself?"

He walked past me into the kitchen. I heard him pour a glass of water. Then he cursed, followed by the sound of cupboard doors slamming. He came back carrying a bottle of whiskey and two glasses.

"I don't want one," I said.

"It will calm you down."

"You're the one who needs calming."

Without looking at me he poured himself a double shot and took a swig. His chest rose and fell. A minute went by. The whiskey was relaxing him, but I was furious.

"Why don't you ask me how I'm going to manage without my weekly *cut*?"

"Cut? What cut? So you're taking money from sleazy bootleggers? What lawlessness is next?"

"Lawlessness? How dare you accuse me of that! What did those bankers do that made some of them jump out of windows? Or shoot their business partners? What was going on there?" Sounding braver than I felt, I pressed on. "Have you had to fire a servant? Stop throwing parties or hiring women to cook for you? Go without a driver? If you have, I haven't noticed."

He put down his glass. We stood facing each other. He took a step forward and tried to embrace me, but I moved away. This wouldn't be settled with a hug, a caress, promises, or tears. And it wouldn't lead us into the bedroom.

"I'm pregnant," I said.

I was aware of the sound of birds and the soft drone of cars passing on the street below. The fan chugged more loudly in the corner, and my heart was audible in my ears. I felt overwhelmed at the same time as my senses were sharpened. But I could no longer stand up, and so I went to sit at the ugly round table, which today looked especially bare without a vase of flowers. There, with my head resting on my arm, I examined the room at a slant.

"Are you sure?" his voice was oddly gentle.

Slowly, I sat up.

"Yes. I'm sure."

"Have you seen a doctor?"

"No."

"Well, then." He took a handkerchief from his pocket and passed it across his face. "Marie…"

We both knew this could happen. Had I been so naïve to think, as we lay together and talked—if not directly about a future, then seductively about our lives—that one day we might be together? What were our sessions of love, if not a kind of commitment? Would he at least acknowledge that a baby was always a possibility? How could it come as a surprise?

He threw back the rest of his drink. He sat down, leaned forward and sank his head in his hands.

"Priscilla was pregnant when we got married. That's *why* we got married. We were in love. Then we weren't. Then she lost the baby." He sounded angry. "Now she can't have children. Believe me I've been thinking about telling her…about us." He looked up and searched my face as though the answer was written there. "How do I say?" His eyes were full of tears. "How do I say, look, what isn't possible with you I'm having with somebody else?"

I didn't know what to say. There were long pauses between sentences, and I fell into every one like stepping off a cliff.

"I don't expect you to answer. I don't expect you to solve this. It's up to me. I know that."

"Then leave her and be with me!"

The words were out before I could think. I was aware of straining toward him as though I could affect his answer. But he only gave me that look of sympathy I hated, like his love couldn't be expressed without the corresponding need to feel sorry for me. When really it was the inadequacy of his actions, how he'd jeopardized first his marriage, then failed to act on our situation that really made him sorry.

Was I meant to behave like those women in the pictures I hated? The heroine, poor and debased, accepts her lover's version of the situation. Instead of the strong woman she believes herself to be, she makes decisions based on shame and the need to hide.

"Marie. You have to be patient."

It was as though he spoke to a child, someone to whom he didn't owe a full explanation.

"Your wife was at the store today."

He stood up. "What did she say? Did you tell her something?"

"What would I tell her?"

"Would you tell me if you had?"

"Of course. She didn't come in. She was outside. Peering in the window."

"That's ridiculous."

"You think I'm lying?"

"No. It's just not like her."

It was almost a thrill, to feel it all coming to a head. He seemed, if not exactly sad, then confused. Maybe he still loved her. Maybe he loved us both.

"Isn't this a good thing?" My voice, strangled, showed too much emotion.

"Marie, calm down."

"Is that all you can say?" I looked directly into his eyes, "I don't know if I want *it.*"

"What?"

"The baby."

"It's my baby," he said.

"No, Beppe. It's not yours. It's mine. *If* I decide to have it."

What did he expect, that I'd sit down and calmly take up a basket of knitting?

"What in God's name are you talking about? I have to think, Marie. Please. Let's discuss this when we're calmer."

"I'm perfectly calm. You have no idea of the shame," I cried. "The whole town is a threat. I look around and think, who's talking about me? Who will stop buying? The town decides whether I eat or not. You have no idea."

I hated the pleading sound in my voice, the all too familiar story of the other woman. I knew I sounded unreasonable, but I delighted in his look of panic, his innocent, clueless surprise.

"I know we can't go on like this," he said.

The situation mocked him, this privileged boy raised to believe everything happens for the best. Isn't life grand? After each rite of passage, a car on his eighteenth birthday, a brothel at twenty, he was assured a smooth path. All he had to do was put one foot in front of the other, like a sleepwalker.

I gathered up my things.

"Marie, please, wait. We have to talk."

"When you're ready," I said, and left the apartment.

I walked home without seeing or hearing, and every normal beat of the heart felt like an emergency.

CHAPTER FORTY-THREE

I needed to distract myself, or I would give in to despair. It had been three days, and still no call. Since it was a Wednesday, I decided to go to the movies. I was still trying to finish my dish set. I was just three flat plates and two bread and butter dishes away from service for six. Oddly for Dish Night, the lobby was filled with young people who seemed to be on dates, so I pretended to be just another young, unattached woman there to meet up with friends. I took my place in line, and when it was my turn I stepped to the counter, ready to collect my plate, but was handed a cup and saucer instead.

"What's this?"

"We've run out of dishes. I'm sorry. This is all we have."

"I'm here to get a plate."

"I'm sorry," said the girl.

"Well I don't want these," I said, handing them back.

A woman behind me sighed, and I turned, ready to commiserate, thinking she, too, had come for a plate, but I could see by her expression that she was irritated with me for not taking what I'd been given.

"What are you staring at?" I snapped. I turned back to the girl. "You can keep it."

"How rude!" said someone from further back. People were turning to stare. I felt the walls close in and the air turn suffocatingly warm. I was hurrying for the door when in walked Angie with Bobby Cavuto.

"Marie! Are you leaving already?"

"It's so hot," I said, looking around and fanning myself with a flyer.

"Are you okay?"

"Fine. I think I got something in my eye," I said, worried they'd notice I was crying. So I made a show of pulling on my eyelash.

Angie said, "These B pictures aren't very good. We just had to get out of the house after a big lunch at Bobby's mother's. Huh, Bobby?" Angie gave him a small affectionate poke.

Bobby Cavuto was older than we were by almost ten years. He was like an old man already, his big frame increasing in bulk, his mother's food destroying the former linebacker's body. He would soon be enormous.

"Look!" said Angie, thrusting out her hand. Bobby pointed, making it known he was the proud buyer of the large, sparkling ring.

"We're engaged!" Her voice rose to a sweet, defiant pitch, and people were turning. "It's pear cut," she declared.

"Congratulations," I said.

Here was my oldest school friend with her big prize, a man with the means to buy her things, to set up her life so it would be as smooth as possible. I imagined when she looked at me she saw a tragic existence. Poor Marie, in charge of a store, and having to manage men and worry every single day about money.

Angie tossed her thick cloud of hair, and with a dramatic eye roll, said, "We spent the morning shopping for furniture, didn't we Bobby? He likes comfortable furniture. So that's what we're buying." She shrugged, as though this was her cross to bear.

I moved to give her a hug, and whispered, "I have to go."

"No, stay. Sit with us. Come on."

"I'd love to, but I can't."

At home, I sat in the living room enjoying the violet dusk. I delayed for as long as possible the drawing of curtains, the turning on of lamps. After a while I went to put water on for tea, and at the moment I returned to the quiet living room, in the fading light, I felt a presence. At first I thought it was Sammy, or I hoped, knowing of course that he was in Camden with Gloria. I waited for the sound of his door opening, his slow shuffle to the bathroom or the kitchen, a sound that, real or imagined, gave me comfort. But when I looked around all I saw was the old furniture, my mother's doilies placed on thinning armrests, and the freshly dusted breakfront minus the cut crystal bowl.

I went into the kitchen and took down the small envelope of artemisia. *How should I grind it? How to disguise a gritty texture or bitterness? Mom, where are you?* She was at rest in the ex-voto lying by the *Materia Medica*, that quarto of frayed leather with its sharp, drying edges. She was among her sweaters and books; she was everywhere. Someone wrapped her arms around me, and with a stirring rattle, I dropped my measuring spoons. Guided by a strange force, I emptied the full contents of the envelope into a pot of peppermint tea.

Yesterday Ruth had casually mentioned that the doctor in Roseview was no longer seeing patients. She was hesitant to tell me, and surprised when I took it so well. Even if we had to travel to Philly or New York, she said, she would help me find someone.

To raise a child alone, without enough to provide for that child, was like baking a cake without ingredients, running a store without stock, or putting food on the table without money. Already I had spent too much of my young life doing these things. Alone, and in the full glare of the town, I would be shunned.

I took a sip of the tea, and with that first taste, only slightly bitter, I went into the ex-voto to check the instructions one more time. The *Materia Medica* fell open to the well-used page. According to a doctor Trotula from Salerno, mugwort was the recommended antidote to the "result of love," along with its mother herb, *artemisia*, named after the Goddess of fertility, marriage and childbirth. Artemis was also known as a protector of women and children, and I saw no contradiction in her many roles, which to my mind corresponded perfectly to the complicated lives of women.

The book recommended the use of both artemisia and pennyroyal, but I'd been unable to get the latter. It said the tea should be taken three times a day for five days, and five days only, after which you were in danger of having your kidneys quit. I took another generous sip.

I went to bed early. My sleep was dreamless.

The next morning I became sick with a powerful nausea that continued even after I'd thrown up everything in my stomach. I was weak, and my eyesight was disturbed. Shapes floated in my peripheral vision. On my way down to the store I nearly fell down the stairs. It was an effort to keep my wits, while the walls seemed to grow up taller and taller, until there was only the barest light above. I told Kenny I wasn't feeling well and would have to go back upstairs, where again I fell asleep.

I dreamt of Ada. She pushed a wheelbarrow like the one Mom had kept filled with geraniums in front of the store in summer. Around and around she went on the sidewalk and, defying busy traffic, wheeled right out into the middle of the road. Heaped inside the barrow was what looked like a mound of soil, but I knew it was herbs. And each time she passed the front of the store, I waved and she waved back, while giving me a look that said, *Do you want me to come in?* This happened several times before the scene changed and Ada stood, not in front of the store, but in front of the mansion on the lake. She was waving to me, inviting me inside. That's where the dream ended. When I woke, it was as if I hadn't slept at all, and I had a vague sense of having left some task undone.

Ruth stormed into my bedroom.

"Marie! Marie! Wake up! What's the matter?"

"Nothing." I looked up and smiled. I had no idea why she was in my room, nor why she was so concerned. It was as if I were still asleep and Ruth was part of my dream. My body grew very tall and thick, and my chest inflated until it reached my chin; it was as though my whole body was swollen.

"Something's wrong. I'm calling Dr. Agnoli," she said.

"No. Don't call anybody."

"I am." With that she left the room and I heard her dialing, but I was too weak to move or protest. When I woke up, Dr. Agnoli and Ruth were standing over me. I asked what was the matter.

Ruth knelt down and took my hand. "You've been asleep for a day, Marie. You almost lost the baby," she whispered in my ear.

Almost?

She leaned closer, "He was here."

"Who?"

"Ashworth."

"When?"

"Last night."

"What happened?" I tried to sit up but Dr. Agnoli put his arm lightly across my chest.

"You rest, Marie. I'll stop in later."

Dr. Agnoli's orders were that I was to stay in bed for a week. I spent the next day sleeping, and was vaguely aware of people coming and going. By the second day I felt well enough to get up. Mimi stopped by with a casserole. She told me not to worry. She was spreading it around town that I had a terrible cold. To Kenny, I pretended I'd tripped on a rug and taken a fall.

Sammy had evidently come down from Camden and sat for hours at a time holding my hand. He'd made me broth and toast, but I was too groggy to remember. Mimi remarked on how good he looked, grown up and happy. She was glad he'd recovered from his injuries, and for a second I thought of Gino.

On the third day, I was in a fit of delirium. I dreamed, and from time to time woke to the unnaturally quiet apartment. Hours later I was feeling better, but then I burst into uncontrollable tears. Finally, without questioning whether I should, I swung my legs over the side of the bed, and paused. What was on the floor?

What looked like tiny seeds formed a neat row, as though some very organized bird had laid a table for a large family. Who would do this? It couldn't have been Ruth. She didn't believe in spirits and wouldn't know the first thing about warding them off. Nor Mimi, though as far as I could remember she had been the last visitor. Nor could it have been Sammy. Then who? I recalled Ada and her wheelbarrow. Was I meant to leave the seeds there? Were they seeds? I bent to inspect more closely and succumbed to the sweet, sharp odor of crushed clove. Purification, love, lust, and wisdom were some of its properties, as were the prevention of nausea and the banishment of negative thoughts. In the end I decided to clean them up, and a good thing too, because minutes later Ruth rushed in. She was anxious to give me the details of Beppe's visit.

"How did he know to come?" I asked.

"I called him. I hope that's okay."

"Was Dr. Agnoli here at the same time?"

"I called Agnoli first. I called Ashworth right after he left."

"What number did you call?"

"The bank. Don't worry, I made up a story. I said I was a cousin. I said I had information about a car he was looking at."

"Was it a new Packard?" I asked, and we both laughed.

"Gersh and I were so worried."

I took her hand.

"Marie. He looked so sad."

Later that afternoon I dialed his private office number. I hoped the right words would come once I heard his voice, but I was caught off guard when he answered right away.

"Are you all right?"

There was the sound of a door closing.

"I'm fine."

"Are you sure? You looked so pale." His words were tender. I wanted him to hug me, to come over and rub my back. He said instead, "I have to go away for a couple of days. I promise I'll call as soon as I get back."

"Where are you going?"

"I have meetings in Philadelphia, and I can't get out of them. I'll be back on Wednesday. I'll call you." Then, after a pause. "I'm glad you're *both* okay."

"I don't want to hang up."

"I know. God, I know."

His voice was shaky, and I felt the distance between us.

"I can't speak to you until after your trip? Why bother calling when everything will be the same? If we don't talk?" I was crying now.

"We will. I promise."

"Why can't you come over now?"

"I can't, Marie. I'll call." He paused. "I'm happy," he said.

"As soon as you get back. Promise."

CHAPTER FORTY-FOUR

I lay on the sofa and thought about what I'd tried to do. I felt shattered and broken, but had no shame. I had dreamed of waking up to a memory tinged with sadness, but with a feeling of relief. I had expected, and welcomed, a different outcome. I wanted to be free to resume my duties in the store, not just for myself, but for Sammy, Kenny, and all future employees. I longed to be the woman I was before I became pregnant. I wasn't reconciled to having a baby, but I also lacked the strength to make an alternate plan. I knew I could count on Ruth's help, but having tried it once and failed, the urge to fight had left me. My botched effort was like waking from a nightmare with the certainty one would rather die than have to repeat the frightening event. I still wanted to be free. Had the tea worked, I wouldn't now have the slightest regret.

When Kenny telephoned to tell me everything was under control in the store, he was gentle. He said I wasn't needed and that unless I wanted to come downstairs, I should stay where I was and rest. I appreciated his sensitivity because I was still feeling so sick. Dr. Agnoli had said I was dangerously dehydrated and ordered me to drink as much water as I could hold down. I took another sip and lay back against the pillows.

I thought about Beppe and his wife. I thought about the town. It was as though there were crowds with me in the room, and I imagined people on the street looking up at my windows. I felt spied on from all sides. Eventually, I would regain my strength, but how would I face my customers? I couldn't remain in hiding.

Sleep had been taking me in short bursts. One minute I had energy, the next I was off on a series of hazy, troubled dreams. I cried for my mother; I summoned her. Then a strange thing happened. I felt a presence, like a spirit had crept into the room. Who was this woman?

I must have dozed off, because I was woken by a sharp sound that was nevertheless a recognizable pattern, three sharp tones followed by a longer one.

I was weak, and moved slowly as I went downstairs to answer the door.

"Ciao," said Ada, gliding past me and up the stairs. I followed listlessly, not caring whether she noticed I wasn't myself, but she hardly looked in my direction. Not even when we stood in the kitchen did she acknowledge me. Ada, with her sharp perceptions and sixth sense, seemed utterly oblivious to the change in me. I was certain now that Ada had sprinkled the herb around my bed, that she had been right here in the apartment, witness to my condition.

"How is Salvie Esposito?" I asked.

She shrugged, a strange glint in her eye.

"You knew him," I said. "I could see," referring to the night of the picnic on the loading bay.

She took from her purse a cookie cutter in the shape of La Befana, the witch meant to bring good luck. I had found an identical one among Mom's things.

"We both have," she said, reading my mind. Then, "Flour?"

I was completely out. All I had was a little potato flour, and I could only imagine the gummy batter that would result.

"Show me," said Ada.

I took out what I had, while she took down my mortar and pestle and began mashing an herb she took from her bag. With a silent aim of her jaw, she commanded me to find my identical cutter.

"I'm too tired," I said. "Besides, *Befanini* is for Christmas."

"Cutter? You have?"

"Why are you making these now?" I asked, leaning against the door jamb and feeling faint.

"Anise. Still fresh from summer," she said. Finally, she seemed to notice the state I was in. She took me by the elbow and led me to a chair. She withdrew a vial from her purse.

"Digitale?" I asked.

"We use. In Campania."

"Then you moved north."

"Yes."

Would she admit she'd known Salvie Esposito in Italy?

"Befanini is northern," I said.

"Si. Your father love them."

I flinched at the mention of Giuseppe Genovese.

Their history was as Sammy had said. My mother and Ada had come originally from the south. This, of course, explained the spells and the superstitions that were considered backward and primitive by Italians from the north.

Gino rejected pasta in favor of risotto and polenta. He wanted to clean up our southern Italian past. I wanted to feel powerful, too, and I wanted to be an American, but I had a foot in two worlds. Mom had worn one of those dreadful scapulars in honor of Our Lady of Mount Carmel. The two holy pictures were meant to be worn, one against the back and one on the chest. "Whosoever dies in this garment shall not suffer eternal fire," read the message, along with the image of St. Simon kneeling at the feet of the Virgin on July 16, 1251. The scapular was a Carmelite tradition and the wearer pledged to observe chastity. Every year on the 16th of July, Italians paraded down the main street of Littlefield and the way they honored Our Lady was by pinning money to her plaster statue and playing their sad horns. I was just a child when I first noticed Mom's scapular, which she wore not on her upper body, but around her waist, pressed against her belly. I was revolted and I refused to wear one.

Ada had settled back in her chair and the mood turned heavy. I detected a secret.

"Were you and Mom close? Did you tell each other things?"

"Yes, oh yes."

"How did Mom meet my father?"

Seconds turned into minutes. I waited.

"Your father. Giuseppe and me. We in love."

My father? In love with Ada?

Why had he married Carmela if he was in love with her sister? Did that mean Giuseppe had never loved our mother?

"Mom never told me," I said.

She spoke slowly. "He tried to find me. After Carmie. But I hid. He wanted both. First Carmie, then me. Ha! I'm here now. I don't need him."

My father alive, as of five years ago?

"Where is he?" I held my breath.

"He has new family," she said.

"Here?"

"No, no. Italy. He move back."

I couldn't remember him—I was too young when he left—but only last night I'd had a vision of us together. Someone who is missing, or long dead, can appear. Even someone you never liked can suddenly fill your heart with the desire to remember. Nothing is ever really gone. Air and ash in a vast bowl. Vesuvius.

Abruptly, Ada leaned in toward me, on her face a look of horror. "Vesuvio!" she whispered. It was more of a hiss. She had read my mind.

"I get out! Mama died. Disease," she said shaking her head. "We were babies. Then our father leave. No mother. No father."

"What disease?"

She didn't answer.

Often I'd heard Italians in town delivering snippets of the past in such random bursts that quite a bit of assembly was required.

"Vesuvius. We scared all the time," she said.

I had heard of these calamities. If it wasn't disease, it was a natural disaster, or the economy collapsing. You could only hope they managed to land one at a time.

She got up and began making the dough. I went to the ex-voto to find my cutter and together we stamped out the cookies. We worked without talking, but once they were in the oven, Ada continued her story as the kitchen filled with the sweet fragrance of Befanini.

"Your father *save* Carmie," she said.

"Save, how?"

She told me how Salvie Esposito had tried to force Mom to marry him. So Ada was finally ready to admit she'd known him from before. She went on. How Mr. E. had promised Carmela money and a good house. He made it seem he was a friend, and he was always hanging around.

"He…" she stopped.

"What?"

"Carmie thought he too old. She only seventeen."

"Ada?" I could tell there was something else.

"She afraid he rape." She shook her head.

Afraid?

"Did he rape my mother?"

"I not sure. I say no more."

"But you were friendly to him the other night."

"It's a long time. He harmless now."

"Did you know he was here, in Littlefield?"

"Noooo. I not surprised. Everyone from Avellino end up in towns. The same."

She explained how, by agreeing to marry Giuseppe, Mom had managed to escape Salvie Esposito. The sisters had talked about it. There were no parents to object nor anyone to protect her from Mr. E. had she stayed. Ada agreed to give up her boyfriend so her sister could flee to America.

"I was sad," said Ada. A dark look flitted across her face.

All those conversations by the back door between Mom and Mr. E. began to make sense. Was she having to fend him off the whole time? I had always thought Mom extremely independent, strong, but there was Mr. E.'s help, the money, the contacts, his interest in the store, and in us. She needed him. I could only imagine how he pressed his advantage. And the other night after Ada had excited him, I was the victim of that excitement. Was he thinking he might work his way through all the Parodi women? If he were in front of me right now I would strangle him.

My head was reeling with the story of such a barbaric old country, of uncomfortable compromises and arrangements. Had Mom ever loved Giuseppe, or did she trade one captor for another?

Ada shattered the silence with an exclamation. "*Le Befanini.* Ready!"

In addition to the aniseed and digitale, what else had she slipped in? Or how could the cookies have turned out so well using only potato flour? We looked at one another as we bit into the delicate crispness. My aunt seemed happy. She seemed free. What did she see when she looked at me?

CHAPTER FORTY-FIVE

Mr. E.'s friend called to tell me the soda fountain was ready to be delivered, and Kenny came up with a good idea for how we could do the installation without closing the store. We would move the racks of school supplies and find a new spot for the bins that were full of knick-knacks, ash trays, and Chinese slippers that weren't selling anyway. The delivery coincided with back-to-school sales, fall was one of our busiest times, but if the counter worked as I planned, the new business would more than compensate.

I was in the middle of making a custard when I heard the squeal of a truck's brakes. Thinking it was the fountain, I ran downstairs. But there was only Kenny on the shop floor, looking worried.

"What is it?" I asked breathlessly. Next to him was Howie, Corley's delivery guy. "What's going on?" I looked from one to the other.

"I'm sorry, Miss Genovese. Corley told me to take back the stock. He said he tried three times to get paid. He feels bad, but he needs a check. Can you give me one today?"

Kenny refused to look at me as Howie began packing up my nice, large pieces of soda glass.

"I can't today, Howie. But I can pay," I added quickly. "Kenny, in the office. Now!" I led the way, before closing the door. "I should fire you on the spot."

"What are you talking about?"

"The missing hundred dollars. Don't pretend you don't know. It was your handwriting. On the check. That money was to pay Feldman, and Corley for this shipment."

"Gino said it was okay."

"So you admit it? And what right…?" I stopped. "Did Gino take the money?"

"I don't know. I guess."

Whatever truth lay at the heart of the matter, I wouldn't hear another word. Kenny would endure torture rather than betray Gino. I disliked him for it, but he was as frightened of my brother as any of us. "You were busy, Marie. It was right before you went to visit your *cousin*…"

I walked out, and said calmly to Howie, "It's okay, I'll call your boss. I'll get a check to him. It's not your fault."

I watched as my beautiful display was emptied. This is how women migrate, I thought, from one catastrophe to another.

The counter was a miracle. The marble was flawless, apart from a couple of tiny chips where you'd expect them to be, along the edge where a cash register had sat. Otherwise, it was perfect, and I pictured customers seated on—how many stools were there—seven? It was with Carmela's confidence that I stood with my arms folded and watched them manhandle the counter into place.

"You're too close to the door jamb. Careful! Don't chip the marble."

They unloaded the stools first, and seeing them come off the truck, with their red vinyl covers and shiny chrome, filled me with hope. But my excitement was nearly ruined by the appearance of Mr. E. I could see he was in a mood, and I thought: Go ahead and be angry because I ordered not just the counter, but the stools. And what, exactly, is your excuse for failing to mention you knew Mom all those years ago? And what about your crime? Ada could hardly bring herself to say the word, *rape*.

"Let's go upstairs," I said, turning away from his sour-looking face.

Maybe it was the effect of being in the kitchen, but he seemed less grouchy once we were seated at the kitchen table. Maybe he was tired. He wasn't a young man. Always old, I imagined, scheming, lining up his next conquest, in business and personally. Always in control, until he wasn't, and then you were treated to a sullen face or worse. I'd sworn not to let him come near me ever again, yet here he was. He peeled back the paper of the cupcake I put before him.

"Mari. Delicious."

"It's my new red velvet. I'm glad you like it."

He ate with his head down, lulled by the sugar and cocoa and my secret ingredient. I'd only had that dreadful hoop cheese, but I'd managed to whip it into the consistency of buttercream. I was getting good at substitutions. And I didn't spare the most important ingredient of all, anise. I watched as he sat back, patted his stomach.

He couldn't know that Ada had told me the story. He probably figured he was safe, since they had been speaking in Italian. So many secrets, normal in Naples, a dirty, ignorant place, according to Mom. She probably thought she had left it all behind, the intrigue, the grubbiness, only to have Salvie Esposito follow her here.

I wished now that I'd added something stronger, the rest of my black hellebore, or a little belladonna perhaps. But a second later I saw the dimming of the light in his eyes, and a confused, vacant expression. His attention drifted to the window and the sky above the loading bay.

"I take care of counter, Mari," he said, like someone wandering the night in search of a place to lay down his head.

"Thank you," I said.

"And lights to help the counter."

"Thank you," I said, again.

"And I send a man down to work out what needs for plumbing. What else, Mari?"

"Corley needs a check," I said.

"Yes, Mari. I take care."

CHAPTER FORTY-SIX

The men worked all day and into the night installing the counter, and I remained downstairs to watch the work. Ruth came in and was very complimentary. It was a day when no one wore a frown or seemed worried. It was the promise of sweet things, of ice cream with toppings, cookies and slices of my baked goods.

The long, black slab held a console with ice cream tubs. There was a neat row of fountains for pulling soda, Coca-Cola and root beer, and it fitted perfectly, as though it had been custom made. My tower of Dell paperbacks looked good at the counter's end, creating a break between where customers sipped sodas and others shopped. For 25 cents, the price of a pack of cigarettes, you could get a novel with a racy cover. I wasn't sure I should be selling books with pictures of women wearing trench coats open clear up to their thighs—some aimed guns, others fainted in men's arms—but the need to drum up business soon settled that question. When a distributor friend of Mr. E.'s offered to extend credit, I ordered the Pocketbook Tower without hesitation. As soon as the books arrived, a group of girls and boys came in and huddled there, whispering. I made sure to leave them alone, hoping they might pool their money and buy one. But if they lingered too long, reading and flipping pages, I called out, "Buy it or put it back!"

I was disappointed that Gersh didn't come. I hadn't seen him for weeks. I had even thought of hosting a small fundraising event, where I would sell cakes on a Saturday, our busiest day, and donate the proceeds to the Oletskys for the repair of their front window. But when I mentioned this to Ruth, she said, "Don't bother. Really, I don't want to hear that night mentioned ever again."

After Ruth left I went upstairs to lie on the living room sofa. I was fanning myself with a magazine when the telephone rang. Knowing it was probably Beppe, I didn't want to seem anxious, I let it ring a dozen times.

"How do you feel?" he asked, sounding concerned.

"I'm much better," I said. And I was. My energy was back. There was color in my face, and I had altered a couple of dresses in an effort to minimize my expanding figure.

"I have your loan papers ready," he said.

"What loan papers?"

"It's time we made it official."

"Make what official?"

"The loan. To give you money for the store. I know you need it, and I like the sound of the improvements. I heard the counter was delivered."

How did he know?

"Wait until you see…" I began.

"Two o'clock?" he asked.

"Yes. Two o'clock."

"I'll bring the papers. I'm proud of you, Marie," he said, hanging up.

It was then I recalled my dream of the night before. Ada had been waving at me from the bus stop. A second later I was running to the ex-voto, where I knelt in front of a pile of boxes. *Mom. I have a name for her. Your middle name, Catherine.* For I was certain I was having a girl, and this would be my gift to Mom. Finally, Beppe understood how important the store was to me. Now our baby had, not just a name, but a future. By loaning the money, he was making a commitment to me and to *her*.

I walked into our apartment, and there he was, smiling like a man about to bestow a gift. The same air of confidence as when he'd watched me open that thin, velvet box at Christmas. This time, on the round table lay a sheaf of papers, and next to them his nice pen, the one he kept in the inside pocket of his jacket. He pulled out a chair for me. He didn't even wait for me to put my handbag down.

"I'm sorry I didn't call sooner," he said, taking me in his arms. "I've been so busy." He kissed me long and passionately. "I wanted to prepare these before I saw you. As a surprise." He held on to me for a minute more before motioning for me to sit in front of the papers.

"You're strong, Marie. You're fighting to keep the store going. I admire that."

"Thank you, Beppe, but why do I have to sign papers?"

"It's a loan, Marie. And I have a board to answer to."

His tone was halting, like that of a patient father working out the right words to use on a daughter who wasn't completely under his control.

"What are the terms?" I asked.

He looked surprised. Don't you dare laugh, I thought. I know all about charging interest. Whenever he became serious, I glimpsed the banker.

"There's a modest amount of interest on the loan, Marie. The payments are spread out over ten years. That's the longest term my board would allow."

I lowered my eyes and began reading, but I had hardly finished the next paragraph when suddenly I couldn't breathe. Seeing my reaction, he said, "I had to, Marie. Before you say anything…"

My eyes had fallen on the signature, Salvatore Alphonso Esposito, in the spot marked co-signer. Mr. E., the co-signer of my loan? And, he had already signed.

Was that how Beppe had found out about the counter?

"I have to have a guarantee, Marie. The board wouldn't…"

"You're the president."

"I have a board…"

"You went behind my back to Salvie? Or did he come to you? The two of you together?"

"No. For God's sake!"

"When did this happen? Why didn't you tell me?"

Now there was a phrase for my headstone. It would read: Here lies Marie who was always wondering, *Why didn't you tell me?*

With a shaking hand I squeezed his fancy pen. I felt the sweat run between my shoulder blades, my head was light. I couldn't fool myself about my intentions. I would welch on the debt. Did he really think there was extra money lying around to pay off a loan? He obviously didn't care who owned the store, but did he realize who he was handing me over to? Of course he didn't know about Mr. E.'s scheming, the attacks, the history. But what about the baby, to whom the man standing next to me owed so much? Yet, if I didn't sign, my floors would never be refinished, the metal ceiling wouldn't get a fresh lick of paint, there would be no money for stock. Worst of all, my child would inherit nothing.

"If I can't pay, who will own my store?"

242 • ITALIAN LOVE CAKE

"He will have to cover the loan. You know as well as I…"

"But you don't like him."

"Marie. I don't think you should worry about that now."

"Not worry?"

I would have told him everything if I wasn't afraid of confirming what Anglo-Saxons already believed about us, that we were all rapists and schemers. I wasn't trying to spare Mr. E., only myself, from the reputation of that brutal Old Country where deals were cut and alliances made in exchange for freedom, opportunity, food. Of course, the same thing went on here, the evidence of which was right in front of me. The unceasing opportunism, vultures hovering, ready to strike. This was how the world worked. I had stopped short of saying I felt preyed upon by Mr. E. The store was the only thing I had control over, and if I signed, I wouldn't even have that. I felt the last of my independence draining away.

"Did he come to you? Or did you go to him?" My voice was low, weak.

"Esposito called me." This wasn't a surprise.

"What about my brothers?" I was almost afraid to hear.

"What about them? Your name is the only one on the title, Marie. You don't owe…. Did you discuss putting in the counter with them? What decisions are they involved in? And where is Gino anyway?"

"I won't sign."

He tried to put his arms around me, to offer comfort. But there would be no comfort, no love making, no celebration of the improvements. I was used to feeling like a child around men, but it took me by surprise every time. I was ignorant of the most basic ways of the world. I got up to leave.

"Marie, wait."

"Can't. Thank you, Mr. Banker."

"Marie, please, don't call me that. This is the future for the store. Sit down. Let me explain."

"And if I can't pay…"

"Default."

"And if Mr. E. covers the debt he will own my store."

"Not entirely. He will have a financial stake, yes."

"Financial stake. What does that mean?"

"It means you will owe him the money he put up to cover the loan."

"And if I can't pay, and he can't, or won't, what happens then?"

"The bank will own the store."

"You?"

"No. Not me. The Peoples Bank. I'm not the bank, Marie. I have…"

"A board. Yes, I know."

I sat down again.

"Marie," he pulled out a chair and sat close to me. "This is your future."

"Whose future?"

"Yours. Please."

He wanted me to sign, take the money and be done with it. The alternative was to be trapped in my present situation. I picked up the papers. I took one last look, then I tore them in half.

Neither of us spoke. I left without shedding a tear, and on the way home I talked to myself: *You think you're in control, but you're not. The men follow the rules, while you break them.* Furbo e fesso. *Clever and stupid. You are both.*

I managed to walk the three blocks without seeing anyone. At home, I made myself a cup of tea and stared out at the loading bay, where I'd left a line of washing flapping in the wind. My underthings were in full view, which had never bothered me before, except once when Gino snatched my girdle down and started waving it around to make Sammy and Kenny laugh. I realized how much I'd ignored in order to maintain what Mom called *positive looking*. What was the point of that, I thought now, when it was so obvious they didn't even see *us*, women, at all. Our emotions, our ambitions, the respect we sought and deserved were a mere pile of crumbs.

CHAPTER FORTY-SEVEN

At the first hint of winter air the street filled with shoppers. I recognized neighbors, classmates, and some new faces. People were suddenly needing warmer clothes, and Ruth was starting to sell scarves and gloves. Now that I had the counter, I looked forward to an uptick in business, and I fully expected Christmas this year to be better than the last.

The counter's first customers were people I knew, but soon strangers began turning up. Had they heard about the fountain? Or had they been on their way to Atlantic City and happened upon us by accident as they stopped in town for gas? I would have been more optimistic were it not for the chain stores that had begun moving into neighboring towns. They were bound to siphon off customers. In nearby Roseview, the family-owned Milners was bought out by Waples, and right away they put in a bigger housewares section. I knew this because Ruth, pretending to be a customer, had made a thorough inspection and reported back. There was no way the Five & Ten could compete, she said, not against their selection of kitchen appliances, skillets, china ware, and range of domestics—tablecloths, blankets and bedding— which only reinforced my belief that putting in the counter had been a wise decision.

I was actually selling more than before, and at the end of the day there was a little cash in the drawer. Nothing like business before the Depression, but people would come in for an ice cream and end up looking around and buying something. Mr. E. was still running goods through my bay and giving me my weekly cut. Thankfully, this week he'd handed the payment to Kenny, so I didn't have to see him. He was avoiding me. I wondered if he'd found out from Beppe that I hadn't signed the papers. If not, I couldn't wait to tell him.

I hadn't spoken to Beppe in days, not since I'd walked out. At least I'd stood up for myself, and over that I had absolutely no regrets.

A fresh tray of cookies was baking, and while I waited for them to finish, I curled up on the living room sofa with one of my paperbacks, careful not to bend the spine or fold a page, so I could place the book back on the rack. The stories were tawdry, and I might have felt embarrassed, except they had begun to sell, slowly at first, before word of mouth got around.

When the cookies were done, I used my heaviest potholders to carry the hot tray downstairs, and I was thrilled to see four people seated at the counter, and it was only a Wednesday. I figured the matinee must have just let out. A woman paused, holding her spoon to her lips, just as her friend leaned in close to her and whispered, "These are delicious." She'd been munching on one of my butter cookies with a cherry pressed into the middle. There was such pleasure on their faces. You occasionally heard the word *war* spoken in subdued tones, on the street and in the aisles at Ferrara's, but never in the Five & Ten once the counter had been installed.

I had gone to stand behind an aisle of merchandise so I could watch Anthony, my soda jerker. Maybe it wasn't the matinee, or my cookies, but rather the polite, lovely looking Anthony, who attracted them.

I went back upstairs feeling pleased. The apartment was welcoming, full of the sweet fragrance of vanilla and butter. I was just settling back into my book when I noticed another smell, this one coming from the stairwell. I followed it downstairs, and when I opened the door to the street, a spiral of smoke curled upwards and wafted past. The fragrance was familiar from countless Masses and holy days. It was frankincense. At my feet was a small metal cup holding a lighted piece of coal, and on top of that a sprinkling of crystals. Using my skirt as a potholder, I lifted the cup and carried it inside.

When had Ada left this?

It was late by the time I got back downstairs and Kenny and Anthony had both gone home. I stood on the warm floorboards and closed my eyes. I placed my hand on the spot where my waist once was, and the future walked into the Five & Ten. I saw a row of nail barrels, and floor-to-ceiling cubbies filled with household fixtures, decorative handles and work gloves. Reflected in my new mirror was a gleaming display of hoes, rakes and spades.

As night came on, the town began to fade as if behind a veil. Street noises were muffled, and one heard fewer cars. It was always like this, that we in our stores were hardly aware of the others, the ones on the farms, down rural lanes, or at the end of a long, winding drive terminating at the lake.

CHAPTER FORTY-EIGHT

Mr. E. called. He had my envelope. We had managed to speak civilly to one another the day the counter was delivered, but at the sound of his voice my stomach fluttered.

As soon as he arrived I thanked him for paying Corley, and he complimented me on the look of the store. I walked him past the new hand tool display, the one Beppe had bought. I knew he thought I'd signed the papers and that these items had been bought with the money from the loan. I let him think it.

He gave me a jar of local honey. His good friend Massimo kept bees, and the hives were healthy; they'd swarmed twice this past spring. He let me know he had several more jars. "I share with you, Mari."

Was this generosity the effect of my cupcake? Or was he worried that Ada might reveal the truth about him and his bad behavior toward our mother?

Anthony was behind the counter serving a customer, so I walked us back to the office where we wouldn't be overheard.

"There's something you should know. I didn't sign your papers. I tore them up."

"What, Mari?"

He had pretended not to hear. He lowered himself into a chair. Was he having a heart attack, or was this drama? But I saw the wheels turning. I knew how these old Italian men thought. They hung around, sticky as fly paper, hoping to wait you out.

I closed the office door.

"I tore up the papers. I don't want your money. And you will never own my store."

"I don't want the store, Mari. I only want to help."

"Ada told me everything."

"What everything?"

He had been sitting, but now abruptly he stood. "I deserve respect, Mari."

Never before had I contemplated a violent act. I took a step closer.

"Mom. Italy. No use lying."

He had a strange look, as though he anticipated what I was about to do, which only provoked me. I raised my hand and brought it down hard against his face. He stepped back, and for a second I thought I'd gotten away with it. I was pregnant, after all. But a second later he was on me. He grabbed a hunk of my hair. He sweated disgustingly, and I almost felt sorry to have provoked him into showing this side of himself. I pictured him pinning Mom as he did me. I could scream, which would summon Anthony, but then everyone would know. I managed to shove him off. Then I picked up a stapler, and stood with it held high, ready to hurl it at his head. In Italy young women had no voice. But we were in America now. He wanted the double prize of taking me physically and financially, but I would never give in to him.

He stepped back. I rubbed my head where he'd grabbed my hair.

"Don't come back here," I said.

"Mari. I'm sorry. We both mad. It's just a mood."

"No."

He took a step closer, but he wouldn't touch me. He was trying to prove he wasn't rattled by what had just happened. First he threatened, a second later his energy seemed to drain away. He backed out quietly and left. Immediately, I went upstairs and sat at my sewing machine. The only way to calm myself would be to sew. I swiped my arm across the table, dislodging bobbins, spools of thread, needles and my scissors, which hit the floor, blades open. I picked them up, hoping they weren't damaged. I grabbed the suit I'd been working on and not being at all careful began hacking away, sewing furiously and stomping on the pedal. The fabric flew beneath my fingers as I ran up new seams. The machine clattered loudly in time to my jagged breath.

CHAPTER FORTY-NINE

We had been warned to save fabric, and I could make two skirts out of one if I removed the pleats and cut very thin panels. It was bad enough to suffer the indignity of an expanding figure, but to wear dowdy clothes seemed an unnecessary insult. The scandal of the short skirt was no longer a scandal, even if the decree was meant more for women who weren't pregnant. So with the War Production Board's permission, my hems rose. And while the new fashion for men was the "victory suit," without cuffs or much lapel, Beppe's suits seemed the exception, generously cut and as roomy as Roosevelt's.

I walked across to the bank and handed Louise, the head teller, a box of cookies. "For you and the girls," I said.

"Oh, how thoughtful. You know we all love the fountain. It's just what this town needed."

They gathered around and helped themselves and while I lingered, making small talk, I looked around the bank, hoping to catch sight of him. Reading my mind, Louise said, "Mr. Ashworth is out of town. Again!" She rolled her eyes and the other girls laughed. She said, "We don't mind. We can take cookie breaks."

"It will be our secret," I said.

Back at the store, I was hardly through the door when I was waylaid by Anthony, my charming soda jerker. He had something he wanted to discuss. I was in no mood, but I could never refuse him, especially when his little paper hat came to such a crisp point at the exact location of a pale birthmark that did nothing to mar his handsome face. I led him into the back room and pointed to a chair, but he refused to sit.

"Marie, I have to quit."

My first reaction was to laugh. Surely, this was a joke. I knew he needed the money. I waited for him to ask for a raise, which I would agree to on the spot. I had been expecting it. Besides, he was always willing to work Fridays and Saturdays, the fountain's busiest days.

"I got another job," he said.

"Where?"

"A shoe factory."

"What shoe factory?"

"Millhurst's."

"The place out on the Pike?"

How was making shoes better than scooping ice cream?

"What's the pay?" I would match it. Anything to keep him.

"Fifty dollars a week and I get to go home at five. No weekends."

"Fifty dollars? How can they afford it?"

I paid him less than half that, and he was always willing to stay as late as I wanted. He folded his nice arms across his chest, across the ice cream-stained apron. The light brown hair on his arms was like the downy fur of a cat.

"They got a big war contract making boots. Boots the soldiers wear. Pretty incredible, huh? They ship them overseas."

I had all but stopped listening as a truth hit home. To own a store was to operate in a different world from the one where money flowed not from customers, but from a big, powerful government gearing up for war. The optimism I'd heard from Beppe and from Mr. E., who always seemed to have money in his pocket, was because of this other economy, one I didn't have access to. They could get contracts and be paid unimaginable sums for manufacturing staples like shoes and olive oil. What benefit could I manage to snag?

"Who owns this factory?"

"The big banker in town. What's his name? Ashworth. Across the street." He plugged a thumb in the direction of Beppe's bank. "Hey Marie, if it's okay with you, I can ask my cousin if he wants this job. He's too young to work in the factory, but he can scoop ice cream."

How come I didn't know Beppe owned a factory? What else hadn't he told me? Did he have another family someplace? A second wife and children, another mansion, more cars? In that second, at the height of my panic, I was convinced my lover had many lives, like a con man.

"Marie?"

I sat down and stared at the wall. After a while, when I still hadn't spoken, he left. I went back out onto the floor to sit behind the register with the Montgomery Ward catalogue open on my lap. I avoided looking in Anthony's direction as I flipped through the pages, while seeing the stock featured there in a new light. How could midget radios sell so cheaply? The black one was $5.75, other colors were $6.55. A five-pound box of chocolates sold for 79 cents, a pound cake for 98. My cakes cost between $1.50 and 2.50, depending on the size. My smallest was twice as expensive as their largest. It was a miracle I had any orders at all. My economy was not only unique, it was precarious.

I was angry all over again. I looked at my watch and was surprised to see it was already noon. I was hungry and feeling a little faint, but I decided to unpack a small box of stock, which I would ask Anthony to put out. For as long as he was here, I would work him hard, and I didn't care if he thought I punished him.

"Can I help you?" I asked just as Mrs. Delfina came in with Mrs. Romasello. But the two only stood there and stared. I was bent over unpacking the stock, my hand resting on my lower back. Normally I would allow myself a small grunt as I straightened up, but because they watched, I sprang to my feet like a teenager.

"What is it you're looking for?" I asked, my tone cheery. Mom always used charm. I watched our customers be fooled by her lightness, her willingness to ignore rudeness, and she always managed to capture their sympathy. That same consideration would never be accorded her daughter, who was part of a younger, bolder generation. Did I imagine it or did their stares settle for a second too long on my expanding middle?

"I don't think you have it," said Mrs. Romasello, sharply.

"What is it you're looking for?" I asked again.

Neither answered me. Mrs. Delfina stared at her watch and said, "Is that the time already? We have to be going."

Would she mention that the priests had liked my fruitcake? I almost asked, but I was still waiting for the difficult errand she always brought to the store. Why didn't I stock a certain color of crepe paper? Why didn't I carry the larger boxes of crayons?

"If you don't see what you're looking for, I can always check in the back," I said.

"Oh, don't bother," said Mr. Romasello, and with that the two turned and left, their backs as stiff as their judgments.

After they'd gone, I put Kenny in charge and went upstairs. I stormed around the apartment thinking I might go crazy. And who would care if I did? I made a cup of tea, then I dialed Ada.

The woman's hello, without the "h," told me she was one of Ada's Italian-speaking friends, one of the Mortellites. I spoke slowly, hoping to make myself understood.

"È Ada lì?"

"Se n'è andata."

"Where? Dov'è andata?"

I was frantic.

"È andata via."

"Dove?"

They didn't know. The woman began speaking rapidly in a southern Italian dialect and I failed to catch another word. Abruptly, she hung up. I stared at the telephone. Why were these Italians so rude?

That night I was agitated and slept badly. I dreamt of Ada. This time she and Mom held hands, and though I recognized my mother, the woman I knew to be Ada seemed a stranger. We were in Italy. They talked about being hungry, but my attention was drawn to the men standing next to us, hunters carrying rifles and trailed by dogs. It was Fall, and the sound of gunfire ricocheted through the hills. Gunfire meant meat: grouse, deer, whatever came into their view. Finally, the woman with Mom became Ada. I recognized her by the way she tossed her raven hair, uncaring as she gave a loud, full-throated laugh.

I woke up hungry, my stomach growling. Then I remembered that Ada had gone somewhere. But where? I was dizzy, and I almost fell over as I readied the coffee while my mind welcomed a slew of worries: Beppe's shoe factory, Mr. E. and my lover conspiring to take the store, the doubtful expressions on the faces of women who had once loved my mother, but who were less sure of me.

When the doorbell rang, I was in no mood for a visitor. Angie barged past me and up the stairs. "You and I are going to set up a bond table in town. We have to start selling war bonds. Don't worry, I'll organize everything."

"Angie, please. What war bonds?" My tone must have alerted her to my state of mind, because she said more gently, "Marie, we can't let ourselves get blamed for Mussolini."

"For God's sake it's thousands of miles away," I said, sitting down.

Roosevelt was making regular pleas on the radio, and advertisements for war bonds were everywhere. He wanted *Americans* to demonstrate their patriotism. He was counting on the shame Italians felt over Italy's support for Germany to get us to work for the war effort. Shame was an effective tool, even if most in town believed a better course was to stay out of it.

I never believed that beast Mussolini and his promises of protection. It seemed men were especially susceptible, though there were plenty of women who blindly followed the dictator. And they were growing bolder. Just the other day I'd heard Mrs. Delfina speak admiringly of Mussolini's uniforms. "He looks so regal," she said. Where had she found that word I wondered? I was standing at the meat counter in Ferrara's when abruptly Eddie Ferrara left his station with the mandolin still running. He stepped to the counter with a scowl and I thought he might challenge Mrs. Delfina. Instead in his most deferential voice, he said, "Hello, Mrs. Delfina, are you still waiting for you order?"

I didn't want to sell bonds for the war effort, but there was such urgency in Angie's expression. We were all frightened. This was perhaps a way to make things better.

"Who else is doing it?" I asked.

She gave me a serious look. "Mrs. Bertolli," she said.

"You're kidding."

Mrs. Bertolli, who once said Mussolini made her proud of Italy, was now joining the war effort against him? Maybe she'd finally come to her senses, since her daughter lived with a violent man and was sometimes seen in town with a black eye. I felt mean for thinking it, nevertheless I would have liked to say *That's what you get for loving a strong man.*

"Mrs. Fiedler, Mrs. Fiorello, Mrs. Giuffre, Mrs. Bellafiore, Mrs. Bertolli, and Mrs. Rizotte. We have to do this, Marie. And we have to wear native dress."

"What native dress? You mean like Indians?"

"No. *Italian* native dress."

I flashed on a photograph of Mimi Rizotte's nieces standing in front of the Quirinal Palace in Rome, ethnic-looking in their ample blouses and those dreadful dirndls. In January, they'd attended the royal wedding of King Victor Emmanuel's daughter, Princess Maria, to Prince Louis of Bourbon-Parma, as part of a contingent of peasants shipped up from the south to show support for the northern king. The dictator himself was there, adorned in gold braid and a cocked hat, and according to the newsreels, he'd been left to sit alone.

Her nieces wore top hats. I couldn't imagine these were the fashion in southern Italy. They'd obviously been given costumes to wear for the pageant of the wedding. "I won't wear a top hat, Angie," I said, picturing their silly grins beneath those hats.

"No top hat," Angie said, laughing.

"And I'm not dressing up."

"Can you at least help me put the posters up? They're coming all the way from New York. Straight from Secretary Morgenthau's office."

"Who's he?"

"Marie! He's the Secretary of the Treasury. That's why we're setting up in the bank." Without looking at me, she pointed toward my front windows. Then, still without looking, she threw her arm around my shoulders and gave me a quick squeeze.

The next day, I mentioned the bond sale to Ruth.

"No. I won't do it. I hate the whole idea of this war. Hate it! And I refuse to help them."

"Well, I won't either, then. They want us to wear native dress. You're right. It's stupid."

"Not stupid," fired Ruth, "Two-faced. The government expects us to hawk their war bonds while this war will do nothing but destroy us."

"That club you're in. They're sponsoring part of it. What's it called?"

"B'nai Brith."

"Remind me what they do."

"It's a women's auxiliary. 12,000 members," she said with sudden pride. "We keep Jewish culture alive. It's a service organization, like the Sons of Italy," Ruth threw me a pointed look. I thought she was about to bring up the incident with Gino, and thankfully she didn't. "I heard the table is going to be at the bank. How do you feel about that? Is that why you're doing it?"

"No. I mean, it's a way to…"

"See him?"

"No!"

"Be accepted?" again, the sly look.

"I haven't seen him for over a week, Ruth. No call. Nothing. I wake up every morning feeling heavy and...old. I feel old, Ruth. I'm not, but it's like my life is over. I'm trapped. I want the baby. And I don't want the baby. I can't decide."

"It's a little late for that."

"You think I don't know?"

Though I wanted to, I couldn't tell her that Beppe had conspired with Mr. E. on a loan for the store. She and Gersh had never trusted Mr. E. and would think me a fool. Nor could I mention how my lover had stolen Anthony away, or that he had a secret business supplying boots for soldiers.

"Ruth, I'm beside myself!"

"They never leave, do they?" she said. "But sometimes there are cases." She leaned in and took my hand. "I knew of a woman once in Roseview. Her boyfriend left his wife. It can happen." She looked off into the distance. "Okay. I'll go with you. To sell the damn bonds. But it's the same with us, you know. They make us feel guilty over who we are. Then we fall in line."

CHAPTER FIFTY

It was an effort to squeeze into the black velvet bustier, and mine happened to be the smallest, scooping low across my expanding breasts. Underneath I planned to wear the costly blouse I'd bought to go with Mom's skirt except it seemed to have shrunk. I went into the ex-voto to look in Mom's old trunk and found an apron edged in lace, coarsely woven in deep purple, green, magenta and black. On the border were garlands of embroidered flowers in softer colors. To fully appreciate such a piece, one had to be a woman, not a girl. I'd often touched, but had never unfolded it to reveal its full beauty. The apron's thick nap of special threads were the result of hours of hand-stitching, and I wondered who had made it.

Unlike my other aprons, with loops that went over the head, and ties long enough to circle the waist at least twice—I had two, one I used for baking, the other for messy jobs like unpacking stock—this one was native, ethnic dress. It would fulfill the requirement. In an effort to slightly modernize the outfit, I lifted from their box my still new looking T-straps, the ones I'd taken to New York. As I stared into the full-length mirror on the back of my closet door, I thought of Beppe. I looked presentable, not too heavily pregnant, and there was good color in my face.

We gathered in the lobby of the bank. I looked around nervously as I tried to catch a glimpse of him. I worried, too, that the others might notice.

"I know," Ruth said, "I look like there's a challah on my head." Ruth's hair was covered in a long fabric scarf, braided and twisted elaborately at the back. "Okay, I'm here. Now what can I do?" She rolled up the sleeves of a long cotton blouse. I recognized the skirt, but her headscarf made her appear an entirely different person, a Ruth from another time and place.

"Mr. Ashworth said we can open the double doors so people can see us," said Angie. Hearing his name, I flinched. *When had she spoken to him?*

"We're ready now," she said, propping a large poster against our fold-out table, which held the pamphlets explaining how to purchase bonds from the bank:

> *Go up to any girl ~ Behind any counter*
> *~ They will be happy to serve you ~*
> **Be An American – Buy War Bonds !**

Minutes later Angie came over to me and whispered, "I saw him yesterday when I came to arrange where to set up. He asked me who would be selling, and when I mentioned you, he smiled."

"I'm sure it's fine," I said, nonsensically.

We finished setting up in the small vestibule between the bank's outside doors and a set of inner glass doors. The weather was cool and blustery, but I no longer felt the cold. Soon, people began coming in, and each time I directed a serious buyer inside, I scoured the bank.

By midday we were all tired from being on our feet on the hard marble floor. I was about to ask for a break when Angie turned to the group, though she looked directly at me. "There's no reason for all of us to be standing at the table."

The women were talking about the president's fireside chat scheduled for that evening, and Ruth wondered aloud if Roosevelt would mention the bond drive. "I'm almost afraid to hear. What if he wants us out here every week?" she joked.

Ruth and Mrs. Fiorello had brought sandwiches for all of us, and we ate right at the table in case people happened by during lunch, which a few did. The day dragged after that, and Angie said we might as well pack up. Though the bank closed at three, the tellers let us know that we could stay later if we wanted and they would keep the bank open. Mrs. Fiorello, who wore a small white doily on her head, which made her look like the woman on the olive oil tins, said she thought we should stay until at least four.

"Okay," said Angie, "But we don't all have to stay." Again, she looked directly at me. I appreciated her concern, but now I didn't want to go. What was the point of doing this tiresome job if I missed seeing him? I felt tears coming, but I fought them.

"Maybe Ruth can go," I said, catching her look of relief.

Mrs. Fiedler, the only German among us, had been quiet most of the day, but now she spoke, "Yes, Ruth has been here the longest. You should go," she said, and Ruth thanked her with a tight smile.

I had always liked Mrs. Fiedler, and I could see she was suffering. Her German outfit was the most elaborate, with rows and rows of lace on a crisp white apron. A lacy shawl was tucked into a tight black corset, and a bunch of fresh flowers was pinned where her large cleavage lay hidden. Out shot a tall white marabou feather from the top of her hat, which was flat and bowl shaped. It seemed the bond effort would succeed due to the efforts of those who felt the most guilty.

Ruth was gathering up her things. Over her shoulder, she said, "Marie, if you want to listen to Roosevelt tonight at our place, just come over."

Mrs. Fiorello was right. Just as people began getting off of work the lobby became crowded. It was our busiest time, and we sold more in that hour than we had all day. The head teller came out to say she and the others were happy to stay open even later if that would help, but at four-thirty we'd already started packing up.

If today proved anything, it was that Beppe no longer wanted anything to do with me. I dreaded going back to my apartment alone, so I suggested we all go to The Sweet Shoppe. But Angie said she had to get home, and Mrs. Fiorello said her feet hurt, which left me and Mrs. Fiedler, who thankfully said she would take a rain check. "You're all party poopers," I said, making a joke, but I was feeling sadder than ever.

"I can store those," I said, indicating the posters. "After all, I'm right there." I pointed across the street.

"I'll help you carry them over to your place," said Angie.

"I can help," came the voice. "I can take them up to Miss Genovese's."

"Oh," said Angie. "That's very nice of you, Mr. Ashworth. And thanks again for letting us set up in the bank."

"Anytime. We have to do this small thing. All of us have to pitch in."

"True, that's true," said Angie.

God knew what showed on my face, and Mrs. Fiedler was staring at me.

"Your costume is beautiful," Beppe said to her, and she blushed.

"It belonged to my mother, who's no longer with us."

"If everything's all put together, I guess I'll go, too," said Mrs. Fiorello.

Angie and I bundled up the last of the pamphlets. I kept my head down. "Tell you what," said Beppe. "Why don't we leave them here in the bank. You'll be doing this again."

"Oh, that would be very convenient," said Angie.

"This way Miss Genovese doesn't have to store them. We've got plenty of room here."

Angie pecked me on the cheek, shook hands with Beppe and was gone. The tellers filed past, said their goodnights and thanked us for our work on behalf of the war effort. Then we were alone. Beppe closed the front door and locked it from the inside.

We stood not two feet apart and studied one another like curious strangers.

"Good to see you, Marie."

"It's good to see you, too."

"Marie, I want to talk. I want so much to talk."

"I do, too."

"Tonight. At the apartment?"

"There's no one at my place. You could come over."

"I'd rather meet at the apartment. Do you want to?"

We set a time.

I had expected to find the place cold and empty, but he was already there and it was warm and dusted, and there were flowers. He was crouched in front of the radio when I walked in. "Roosevelt's speaking," he said, turning toward me with a smile. I had forgotten all about the fireside chat.

At the sight of him—he didn't have to drag his fingers along my arm—there was a familiar spark, and with my body full of his baby it was as though a fire burned. He came toward me, helped me out of my jacket, and we lingered for a few minutes pretending nothing was wrong.

"Why didn't I hear from you?" I finally asked.

"I'll be right back," he said and headed for the kitchen. "Do you want a drink?" he called out. Then the familiar thud of the icebox door. "The broadcast starts in fifteen minutes."

"I shouldn't have anything to drink," I said, my body heavy as I sat down on the sofa.

He came back and handed me a glass of water.

"Where have you been, Beppe?"

He took a seat across from me, cleared his throat, and leaned forward. "My father ran a couple of businesses. Actually, he ran them into the ground before he bought the bank. I learned early not to do things the way he did. I aimed higher. He taught me not to get over extended." He paused. He was looking out the window, though it was already quite dark.

"Marie, sometimes it's tempting to borrow more and more money, but it never works. I know the tough spot you're in. We just have to stay the course. That's the ticket."

"What about taking my soda jerker?"

"What?"

"Anthony. He's going to work for you."

"I don't know Anthony. Working where?"

"Your shoe factory. When were you going to tell me?" He looked shocked. "Are you saying you didn't know about my worker?"

"No. God. I would never take your employee. Never."

"Well, you did. Now who can I get to run the fountain?"

His face contorted. I waited for his explanation. He was staring at the floor. He took a sip of his drink.

"He's making a lot more money with you. That's for sure," I said.

"I don't know what to say. I'm sorry."

"You didn't know? How could you not? What else haven't you told me?" I struggled to keep my voice calm, neutral.

The room was warm. He began loosening his tie, working free that perfect knot. "I don't want you to worry." Then nonchalantly, as though it didn't require my full attention, he said, "I drew up new papers."

"Papers?"

He got up and took a document from his briefcase and placed it beside me on the sofa. A set of loan papers.

"Go ahead," he said.

Without hesitation I flipped to the signature page.

"Everything is going to be all right," he said quickly, as my eyes fell on the name of the new co-signer: Mr. Joseph P. Ashworth. Then he pointed to a paragraph he wanted me to read. It stated that he would own seventy percent of the store if the loan wasn't paid back in three years. *Only three years.* The previous note had been for ten.

"What happens if I can't pay it back? Who will own the Five & Ten?"

"I will own the store. But read on, Marie. You'll like this."

Joseph P. Ashworth, as the main investor, "will undertake repairs and upgrades as needed in keeping with Miss Marie Genovese's plans for expansion."

"You'll pay to turn the Five & Ten into a hardware store, and that's money I don't have to pay back?"

"That's right," he smiled happily.

The amount of the loan was considerable, sufficient not only to add hardware, but to do a complete overhaul of the outside, new paint and awnings. I could afford new bins and shelving.

"I'm having the kitchen repainted," I said.

"I suppose there's money for that."

"I mean I'm already doing it. I hired a man."

A special craftsman, an Italian newly arrived from Naples, was adding feather-light sheets of gold leaf to my new kitchen cornices in the shape of ivy. The gold leaf was a gift from Ruth and Gersh from the notions show in Philly where they bought accessories for the haberdashery.

Beppe listened. He pushed the papers closer.

"I'll put water on for tea," I said, needing a minute alone. We should have been talking about the baby. Like a *folletto*, she blew mischievously about the apartment, as alive in the air as she was in my body. The same experience as on the day Ruth and I had sat in my kitchen, when I first knew I was pregnant. That day, too, we had been discussing my options.

I was calm, so calm, as I set in front of us the cupcakes I'd brought, two perfect cakes made of the most delicate vanilla chiffon. The icing was a rich, velvety chocolate. I placed them on the small bone china plates decorated with African violets, castoffs from the mansion.

I took a bite. "Talk," I said, "I'm listening."

"Don't be like that. Please." His arms went around me and I let him hold me. "You're right," he said, "Everything you're planning is good." He took my hand, looked intently into my eyes. "I can see it."

I waited.

"I believe in the store, Marie. And I like your plans for adding hardware. It's going to be needed, and you're in an ideal location. With this money you can pay for a lot of improvements."

He was restless and went to stand by the window. Unconsciously perhaps, he caressed the brocade runner I'd placed along the ugly brown chest of drawers. "But you have to watch your spending, Marie. We're still in a Depression. Things could be shaky for a while."

I picked up the pen. I had already decided to sign. To him this was debt. To me it was one more brick in a wall of well-executed masonry. It was a small miracle that we still felt as we did for one another, plus this new feeling, that we were destined to be in each other's lives. I scribbled my signature and went to stand next to him at the window. He was looking down at my belly. He placed his hands there, and we forgot all about the fireside chat.

I had just put my dress back on and was sitting on the edge of the bed and adjusting the straps of my shoes, when he said, "I have something else for you. But I don't want you to open it now."

He handed me a small box, the size and shape suggested it contained a ring.

"Why can't I open it now?"

"After you get home," he said.

On the card was his neat and precise handwriting, *For Marie.*

We kissed goodbye. He said he would call the next day. He wanted me to leave first. As I walked home, I imagined what people would say if they chanced to peer out their windows and see me out on the street in the dark. *There's that poor woman, alone, and with the war coming. I hear she's pregnant.*

Back in my apartment I made tea and went to sit by my front windows. I took the small box from my pocket. Nestled in a curl of black velvet was a gold ring set with a small garnet surrounded by tiny diamonds. I held it up and inspected it, admiring how it caught the light.

The card read:

> *I am helpless, Marie. Without you I am nothing and no one. I hope you know that.*   Love, Beppe

Having long ago given up the hope of spending every waking minute with him, having abandoned the satisfying picture of the two of us seated opposite one another, our chairs separated by a warming fire or radio console, the ring represented only confusion. I looked around, and in that moment I realized how much I loved the solitude of my home. Maybe only a certain amount of suffering was possible and after that one had to let go. I slipped the ring on and sat with my hands in my lap. Then I thought about Priscilla Ashworth, how there was nothing fair about life, nothing fair under the sun.

CHAPTER FIFTY-ONE

I notified my regular cake customers that I would be out of commission for several weeks while I was having the kitchen painted. If this seemed an incredible luxury, it was. Even as people were saving money, or trying to, warned over and over again by the government to *use it up, make do, or do without*, I was happily spending. And I began wearing the ring Beppe gave me in public. Why give such a present if he didn't intend me to wear it?

But I soon learned that having cash didn't necessarily guarantee I could get the stock I wanted—the chain stores were taking up more and more distribution, and what they didn't grab, the war was gearing up to take. Rubber products like spatulas and kitchen gloves were becoming scarce. Fortunately, people were still willing to trade, and once my kitchen was back in commission I began baking seventy-two cupcakes once a fortnight for a supplier up the line who, in exchange, sent slide rules, women's fedoras, costume jewelry and Zippo lighters. I needed to offer practical items as well as small, seductive trinkets. Other products, such as undyed linens, were coarse and of poor quality and only available at exorbitant prices, and I could no longer get women's slippers at all. I'd always stocked them in a modest selection of sizes, but shoes of any type were becoming impossible to find.

Yet I'd managed to sell a frying pan that was badly dented on one side—the result of Kenny's careless handling—to a customer who didn't complain or ask for a discount. It was true I had marked it way down, but it seemed a miracle that, rather than becoming more discerning, some of my new customers complained less. Then, recently, a woman I didn't recognize came into the store and, after looking for a while at my pots and pans, cupped her hand and whispered to her friend, "Cheap! But what do you expect from *them*?" When she approached the counter to pay for a set of hand-crocheted coasters made by Mrs. Bertolli, *I almost said, I see you're buying nice handmade items with perfect stitches and beautiful yarns, made by us.* Of course I said no such thing. I smiled and thanked her, while wishing I'd put on a fatter price.

Women I didn't know began dropping in to inquire about my cakes. Who were these people who had never been inside my store before? I credited the counter. And it was a great relief when Anthony's cousin Mimmo wanted the job. He wasn't as cute or efficient, but he was always on time and never complained.

A cake for Father Barnes was a success, as was a tray of cookies for Mrs. Fiedler, and the way I found out they liked them was from the Ashworths' maid, Ella, who stopped by one day. Not only did she know what women in town were saying about my cakes, but the shy, uncommunicative Ella was full of praise. "Oh, yes," she said, "I gave them your number." Just as she was leaving, I was about to risk inquiring why the Ashworths hadn't asked for another cake, when Ella said with a shrug, "Mrs. A. is hardly at home these days."

I thought it must be a mistake when I noticed that Beppe's loan had been deposited in full directly into the Five & Ten's account, over which I had sole control. I thought it must be an error, but then I wondered if maybe he was demonstrating his trust, his belief in me and the store. Whatever it was, I decided not to mention it. I went ahead and splurged on linens imported from France, two small tablecloths, a set of napkins, and nicer candles. I even stocked a fancy nativity set that was unlikely to sell, but I was determined that this year's Christmas would be better. The store needed to appear prosperous. I pictured a line forming clear around the block once word got out that the Five & Ten was fully stocked.

But when Beppe called, he skipped over the usual pleasantries. "Marie, all the money went in. We weren't planning to release…"

"Everything will be fine," I said, using one of his expressions.

"But you want to pace yourself."

"I'm always careful, Beppe."

Whenever he neglected to cross a "t," he acted as though the sky might fall in. Whenever I made a decision without consulting him, I felt a surge of strength.

"You don't have to worry, Beppe. I've got it under control. See you Thursday?"

"Yes. See you Thursday."

With so much money in my account, I went further. I wrote up a list of items I'd only dreamed about, like the new Breakfaster, a machine that could make toast at the same time as you could fry an egg on the top hot plate. I planned to stock chaffing dishes and shower curtains. I combed through catalogues I'd once considered too expensive and ordered hand tools, a couple of ladders, and packets of seeds. There was no stopping me. I was exhilarated, exhausted, happy and overwhelmed. It was the baby. It was also the freedom of having money.

Yet I was alone, and just when I needed her the most, Ada had gone away. I'd called again and gotten the same response from the rude woman with the heavy Italian accent. Meanwhile, the pregnancy was moving along, and I felt different each day. A little shortness of breath, a small dizzy spell, but I didn't alter my schedule. I was in the store early each morning and more optimistic than I'd ever been. The counter shone like a shiny new railway car, and with customers coming in, the hum and buzz of the Five & Ten told me that the world would not stop for long, even with a war. We would somehow get through whatever came our way. Some days I felt invincible.

I asked Ruth how far along she thought I was. At Beppe's insistence I had been seeing a doctor. But Dr. Agnoli, whose kind and patient expression was comforting, offered no information apart from, *Everything looks fine, Marie.*

"Doesn't he explain anything?" asked Ruth.

"No."

"My God. Make him!"

"I get the impression he thinks it's none of my business," I said, laughing.

"You're kidding. I'll go with you next time."

In truth, I didn't know what to ask him, and I was embarrassed to admit I knew so little about the process happening to my own body. I only noticed my weight, which seemed to increase dramatically each week, and the violent activity inside that fell like a hammer when I least expected it. Why, when I was just getting ready for sleep, did the baby suddenly wake and kick? Why couldn't we manage to sleep at the same time?

With Ruth's help, I was preparing to give birth at home. She knew a midwife who lived just up the road in Franklin. The date was still months away, but with Christmas upon us and all the work still to do, we were already planning.

I was cleaning up a mess of packing material and sweeping up the dust left by a delivery, when I noticed a pile of crumpled tissue paper just where customers would have to step. I was out of patience with Kenny, and about to give him a sharp talking to when in walked Mr. E.

"Mari, I have some bad news. I try to bring the money. I don't know if I can. For how long…"

"I don't need your money," I said, wanting to get him out of the store as soon as possible. The men I'd hired to refresh the woodwork around my displays had arrived. They were setting up ladders and unpacking painting gear.

"Mari, my God, what's this?" he asked.

"I signed new papers."

"What new papers?"

"A new loan."

"What loan?"

"Mr. Ashworth and I are the only names on the paperwork," I said, in triumph. As much as I resented having any name on the paperwork other than my own, to be able to eliminate Salvie Esposito from my life gave me an intense burst of pleasure.

He stared in shock. So I decided to risk it.

"Did you follow her here?" I asked.

"What, Mari?"

I hadn't planned to bring it up, but now I seized my advantage.

"Did you come to America to try and snag Mom like you couldn't in Italy?"

"Madonna mia!" he exclaimed and threw up his hands.

"I know all about you and Mom," I said.

"Mari, we talk. If you want."

"No need," I said. "Don't let me keep you."

*

Sammy and Gloria invited me to Camden for Christmas Eve, but when Sammy told me he'd arranged for me to drive up with Mr. E., I made the excuse that I was too tired. I still held out hope that Ada would get in touch, but after my most recent call to the Mortellites, who again said they didn't know where my aunt was, I gave up. Feeling despondent, but determined not to let my disappointment spoil Christmas, I told Sammy not to worry. Since they would all be coming down on Christmas day anyway, there was no need to get together two nights in a row. At first, the prospect of spending Christmas Eve alone made me sad, but soon I began to savor the idea until, at the last minute, Ruth and Gersh invited me to their house for Christmas Eve. I said yes right away.

"Don't worry," Ruth said, with her usual cynicism. "We won't be studying the Torah." She explained that Nittel Nacht, named in the 17th century by a Jewish scholar, was their Christmas Eve, and that it began a period of restricted activity. It was also, according to Ruth, recommended that Jews play cards!

"What can I bring?"

"Nothing. We're doing it."

A friend of Ruth and Gersh's who lived in New York was coming down to visit relatives in Roseview and would drop off Chinese food from a restaurant they all loved.

"I'm going to reheat it," said Ruth. "I hope it's okay."

When I arrived Ruth said, "There's no milk in anything, so we're almost kosher. And the shrimp and pork," she shrugged, "they're disguised." She and Gersh were both laughing. I had never seen them so happy. Having decided our friendship was worth more than the dangerous ideology spreading like a flu, we'd decided to put aside the terrible incidents, and none of us ever mentioned Gino.

Ruth said, "We had to do *something* today, while all the rest of you are with your *group*."

"Ruth, I hate that. I'm not with *my group*. I'm here."

"I didn't mean that," she said, and took my hand. "I want you here, and I'm glad you didn't drive all the way up to Camden in this slushy weather. Now let's play cards!"

I compared this Christmas to the previous one. It was exactly a year ago that I'd dressed as a fashionable woman to deliver soup to my lover's home, and met his wife. This year I felt heavy as a millstone. Once or twice I'd pictured Beppe in the big house with an enormous tree, and a party, though this year no one had called to order food. And once I decided not to dwell on it, Ruth, Gersh and I had a lovely night.

What a different ritual this was. Ruth told me that the day before the Sabbath they were meant to be tearing up toilet paper in advance of the forbidden *work* of doing it on a Saturday. "All our toilet paper is pre-torn, Marie. We're all set." I was sure our bursts of laughter could be heard on the street and beyond. I never remembered having so much fun. I stayed late, well past eleven, and I wasn't even tired.

The next day, on actual Christmas, we gathered as in years past, Sammy and Gloria, Kenny and Loretta, and Mr. E., whom I'd hoped would stay away, but he was Gloria's uncle, after all. If it seemed strange to be without Gino, we soon forgot. But when Mr. E. produced a nice bottle of Four Roses and said it was a gift from Gino, I wanted to take it from his hands and smash it. Nor did I believe him. Mr. E. seemed different again, or maybe he chose to pretend I hadn't asked him about his relationship to our mother. He pretended we hadn't clashed. I decided he must be crazy.

My figure was in full bloom, and I was self-conscious. But after a small glass of wine I relaxed. There was also nothing for me to do. For once, the cooking hadn't been left up to me. Gloria and Sammy brought a lasagna Bolognese, salami, cheese and olives. Mr. E. brought wine, flowers, artichokes and roasted veal. Kenny and Loretta brought their leftover *baccala*, the salted cod that was traditional on Christmas Eve. All I'd had to do was make a dessert. So I baked an Italian Love Cake.

The evening passed without incident or tension. I wondered if I was the only one to miss Ada. I had hoped for her casting of intentions to give us a better next year. But my greatest wish was for all of us to get along, for the store to do well, and for Beppe and me to come to some agreement.

1940

CHAPTER FIFTY-TWO

Christmas sales were nothing special, but it didn't matter, because I was awash in cash from Beppe's loan. Still, I wondered why all the extra stock, the fresh paint and gleaming new counter hadn't made a bigger difference in our sales. Ruth and Gersh said that for their store, too, it had been a poor Christmas.

Cushioned by Beppe's loan, I was able to pay Kenny, Feldman, Corley, and Mimmo, my new soda jerker. The loading bay continued its midnight hum with whatever goods Mr. E. was running through. But these days, whenever I heard the trucks, I rolled over and put a pillow over my head to block out the noise, but also to dampen thoughts of the illegal activity.

Twice in a month I'd gone to the doctor complaining of odd twinges. The kicking had stopped, which concerned me, but Agnoli was reassuring. "The baby is coming soon," he said. Oh, thank you very much, I thought. I could have told you that. But I was having terrible leg cramps, and I became extremely tired every day around four. Whenever I could, I took a nap. Yet my urge for sex was incessant, and Beppe and I were meeting twice a week. I wondered what he told Priscilla when we got together at night in my apartment or in the apartment on Bellevue, because often we didn't part until very late.

Beppe seemed distracted, and we continued to argue. I was determined to have the baby at home, but he thought I should give birth in a hospital; of course he would pay, it was all arranged. I was to call him the second I went into labor and he would drive me there. He gave me a telephone number, and this person, a secretary or a friend, would know where to get in touch with him.

"What about Priscilla? What if it's in the middle of the night?"

I recalled Ella saying that Mrs. A. wasn't often at home these days. I took a sharp breath and waited for his response.

"Let me worry about that," he said.

"I don't want to go to a hospital."

"Don't be ridiculous, Marie. You have to."

We were dressed and ready to leave the apartment after an intense session of love, when he moved closer and tried to take me in his arms.

But the baby pressed so uncomfortably against my ribs, cutting off the next breath, I was unable to respond. He looked alarmed, and raising his voice said, "What do you expect me to do?"

I matched his tone. "You honestly don't know?"

Just then a mouse flitted across the carpet and skirted past my shoe before disappearing behind the sofa. With a rapid step forward Beppe got down on his knees and bent to peer underneath.

"Leave it alone!" I cried.

"Are you kidding? I'm going to catch it. We have traps in the kitchen."

"No. I don't want you to."

"Why? For God's sake…"

I burst into tears. "You can't kill it!"

"Marie, it's a mouse."

What if it was a friendly spirit? A *fata* bringing me good luck? Again, he tried to put his arms around me, and again I pushed him away. He stood and adjusted his suit. "Tell me what's wrong."

The baby kicked with terrible force.

"When will you leave her? When?"

"Marie. Not now. Please."

Was any of this real? And who was he, really? I could have ended it right there. It mattered little whether we said the words *I love you*, or didn't. That would always be secondary, if not beside the point.

CHAPTER FIFTY-THREE

I had been feeling heavy all day, unable to breathe. Dr. Agnoli had been vague about the due date, but I believed the birth to be at least a month away. After our last meeting, Beppe and I decided it was futile to discuss his marriage, the store, or the baby's birth. We were too emotional, our minds squirrely with impulses and worries. Neither of us wanted to risk another argument.

I had a list of things to do before the baby arrived. I intended to give the apartment a good, deep clean, and repair a tear in my winter coat. But I was coming slowly up the stairs from the store, having finally packed up the last of the unsold Valentine's Day stock—a job Kenny was meant to have finished weeks ago—when I had to pause in the hallway. I felt a warm liquid run down my legs. I checked quickly to make sure it wasn't blood, and I was relieved to find only clear water. The contractions began immediately and were much deeper than those mystery pains I'd had early on in the pregnancy. The pain wasn't confined to one side of my belly, nor was it connected to the frightening appearance of an elbow or a knee. Rather it was like a hotwire traced the outline of the baby in my stomach, radiating across my entire midsection like lightning illuminates the sky. I was doubled up with pain and just managed to drag the telephone into the living room, where I sat down and called Ruth.

She said she would call the midwife, and not long after we hung up Ruth was there with me. Then the midwife arrived. I explained that I thought the baby was early, but they ignored me as they set about preparing the apartment, arranging towels and putting water on to boil. In the midst of this activity, while they were making me as comfortable as possible in bed, the doorbell rang.

"I'll go see who it is and get rid of them," said Ruth.

I thought fleetingly about Beppe. I knew I wouldn't call him. I wondered if perhaps it was he at the door.

"What beautiful flowers," I heard Ruth say, followed by two sets of footsteps on the stairs, women's footsteps. So it wasn't Beppe, which made me feel relieved but also sad.

Ada stood in the doorway holding a wild bundle of flowers, hellebore and witch hazel that looked as if they'd been yanked from a neighbor's garden, except it was the wrong season. Where had she been, and why hadn't she called? And how did she know I was in labor?

"I come," she said, just as a contraction gripped me with such force that I was taken completely out of the picture. When I was finally able to speak, I said to Ruth by way of an introduction, "Ada is Mom's sister."

Ruth stared at me like I'd fallen down a flight of stairs. A second later she was peppering Ada with questions. "Have you been here long? When did you arrive? How did you make the trip over?"

"I come one year," Ada said. "Then I go back."

"What's going on in Italy?"

"How?"

"With Jews."

"The baby is early," I said, anxious to remind them I was in labor.

"Not bad like Germany," said Ada.

Ruth was getting ready to ask another question when I was felled by the next contraction. I stifled a scream. "Can I please have a drink of water?"

"Yes, Marie. I'll get you some," said Ruth, as if she was annoyed to be pulled away from questioning my aunt." Then, to Ada, "I think there's some grappa."

Ada nodded, and Ruth hurried from the room.

"*É forte!*" exclaimed Ada, swallowing the whole shot in one gulp. "*Si, si,*" she said, pushing her glass forward for a refill. "I go and wash." She threw her coat onto a nearby chair and rolled up her sleeves. The midwife looked from Ruth to me, unsure what to do as Ada took charge.

My labor lasted through the night, but I never felt afraid or alone. The pain was excruciating, but I could sometimes trick myself into believing I was separate from it. I would live through one contraction, thinking I could bear it, then the room would abruptly tilt. I fixed my gaze on the curtains swaying in the heat rising from the radiator, and this distracted me for a second.

Ada had given me a tincture to sip, which caused me to see a collection of small animals gathered on my bedroom floor. They were see-through, with glowing outlines like the neon Packard sign in the magazine advertisements. But with my next breath, the vision dissolved and the pain resumed.

Once Carol, the midwife, realized that Ada knew what she was doing, the two began working together. One would whisper in my ear, then the other would reinforce what the first had said, and so I was carried through each threshold with commands: Breathe. Don't push. Not yet. Push! Ruth kept water boiling and brought fresh towels. She made snacks and allowed me the occasional sip of tea made from Ada's concoction. The hours went by slowly. Gradually, light began appearing between the curtain's folds; I watched it change from deep blue to gray to a lovely lemon, through eyes so full of water it was as if I were crying. As dawn broke, I realized I'd lost all sense of time, while trying to temper my cries so it didn't seem as though the pain overwhelmed me.

Occasionally, I looked up to see Ada peering into the corner of the room, but it contained only my small nightstand, a copy of the *Ladies Home Journal*, and the Bible; the latter I kept out of superstition but had never opened, nor would I.

Mom was there, too. Her phantom hands were outstretched like she was ready to catch the baby, and on her face a look of sympathy.

Between Ada's forceful commands, there was the comforting feeling of warm towels pressed into the delicate crevice between my legs, still empty of a baby as far as I could tell. When suddenly, Carol and Ada both said, "We can see the head!"

"It's time to deliver this baby," said Carol, with a warning look.

"Here it comes!" cried Ada.

With the next push I fell back as the mass slithered from my body. After so much agony, it seemed easy, satisfying, even soothing.

"She's perfect!" said Carol. Having worried about missing fingers and toes, I was flooded with relief. It took me a second more to digest the glorious sound of the word *she*.

Ada placed the tiny thing on my stomach, her lovely, wrinkled body snugly wrapped in a receiving blanket. We stared into each other's eyes. Hers were unseeing, though I didn't really believe this. Mine were full of amazement and gratitude at being granted my wish. *A daughter*. I would have been shocked to learn otherwise. I had known I would have a girl.

Carol appeared with a prepared bottle, and Ada practically screamed, "No Similac!"

"Sobee," said Carol. "It's better."

"No Sobee!" said Ada.

"The mother isn't breastfeeding." Carol held her ground.

"Yes she is." Ada stepped forward, and scooping Catherine up, positioned her at my breast. Before I knew what was happening, Ada had taken my nipple between her thumb and forefinger and squeezed savagely, which caused tiny droplets of a thick white ooze to appear. "Look. So rich! Baby, here," said Ada, ignoring my pain and glaring at Carol. Ada pushed Catherine to the nipple, while pointing at my breast with the wild eye of a witch.

CHAPTER FIFTY-FOUR

Before the birth, Beppe had taken to calling me every day. But because she was early, he didn't yet know she'd been born. Still, I had been expecting his call. I'd slept for most of the two days after giving birth, and when I was awake the baby completely took over my life. The gentle pulling on my nipple was constant and also sexual, and I was filled with deep feelings.

Ruth had been staying the night, waking and sleeping when I did. *Mom, what did we do to deserve such a friend?*

Kenny was the first visitor. He brought me a bouquet of bright yellow winter jasmine. He seemed embarrassed. I could tell the milky atmosphere was a difficult place for him, and he didn't know how to approach his boss, in bed, with a tiny baby in her arms. Loretta and her mother, Mrs. Monastra, hovered behind the door. They were dressed all in black like crows, which made me wonder whether they might be heading to a funeral straight after. I motioned for them to come in.

"Who called your Aunt Ada?" Ruth asked, when we were once again alone.

"I didn't," I said.

"When were you going to tell me about her? She looks like Carmela." Ruth stared off, and neither of us spoke. She was angry with me, and if it weren't for my fragile state, she would have said more.

The baby was asleep in the crook of my arm, and I felt Mom in the room. "I wish she could see her," I said. The tension of the previous weeks and months broke suddenly, and I cried uncontrollably in Ruth's arms.

"Now, now," said Ruth. "Everything is okay."

"I have to call him."

"Do you want me to?"

I nodded yes, and Ruth slipped out into the hallway.

"He's coming right over," she said, returning. She went to find my lipstick and helped me fix my hair.

"My bed jacket. The silk one. Over there," I pointed at the hook on the back of the door. The jacket was made of soft, peach-colored silk, padded, with intricate embroidery on the collar and cuffs. For months, I'd been planning to wear this on the occasion of his first visit after the birth.

The baby wanted feeding again, and Ruth offered to heat up a bottle. So long as Ada wasn't here, we could do what we wanted with the feeding. But my breasts were protesting, and I stuffed cloths into my nightgown to absorb the leaking milk.

I was fussing and feeling anxious when Ruth came back with the bottle. "Calm down," she said. "Have you thought of a name yet?"

"Yes. Catherine. I'm calling her Catherine."

I held Catherine as she took the bottle. It seemed she might sleep.

I waited, my eyes trained on the door. It was the strangest thing after such an ordeal to hear my lover outside in the hallway talking with Ruth. So much had changed in so short a time, as though it were now accepted fact that Beppe and I were together.

"Marie, dear Marie."

There was a look of surprise on his face. He paused in the doorway, in his hand a large bouquet of pink roses, which Ruth took from him before disappearing.

"I'm so happy. I'm so glad you're all right."

"Of course I'm all right."

I pictured what we looked like—me in my silk bed jacket and Beppe in his suit—like Loretta Young and Tyrone Power in *Love His News*.

At first I thought Beppe might frighten the baby, his face was so close to hers, but her teal-colored eyes drifted blindly. We, her parents, were staring transfixed, when suddenly her tiny face scrunched and turned bright red, followed by the sound of the diaper filling. Beppe and I dissolved into uncontrollable laughter.

"Was it terrible, Marie?" he asked, his face attempting seriousness.

"No, Beppe. Not terrible."

I couldn't describe the pain because it had faded from memory, replaced with a sore bottom and aching limbs and the agitated excitement of getting so little sleep.

"That's good," he said, peering down into the tiny face. "What will we call her?" He seemed so earnest I didn't have the heart to say I'd already chosen a name. It hadn't even occurred to me to wait, to consider him in the decision. Of course she should have Mom's middle name; there had never been any question that she be named Catherine.

"What do you think of the name Catherine?" I asked.

"I love that name. I think it's perfect. She looks like a Catherine," he said, leaning in closely. "But Marie, this diaper definitely needs changing."

"Could you ask Ruth?" I said, laughing.

When we were alone again Beppe looked around as though he stared at a jail cell. "You had her *here*?"

"Of course," I said, ignoring the implication that I'd risked Catherine's life and my own by not following his plan to go to the hospital. Besides, my room looked lovely, especially with so many flowers. Mimi had dropped off hyacinths, and Mrs. Vitolo had sent her cousin Vincent, who'd brought me a bouquet of silk flowers I recognized from the store. I was glad Beppe was here to witness the love and thoughtfulness that flowed toward me from people in town. I wanted him to appreciate that I had a life outside of *us*, and for him to see that my friends and my customers cared for me.

"I love you so much," he said.

A pale winter sun filtered in through the sheers, which I was glad blocked out my not-so-clean windows.

"I love you, too."

I wanted to confide in him, but I couldn't say how unprepared I felt caring for this small, fragile new life. To admit that Catherine seemed like a stranger to me, while I was expected to respond to her every cry, and to feed her so often I thought I would die—to try to explain any of that would sound harsh. So I said instead, "I'm the happiest woman in the world."

His head was in his hands and he was crying. Next we were clinging to one another as though we'd survived a plane crash. He had to go, he said. He had appointments. I said I understood. Besides, I was tired. He looked back from the doorway and gave a brave smile. Ruth walked him out, and I listened to the sound of his footsteps receding down the stairs.

The next day Sammy and Gloria came, and behind them stood Mr. E., holding his hat in his hand.

"Come in. Come in. All of you."

Catherine made lovely gurgling noises, and Gloria was entranced. I almost said, be careful, you have no idea of the energy they take.

"Beautiful, Mari," said Mr. E., stepping forward. He handed me an envelope containing not cash, but a war bond, the sum considerable.

"Thank you," I said.

He bent lower, and whispered, "Don't worry, Mari, I not leave."

Sammy wanted to hold Catherine, and without waiting for permission took her with expert hands. How I longed for Mom in that moment, not only for her to see Catherine, but for the three of us to be together just this once.

Sammy rocked Catherine from side to side. His eyes never left hers. "Gloria and I have some news," he said.

"I'm pregnant!" Gloria announced. She went to stand next to Sammy and took his arm. They huddled over Catherine and I almost couldn't bear it, because I was thinking about Beppe, who was either at the bank or at home, but not here.

"Before you say anything, Marie, Gloria and I are getting married. Next weekend. Nothing fancy. A registry office. Will you be our witness?"

I couldn't disguise my shock. A registry office? No church? No priest? Though who was I to talk?

"Yes, oh yes," I said.

A week later, Ruth and Gersh came to get me. I was nervous and hesitated at the downstairs door. This would be my first time outside the apartment since Catherine was born, only now instead of a stomach to hide, I had a living, breathing baby. It was also the first time since the pregnancy that I'd worn regular clothes, one of Mom's suits, and on top her old camelhair coat. I looked across to the bank and back to our little group, Ruth and Gersh, Sammy, Gloria, and me, the only one not in a couple. I was surprised not to see Mr. E. Hadn't they invited him? I decided not to ask.

Catherine was well swaddled, but as soon as we were out on the street, dainty clouds of steam escaped from her tiny mouth, which formed an adorable little "o." I tickled her chin all puckered up with cold, and said, "Today, my little one, you are Mommy's date."

CHAPTER FIFTY-FIVE

Beppe wanted to resume meeting at our tryst apartment, but I tried to find reasons why we should still meet at my place. It was difficult transporting all I needed for Catherine, who was still too young to be left with Ruth. But the real reason was that I wanted to be at home and near the store, which I couldn't explain and was afraid he wouldn't understand.

One day after we'd made love, he went to my closet and opened it, something he had never done before. My first impulse was to shrink. There hung my worn housedresses, the clothes of a woman who worked in a struggling Five & Ten. I was ready to tell him how much satisfaction I got from my work. Sure, I became disgusted. I sometimes hated Kenny, just as I had once hated Gino. Even Sammy was capable of driving me crazy. But these days I had less time for aggravation. The sight of those dresses had given him a glimpse of what my life was like; they also represented the part that made me most proud.

"I can hire you some extra help, Marie. You shouldn't be working," he said, closing the closet door. We were putting our clothes back on, getting ready to resume our separate days.

"I like to work," I said. "And I plan to spend more time downstairs, as soon as Catherine is a little older."

He looked surprised. Poor Beppe, I thought, trapped in his old fashioned ideas. He wanted to take care of me, but there would always be a compromise from my end. I flashed on the loser in that poker game, when my father won the deed to the store. Beppe would see it as a successful business transaction, whereas I could almost feel that change in fortune that had robbed the man of his property, his livelihood, his family's inheritance. I had never thought of him before, the man my father ruined.

How could I explain to my lover that Catherine wasn't a substitute for the store. She was the biggest part of my life, but the Five & Ten was what got me out of bed in the morning. In fact, I considered the store's wellbeing essential to hers. An almost daily concern was whether I would one day be able to leave her an inheritance. How could I explain to Beppe the line that stretched from Carmela, and through me to Catherine, an unbroken umbilical that not only connected us as women, but as the Five & Ten's owners. For a woman to pass her property to a daughter was too far outside the normal order of things. He would think it was silly.

Neither of us mentioned that he was still with Priscilla. Nor did we talk about what was always a possibility, that I could become pregnant again. There was much we did not talk about. But how I loved watching him and Catherine together. She brought out the best in him. If she happened to wake and start crying while he was there, he would run into her room and pick her up. Other times he hovered by her bassinet. She was all he wanted to talk about. If it annoyed me that he sometimes became bored when I recounted my day, a trip to Ferrara's, a problem with a shipment, I knew I could always entertain him with details of crying, soiled diapers, and cradle cap.

He turned to me, his tone combative, "Kenny is working harder. Why don't you give him a small raise? Marie, did you hear me?"

"I heard. And I'm not giving Kenny a raise."

I got up and walked around the room picking up clothes. How I handled Kenny was my business. In that moment I felt strong. I also looked good. I'd gotten my color back, and my figure was returning. I had a waist, and could even fit into some of my skirts, those with larger waistbands. Naked, I looked even better.

He let the subject drop. He told me he was shopping for a new car, considering a Cadillac Fleetwood. I didn't understand this male obsession with motorcars. Just the other day I'd overheard two men in the street talking about Ford, how it had just sold its 28 millionth automobile. How were so many people able to afford them?

"Would you ever buy a Ford?" I asked.

"Never," he said, shaking his head.

"Why not?"

"Ford is a supporter of Germany, which these days means Nazis."

I looked out the window, thinking that Spring might never come. Freezing rain was turning into snow and accumulated on the windowsill. "I'm sick of this weather. It should be warming up. I need to go and check on Catherine," I said, in a bad mood suddenly.

Catherine was napping for longer periods, but I never trusted it, thinking I would go in and no longer find her breathing. Beppe followed me into her room, which had once been Sammy's.

"I ordered the Ellery Queen series," I said, wanting to steer the conversation away from war and Nazis. "And some exploding cigars and water-squirting rings. They come from an Italian toy manufacturer who's set up in America. He's doing very well…"

"Did you know Ellery Queen is really two people?" Beppe asked.

"What do you mean?"

"Ellery Queen. He's Manfred B. Lee and Frederic Dannay."

"Really? Then who is Ellery Queen?"

"A made-up name."

"I love the Sunday night program," I said.

"Me, too."

I pictured him at home, Priscilla sitting next to him.

"Did you know they argue while they're writing?"

"How do you know?" I asked.

"I read it. Say, Marie, why don't we go out? Why don't I take you and the baby someplace?"

"In this weather?" Snow was falling steadily.

"I guess it's a silly idea, huh?"

"I think so."

"Let's do it anyway."

"I guess I could bundle her up," I said.

Catherine's eyes were open wide, staring up at us. Soon she would begin to cry, wanting to be picked up and fed.

"She has a new snowsuit," I said. "It's red." It felt strange to describe his daughter's clothing to him, as though he might never see her wear these things. "Did you know it's a crazy year for static electricity?"

"What?" He laughed.

I hoisted Catherine up and held her.

"The suppliers are complaining. They say they've never seen anything like it. The other day when I shook hands with Feldman I got a big shock. I even saw a little spark."

"Sure he doesn't have a crush on you?"

"He's twice my age."

I carried Catherine to the chest of drawers and put her down on the soft mat where I changed her. Beppe stared and it made me uncomfortable. I wondered if he disapproved of me putting the baby on the bureau. Or was he still thinking of the electrical jolt from Feldman? He often asked me the age of the men who sold me stock; he was even curious about the immature Mimmo. I was flattered, but also annoyed.

"I definitely think we should take a drive," he said.

"First I have to feed Catherine, then get all her clothes on."

"I can wait." He sat on what was once Sammy's bed.

I felt self-conscious tending to the baby in front of him. The other day he'd refused to leave as I fed her. It was the first time he'd seen me take out my breast and position my nipple in Catherine's mouth. He seemed embarrassed by her little noises of pleasure, humming away like a motor, but soon we were laughing.

A baby required several pairs of hands, but then so did the store. In the days following Mom's death, I was afraid, but I never really doubted I could do it. But this? Catherine was so lively. Too lively.

We left Littlefield on the Moss Mill Road heading south toward Atlantic City. The roads were a mess, full of slushy snow, but inside Beppe's car, with the heater set to full, and a woolen car blanket to tuck around the baby and me, it was our own little world, ordered, comfortable.

"Do you want to walk on the boardwalk?" he asked. "Marie, I want to see the ocean. Do you?" He looked across at me.

"Yes I do," I said. But I worried about Catherine, who was in a good mood now, having had a nap and a feed, but there was no predicting the next hour.

The closer we got to the shore, the better the weather became. It was no longer snowing, and here the old roads seemed to be recovering, glistening where the snow had melted. On the shoulder were piles of ugly brown slush, but the light was strong and bright.

The ocean was like a huge, swaying animal moving forward and back. Because it was so cold we couldn't spend long, so after a brief glimpse we got back into the car. Beppe seemed to understand that outings with a small baby had to be kept short. I wondered if he was thinking the same thing I was, about our trip to New York and all the time we'd had.

Before we knew it, we were back home, standing in the stairwell. He kissed me chastely on the top of the head. Then he kissed me again more fully on the lips. Catherine gave a little yelp.

CHAPTER FIFTY-SIX

Beppe came over every day after lunch, and on one of his visits he brought me a better radio. Because we hadn't been going to our apartment, he wanted to make sure we could still listen to the president together. In his latest fireside chat, Roosevelt had gone from talking about remaining neutral to reassuring Americans that not only did we have the strongest navy, but it was ready to deploy. He went down a list of costs in great detail, describing every upgrade, the new ships and planes. I couldn't believe how much was being spent on the war—all the country's money, it seemed.

Usually, I didn't pay much attention to politics, but two things happened to jar me awake. I was shopping in Ferrara's and I heard the words France, Paris, and allies. The women were usually preoccupied with how much meat they could afford. Rarely did they engage in conversations having to do with the world outside of Littlefield. But on that day Eddie Ferrara talked nonstop about the Germans entering Paris and how Hitler had marched with his army straight down the Champs Elysee. I looked around at the faces of my neighbors and saw their looks of horror. If France fell, we could no longer pretend the war wouldn't touch us. The next piece of news sent me running into the store in search of Kenny. Mrs. Monastra, Kenny's mother-in-law, had been telling another woman that the Sons of Italy planned to march up the main street this coming weekend. They planned to wave Italian flags and protest America's support of the allies. I couldn't believe what I was hearing. How could we not side with England and France? It was shameful, and dangerous. For Italians to support such a thing would invite scorn and give our Anglo-Saxon neighbors one more reason to single us out.

When I asked Kenny whether this was true, he tried not to betray much interest.

"Yeah," he said, but I could tell he was excited. He turned and gave me a piercing look. "Gino is coming."

"Here? For this march?" I took hold of his arm so he couldn't walk away.

He would always side with Gino, but I also knew he feared the loss of peace and quiet should my brother reappear. We all worried about another incident of violence.

"Is Mr. E. behind this?" I asked.

Without answering, Kenny backed away, with the excuse he had work to do.

I set up Catherine's playpen behind the soda fountain and left her to be watched by Mimmo while I rushed over to the Oletskys to warn them. Ruth told me she had already heard about the march, which she called a parade. She had a way of minimizing the harshest facts. Nevertheless, she and Gersh would be closing the store. They planned to board it up, after which she said they might go away. I was mortified. I wondered whether I should warn her that Gino might come. But why upset her further, I thought, especially as I intended to stop it.

It was sickening to learn the extent of the anti-Semitism among members of the Sons. If questioned about their shadier activities, they reeled off a list of the good they did: they were a service organization, they helped the poor, they made sure the town's streets were swept. All this was true, but so were their fascist beliefs and their hypocrisy. Some of these same men, with the nerve to march on the main street in support of Mussolini, attended a regular poker game in Philly where Jews played. Many of us Italians had built up close personal relationships with our Jewish neighbors and shopkeepers over many years, all of us in it together as we struggled with the Depression.

I'd heard Gino was still at the shipyard, his job more secure than ever with the war coming. I wondered if his fellow workers knew he read *Social Justice*, and that he sided with fascists. Would he dare say to them what I'd heard him say in the back room of the store? That he was working to turn public opinion against the United States becoming involved in the war?

I'd been silent for too long. I was ashamed of Gino's behavior and afraid of what he might do, but I dreaded taking on another battle with Mr. E. When he visited me after Catherine's birth and presented his gift of a war bond, I was polite. I knew he took that as a sign I was ready to move past our disagreements. The truth was I never wanted to see or speak to him again. Still, I knew what I had to do.

I clutched the receiver and dialed his number. When he heard my voice his hello was frosty. Fine with me, I thought. My resolve nearly left me until I remembered I had to stop him. I dug my fingernails into my palm and said the words. I told him if he allowed the march to go ahead, I would tell everyone in town he had raped my mother. A long pause.

"Did you hear me, Salvie?"

A sharp intake of breath. "Yes, yes. I hear. It nonsense, Mari."

"I believe it," I said.

"A lie!" he roared.

"Ada told me."

Silence.

"Is Gino staying with you? And don't make up a story."

"He is family, Mari. Time to patch things."

"Never," I said.

"I can explain…"

"No need. You heard me," I said, hanging up.

I went straight back to work, but my hands were shaking. I had accused him of a terrible thing. Ada had merely hinted at rape, but I could tell there was more to it than she was willing to say. My own clashes with him had given me confidence. There was always a tendency to paper over the worst that had happened to us, and speaking the truth was a double blade, one aimed at our attacker, the other ready to pierce our own flesh. Even if I hadn't had those experiences with him, I knew Ada had spoken the truth.

After the call with Mr. E., the old Marie would have had to sit down. The new Marie went to the cupboard and poured herself a grappa.

CHAPTER FIFTY-SEVEN

In response to my threat, Mr. E. convinced the men at the Sons to cancel the march. Or maybe he was powerful enough to simply issue an order. I couldn't help but marvel at his courage when he telephoned to assure me that Gino wouldn't be showing his face. He was far from contrite and delivered the news matter-of-factly, without a hint of the horror he'd been prepared to unleash. "Now you can relax, Mari," he said. A silence opened up. He expected to be thanked.

"Fine," I said, hanging up.

Ruth and Gersh didn't have to board up their store and leave town, which would have destroyed their business, the Five & Ten wouldn't suffer another boycott on account of Gino's actions, and I'd avoided a scold from Beppe. Best of all was my revenge on Mr. E. for the pain he'd caused our mother. On the day of the scheduled event, as I looked out onto a peaceful main street, I felt proud of what I'd done.

Mimi Rizotte stopped by and asked if she could come upstairs. I could always tell when Mom's old friend had something important to say. I put the coffee on and braced myself, thinking maybe she wanted to talk about Gino. We sat at the kitchen table and Mimi leaned forward, her expression just as stern as Mom's would have been. She took my hands in hers.

"Everyone knows, Marie. About Catherine."

"Yes," I said.

"I mean who the father is."

"Yes," I said again.

Then she told me something I had suspected, but could never be certain of. That Priscilla Ashworth knew, not just about the affair, but that my baby was her husband's. She'd evidently known for quite some time. The shock was hearing Mimi say her name. Littlefield was made up of two distinct social classes, and part of her warning was to let me know I'd crossed into that other one.

"I don't know what I can do, Mimi," I said.

I felt more sympathy for her discomfort than I felt shame over the damage to my reputation. But what Mimi said revived questions I'd brooded over but had been reluctant to ask Beppe. If Priscilla had known for a long time, did that mean he and his wife had come to some arrangement? Had Priscilla agreed to look the other way in exchange for him staying with her? Why had I never asked him?

Thankfully, the summer passed without incident, though I remained vigilant if I noticed unusual activity on the street, or if a group of men had stopped to talk, engrossed in what looked like a meeting. As far as I knew Gino had stayed away from town, and I hadn't seen or heard from Mr. E.

The August heat was at its most oppressive when Gloria gave birth to a baby boy, which she and Sammy named after his birth month. August was almost ten pounds at birth, with long legs like Sammy's and Gloria's cherubic face. I would have to wait to see a hint of my brother in his round features, but a baby's appearance often switched back and forth. Catherine, having looked more like her father at first, now looked like me.

Back-to-school sales were brisk, and I credited the fountain and word of mouth. My cookies were in demand and I had more baking commissions. The store was full of new stock displayed on new shelving that Sammy had built. I harbored a wish that one day he might move back to Littlefield with Gloria and help me run the store. Just last week he'd brought me several boxes of stock from a friend in Camden, who could get his hands on returns from the chain stores. I watched from the doorway as he unpacked work gloves, spades, shovels, and an assortment of small tools, and I was touched by his thoughtfulness.

At six months Catherine seemed determined to walk, and once she'd made the decision she was unyielding. In the apartment she crawled towards any piece of furniture, latching onto whatever she could as over and over again she tried to pull her herself up. I made sure to take time to play with her in the piles of newly fallen leaves I had Kenny gather and deposit on the loading bay. As she rolled around I held onto her so she wouldn't fall off the bay. She liked to spread the leaves everywhere while sending up high-pitched screams. Afterward, Kenny would have to rake up all the leaves, but he only laughed. Catherine had him completely under her control.

But not everything was carefree. Beppe was generous, and I no longer felt such terrible financial pressure, but despite the new stock, the counter, and Beppe's loan, I realized we would always need more money for stock, that is until the economy improved or we were finally able to expand. Women and men once dissected every word of Roosevelt's fireside chat, but with worsening news coming from Europe, our collective worry gathered in an eerie silence. Gone was Roosevelt's lofty rhetoric, replaced by hard numbers, timelines, and demands that we be ready to make sacrifices. We watched, and waited, unbelieving, even as we felt the mayhem heading our way.

As winter came on, I needed cheering up, so I invited Sammy and Gloria to come down for lunch with baby August. He could barely lift his wobbly head, but Catherine was enchanted and he was equally interested in her. She performed for him constantly, becoming louder, hurling herself about the living room and falling over until finally I had to restrain her. The other reason for asking them to come was so they could give me their opinions on the mural I was planning for the loading bay. I'd found a local artist who, come spring, would paint the rear cement wall to look like an Italian garden with a grape vine, trellis, and the ruin of a pillar.

We were in the living room preparing to go downstairs to look at where the mural would go. Maybe it was the idea of change, of improvements, and hope, but I could hardly contain my excitement as I pulled on my coat. Gloria was bundling up August and helping Catherine with her gloves, when Sammy stopped abruptly in the doorway. He turned to look at us with the strangest expression, and said, "I got my number."

"What number?" I asked quickly.

"The draft. I'm waiting to be called up."

It couldn't be true. Catherine let out a scream, and all eyes were on her as we let ourselves be diverted.

My God, I thought, couldn't it have been Gino instead?

Sammy began pacing, and we took off our coats. Gloria picked up August from the floor and went to sit on the couch, where she lay back against the cushions.

"What about Gino?" I asked.

"He's at the shipyard. Automatic deferment."

"He won't have to serve?"

"No."

Mr. E. had gotten Gino the job. He had tried to get Sammy to take a job there, too, but Sammy wanted to stay at Campbell Soup in Camden. He was avoiding looking at me as he dropped to the floor and began roughhousing with Catherine.

"Everybody has it bad right now," he said from flat on his back with Catherine on top of him.

"Not everybody," I said.

No one spoke for a full minute. Catherine continued climbing all over Sammy, and he made a show of shielding his face or risk an elbow or a foot in the eye. We tried to laugh, but the mood of optimism had been destroyed.

"They're dismantling the rest of the World's Fair," Sammy said.

Gloria looked off to the side, as if to say there's no point in trying to change the subject. His comment got me thinking about the previous two years. First, the glorious trip to the World's Fair, then finding myself pregnant and Catherine's birth. I had been a different woman then. I knew it wasn't cruelty on Sammy's part, but with the mention of New York, I felt another piece of my youth slip away.

I looked down at my handsome brother and thought how selfish I'd been to be so obsessed with the mural. Here was Sammy about to become a soldier. He didn't want to play anymore, and Catherine started crying. I lifted her into my arms, and with the excuse that I needed to check on the soup, I rushed from the room.

CHAPTER FIFTY-EIGHT

Patience, a quality I'd never had, nor particularly respected, crept into every exchange, every decision. I was no longer short tempered with Kenny, or Mimmo, who too often failed to fill the ice cream tubs in the evening to be ready for the next day's sales. And when Kenny's stupid look of confusion threatened to aggravate me, instead of snapping at him I served him a cupcake. Often right after that he began working harder and complaining less.

Ada was visiting for the second time in two weeks. We were in the kitchen and I was looking for a recipe, when I remembered what I searched for was in the ex-voto with Mom's things. Ada had never been inside the little room, so I scooped up Catherine and motioned for Ada to follow.

My aunt's gaze wandered over every square inch, and I saw Mom's room and her things through Ada's eyes. There were the boxes I'd yet to unpack that I used as tables. I'd added homey touches, a vase of silk flowers, and a ceramic ashtray into which I'd placed an assortment of Mom's mismatched earrings. An old cookie tin held a store of buttons—a favorite toy of Catherine's. But it was very heavy, and I worried it might slip from her hands, so I'd filled a jar with raw pasta and she shook that instead. I hadn't slept well the night before and the din of the pasta clattering in the can got to me. Sensing my distress, Ada took Catherine from me and held her. My aunt was expert at noticing what needed to be done; often, seconds before Catherine let out a hungry cry or soiled her diaper, Ada was already at the task.

There was not a stir of air in the room, yet I felt the tiniest knot of wind, a *folletto*, or some other shape-shifting *fata* demanding to be heard. The three of us looked around. No one spoke. Catherine had stopped shaking her jar. Abruptly, Ada sat down and adjusted Catherine on her lap.

"Too many things," said Ada, looking around.

Did she mean I needed to get rid of some? These were Mom's things.

Then, with a twirl of her right arm above her head, as though she could whip the apartment and its contents into a whirlwind and send it flying, she leaned in close to me. Catherine began to squirm; she didn't like being crushed between us.

"I dream," she whispered.

After days or weeks, when Ada breezed back into our lives we were grateful. She came when I needed her, waving her herbs and delivering bursts of Italian that in the moment turned my thoughts crystal clear. Right before one of her pronouncements, however, there was a second in which I became afraid.

Before I had time to think, the words flew from my mouth. "You could live here," I said. Ada looked around as if I'd meant the tiny room. "Not here," I said, smiling. "In the apartment."

Had I lost my mind? If she came to live with us, I would be welcoming augurs, old ways, an old country. This aunt with her worn skirts and shoes. She'd even resisted my present of a new velvet hair ornament and a tortoise shell barrette. Though obviously pleased, she'd stared at them as though they were foreign objects.

"I dream," she said, again. "Suitcases."

Did she mean she would pack up her things at the Mortellites and move in here? Or was someone taking a trip?

"You have new life," she said. "We go."

She got to her feet, gathered Catherine up and led the way back to the kitchen. Several times I tried to get her to say more, but she was quiet. She began tidying, then took out her portable apothecary and motioned for me to take down the tin where I kept the flour. She sat at the table and began making a dough.

For the rest of the afternoon, whenever the phone rang or the buzzer sounded, she looked at me with a raised eyebrow, as if she were expecting someone. Kenny telephoned to advise me of a shipment, then called again to say he'd locked himself out of the office. Both times, hearing the phone, Ada sat bolt upright, listening intently. It was only after the downstairs buzzer sounded, and Ruth stormed upstairs that Ada finally relaxed. Was Ruth the visitor she had been expecting?

"Guess what?" said Ruth. "Your boyfriend's wife has a boyfriend!"

"What in the world, Ruth?"

"Before you say it's nothing but gossip, let me just tell you, they were *caught*."

Ada took Catherine and left the room.

"What are you talking about?" I asked.

"Guess who caught them? You'll never guess."

"Ella?"

"Her husband!"

I asked who this boyfriend was.

"Does it matter?"

"When did this happen?"

"Not sure. I heard it from…guess who told me? Louise, the head teller. I went in to make a deposit, and they were all talking. When they saw me they stopped. They seemed…glum. Like the bank might have to close or something."

"I'm going to meet Beppe in an hour," I said.

"Well, make him tell you who this boyfriend is. Then promise to tell me."

I rushed to the apartment where I found Beppe standing at the window. When I entered he looked up, gave a tight smile and looked away again. He ran his fingers along the inside of his collar, smoothed his hair. Then he went to pour himself a Scotch, and when he came back into the room I hurried toward him and took him in my arms. He submitted, but it was brief. He pulled away and collapsed into a chair.

"Priscilla left. She's gone," he said, leaning forward, his head in his hands.

"How long will she be gone?"

"She's gone, Marie. For good." He looked at me as though I were crazy.

I saw again the hand cupped against the glass of the store's window. An Italian woman would never be able to ignore her husband's infidelity. There would be screaming. Had there been screaming?

"You're scaring me, Beppe. This isn't terrible. I love you, and you love me."

What bothered him more, that she no longer loved him, or was it the scandal? I didn't know what to make of his mood. Rarely did scandal touch him, not in the way it touched me. He was an important man, and I, of course, would be blamed, a young woman who struggled financially and who was too attractive for her own good. And he would hardly be condemned for allowing normal, masculine weakness to get him into trouble.

"It's been hell since Catherine was born, but she would never talk about it. She told me she didn't love me anymore. That she had already planned to go."

"You wanted to leave her. That's what you said. Are you telling me everything?"

"What does that mean?"

Would he admit his wife was in love with someone else? There were few things more embarrassing than people finding out you'd been left. I recalled Mom in the days following our father's disappearance. She was angry and embarrassed. She also didn't have someone else in her life, and that's what confused me. Beppe had me; he had us. He'd underestimated Priscilla. Women were strong. Why didn't men understand how strong we were?

In contrast to our moods, the apartment filled with sun. I had so many questions, but I read his temperament. He was sad. I wanted to feel sorry, but I wasn't. I knew he wouldn't answer a single question, nor would he elaborate on the information already given. And if I persisted, we would only argue, and there was so little time.

He stood up and led me to the bedroom. There we embraced, and our bodies began what had become so familiar. We made love with abandon, with a new, violent energy. There was a change, and we both felt it. But afterwards we found it hard to look at one another.

1941

CHAPTER FIFTY-NINE

Sammy received notice that he was to report to Marine Barracks, Parris Island, North Carolina in April. Beppe tried to explain to me what was going on in Europe and North Africa, but it was confusing. Roosevelt didn't yet have a clear plan on how he intended to respond to Hitler's aggression in the Atlantic. All we knew was that Britain needed our help and that the United States was already giving substantial material aid, which it was generally assumed would eventually drag us into the war. Beyond basic training we had no idea where Sammy might be sent. I had a bad moment when Gloria told me Roosevelt had just extended the soldier's term of duty to twelve months.

The day Sammy left, we stood shivering in a cold rain outside Sammy and Gloria's apartment in Camden. We waited for a taxi to arrive to take him to the bus. Mr. E. had volunteered to drive him to the station, but Sammy wanted to say goodbye to all of us while still at home. The children were crying, and I'll never forget the look on Gloria's face. This was only the second time I'd said goodbye to my brother, the first was when he'd moved out of the apartment to go and live with Gloria. This time, I wondered whether he would come back.

He wrote regularly to us from boot camp, and Gloria and I shared our letters, except for the intimate pages meant only for her. These she held to her breast, her face flushed with pleasure and desperation. I tried to joke and made a show of grabbing at the pages, and we laughed at first, before the tears came. Neither of us believed his upbeat tone. He was on a seven-week training schedule and had just started a second round, because he hoped to become a rifleman. The training was grueling. He was using his arms and legs like a monkey to navigate a structure of metal bars, or made to crawl inches from the ground as fast as he could wearing a heavy pack, but he loved rifle practice. Then, after weeks of no word, Sammy finally wrote. He would be deployed to Iceland in a matter of days. He was excited. He promised to write.

At twenty months, Catherine's little hands were always in the cases behind the fountain. Nor could I stop her from following Mimmo around as he served customers. Beppe had bought us a small oven and a portable griddle for the counter, and Mimmo began offering toasted sandwiches at certain times of the day. When it was cold there was nothing nicer than having a toasted cheese with a nice cup of hot chocolate. Beppe sampled the first one, and Mimmo seemed thrilled to have the banker eat his food. Catherine was busy playing, and fortunately she was leaving her father and me in peace. It amused me to watch Mimmo pretend that Mr. Ashworth was nothing more than a family friend. By now everyone knew of our relationship, but when Beppe picked up Catherine and she swung her little arms around his neck and screamed Da Da, there was the inevitable moment of awkwardness.

Kenny had started calling Catherine little Carmie, which shocked me every time I heard it. I thought of asking him to stop, but I somehow couldn't bring myself to do it. For once, we were thriving in our little store, and I didn't always have a knot in my stomach. And I no longer feared the biddies who'd once come in to stare. Having been completely won over by Catherine, they now smiled when they saw us together, and quite a few bought something, which told me I was right to believe they had been boycotting me. Nor did I fret over my suppliers' bills. Not that all my worries were gone, but for the first time I had control over my life, our lives, Catherine's and mine.

Beppe and I continued to meet at the tryst apartment when Ruth was available to babysit. We had crossed into a settled life, if not together, then separately with the shared responsibility of Catherine and the store. But the terms of the loan felt more and more onerous as time went on, and there were many nights when I lay awake, picturing the Five & Ten with a new name, or no longer a store at all, because the bank had taken it. Beppe and I hadn't talked about this again. He believed I was content, and I was. We also never discussed our future together. Some days I thought there were too many unknowns, too many questions. I wanted the answers, but my next thought always was, why borrow trouble?

Beppe was sending a man around to repair the heater in the apartment, which had stopped working right in the middle of a late cold snap. I'd gone to sit with Catherine on my lap in Mom's mohair chair, and over us I'd thrown her old camelhair coat.

When Beppe walked in, Catherine jumped up and demanded to know whether he'd brought her anything. "Da Da? Present?"

The repair man, whose name was Frank, shot us a look.

Beppe said, "You know I forgot. But there's a little thing I saw the other day…"

Her eyes widened and she threw her arms around him. "Get it for me! Get it for me, Da Da!"

"Catherine!" I spoke sharply, but Beppe interrupted.

"She's okay, Marie. Aren't you, little one?" he asked, chucking her under the chin.

I took Catherine out of the room so Beppe could discuss the heater, and also so that Frank wouldn't witness any more of our domestic conversation. Once Frank had left, Beppe brought up the subject of the store and I was immediately nervous. But he only wanted to tell me that the shop next door was still for sale following the death of the key cutter.

"It's very narrow, Marie, so we might be able to get it for a good price."

"We can do the tool annex," I said.

"That's exactly what I was thinking. And we could put new railings on the upstairs balcony. Marie, you could move your office up there if you wanted." He waited for my response. Of course I would answer yes to everything.

"The floor needs replacing," I pointed out.

"We could do that, too."

Everything was so positive, with plans and hopes. I pictured wheelbarrows stacked one on top of the other, like the red and green ones I'd seen in the Mom and Pop store in New York.

Catherine was growing fast, and every day it seemed she developed a new interest. She spent more and more time in the store with Mimmo and begged to be allowed to help him cook. She'd gotten very good at opening the small cold storage beneath the counter, so we had to watch her closely or risk the heavy door closing on her fingers. But we always knew exactly where she was, because she talked nonstop. She performed for customers, and sometimes I had to pick her up to restrain an outburst, especially if I happened to be serving someone who was more reserved or from out of town.

I was happy, and so was Beppe. Still we avoided talking about our future, a fact that confused Ruth, who claimed I gave him license to stray. We were sitting at my kitchen table sipping tea, and she kept asking, "So what now?" I explained that both of us were content with things as they were. "Is he?" she demanded. "I can't believe that, Marie."

With Priscilla out of the picture, Beppe and I had lost some of our urgency, but I couldn't really explain this to Ruth, when I myself didn't fully understand how ordering and arranging stock, planning the tool annex, and combing through endless to-do lists, seemed enough for me. My life was full. Ada visited more often these days, and as usual she turned up unannounced. Though she could annoy me as she talked on and on about Italy, storms, and how children were frightened by lightning and thunder, an outpouring she delivered with her usual certainty, I managed to be patient. Sometimes we liked to sit in companionable silence in the living room, a plate of cake on each of our laps. When the visit was over and I watched her make her way to the bus stop, I felt sad. The way she walked with unapologetic defiance reminded me of Mom. I hadn't asked her again about the idea of moving in, and she appeared to have forgotten it. Ada was like that, always in the present. After every visit, when I went to put our dishes in the sink and I looked around at my little engine room, my kitchen with its glowing paint, right there, in the middle, was a brilliant spot of light.

CHAPTER SIXTY

I was laying out tea and cake for Beppe and me in the tryst apartment when he leaned forward and grasped my hand. "Marie," he said with some urgency, "move in with me."

"Here? How can the three of us fit into…"

"No. I want you and Catherine to come and live with me in the big house."

In my daydreams I sometimes stood on his dock and stared at the lake, at the calmness and beauty, but I never pictured myself inside the house.

When I didn't answer right away, rather than show disappointment, he stood up, "I'm going to have a shave."

He headed for the bathroom, and I unbuttoned my dress. As soon as he came back, we started kissing.

"We have a lot of planning to do," he said, his lips on my neck.

He had removed his shirt and was taking off his trousers. His eyes held mine, and I could see how pleased he was to have finally spoken his idea. He was ready to make a move, to arrange our future. We made love, and afterward he said he wanted me to go with him to the mansion. He suggested the following week. "Just to look around," he said, making it sound casual.

The car was warm and I loosened my coat. He looked over and took my hand, in his eyes an intense look of pleasure. When we got to the house, he swung the car around in the rear drive, a practiced swerve at too fast a speed, and I sensed a habit from the past. What else would I learn? How he crunched his toast in the morning, leaving little hard corners on the edge of his plate? His preferences for china and silverware? Was he as fastidious in his standards for the house as he was in his dress? I would find out.

It was a gray day and the lake was a band of silver; a lone beam of sunlight shone on its surface. I had the same thought as on the day I'd delivered the soup and had stopped to stare at the lake. Could this be the same lake where Angie and I had gone as teenagers? The Lake Park existed on this same stretch of water, but here was a completely different world, and town seemed a million miles away with its Dish Night, the commerce on Bellevue Avenue, the Sweet Shoppe, and people out on the street, Mrs. Tilton in a new hat, Mrs. Mastri walking with a cane. If I had been with Angie, I could have shared these thoughts.

"Marie, aren't you cold?" The wind had come up. He took my elbow and steered me toward the house. He seemed anxious for us to get inside. He said he had a surprise. We entered the kitchen that had been full of yellow light the night Gino and I delivered the soup, what had been my first glimpse of my lover's world. Today the room was cold and there was no evidence of recent cooking. It occurred to me that I didn't know where he ate most of his meals when he wasn't with us.

I couldn't picture him in this unloving house. The vast living room with the vaulted ceiling was as hollowed out as a cave in the dim light. The gargantuan furniture, the stuffed breakfronts, and two pairs of French Provincial chairs, all of it covered in sheets like a sea of ghosts.

"What is the surprise, Beppe?" I pulled my coat tighter around me. "You'll see."

I followed him down the corridor until we came to a tall, wood-paneled door, which he opened and we were hit by a welcome blast of warm air. He stood aside and motioned for me to enter a small den furnished with a suite of leather chairs and a sofa. Heavy curtains depicted a hunting scene, with red-jacketed riders and packs of dogs. In the middle of the room was a small table set for two, steam escaping from a silver chafing dish full of the welcome smell of food. Ella entered. She looked briefly at her employer, not in disrespect but in embarrassment. I tried to catch her eye. *It's me. Marie.* But she looked quickly away.

Beppe pulled out a chair for me, leaned across, and took my hand. He seemed about to laugh, expecting me to join him, but I was thinking about Ella and wondering what she thought. Here I was the young woman who'd gone from hired cook to perhaps the reason Mrs. A. had left her house and her husband. Ella and I had formed a bond around our shared stations. Would she now be serving us? I drowned in shame.

Again I tried to catch her eye, but again she looked away. Then in came the young woman Gino had been flirting with the night we delivered the soup. As the two began serving us a lunch of Welsh Rarebit and salad, Beppe poured champagne and proposed a toast. "To my beautiful, lovely, Marie."

"And to you, Beppe," I said in a lowered voice, grateful that at that moment the women had stepped away, presumably to ready another course in the next room, which I realized must be a second kitchen.

He took my hand. "I love you, Marie. I want to be with you. I want us to be together." Though the women were hardly out of earshot, he didn't seem to notice or care. We ate quietly and took our time, but I couldn't rid myself of the thought that the house frightened me. Surely, we had to talk about this before a decision was made. Only in the movies did women succumb as though they'd been drugged or hypnotized. "Oh yes, oh yes," whispered Myrna Loy in *Manhattan Melodrama*.

The room was too warm. Beppe was smiling, waiting for me to match his mood, to catch up to the wonder and excitement of what he proposed. But all I could think of was Mom in the ex-voto. How could I move her here, and would she come? I couldn't picture her furniture in this house. I had once dreamed of a chariot, our mother standing behind its shield, buffeted by wind, her long hair cascading back, her eyes steadily forward as we flew higher and higher. The three of us, her children—Gino, Sammy and Marie. We would glide in her slipstream, and we, the next generation, would be better than the last. We, the owners of a store on the main street of Littlefield, finally self-sufficient after years of struggle.

I adjusted my bracelets, Beppe's, and one that had belonged to Mom. Not a valuable thing, but in an elaborate filigreed style from Italy.

We had eaten too much and leaned back in our chairs.

"It's like New York," I said, thinking of the rich food.

"It's better than New York," he said, with a meaningful look.

He meant our being together, that what we had wanted for so long was now possible. He was ready to make a plan. But at some point I'd stopped dreaming beyond the hope that the store would continue to improve, and that with the ease of Beppe's money a future stretched out ahead of us, past the frightening present and the threat of war. And there was the glorious presence of Catherine. With all of that, I wanted for nothing.

"Come upstairs," he said. "I want to show you something."

We walked out of the overheated den into the cool hallway. Off to the side was the huge living room, and I saw again those dust sheets and wondered why he hadn't removed them. I followed him up a sweeping staircase that resembled those in the movies I loved, but in the gray light the beauty I'd expected was missing. We walked along a book-lined corridor to a door at the far end, and here Beppe stopped. He turned to look at me, took my hand, and with the other he opened the door. "This is Catherine's room," he said, pleasure on his handsome face. I saw the man I had first met, with the thick sandy hair and strong, smooth neck. This man I recognized, so different from the moody version whose thoughts and feelings were hidden.

I went to the window and looked out. This room didn't have a view of the lake, but of a network of stone paths bordered by a box hedge, ravaged by winter and hollowed out in sections. I looked around at the furniture, and Beppe said quickly, "We'll buy a layette and everything she needs."

A layette? She was no longer a baby. I smiled. He didn't know, but he would learn. I would teach him what a young daughter needed. I would give him time. Yet, I felt different suddenly. Though I couldn't have said exactly, the mansion put me at a disadvantage.

CHAPTER SIXTY-ONE

Shortly after I returned home, Ruth brought Catherine back to the store. They'd had a nice day together. Ruth winked at me when Catherine explained how she'd helped fold handkerchiefs. Ruth had tried to teach her how to place them neatly in the shallow wooden drawers of the men's valet. I took Catherine's hand and we walked Ruth out. At the door, Ruth turned and shot me a look that said, *I want to hear all about it.*

Strangely, at that exact moment, the sun made its first appearance of the day, and a violet light streamed through the windows. Catherine noticed, too, as we paused to look.

"Where were you, Mommie?" she asked.

"Visiting Beppe."

"Where?"

"At his home."

"He could stay here."

"In the store?" I laughed.

"There," she said, pointing toward the back room where the old sofa was. I laughed again, picturing my lover, that precise man, on that sofa.

"I don't think he'd like that."

"He can sleep with us."

"In the apartment?"

"Someplace, Mommy." She looked up into my eyes, the way children look at you when they want a better answer. I leaned in and kissed her cheek, which was dry and gritty with food particles.

"Let's go wash your face," I said.

I allowed her to pick out some penny candy, which she clutched to her chest, while I took the other hand and we went upstairs.

"Let's bake something, Mommy."

"I don't think I have what we need."

"Let's go look," she said, dragging me into the kitchen.

I had a little flour and sugar, but only a small amount of Crisco, and no eggs. "I don't have the ingredients, sweetheart."

"Yes you do!" she cried out.

"Look," I said, showing her the meager pile. "We can't make anything with this."

"Yes we can!" This time she yelled, and I scolded her.

She struggled to climb up onto a kitchen chair and rested her head on her arms. She wasn't crying but she was disgusted with me; I remembered behaving similarly with my mother. And this sorrow led to another, how I would regret leaving this place, especially the ex-voto. I recalled the crumbs around my bed, the frankincense on my doorstep, the *folletto* that snatched my breath away but gave me courage and hope; all that had taken place right here.

"We can try," I said, eyeing the pathetic ingredients.

What would Ada do?

Catherine smiled and began kicking her legs. "Goodie," she said, pounding the table, having fully recovered from the previous minute's drama.

I knew exactly the kind of cake we would make: gummy, failing to adhere, and so dense it would bake into a solid mass only to fall apart upon cutting. I decided to simplify the recipe, if one could even call it that. We would bake a small tray of cupcakes. I mixed the ingredients as fast as I could while the oven came up to temperature. Catherine insisted on measuring the flour, but really we needed it all. Apart from that, the main ingredient was water! I set up the equipment on the kitchen table and let Catherine think she was making the cake all by herself. At the last minute I added my remaining fennel, my last pinch of anise.

"Who is that, Mommie?"

"Who sweetheart?"

"Is it Aunt Ada?"

I turned around, thinking someone had snuck inside without us hearing, but there was only the quiet kitchen and the light falling on familiar objects. I turned back and caught Catherine staring at the doorway, her eyes wide.

"What is it, Catherine?" I tried not to allow panic into my voice.

"Aunt Ada," she said. "Her hair is like yours, Mommie."

Who was she seeing? What had made her think of her aunt in that moment?

Once we'd put the tray into the oven, I suggested she take a bath, and she didn't protest. It was cold in the apartment and she had started to feel it. I soaped her little body, her face turned up to look at me with that goofy expression designed to make me laugh. I rinsed her off, dried and dressed her in a warm sweater and dungarees. She ran into the kitchen and took up her spot at the table, kicking her legs and drumming with her hands. She appeared to have forgotten about the presence in the room. I stood by the oven with my hands over the rising warmth.

The cupcakes needed another five minutes. I wanted to be alone with my thoughts, so I grabbed one of Catherine's dolls and a change of outfit and placed them on the table in front of her.

Mom, what should I do about Beppe's offer?

For as long as I could remember, I'd had so little time to myself. How much would that change? Beppe made sure to tell me I would have my very own sewing room down the hall from the nursery, but I was already sewing less and less. I could, if I wanted, buy new clothes. I loved him, and he loved me. He seemed confident everything would work out.

Mom, if everything in our lives is determined by him, I already feel the tightness of that.

There was the money to consider. Mrs. Bertolli could use more sales for her beautiful crocheted items; I would pay her more, and up front. And Mimi could finally get a fair price for that superior grade of wheat she was still somehow able to get. She and Ron were wanting to expand the mushroom house. Maybe I could convince Beppe to become an investor.

We've been happy here, haven't we, Mom? I regret, just as you did, the dust moats. But we both know that living on the main street they're inevitable. And we refuse, don't we, to be daunted by poverty, which by the way isn't my word. I have never, nor will I ever, see anything poor in our lives as they were.

Carmela said nothing. No word, not even a feeling. For weeks now there had been this ghost silence. I might as well have been speaking to the Ouija, with its unsatisfying 0 to 9, the simple Yes, No, Hello, Goodbye. Without Mom's guiding hand, I felt frightened.

I turned to check on Catherine and caught a look of terror that lasted barely a second before she slid down from her chair and came to stand next to me.

"What is it, Catherine?"

"Mommie, Aunt Ada is here!" she called out in her most urgent voice.

Why had I not heard the downstairs buzzer? I looked around and saw no one. I had just crouched down to peer into the oven, when I turned and saw Ada in the doorway.

"Ciao," she said, smiling. "Si, I come."

"How…"

"The cakes. We finish."

"Is it done? Is it done?" Catherine stomped on the floor next to me.

"Let's check," I said, and Catherine scooted down. "Be careful," I said, "it's very hot." I put on my glove and slipped my hand inside the oven. I felt Ada behind me.

"Oooooh." Catherine gasped.

The crowns were lightly cracked where the batter had split, revealing a steaming, moist but firm cake underneath. How in the world? The smell was heavenly, as though I'd added treacle or maple syrup, though I had neither.

"Can I eat one now? Can I? Can I?"

"Yes," I said, "but let's let them cool for a minute."

The kitchen was warm from the baking. Ada pulled out a chair. She smoothed Catherine's hair, which was tangled from her bath. Then she hoisted her heavy purse up onto the table and began rooting through its contents with purpose.

We were waiting for the cakes to cool. I looked out the window at the birch tree and noticed new spring growth. The willowy branches slapped against the window. I would have to get it pruned.

Ada peeled the paper from a cupcake and handed it to Catherine, who began kicking and pounding to beat the band. Gently, I put a hand on her legs and with the other stilled her small hands. She looked up and smiled as a curl of warm, fragrant steam reached our noses. Ada got up to pour Catherine a glass of milk. Then she set a cake in front of me and took one for herself. They were perfect and smelled delicious. I waited for Catherine's ungrateful "yuck," ready to explain that the ingredients were poor.

Catherine took the first bite, her eyes wide.

"Ummmmm…" she exhaled with a long, slow breath, then threw herself back dramatically against the chair. "So good, Mommie."

Ada found what she was looking for in the depths of her purse, a vial of a mossy-looking substance she turned over and over in her hand. "La protezione," she said, holding the vial up to the light, as her eyes drifted to the fourth chair at our little table. Things were in motion. She was looking at me with the same expression as on the day she'd commanded me to state what I most wanted, my *intention*. As had happened then, a single thought obsessed me. I wanted the best hardware or variety store on the main street, and I wanted to compete with the likes of Millers, Woolworths, Kress, and Waples.

Ada's hands flew about her face, as though she was clearing smoke or a foul odor. Then she aimed her sharp nose at the vial, which she'd placed in my hand. This time she didn't make me state my intention out loud, but in an abrupt change of mood she took the vial from me and instructed us to close our eyes. I heard her get up from the table, then the opening and closing of a cupboard. "Okay, now you look," she said. The vial was gone. She had hidden it.

Ada sat down and smiled at Catherine. I looked at them and noted the family resemblance. Ada appeared to have forgotten all about me and I felt as if I dangled from a great height. Her hair was sleek and pulled back, the long mane resting on her right shoulder. Pinned to her sweater was a brooch, in the shape of a sprig of an herb studded with rhinestones. It was junk, you could tell, and it was the first costume piece I'd ever seen her wear. It was *American*, and so unlike her.

She got up to brew a pot of coffee. Catherine was busy with her cupcake, and I was thinking about Beppe's proposition. Suddenly Catherine became attentive with the same panicked look as before. Ada, too, sat upright, her back rigid, her eyes hard as flint.

"Are you all right, sweetheart?" I touched Catherine's arm, while my eyes never left Ada.

Catherine touched my hand. She said, "I love our house, Mommie. I love our store."

"I know you do," I said.

I felt Mom pull up a chair.

Ada was studying Catherine with the same adoration I felt at this small being, the next in a line of Parodi women. Sammy would approve of Ada living here in the apartment with us. How he loved family, the same old conversations, the feuds, the histrionics.

Ada brought coffee to the table and sat where Mom was already sitting. The three of us nibbled our cake, and Catherine asked to have some coffee. Ada poured a tiny amount into a cup and added plenty of milk. Catherine tasted it and made a funny face, which prompted our giddy laughs. I never remembered feeling so happy. There would be time to give Beppe an answer. Rarely was I so indecisive. There were only two things I knew for sure: I would continue to work in the store, and the Five & Ten would eventually pass to Catherine. Neither of these decisions had I discussed with him, but there would be time for that.

The kitchen filled with afternoon sun. I felt the store breathing beneath my feet.

ACKNOWLEDGEMENTS

I am deeply thankful to those who helped me realize this novel.

Most profoundly to my partner, Nick Bogle, for his rock steady belief, patience and unflagging support, and to my daughter, Ava Bogle, my soul mate, fellow writer, and creative muse. To my dear friends, the authors Kim Chernin, Renate Stendhal, and Muriel "Aggie" Murch for multiple reads and hand holding, I'm eternally grateful for your time and care. To the gifted illustrator, Jenny Kroik, for my beautiful cover art, and to Bordighera Press and the multi-talented Nic Grosso, whose guidance in all things I was able to trust.

And through your friendship, support, and sensibilities, you have helped contribute to this book: Suz Lipman, Else Johnson, Judith Lowry, Cathy Cook, Maria Laurino, Bathsheba Monk, Mary Lawler, Jennifer Martelli, Kathy Curto, Jane Mickelson, Susan Dalsimer, Jane Silvia, Cathy Sanchez-Corea, Liz Kay, and to my late friend, Joanne Kyger. To Brett Hall Jones and the wonderful family that is The Community of Writers—thank you for years of inspiration and encouragement. And to Myn Adess for valuable editorial assistance in the home stretch.

To a spiritual mentor, Elena Ferrante, whose work gave me permission to write the story of my own Italians, and who helped me discover our deep connection to Italy, an inheritance that wasn't always obvious to this third generation Italian-American.

To my dear sisters, Lisa and Donna. To my mother, Lorraine Reitano, who taught me that it was possible to be an artist, and to my late father, John, a natural storyteller if ever there was one.

Finally, to my maternal grandmother, Anna Renzi, whose struggles and triumphs were the essential ingredients in shaping the flavor and texture of *Italian Love Cake*.

ABOUT THE AUTHOR

GAIL REITANO was born and raised in the southern New Jersey Pine Barrens and currently lives on the West Coast, north of San Francisco. Her work includes fiction, memoir, and the personal essay, and has appeared in the anthology *Songs of Ourselves: America's Interior Landscape*, *Glimmer Train Press, Catamaran Literary Reader*, and *Ovunque Siamo: New Italian American Writing*, among others. *Italian Love Cake* is her first novel.

VIA FOLIOS

A refereed book series dedicated to the culture of Italians and Italian Americans.

GARIBLADI M. LAPOLLA. *Miss Rollins in Love*. Vol 119. Novel.

JOSEPH TUSIANI. *A Clarion Call*. Vol 118. Poetry.

JOSEPH A. AMATO. *My Three Sicilies*. Vol 117. Poetry & Prose.

MARGHERITA COSTA. *Voice of a Virtuosa and Coutesan*. Vol 116. Poetry.

NICOLE SANTALUCIA. *Because I Did Not Die*. Vol 115. Poetry.

MARK CIABATTARI. *Preludes to History*. Vol 114. Poetry.

HELEN BAROLINI. *Visits*. Vol 113. Novel.

ERNESTO LIVORNI. *The Fathers' America*. Vol 112. Poetry.

MARIO B. MIGNONE. *The Story of My People*. Vol 111. Non-fiction.

GEORGE GUIDA. *The Sleeping Gulf*. Vol 110. Poetry.

JOEY NICOLETTI. *Reverse Graffiti*. Vol 109. Poetry.

GIOSE RIMANELLI. *Il mestiere del furbo*. Vol 108. Criticism.

LEWIS TURCO. *The Hero Enkidu*. Vol 107. Poetry.

AL TACCONELLI. *Perhaps Fly*. Vol 106. Poetry.

RACHEL GUIDO DEVRIES. *A Woman Unknown in Her Bones*. Vol 105. Poetry.

BERNARD BRUNO. *A Tear and a Tear in My Heart*. Vol 104. Non-fiction.

FELIX STEFANILE. *Songs of the Sparrow*. Vol 103. Poetry.

FRANK POLIZZI. *A New Life with Bianca*. Vol 102. Poetry.

GIL FAGIANI. *Stone Walls*. Vol 101. Poetry.

LOUISE DESALVO. *Casting Off*. Vol 100. Fiction.

MARY JO BONA. *I Stop Waiting for You*. Vol 99. Poetry.

RACHEL GUIDO DEVRIES. *Stati zitt, Josie*. Vol 98. Children's Literature. $8

GRACE CAVALIERI. *The Mandate of Heaven*. Vol 97. Poetry.

MARISA FRASCA. *Via incanto*. Vol 96. Poetry.

DOUGLAS GLADSTONE. *Carving a Niche for Himself*. Vol 95. History.

MARIA TERRONE. *Eye to Eye*. Vol 94. Poetry.

CONSTANCE SANCETTA. *Here in Cerchio*. Vol 93. Local History.

MARIA MAZZIOTTI GILLAN. *Ancestors' Song*. Vol 92. Poetry.

MICHAEL PARENTI. *Waiting for Yesterday: Pages from a Street Kid's Life*. Vol 90. Memoir.

ANNIE LANZILLOTTO. *Schistsong*. Vol 89. Poetry.

EMANUEL DI PASQUALE. *Love Lines*. Vol 88. Poetry.

CAROSONE & LOGIUDICE. *Our Naked Lives*. Vol 87. Essays.

BASSETTI. ACCOLLA. D'AQUINO. *Italici: An Encounter with Piero Bassetti.* Vol 55. Italian Studies.

GIOSE RIMANELLI. *The Three-legged One.* Vol 54. Fiction.

CHARLES KLOPP. *Bele Antiche Stòrie.* Vol 53. Criticism.

JOSEPH RICAPITO. *Second Wave.* Vol 52. Poetry.

GARY MORMINO. *Italians in Florida.* Vol 51. History.

GIANFRANCO ANGELUCCI. *Federico F.* Vol 50. Fiction.

ANTHONY VALERIO. *The Little Sailor.* Vol 49. Memoir.

ROSS TALARICO. *The Reptilian Interludes.* Vol 48. Poetry.

RACHEL GUIDO DE VRIES. *Teeny Tiny Tino's Fishing Story.* Vol 47. Children's Literature.

EMANUEL DI PASQUALE. *Writing Anew.* Vol 46. Poetry.

MARIA FAMÀ. *Looking For Cover.* Vol 45. Poetry.

ANTHONY VALERIO. *Toni Cade Bambara's One Sicilian Night.* Vol 44. Poetry.

EMANUEL CARNEVALI. *Furnished Rooms.* Vol 43. Poetry.

BRENT ADKINS. et al., Ed. *Shifting Borders. Negotiating Places.* Vol 42. Conference.

GEORGE GUIDA. *Low Italian.* Vol 41. Poetry.

GARDAPHÈ, GIORDANO, TAMBURRI. *Introducing Italian Americana.* Vol 40. Italian/American Studies.

DANIELA GIOSEFFI. *Blood Autumn/Autunno di sangue.* Vol 39. Poetry.

FRED MISURELLA. *Lies to Live By.* Vol 38. Stories.

STEVEN BELLUSCIO. *Constructing a Bibliography.* Vol 37. Italian Americana.

ANTHONY JULIAN TAMBURRI, Ed. *Italian Cultural Studies 2002.* Vol 36. Essays.

BEA TUSIANI. *con amore.* Vol 35. Memoir.

FLAVIA BRIZIO-SKOV, Ed. *Reconstructing Societies in the Aftermath of War.* Vol 34. History.

TAMBURRI. et al., Eds. *Italian Cultural Studies 2001.* Vol 33. Essays.

ELIZABETH G. MESSINA, Ed. *In Our Own Voices.* Vol 32. Italian/American Studies.

STANISLAO G. PUGLIESE. *Desperate Inscriptions.* Vol 31. History.

HOSTERT & TAMBURRI, Eds. *Screening Ethnicity.* Vol 30. Italian/American Culture.

G. PARATI & B. LAWTON, Eds. *Italian Cultural Studies.* Vol 29. Essays.

HELEN BAROLINI. *More Italian Hours*. Vol 28. Fiction.

FRANCO NASI, Ed. *Intorno alla Via Emilia*. Vol 27. Culture.

ARTHUR L. CLEMENTS. *The Book of Madness & Love*. Vol 26. Poetry.

JOHN CASEY, et al. *Imagining Humanity*. Vol 25. Interdisciplinary Studies.

ROBERT LIMA. *Sardinia/Sardegna*. Vol 24. Poetry.

DANIELA GIOSEFFI. *Going On*. Vol 23. Poetry.

ROSS TALARICO. *The Journey Home*. Vol 22. Poetry.

EMANUEL DI PASQUALE. *The Silver Lake Love Poems*. Vol 21. Poetry.

JOSEPH TUSIANI. *Ethnicity*. Vol 20. Poetry.

JENNIFER LAGIER. *Second Class Citizen*. Vol 19. Poetry.

FELIX STEFANILE. *The Country of Absence*. Vol 18. Poetry.

PHILIP CANNISTRARO. *Blackshirts*. Vol 17. History.

LUIGI RUSTICHELLI, Ed. *Seminario sul racconto*. Vol 16. Narrative.

LEWIS TURCO. *Shaking the Family Tree*. Vol 15. Memoirs.

LUIGI RUSTICHELLI, Ed. *Seminario sulla drammaturgia*.
    Vol 14. Theater/Essays.

FRED GARDAPHÈ. *Moustache Pete is Dead! Long Live Moustache Pete!*.
    Vol 13. Oral Literature.

JONE GAILLARD CORSI. *Il libretto d'autore. 1860 - 1930*. Vol 12. Criticism.

HELEN BAROLINI. *Chiaroscuro: Essays of Identity*. Vol 11. Essays.

PICARAZZI & FEINSTEIN, Eds. *An African Harlequin in Milan*.
    Vol 10. Theater/Essays.

JOSEPH RICAPITO. *Florentine Streets & Other Poems*. Vol 9. Poetry.

FRED MISURELLA. *Short Time*. Vol 8. Novella.

NED CONDINI. *Quartettsatz*. Vol 7. Poetry.

ANTHONY JULIAN TAMBURRI, Ed. *Fuori: Essays by Italian/American
    Lesbiansand Gays*. Vol 6. Essays.

ANTONIO GRAMSCI. P. Verdicchio. Trans. & Intro. *The Southern Question*.
    Vol 5. Social Criticism.

DANIELA GIOSEFFI. *Word Wounds & Water Flowers*. Vol 4. Poetry. $8

WILEY FEINSTEIN. *Humility's Deceit: Calvino Reading Ariosto Reading Calvino*.
    Vol 3. Criticism.

PAOLO A. GIORDANO, Ed. *Joseph Tusiani: Poet. Translator. Humanist*.
    Vol 2. Criticism.

ROBERT VISCUSI. *Oration Upon the Most Recent Death of Christopher Columbus*.
    Vol 1. Poetry.

CPSIA information can be obtained
at www.ICGtesting.com
Printed in the USA
FSHW020000030222
88090FS